CHILDREN OF THE EARTH

David C. Corbett

PRISTINE
PRESS AND MEDIA

Children of the Earth
Copyright © 2025 by David C. Corbett

ISBN
978-1-964804-85-9 (Paperback)
978-1-964804-84-2 (eBook)
978-1-964804-86-6 (Hardcover)

Table of Contents

CHAPTER 1

Star Gazers

1 January 2024 Kitt Peak National Observatory

Seven thousand feet above the Arizona plains, two men stood over a large worktable littered with working papers, photographs, and graphs. Their office is part of the Kitt Peak National Observatory, located fifty-two miles southwest of Arizona's capital. The men looked and felt drained. They had every right to be exhausted, for they had been together for the past forty-eight hours, working in the confines of their small office. Earlier, while using the one hundred and fifty-eight-inch reflector telescope, the two scientists happened upon an anomaly that frightened them both.

Doctor Ellis looked up from his desk, a worried and perplexed look in his seventy-year-old eyes. Financial grants from the U. S. National Science Foundation, as well as his profound abilities, had earned him the position of head of the institute's asteroid research program. Over the past twenty-five years, Ellis had published hundreds of scientific papers on asteroids and was considered the most prestigious scientist in that particular field of astronomy. Now he looked over at his young assistant, Doctor Benjamin Duke.

"Ben, what in God's name are we going to do with this?"

"Hell, Doc, I don't know. This is the sort of thing that could cause world panic, and I'm sure every major observatory on the globe has the same pictures as we do. What do you think they'll do with them?"

"Same as us, I guess. The big question is what will their governments do? What will our government do, for that matter? Damn it, Ben, a rock this size has never hit earth in millions, maybe billions of years. The last large asteroid to punch us was about 2.3 million years ago. That one caused an ice age, and Lord knows what else, certainly the extinction of practically every living thing on earth."

Ben glanced at the man who had been his mentor for the past five years. Funny, he thought, how the old doctor looked like Pinocchio's dad, Geppetto. Ellis' glasses slipped down his nose, and his long, snow-white hair hung to his shoulders. Ben's heart went out to him, for tomorrow he would have to reveal the facts of their discovery to the Foundation's directors, and then what? They had been over the calculations so many times in the past few days that he could almost recite them by heart. The two of them had taken hundreds of pictures of the southern sky in the past two weeks. Around the clock, they had worked, trying to find a fallacy in their figures, but no matter how they viewed it, the flying nightmare would hit Earth.

"Doc, it's 2025 anyway you look at it. That hunk of iron and nickel," pointing at an eight-by-ten, black and white photo lying on their work table, "will hit Earth, and it's twice the size of Ceres, the largest known asteroid we've ever observed. I still can't believe it is nine hundred and fifty miles across the diameter and moving toward us at 40 miles per second. It won't make a tinker's hoot where the thing strikes; it will be the end of everything!"

"I know it, you know it, but should we tell the world? Can the men and women of this tired old planet handle this kind of news? Hell, we've been trying to bring some semblance of peace to the world since old Clog first hit his new bride on the head. Still, the whole blasted population is trying to kill each other off, and now we'll just pop up and say, 'Oh, by the way, the world is going to end in two thousand and nineteen. It would be utter chaos, social shambles, and possibly, uncontrollable violence. He shook his head, his silvery, white hair stirring silently.

1 February 2024, The White House

"Mr. President," Bob Whitman, the nation's top security advisor, began, "what I'm about to tell you is one of the best-kept secrets of modern times. I would venture to say as few as a thousand people have any idea about this event."

"Sounds rather grave," smiled the President. "Go on!"

Whitman squirmed in his seat. He was uncomfortable, though the chair was deep and plush. He looked at the other men in the room. There was the Chairman of the Joint Chiefs of Staff, and a very drawn-looking old man… Doctor Ellis. Poor Ellis, Whitman thought, he has aged decades since I last saw him.

"Mr. President, I'm not going to beat around the bush. Frankly, you'll never see the end of four years in office."

"I beg your pardon," interrupted the newly inaugurated President.

"Please, sir, let me finish."

The President nodded, but the look on his face said do not be coy with me, just give me the facts.

Whitman began again. "Sir, in about two years, the world will have an event that will virtually end life as we know it."

"What in hell are you talking about?" The President asked in a tight, irritated voice. "Event, what event?"

"Mr. President," Doctor Ellis almost whispered. "What Mr. Whitman is trying to say is that the Earth will be struck by the largest asteroid science has ever recorded. It was first sighted in 2023, and we have been tracking its movement ever since. There is no doubt that it is going to hit Earth. Of course, every world government is aware of the situation, but none wish to experience the total societal breakdown should the word get on the street."

The President, his fair-skinned face turning scarlet, stared at the men before him. "You're trying to tell me that for the past three years there have been men and women who have known, or thought they've known, that the world is in terminal peril… I don't believe a word of it. I don't see how that kind of information could have been kept under wraps."

"Actually, it hasn't been too hard," General Gilmore spoke for the first time. He'd been the Chairman of the Joint Chief's for two years, and was a respected military and political adversary in the Washington arena. "The fact that we were able to suppress the information from the first was in large part due to the scientific community. They recognized the problem, and elected to contain the information themselves. In fact, it was well over two years before a few of the world's lesser governments became privy to any knowledge of the event."

"General, you're trying to tell me that we've had a massive cover-up on this issue?" The President's voice was like ice, cold and unrelenting. "How in heaven's name could information of this magnitude be kept quiet for so long, and how much longer will it be possible? You're telling me that amateur astrologers, religious nuts, or whatever haven't taken issue and raised cane? I'm not that naive."

"Please, sir," Whitman was pleading, "stop and think for a moment. Can't you see what would happen if you went on TV tonight and told the American people that the world was ending in 2025? We've been able to contain the knowledge of this damned asteroid by carefully screening every individual that has information, or thinks he has information, on its appearance. Amateur astrologers normally report their unusual findings to an observatory nearest to their sightings. We would then stress to them the wisdom of staying quiet."

"How may I ask, did you accomplish that? Keeping them quiet!"

"Mostly through my efforts," sighed Ellis. "I have traveled a great deal these past two years, and talked to some very well-meaning and, I might add, intelligent folks. Most agreed that it was going to pass us by, just as I explained to them. That has been the bottom line. It isn't going to hit, but simply pass harmlessly. Sure, there have been skeptics, but with the scientific community behind the deception, well?"

"And those that didn't believe your 'pass-by' theory?" The President's eyes bored a hole into Doctor Ellis'.

Doctor Ellis slowly lowered his head. "That's Mr. Whitman's department. I merely passed on the information to him." Ellis shook his shaggy head sadly, "not an American thing to do, but...?"

The frown on the President's face chilled Whitman. He knew, all too clearly, how the President felt about human rights. "Doctor Ellis did a superior job of convincing ninety percent of those who questioned our findings. Those that we felt would not cooperate have been detained."

"Detained? Detained where?" The President was losing control.

"Sir," General Gilmore interrupted, his big frame unwrapping itself from his chair as he stood. "I think that you should have the whole story before you start judging anyone here. Not one individual has been mistreated." Gilmore was an imposing man, black as night, with piercing eyes capable of holding lesser men at bay. Those eyes now burned into the President with the desired effect. "Doctor Ellis, would you be so kind as to bring our President up-to-date?"

Doctor Ellis, though never big, had shrunk into a withered old man since his disturbing discovery. His trusting blue eyes seemed to carry the entire weight of the world in their depths. He stood, shoulders slumped, his glasses slipping down his nose, looked at the men about him, then turned to the projector sitting next to him and switched it on. The room seemed to dim and grow smaller as the screen filled with a picture of a gray mass of rock.

"That, sir," pointing at the screen, "is going to slam into central Africa on the second day of June 2019. *That thing,* "he pronounced the word *thing* as if it were a living entity, "we now call The Devil's Face. Science classifies it an asteroid, though in reality, it is more akin to a small planet." Ellis' voice was rising in strength with every word. "It's the size of a small moon. In fact, in all probability, this chunk of rock has been hiding behind Jupiter since time began. Regardless of where it came from, some phenomena, probably an asteroid collision, moved it out of its normal orbit, and it is headed straight for our tiny planet. Sir, if I may be so crass, in layman's terms, this gigantic piece of space shit is going to destroy every living thing on earth."

"You're trying to tell me that some damned meteorite is going to destroy earth? That's preposterous," interrupted the President.

Doctor Ellis shook his head. "No, Mr. President, this isn't a meteorite; it is an asteroid, which is totally different, though it is composed of much the same matter . . . iron. An asteroid and a meteor do have several things in common, such as their composition and the speed at which they move through space, but that is about the end of the similarities. This particular asteroid is a sixteenth of the size of our moon and aimed directly for Earth at a speed of 40 miles per second; that's 144,000 miles per hour."

There was silence in the Oval Office as each man looked to the other for an answer to a question, but neither knew just what the query might be.

"The size of The Devil's Face," continued Ellis, "is of such magnitude that when it hits, the collision will be felt from pole to pole, and on every continent. The immediate effects will be floods, earthquakes, and exceedingly high winds. Cities, no," Ellis stopped and reflected a moment, "perhaps whole countries will just disappear. Nothing, Mr. President, in your worst nightmares will compare to that impact, and there is nothing, absolutely nothing we can do about it."

Quietly now, "What do you mean, nothing? Why not use our arsenal of nuclear weapons against it?"

"Yes, sir," interrupted General Gilmore, "certainly we have thought of that. Our dilemma involves with what, how much, and when. If we wait too long, then we risk doing as much damage as the asteroid itself. Asteroid fragments would strike earth just the same, plus we have the real problem of gross radiation fallout." Gilmore paused momentarily before he continued. "To destroy The Devil's Face would require one mammoth nuclear device. To reach it in deep space, far enough away to reduce any real threat to Earth, would require a rocket and payload beyond our technological abilities. President Obama ordered such research in 2015. Unfortunately, though we have a little over a year left, we are still ten years too late. Frankly, I don't believe we can stop this monster."

"Well, what in God's name have we done? I mean, beyond hiding the fact that it is on its way."

"That may be the only bright side to this affair," Whitman answered. "On the recommendation of the Security Council, President Obama approved funding for the construction of an underground city in Colorado. Built on the same order as the National Strategic Command Center, and under that guise, the city will be completed by late 2024. Though small, it will only support fifteen hundred souls, we might be able to save enough to keep the human race going for another millennium. Maybe, is the big factor here. The city is designed to withstand a 'best case' scenario, but not, for instance, if the Rockies come tumbling down."

"And just how do you propose to select those lucky enough to go below," asked the President, tight-jawed.

"Why, those that could best start a new civilization," replied a slightly surprised Whitman. "The best of our scientists, government officials, teachers, historians, and the like; in fact, the list has largely been prepared."

"And I suppose you and I are on that list, Mr. Whitman?" the President asked.

"Of course, sir!"

"Like bloody hell we are," screamed the President.

The room sparked with hostility emanating from the headman in the oval office. The other three could feel the disbelief and indignation seething from the man behind the desk. "If my people die, I'll die with them," exclaimed the President flatly. "And so will you! I want to see that list before this day is over, and don't think for a minute that this so-called 'list' is by any way locked in concrete . . . understood?"

"Yes sir," Whitman answered.

August 2024 Ponto Lake, Northern Minnesota

Jason was having the time of his young life. He always looked forward to the family's summer weekends on Ponto. Ponto Lake was as much a part of his life as was his sister or his computer. This afternoon had really been special, for in all of his fourteen years, he had never caught a bass the size of the one now hanging on his stringer. Five and a half pounds of large mouth was something to be proud of . . . period.

Fred Collyar, Jason's dad, taught his boy to fish when he was a mere five years old; hardly big or strong enough to hold a rod. And it was not just bobber fishing for bluegill, but with a casting rod and reel for bass and walleye. Jason had been a quick study, as he had been in most things involving the outdoors or sports. Learning to shoot a shotgun at nine and able to navigate through the north Minnesota woods with ease by the time he was twelve, Fred's son was one of those boys that would make any father pop buttons on his shirt with pride. Looking at him now, strutting up the path to their cabin, Fred saw an adolescent about to bloom into manhood. Standing 5'6" and growing, blond hair blowing in the breeze, he looked every bit like a returning hero from some great war. Bass in hand, Jason was off to show his mom just who the greatest bass fisherman in the world was. Fred laughed to himself. Jason was special, not just because he was his son. No, everyone that met him felt his presence. Jason radiated life, power, and confidence.

"Mom! Mom! You've got to come look at this," yelled Jason through the screen door. "I don't think Dad has ever caught a bass this big before, and if he said so, he is probably lying about it," he laughed.

As June Collyar came to the door, she could sense the excitement in her son's voice. When she saw the fish, she understood why. "Jason, did you catch that?"

"Absooolutely! Plus three more. You'll notice," the wicked gleam in his eyes showed an ongoing, father-son needling, "there are five bass here. Let me see, that means I caught four and Dad caught only one. My, my, isn't that too bad. Getting old I mean."

They all laughed, a good hearty laugh, as was normal in the Collyar household. The family was stable, something even they remarked about at times. The Collyar's had found the key to being happy as a family, and, according to Sally Jesse Raphael and other ridiculous talk show hosts, that made them unusual.

Jason grew into adolescence reasonably happy and well adjusted. His interests ranged from hunting to immersion into the world of the computer. He loved to read, something about which his friends often gave him grief. Though unable to ascertain why, his peers naturally turned to him for leadership and guidance. He felt comfortable in this role of peer pacesetter, and never gave it much thought one way or the other. Jason, with his sense of humor, innate leadership abilities, and intelligence, was just Jason.

Later, as father and son were putting their tackle away, Jason asked, "Dad, are you planning to come up to the cabin for partridge hunting this fall, and maybe for bow season?"

"Yeah, I suppose so," answered his father. "I might even bring you along, if you promise not to shoot more birds, or the biggest buck. I couldn't stand the razing if you out shot me. Lord knows, it's bad enough I'll have to live with you over that puny little bass you caught today."

"Sure, sure! You know what they say, 'if you can't stand the heat, get out of the kitchen'. Seriously, Dad, it really means a lot that you treat me as one of the guys when we're in the woods. I wish sometimes I could stay thirteen forever, but most of the time I want to be twenty-one."

Again, his father laughed. "Son you're a wonderment!"

CHAPTER 2

Bitter Times

1 June 2025, The White House

"You're up early this morning, Mr. President," Bob Whitman exclaimed. "But I guess none of us have slept very soundly these past few months."

"No, I guess not." The President looked as if he had aged fifteen years since he first sat down in the oval office. His close-cropped hair was now completely gray, but he would not allow it to be touched with dye. "How do you think the broadcast went last night?" He was speaking of his latest TV chat with the American people.

In that telecast, he professed his final lie to the world. "No! The fears of a few zealots and fanatics that a meteor of monumental size is going to hit earth are without foundation. I am told there is a large asteroid that will pass very close to Earth's orbit, but it is of no real threat to the planet. I assure you it will pass harmlessly by, causing nothing more than some unusually high tides." He bitterly smiled inwardly at those words. *Boy, are we going to have some high tides,* he thought.

Doctor Ellis' gentle, grandfatherly face was then introduced. Taped earlier, before the doctor's departure for Africa, Ellis had, with the help of charts, pictures and scientific gobbledygook, further strengthened the deception.

This final attempt to keep the truth from the people of the United States was the end of a series of such broadcasts. A leak in the dam of silence had begun to seep rumors of the asteroid in late 2017. Since that time, Doctor Ellis, along with world leaders everywhere, had kept the wolves at bay with lies. This would not have been possible, was it not for the help of the scientific community. For once, perhaps for the first time, scientists all over the world agreed on one thing . . . information of the magnitude concerning the end of time should not become general knowledge.

"Mr. President, I would say you have the vocal presentation of a genuine magician. The stock market, certainly an essential index to public opinion, has not changed, and we have no riots in the streets. Sir, we've succeeded in keeping a lid on this, and in my heart, I know it was the right thing to do."

"You're correct, Bob, but I still can't fathom it's all going to end in a little over twenty-four hours. Does Ellis still confirm it will strike at 10:02 EST tomorrow morning?"

"Yes," replied Bob Whitman. "The good doctor has it calculated down to the second, but frankly, who cares? I told my wife this morning; I mean, I told her the truth. I think she suspected, but the knowledge sent her over the edge. Mainly, she is concerned about the kids. I asked her, 'Why be concerned? It's going to happen to everyone, not just us.' Nevertheless, that did not seem to help matters. It did prove to me we've done the right thing by not telling the world. Mr. President, I'm scared. Not of dying, you understand, but what is after. Do you think this is God's punishment on mankind?"

"Bob, you have been my friend and advisor for years, but I can't answer that question. Thinking on it though, Revelations tells us there will be one heck of a big fire, and Lord knows when that rock hits the atmosphere, we're going to have a fire. Have we got 'The Few' safely underground?"

"Yes, they have been secure in their new home for over a week. I still wish you would join them."

"No, that's not my style. Actually, I don't believe I could handle being one of those taking to the caves. The thought of being one of the few left alive on the planet doesn't appeal to my political heart." The President chuckled for the first time in days. "You know, not enough people around to boss." He paused, his brow wrinkling in concentration. "It still worries me that I approved General Gilmore as the man in charge of that gaggle."

Bob nodded his head in understanding. "It seemed a good solution to the organizational problem at the time, but now? He's a good man, but the thought of a military man leading 'the chosen' from below, well, you know what I mean."

"Yes, I suppose I do. Why interject the thought of war into the new era, or something like that. He'll have his hands full, though. I don't think I would care to be in his shoes the day after tomorrow."

"Nor I," Bob replied.

1 June 2025 Somewhere, Five Miles Under the Rocky Mountains

General Harold B. Gilmore sat behind a large metal desk. His eyes, a source of his control over others, burned dimly . . . no man to stare down today he thought. Gilmore had risen through the officer ranks, not because of his color, nor despite it, but because he was the best. His analytical mind, his superior strategic abilities, and, most importantly, his ability to influence people brought him to the highest position any military man could hold in the world . . . Chairman of the Joint Chief's. Those days were gone forever.

"Never have I ever had to lead so few into so much." He grinned ruefully at Doctor Benjamin Duke sitting across from him in the small room carved from raw rock. "I just hope you will once again reiterate to 'The Few' why we will have to live in the caves for such an extended period."

"Damn it, General, I keep telling you and everyone else who will listen, it could be several generations before anyone will see the sun again. It certainly won't be us. Why won't you or anyone accept that as fact?"

"Because, my dear Doctor, we can't. At least not yet! We are not moles by nature."

Benjamin shook his head in disbelief and took his leave with a wave and a sigh. They had been living underground for only a week, and yet he could understand why others were rejecting the idea. He missed Doc Ellis, he missed his work, and he missed the sun, he thought to himself as he walked back to his small eight by eight cubical, and his wife Margaret.

Doctor Duke was the only married man in New Land. Following the first report he and Doctor Ellis had generated on The Devil's Face, he'd submitted several studies regarding what the aftermath of the strike might be, and how humanity might save itself. His detailed and analytical analysis much impressed the President, who had the absolute final say on the names of The Few. Benjamin was completely surprised when his name appeared on the final draft of those to retreat to this underground home. Tall, almost frail, he had always considered himself the ultimate "nerd," the type who wandered halls of universities with fourteen pens in their left breast pocket. Never a woman's man, he had been overwhelmed with astonishment when, in 2008, he had asked Margaret to a movie and she said yes. They'd been married two years later, and built a union on a firm foundation of trust and love. More than that, each had understood the other's personal need to excel professionally.

Now here he was the foremost advisor to General Gilmore on subjects concerning New Land. He should have felt elated. He did not! He was not sleeping well knowing those residing in the tunnels of New Land would soon be the only living humans on earth. He didn't enjoy the role of a demigod; he didn't much care for Gilmore, and the thought of living his life surrounded by cold, clammy rock reached into cracks of his psyche which he would have rather left untapped. At least he had the good fortune of Margaret, he thought as the plastic door slid shut to the tunnel outside.

* * * *

Left alone, General Gilmore looked around his tiny office. Very austere, he thought. What a difference from his huge Pentagon department with its 24-hour staff. Here he was stood by himself, a leader of fifteen hundred men and women. As the past year rushed by, the President had revised the list of those to survive a dozen times. Should there be children? More women than men? And what about animals? Plus, a thousand other questions. In the end, the decision was to establish a colony of one thousand women and five hundred men. Survival of the species was paramount. Except for him, the entire community was between the ages of 25 and 31. Again, the thought of childbearing years was the influencing factor. Only the brightest of minds and those with reasonable sex appeal survived the list's final cut. Extensive psychological testing was performed on over six thousand individuals before the final roll was handed to the President for approval, and now they were his charges. An attempt was made to include most of the races on earth. Of course, regardless of color or eye shape, they had all been raised in the U.S., but the effort had been honest and real.

Not to his surprise, the Presidential committee selected him to be the leader of "The Few," as they would come to be known.

Interviews of potential New Land inhabitants had been done under the pretense of a government project relating to the colonizing of a future space station. In that regard, there had been enough similarities to their present situation to make it a reasonable cover. Margaret Duke, Benjamin's wife, acted as the sociologist and psychologist in the development of standard qualification tests. From the six thousand screened, fifteen hundred were selected to move into the tunnels of New Land.

When it came time for The Few to gather in the tunnels of their new home, each was provided a cover story such as a vacation, business trip, or the like. Still, the problem of saying good-bye to parents and friends created last minute difficulties. Bob Whitman's department solved those inconveniences as best they could, though not to the liking of some going underground. That is, it would not have been to their liking if they had known what actions were taken. There had been no deaths as families left parents, friends and their jobs, but a great number of Americans were being detained prior to the strike. The detention was well meaning, if inconvenient for those who suffered internment. However, it did stop possible internet rumors which would undoubtedly cause mass hysteria throughout the country and the world. Un-American at best, but something that had to be done to keep the world sane.

"Leader! Leader of what?" Gilmore thought aloud, as he stretched his six-foot six frame. He had always been an active man, reveling in physical sports. He played football at West Point and made an early and respectable name for himself by doing so. As a fullback, he had shown his contemporaries just what type of leader he would later become; one that bullied his way through obstacles. A 2nd Lieutenant during the war known in Afghanistan, he had been highly decorated, as much for his innate ability to accomplish any mission or task assigned, as for his bravery. He had been and still was a "man's man." General Gilmore was the embodiment of a soldier who could be counted on during any crisis. "Well, Mister Hot Shot," he wondered? "What are you going to do about this mess?"

Both he and his chief advisor, Doctor Duke, had viewed the looks of awe and uncertainty on the faces that came to fill the cubicles of New Land. " 'New Land,' what a God-awful name for this underground labyrinth of hell," Gilmore whispered. Tunnel beyond tunnel connected the small living cubes with dining halls, entertainment centers, and storage facilities. Sixteen square miles hollowed out of the earth's protective crust under a mountain. Sixteen square miles, most of which was dedicated to the cache of survival necessities. For the past thirty-two months truckload upon truckload of canned and packaged foods were shipped and stored in New Land. Water had been another problem altogether, but solvable through the diversion of underground springs. Ventilation and the production of oxygen created yet another major obstacle, but through the use of space technology, that dilemma was unraveled like most others. By dedicating a large percentage of tunnel space to the growing of plant life, and using artificial lighting, they ensured the oxygen levels would stay acceptable. The production of power was the most difficult to overcome.

Several theories were considered concerning the power issue. Would Earth's atmosphere, after the strike, be suitable for breathing and/or running of diesel power plants? What if it was? Where could diesel fuel be stored in enough quantity? Strike that plan . . . and so it went. Finally, the logical solution was nuclear power. A small, but powerful, plant was built within the confines of New Land, which produced three times the power required. Having the plant did necessitate a careful watch on radiation levels, but that was a problem Gilmore could easily handle.

The city itself would survive; the developers decided. That is if it were to make it through the initial trauma. But could those living in the complex make it through and live on to see another day, reflected Harold Gilmore. Could anyone reasonably expect the human psyche to adapt to living underground for generations? It was a mute question in many ways. They would have to learn to live in this nether land of gray rock, or die. Later generations would have adapted, but these fifteen hundred, of which he was one, were the first entombed, and that will be where the problem lies. We know what it is to look at the sun, and run through a green field.

Gilmore glanced to the far wall of his office. Spreading over an entire wall was an electronic layout of New Land. Laser optics depicted a labyrinth of tunnels, cubicles, and common rooms, a city laid out as a giant wheel. At the wheel's Hub, the operations department. A large room filled with the necessary electronic equipment to influence everything from oxygen levels to the amount of power the nuclear reactor put on line. A maze of computer monitors, some the size of movie screens, provided enough illumination to the interior that little overhead lighting was necessary. Operations, The Hub, was the heart of New Land, with Gilmore its brain, his office built into part of the wall which overlooked the entire compartment. Here, towering above his domain, he was at home. His duties for the past fifteen years as a general were not unlike overseeing the men and women inhabiting New Land . . . he was comfortable with his duties as a commander.

Surrounding the inner Hub, a tunnel ring from which radiated thirty-two spokes, which in turn ended at what would be the rim of a wheel. The entire rim measured fifty feet across, wall to wall, housing the oxygen generation conservatory, a virtual jungle of various sizes, shapes, and species of living plants. Cultivated under extremely controlled conditions, each plant was scrutinized for disease and infestation of unwanted fauna before shipment to New Land's rim.

"Let's see if cockroaches can withstand The Devil's Face," chuckled Gilmore to himself, as he thought of the amount of work that had been necessary to ensure no unwanted insect came below with The Few.

Recalling from memory every detail of New Land, Gilmore looked closely at the radiating spokes. Four spokes housed three hundred and seventy-five souls each, with two hundred and fifty women and one hundred and twenty-five men making up their population. If the wheel were to be viewed as a clock, the dormitory tunnels were located at 12, 3, 6, and 9 o'clock, with a variety of housekeeping tunnels separating one dormitory from another. The vast majority of the remaining of these "housekeeping" tunnels were dedicated to storage of food, repair parts, and both hard and soft goods necessary to sustain life on a level thought to keep humans happy and content. Other tunnels were dedicated to entertainment, hobbies, food services, and medical requirements. New Land was a city, built underground, with most of the amenities any small municipality might boast. There was even a tunnel, small by comparison to the rest of the great wheel's spokes, dedicated to weapons. Weapons only Gilmore knew about. This small tunnel opened through Gilmore's office. The single key to the door's lock hung around his neck on a golden chain.

General-No-More, Harold Gilmore turned his head skyward, though there was nothing but hard rock at which to look, closed his eyes and whispered, "Lord, Our Father, please, I beg of you, give me the knowledge to guide, the strength to control, and the courage to maintain what is to be left of human life on this, Your world."

1 June 2025 Anoka, Minnesota, a town north of Minneapolis

Whistling an unrecognizable tune, Jason strode for home. He had been shopping at the Mega Mess, the kid's nickname for The Mall of America, with a bunch of other teenagers. Well, not really shopping per-se, but rather just hanging around with friends, although he had made time to purchase the newest Avengers VII computer game. He'd gotten off the bus at Sunny Lane and paused long enough for a coke at Belerr's Drugs, and headed for home on Norwood Street. He paid little attention to the soft green leaves, which now sprouted on the maple trees lining either side of his street. Spring was in its glory and the air was fresh, clean, and clear in the medium sized town of Anoka. His pace matched the mood of a happy teenager with nothing more to worry about than whether he should ask Judith or Bethany to the movies on Saturday. Secure in the knowledge that either would say yes, he was in hog heaven, ready to take on the world.

Ever since I caught that big bass last summer, Jason mused, everything has been going my way. Thinking back to the start of school, as he swatted at one of the season's first mosquitoes, Jason wondered how his life could be so perfect. On the long drive home from Ponto, his dad had finally given him permission to use the family's bomb shelter as a computer workroom. He had been begging for the use of the underground bunker for the past two years, but always lost the argument to his Mom. She used the space to store her homemade canned goods.

The Collyar's home had been built in the early fifties; a time when the world was about to be blown apart by H-bombs rocketed in from Russia. The threat, real or imagined, enticed government officials into recommending bomb shelters be constructed by the American people. So it was the Collyar's inherited an eight by ten concrete room off their basement. Over the years, the shelter reverted into a storage area. When the Collyar's bought the house, in 2015, they installed electrical outlets, shelves, and a large desk-like workbench. It was, thought Jason, the perfect hide-away for his computer work.

Upon arriving home from Ponto, Jason began the work of changing the shelter into "his" special place, though his mother insisted on maintaining one wall for canned vegetables from her garden. Then school had started!

Jason had been looking forward to the start of a new school year, his second in high school. He had tried out for football and was pleased to make the varsity team. Though only a sophomore, he occasionally played first-string halfback, starting his first game on his fifteenth birthday. His prowess on the field made him especially attractive to the fairer sex, and though he was still a bit shy about the process, he allowed as how dating wasn't half bad. Girls were wonderful creatures, after all. Scholastics present him with little challenge, as he had always been a good student. He even learned to enjoy English, a subject he always hated in the past. School and football took a major chunk out of his daily routine, but he had still been able to go hunting with his dad.

Ponto Lake in the fall was a remarkable time. He, along with his father and two other hunting companions, made the four-hour drive to the heart of Minnesota's lake country the day before the season opened. Ostensibly, their purpose was to shoot a few grouse, but the main objective was to enjoy the companionship of hunting together and the vibrant fall colors of October. Though the birds were scarcer than hen's teeth, they had seen and shot enough for a couple of meals at the cabin.

Fred Collyar loved to show off Jason's abilities with a shotgun, and at one point, bet a friend five dollars his boy could hit three clay pigeons in one throw. Jason stood nervously at the edge of the lake while his dad threw the targets into the air. He'd done it . . . three shots, three broken pigeons.

The men spent their evenings swapping lies and joking with and about each other. It was a time Jason would always treasure.

In early November Jason and his father returned a final time to the cabin. It was deer season. Three days of sitting morning and evening in a cold deer stand could not deter his enjoyment of being outdoors. He had not shot a buck, but his Dad had, and the two of them hung, skinned, and butchered it at the cabin. It was the first time Jason actually helped clean a deer, and he'd been pleased it hadn't bothered him . . . stomach wise. The day they had left it snowed hard, covering the cabin with a white blanket of purity. Driving into Pine River, they had taken the deer hide to Shamp's Meat Market where they traded it for a new pair of deerskin gloves. It had been a great hunting season.

By Christmas, Jason had grown out of his fall school clothes. He now stood five foot nine inches, his body filling out to match "the new view from above," his mom would say. One only had to look at the fifteen-year-old Jason to know he was going to be a fine-looking man . . . tall, blond, and well-muscled, with bright blue eyes.

Under the Christmas tree, Jason reaped a bounty of computer gadgets and games, but the biggy was a new 12-gauge shotgun. His dad told him warmly, that he'd earned the right to carry the big gun. His Grandmother Collyar presented him with the complete set of "The Foxfire Books," edited by Eliot Wigginton. Jason found these books a new experience in reading. He thoroughly enjoyed the mountain folklore that the volumes covered in detail. The books encompassed everything from making medicine out of rootstock to producing the finest of moonshine. He marveled at how the pioneers survived and the ingenuity they displayed in their daily lives.

The year, 2025, blossomed with snow, snow and more snow. Much as he loved Minnesota, winter did have its drawbacks. As May approached, news broadcasts began mentioning rumors of a meteor passing near the Earth. Some religious organizations even went so far as to predict the end of time. However, the President, on several occasions, reassured the country to the contrary. Jason hadn't given it two minutes thought one way or the other. Life was good, and he was going to ask Bethany to the dance.

1 June 2025 National Institute of the Medical Sciences, Atlanta, GA

Sam Carlon and Luke Lipsy were working late into the evening. Several hours had passed since other scientists employed at the military's "Chemical, Biological and Nuclear Warfare Research Laboratory" had turned their Bunsen burners off and left for home. It was the end of an extremely long day for the two remaining men; in fact, it had been a long week. It was just eight days past when Carlon and Lipsy determined they had indeed developed a new biological virus. A virus they both feared would possibly be added to the arsenal of the United States Armed Services. They, along with the twenty members of their team, had been working on the development of this new virus for the past five years. Now it was a reality. The virus lived, and its lethality frightened the crap out of them.

Doctor Sam Carlon was a man of reputation in the research field of bacteria and viruses. He had been recruited by the government in 2012 for the specific purpose of developing a new, highly potent, and extremely lethal virus for military use. The promise of his own lab and staff seduced him to accept the proposal, though he'd given little thought to the actuality of causing deaths on a future battlefield. Now the reality was hammering home with the thudding of a migraine headache, the likes of which he would just as soon forget.

The two were talking about their recent discovery. Where and how to permanently store the small vial of death was of major concern. This virus, code-named, "Lex Luther," after the nefarious criminal mind of Superman comics, was an airborne bug with no known enemy in the human body's defense system. Developed to attack only the human mammal, it began disabling a host in twenty-four hours or less, and killed within three days after contact. Seventy-two hours from first contact until the body destroyed itself from within. The virus attacked the internal organs, causing them to rupture and bleed. Once the virus infected an individual, there was no cure; nothing to ease the pain and nothing that could stop the unfortunate from dying.

Carlon and Lipsy were working not over a lab table, but rather discussing the ramifications of the new virus. The men felt that it should be destroyed outright . . . there was just too much danger of their new "child" escaping into the real world. They were very aware of the catastrophic consequences if "Lex Luther" should find its way out of their laboratory . . . it could well destroy humanity. The issue was too weighty, and in the end, they resolved to report their findings to Washington the next day. It was, they agreed, really a decision for men much higher in the military and governmental structure. The vial was gently placed in the facilities' security safe . . . locked away for yet another night. The small flask of man-made death would spend another night in its specially designed container, incarcerated in the environmentally controlled confines of a vault in Atlanta, Georgia.

CHAPTER 3

Avengers VII2

June 2025 8 AM, EST / Anoka, MN

Jason opened one eye to the world, and elected to snuggle deeper into his covers. School was out, and he did not need to leap into the day. As the cobwebs of sleep began to clear, he remembered he had a new game to load on his computer . . . Avengers VII. He had been looking forward to killing off the demons of another land ever since he had seen the game on a friend's computer. He had finally scraped up enough money to buy his own copy, and this morning he was going to load it up and play to his heart's content.

Uncovering his head, Jason looked out on the Minnesota spring, morning. It was raining . . . a real frog strangler, as his grandmother would say. "Good," he thought, "a perfect day for laying low in the office;" the *office* being his hideaway in the shelter. "Up and at 'em," he hummed to himself as he rolled out of his twin bed, and headed for the bathroom.

"Get out of there, pest," Jason yelled at his sister, Sally. "You've been in there long enough, and if I don't reach the stool soon I'm going to pee under the door, got it!"

Sally, who had recently turned the ripe old age of ten, decided, much to Jason's frustration, she needed to primp in the bathroom each morning. Now he was just out of the rack, standing in front of the bathroom door with his legs crossed to keep from peeing in his underwear. "Come on, twerp, I'm serious, I need to get in there. Now!"

The door swung open with a bright-eyed, blond-haired girl standing firmly in the doorway with her tongue stuck out. "Cute," Jason sighed, as he rushed past her to the toilet. "Shut the door on your way out."

"You're gross," cried his sister as she ran down the hall, leaving the door open.

"Sisters," thought Jason, "are a royal pain in the butt."

2 June 2025 8 AM EST / New Land

"Yes, I agree," Gilmore stated to the group before him. He had called a final meeting of his small working staff before The Devil's Face struck later that morning. Gilmore was attempting to organize The Few, using a military structure as a reference point. Using the natural layout of the tunnels, he decided to have each housing spoke elect their own leader. The four elected officials would then be accountable to him as the ultimate decision-maker of New Land. Doctor Duke, his newly appointed Chief of Staff, was to hand pick individuals from the four tunnels to sit as heads of various administrative and work-a-day functions. The command staff duties were over and above those already assigned these individuals when they were selected as one of The Few. Every man and woman who passed through the huge steel doors leading into his or her new home under the mountains possessed a special skill. New Land was staffed with doctors, psychologists, nuclear specialists, contractors, electricians, and a myriad of other talents necessary to operate and administer a city.

Gilmore gave names to each of the tunnels, Alpha, Bravo, Charlie, and Delta. Basically, a miniature government was being established along the "chain of command" structure of the military. Two factors in Gilmore's mind determined the organization from which he would control the residents of New Land: First, it was an arrangement with which he was intimately familiar, and therefore he could work smoothly within its composition. Second, it was a means of providing an identity for each four living areas, thereby fostering a team-like atmosphere for the vast majority of men and women who now lived underground. Keeping "his" people happy and busy was his major concern.

"Yes, I think gathering all the residents into the common areas is a good idea. If we do have tunnels collapse, we'll have a work force at hand to start a dig out. We have less than three hours; so let's get cracking. Doctor Duke, would you hang with me for few minutes?" Gilmore said, as a means of dismissing the others.

"Doctor, what's the word in the caves? How are our people reacting toward the life style we have structured?"

"Frankly," Duke replied, "I'm surprised at how well they have accepted you as a near dictator, but under the circumstances, I guess your way of creating order from a chaotic situation is by far the best, and has been accepted exceedingly well."

"Good, good, but what is your personal opinion?"

"I've been too busy to give it much thought, but Margaret has made several comments about separating our people into groups. Being a sociologist as well as a psychologist, she is concerned that by dividing into cells, with separate leaders, we will develop special interest groups. If that should happen, your job of keeping the peace is going to be much more difficult than if we all remained a single entity.

"I suppose she is right," Gilmore mused, "but I have to get some control, or we'll have dissension in the ranks. Perhaps Margaret could provide me with some thoughts and recommendations after the big bang."

"I'll certainly ask her to put something on paper for you, if it will help."

"Thanks. Now, I guess it's time we start heading for our stations in The Hub. May the Lord be with us."

2 June 2019 9:10 AM EST, Anoka, MN

Jason chewed his last bite of muffin with gusto and flurry. Never much of a breakfast eater, greatly to his mother' chagrin, he finished his morning English muffin and honey. Gulping down the last few swallows of OJ, he slid his chair away from the table.

"Where ya going?" asked Sally.

"Down to the office. I've got the new Avengers VII to load into my computer."

"Cool! Can I help?"

"No way! Why don't you go play with Jennifer next door? After I get it loaded, and after I've had a chance to blast my way through the creatures trying to destroy Earth, maybe I'll let you have a go at it. But you'll have to promise you'll get out of the bathroom when I need to go. Deal?"

"You promise?"

"You bet," Jason smiled. Actually, he got along with his younger sister quite well. He, without realizing it, was a very protective brother, and even enjoyed her company at the computer.

Gathering the game from the kitchen counter, Jason headed for the basement. "Did Mom tell you when she would be home?" He asked over his shoulder.

"No, but she left a note by the phone," Sally mumbled through a half-eaten spoonful of Cap'n Crunch. "She went shopping with Mrs. Frazer."

Jason detoured through the kitchen into the den to read his mother's note.

Kids,

Went shopping at Northtown Mall with Mrs. Frazer. I plan to stop by and see Dad at his construction site on University Ave. before I come home. Should be back by 2.

Love,
Mom

Great, thought Jason as he walked back through the kitchen to the basement door; six whole hours without Mom asking me to take out the garbage or something. Taking the basement steps two at a time, he hit the switch that lit up his office. There stood his pride and joy, a HP 5500 computer with CD-ROM, HD DVD, and Multi-Media pack. Next to his fishing tackle and shotguns, nothing was more precious. Well, maybe girls, particularly Bethany, might fit into the picture of importance somewhere, but for now it was time to play Avengers VII. Switching on his machine, Jason began the process of loading his new game.

2 June 2019 8:30 EST / The White House

The President and Bob Whitman sat in silence. There was not much to talk about since their last encounter just a few hours ago. They both knew it was near the end, but were determined to see it out. Sitting around the two men were their wives and grown children.

"How long after the asteroid hits will we feel the effects?" the President's wife broke the hush.

It was Bob Whitman who looked up from his lap, where he had been silently staring, to answer. "We really have no idea. It could be immediate, or it could be hours. Estimates contrived by experts range from total Earth destruction on impact to a slow death by an ensuing ice age."

The telephone rang and the President reached for the hook. "Yes, put him through. Doctor Ellis, I take it you made the trip all right?"

"Yes, sir," replied Ellis from the other end. "I'm as close to ground zero as I can hope to be. Professor Dacha, here at the University of Bangui, has been very helpful in setting up the arrangements for transmissions to you and others. How goes it on your end? The Few are safely tucked away under their mountain and we're waiting as best we can," answered the President. "Have you been able to see the damn thing yet?"

"Oh yes, it has become quite visible in the Southern Hemisphere, even though we are located at the very northern extremities. The Devil's Face is moving towards us at a very predictable rate and dead-on course."

"I see," replied a President resigned to losing his country and his life. "Please stay on the line as long as you can."

2 June 2024 9 AM EST / Atlanta, GA

Doctors' Sam Carlon and Luke Lipsy stood before the great steel door leading to the cold storage safe on level three of the National Institute of Medical Sciences. The men, with deep lines etching their faces, looked as if they had had little sleep. As the two-and-a-half-ton door swung open on its hydraulic hinges, they exchanged knowing glances with one another. The haze of green light reflected their haggard looks. Housed within the safe's walls lived some of the most dangerous biological agents known to man. Their terrible "Lex Luther" sat along with rows of vials and flasks of bacteria, viruses, and molds that even Satan himself would not have thought possible.

"Well, Sam, what do we work on today, death, destruction, or both?"

"Neither. Let's have a cup of coffee and think about it first," Doctor Carlon replied. "Besides, I've got a couple of phone calls to make." He turned, with Doctor Lipsy in tow, and moved toward the elevator, leaving their colleagues to gather other vials of death from the safe.

2 June 2024 1000 AM EST / The White House

"It's clearly visible now, probably just seconds from reaching our atmosphere," spoke the sad, yet strangely excited voice of Doctor Ellis. He had been on the phone with the President and perhaps two-dozen colleagues for the past hour. Conversation ranged from general small talk to the scientific ramifications of The Devil's Face. Now, here it was, a great planet-like object actually blocking part of the moon's light in the nighttime darkness of the African continent.

"There, there, it just hit the atmosphere. It is burning like something from hell. The whole sky has lit up in cosmic fireworks. My God, but it's huge! It is coming, oh Lord, it's coming. Oh Lord, it really is the Finger of God coming to touch us . . . ." Static and then silence.

CHAPTER 4

The Strike

2 June 20225 at 1020 EST

The Devil's Face, a mindless hunk of iron and nickel, a massive ball of fire a quarter the size of Earth's moon, struck the waist of Africa with a power few living men could begin to comprehend. If it were possible, the "thing" hit with the magnitude of all the world's nuclear weapons detonating at the same instant multiplied by a hundred million. Or like a six-foot boulder hitting the windscreen of an automobile traveling four hundred miles per hour; Earth would be the car.

In the past, when an asteroid struck Earth, a crater was formed with a corresponding ring around the cup-shaped depression. This collar was formed by the remnants of the asteroid and the collision site, as both disintegrated on impact. The Devil's Face did not vaporize, as it should have. At least not all of it. Its central core drove for the very heart of the planet. Africa, or the vast majority of this continent, disappeared into the molten rock of Mother Earth. The planet shuddered under the impact, listing six degrees off its normal twenty-three and half tilt, and, for better or worse, moved a fraction out of her orbit. The deviation from orbit, in all probability, saved what little life remained, for at least ninety-five percent of the debris created by the strike was hurled back into space. The remaining dust would be sufficient to shade the sun's rays, but not enough to create an ice age.

Shifting on its axis created a severe strain on the polar ice caps. At the North Pole, cracks and fissures began to develop deep within the cap itself. As millions of tons of ice began to fracture and drop into the surrounding waters of the Chukchi, Brents, Norwegian, and Greenland Seas, mammoth tidal waves began to form, helped along their way by winds of more than three hundred knots. While the Arctic cap formed its waves of destruction, so too did the disappearance of Africa. Two waves over a thousand feet high moved into the Indian and Atlantic oceans. Again, strong winds, higher than man had ever known, helped push and build these mountains of water.

The core of The Devil's Face pushed its way into the very heart of Earth, disrupting and destroying the various supportive crusts that are layered from the surface to the magma. The faults, boundaries of two major plates that make up the Earth's crust, began to shift, slide, and break away from each other. The mid-oceanic ridge, the largest mountain range on Earth, sinuously winding its way through all the world's oceans, began to shear in both the Arctic and South Pacific oceans. Molten magma began pouring onto the ocean floor. Islands, such as the Fiji and Hawaiian chains, simply vanished beneath the waves. The San Andrea's Fault, one of the few active faults in the world, blew apart within minutes after the strike. The quake was beyond what the Richter scale could tabulate as California, Oregon, most of Washington State, and well over half of Mexico slipped into the Pacific Ocean. Great mountain ranges throughout Europe, Asia, and South America shifted on their twenty-six-mile-deep supportive crusts and toppled or sank beneath the surrounding landmasses. New fissure lines spread from the mid-oceanic ridge, many following mountain ranges or ancient riverbeds, such as the Mississippi. Volcanoes sprang up like wheat in a fertile field, only to die and be swallowed back into the Earth moments later.

By 10:30 EST, a mere twenty-eight minutes after The Devil's Face struck Earth, fifty percent of its human inhabitants were dead or dying. It was only the beginning of the devastation. The sun's gravitational pull moved Earth inexorably back into her proper orbit within two hours, and its axis was reestablished. A gray haze blotted the sun's rays to a whisper, and seventy-five percent of all life forms were swallowed into history. Continents moved, broken apart, or merely faded into oblivion. Ocean floors heaved their muds and sediments to the surface, covering low-lying lands, which in turn were washed clean by a passing tsunami. If the anguished cries of the continents destroying themselves had not wiped the life slate clean, the following wind of over three hundred knots scoured the land of everything in its path.

Extending from Cape Lookout, North Carolina, to well south of Cape Fear, the coast bears in an east west direction. Tracing a line due south of Cape Lookout's hook, the waters slowly deepen to ninety feet at the Sea Buoy, which is secured to the bottom fourteen miles offshore. Three miles further south lies a trench where the ocean floor drops suddenly to two hundred and fifty feet, and then rises equally rapidly to ninety feet once more. It is another fifteen miles to the continental shelf. That shelf, the part of the American continent that extends seaward, is a true cliff that drops over six hundred feet into the depths of the Atlantic Ocean. Fifteen minutes after the strike, the East Coast of the U.S. began to feel the effects of the asteroid's devastation. The Devil's Face, as it bore into the protective crust of Earth, opened a weakness in the Continental Shelf perpendicular to the trench. The strains on rock, limestone, and substructure plates became too intense and gave way. The ensuing fissure rapidly gained velocity in a westerly direction, splitting a fracture which, at first, was but a few feet wide, and then grew to one over a hundred feet across. The fracture touched land at Harkers Island and turned southwesterly, destroying Morehead City, Havelock, and Marine Corps Air Station, Cherry Point. The quake, driven by the rumbling of the entire substructure of the inner Earth, drove for Cape Fear. Southport, North Carolina, disappeared as the subterranean plates slid against each other, and the fissure turned due west. By the time it hit the hard supporting crust under the Blue Ridge Mountains, the crack had swallowed dozens of towns and cities, great and small.

The monumental earthquake bumped the mountains and turned to the southwest, forcing its violence toward Georgia. Atlanta felt the trembling of the planet and passed into history. Left in the quake's wake was a broken and shattered cold-storage safe in the Nuclear, Chemical, and Biological labs of Doctors Carlon and Lipsy. A small vial of deadly virus, named Lex Luther, teetered and fell to the safe's floor. Spreading on the ground, the liquid evaporated into the swirling winds that were carrying dust, debris, cars, and trains at three hundred and fifty miles per hour.

The serpentine gap found a weakness under Alabama and moved northwesterly for America's mid-west. Roaring through Nashville, tearing the ground like a child ripping a sheet of paper, the quake zeroed in on the Golden Arch of St. Louis and the Mississippi River. The mighty river had, over millions of years, etched a natural groove, and northward the quake hurled its destruction. Through the hearts of cities such as Keokuk, Davenport, and Dubuque, it raced. Reaching the twin cities of Minneapolis and St. Paul, it fell on them as it had others, leaving little but rubble, fires, and death. Cutting its way north, the great quake began to lose vitality, finally dying at the Mississippi's headwaters in Itasca State Park.

As Cape Lookout's earthquake dealt destruction in its deadly travels, three great tidal waves were traveling hell bent for leather towards the East Coast of the U.S. At 12:30 EST, the first two walls of water arrived from the north. These mighty waves, given birth in cold Arctic waters, bore down on the northeastern states of the U. S., their western edges sweeping the corners of Canada. By the time the third barrier of moving water pressed in from Africa, the two Arctic waves had struck beaches from Newfoundland to the Virgin Islands and Maine to Virginia, rinsing them clean of every living thing. However, the Arctic waves were but children compared to the tsunami from the east. By the time this wave began its rise up and over the shallow waters of the Continental Shelf, it towered a mile high. When it hit the shores of North America, nothing but the mountain ranges of the East Coast could stop its movement westward. The wave swept across Florida, exposing a bone white substructure of limestone. Between the earthquake and tidal waves, there was little left of the eastern coast of the United States and Canada.

The Devil's Face was destroying Earth faster than the planet had come into existence millions of years past.

2 June 2025 Anoka, Minnesota, 1045 EST

Jason was well into solving the mysteries of the Avengers robotic enemies, and the ways and means of destroying them. After loading his new game and completing the necessary setup requirements, he was totally immersed in the fast-paced computer game. The only interruption in his concentration was Sally yelling down the basement stairs that she was going next door to play with Jennifer. Suddenly, he looked up, startled.

"What was that?" Jason thought aloud. It was if some primal fear passed through his body, producing goose bumps on his arms and causing the hair to rise slightly on the back of his neck. Looking around the small concrete enclosure all seemed proper, with his mother's canned vegetables lined neatly on the far wall shelves. Glancing back at his computer paraphernalia, nothing appeared to be wrong; still, all of his senses were casting about for something not quite as it should be. Perceiving it in his posterior first, as tremors moved along the wooden legs of his chair, Jason leaped to his feet. Something was very wrong!

The basement started to heave and roll as the quake came nearer. Jason reached out with his right arm to steady himself on the desk. Instincts began relaying signals to his feet to run out of his basement hole in the ground. He began to move, only to be struck by several jars of canned tomatoes. The heavy glass containers hit his left shoulder, knocking him off balance. His left hip struck the sharp corner edge of the desk, splitting his leg with a nasty gash. Trying to regain balance, he made another attempt for the heavy door. It was too late! The door was swinging shut as a large support beam gave way under the house. Jason, his fear rising with each microsecond, knew his only chance was to get clear of the house. The door moved a fraction as he slammed his shoulder into it. Backing up a step, he rammed the door again, moving it yet another inch or two. He backed up once more thinking "this will be the one," and leaped forward. Jason's peripheral vision registered a glimpse just before it crashed into his head... a quart jar of canned green beans. The world turned to blackness.

2 June 2025 New World, 1055 EST

The screeching of Earth's living rock in its death throes would have brought insanity to hell's wraiths. What it was doing to The Few was just that, causing momentary aberrance throughout the common areas of New Land. Men and women were rolling on the cold granite floors holding their ears with both hands. Some were clawing at the walls or each other trying to get away from the horrific din reverberating from tunnel to tunnel. California was plummeting into the inky blue of the Pacific.

Gilmore was terrified for the first time in his fifty-five years. The noise forcing its way into his brain was beyond anything he would ever again experience. The mountains, under which their new home was dug, shook and trembled with increasing intensity. He could not have been more frightened if he were standing in an open field, caught between the rifles of two enemies.

Doctor Duke, eyes watering with fear, hugged Margaret close to his chest. Looking up at the big black man he wondered, how can he be so calm? What's the man made of . . . steel?"

"What the hell is going on Doctor," Gilmore bellowed over the din of crying rock. "Nobody told us it was going to be like this. When is it going to end?" His voice was as regulated as his demeanor appeared, but his heart was pounding with the adrenaline of fear. "We've got to get this crowd under control before they start tearing each other apart," he demanded, grabbing his Chief of Staff by the shirt collar and shaking him like a leaf.

"What do you expect me to do?" screamed Duke.

"You head for the common areas of tunnels Alpha and Bravo. I'll take Charlie and Delta. Get in there and try to calm them down. Tell lies, hit them if they need it, but get them under control."

Duke nodded and stood slowly. "Margaret, come on, we've got to go help."

"Like hell we do. We're going to die right now and I don't have to be running off just because 'he' says so." She was mad, her anger circumventing the terror she felt.

"Come on, honey, help me. I need you." He stood, pulling her with him. Using each other and the walls of the tunnel for support to overcome the shaking ground, they started for the common room of Alpha tunnel.

Gilmore entered the large rock room of Charlie tunnel. If the sounds piercing the air were not enough to frighten, then the sight of men and women going crazy certainly was. He strode to the closest man and yanked him off his knees like a rag doll. "Get it under control, mister," Gilmore howled, his eyes burning into the terrified man.

The man went limp. His head dropped to his chest. Then, after a moment, he looked up at Gilmore with red fury. "Yes, sir," he saluted, his spirit broken because of the strength Gilmore displayed. "What is it you want . . . sir?"

"Help me get this bunch under control. Help me calm them down," he ordered, dropping him and moving to a woman banging her head on the rock floor.

The two men moved rapidly through the room. Gilmore forced his will on others; his unwilling assistant worked slower, but with equal effect by quietly soothing those around him. They would become his friends, the men and women with whom he was going to live with the rest of his life. Soon, the only sounds from Charlie tunnel were that of ripping rock. Gilmore, in control of himself after having conquered his own internal struggle, once again grabbed the man he had first imposed his iron will upon.

"What's your name?"

"Jack."

"Well, Jack, let's get to Delta."

They ran for the door when, suddenly, it was quiet. The lack of sound was almost as frightening as the screaming rock had been. It was over, thought Gilmore. He had overcome yet another crisis, this one unlike anything combat or Washington's politics had wrought. He stopped and turned to Jack.

"Thanks for the help, Jack. You did an outstanding job. Come see me when things have settled down."

"Right, sir," Jack said, with a sarcastic tone. "Sure I will."

Gilmore took no notice of the man's acerbic tone, as he rushed back to the Hub to find his command post in complete chaos. The staff on duty had been subjected to the same psychological demons that possessed all of The Few. Stations were vacated, lights of warning flashed on instrument and monitor panels, and small electrical fires plumed acrid smoke into the room.

"Status of the power plant?" demanded Gilmore. "Come on, people, let's get cracking." He strode through the large room radiating determination and dominance.

Slowly, chairs filled with duty-bound experts.

CHAPTER 5

The Awakening

Jason, his head exploding with flashes of colored light, tried to move his arms. Though stiff and sore, they seemed intact. He had no idea how long he'd been lying on the cold cement floor, but his instincts told him it had been a long time. Everything hurt, particularly his leg and head. Something heavy pinned his legs, but he could still feel them. Though the pain hurt like all get out, he took the soreness to be a good sign. He opened his eyes. It was dark, darker than the inside of an inkwell.

"Jesus, what happened?"

Slowly he began struggling under the weight on his legs. With a clatter that echoed through the small room, his computer and monitor rolled to the floor. Jason sat up, right hand going to his head. He felt blood crusted to his scalp and down his face. "Dried," he thought. "It has been a while since I got knocked out." Feeling into the darkness, he found his desk and using its corner as a support, he pulled himself to his feet. "A bit wobbly," he mused, but his legs held under him

"I can't see a thing." His eyes opening as big as saucers tried to gather a glimmer of light. Nothing! He felt an overwhelming fear welding from his gut. What if I'm blind? No, his reason was soothing him. It's just dark. The electricity must be out, he thought. He reached out into the blackness, trying to locate himself in the small room. Taking a step, he slipped on a jar, and tried to catch himself, only to step on another. It was like a cartoon character running on ball bearings, and down he went, breaking his fall with his right hand. Pain exploded in his head, already saturated with confusion. He slipped into unconsciousness yet again.

When Jason next opened his eyes, there were small streaks of light streaming through the shelter's door. He could see enough of his small room to learn that it was a disaster of broken vegetable jars and computer equipment. Moving slowly, he sat upright and took stock of his situation. Stabs of fear shot through his senses, his heart seemed to be racing in his chest, and clamminess lay heavy about him.

"Why hasn't anyone come looking for me?" he thought aloud. With shaking hands, he felt his head again, and wiped more dried blood from his face. Jason stretched his legs and groaned. Reaching down to his right hip, he felt the laceration inflicted by his desk when he went down the first time. Touching it gently through the rip in his jeans, he found that it was neither deep nor dangerous, but it had bled profusely, soaking his pants. From his vantage point on the floor, Jason felt a pang of heartache, as he realized his computer was destroyed. What happened? What in the world happened, he wondered again?

Swallowing his fright, he yelled, "Mom! Dad! Mom, Dad, I need some help down here." Nothing but a shifting of something heavy above him. "Sally, are you there? Come on somebody, give me a hand."

"I wonder how long I've been down here." Jason spoke aloud.

It was dark the first time I woke up; he struggled to put the pieces together. Now at least I have a splinter of light. It must have been night the first time and now it's the next day. Okay, why haven't Mom and Dad come home? Pondering this question, he began controlling his fear. There must be a reason why no one came to my rescue . . . a perfectly good reason. Maybe it hasn't been very long since I passed out; I just think it has. Dad will be here anytime now, and we'll be eating supper soon. Yeah, that's it, he thought.

Painfully standing, Jason pushed several jars out of his way and moved to the heavy door. Peering at the basement, he drew in his breath with a sucking sound of surprise. His head reeled, and the anxiety returned. "My God, no wonder no one can hear me," he whispered. The basement was nothing but a caved in house.

Jason pushed on the steel door. It would not budge. He looked through the two-inch opening and could see the problem. A ten-foot 2 x 6 was wedged between the door and his Mom's washing machine. He would have to knock it away from the door. Looking around his office, he found nothing long enough to reach.

"There's got to be a way," he thought frantically. "But how?" He moved to his overturned chair and stood it upright. "I've got to get control of myself."

Profound mind-numbing dread was beginning to steal his ability to reason. He sat and took long deep breaths, trying to calm himself into a thinking mode. Taking stock of his situation in a realistic, one step at a time way, he wrestled his fear down where it would work for him rather than against. Swallowing his heart back into his chest, he found he was hungry.

"Ridiculous," he reflected. "Thinking of my stomach at a time like this." Absentmindedly, he picked up a jar of tomatoes, unscrewed the top and began drinking the cool goodness of his Mom's garden fruits. "The shelves. The shelves are long enough to pry with."

Leaping from his chair, he sagged under the pain of his leg. "Got to move a bit slower if I'm going to get the job done," he grunted to himself, seizing the bottom board.

Jason pulled against the nails holding it in place. Straining with frustration, he heaved again, this time with success. The long plank succumbed to his strength and broke free with a snap. Carefully, so he would not fall ass-over-teakettle, he made his way to the door and stuck the shelf through its small opening. With all of his strength, he rammed the shelving into the wedge holding him prisoner. Thud! The two boards collided, neither moving, but sending the power of his stroke back into Jason's arms. He winced under the sudden pain it brought to his head, arms and injured hip. Three more times wood hit wood without influence beyond his own pain. Then, on his fourth swing, the shelf broke, but the jammed wedge moved slightly.

"It's going to work," smiled Jason. He grappled at another shelf, spilling what few jars were left. "Dumb, dumb, dumb! I can't be throwing food away like that. No telling how long it's going to be till I get out of here."

Carefully, he gathered the unbroken canned goods from the floor and off the three remaining shelves. A total of fifteen jars now sat neatly on his desk. At least I won't starve for a while. I just hope Mom, Dad, and Sally are okay. What could have happened to them?

Turning back to the door, he found the light he required was fading fast. It was cold he realized for the first time since awaking; too darn cold, even if he was in the cellar. Shivering, Jason thought it best to quit for the time being. He needed sufficient light to aim his battering ram against the board locking him in. Cleaning a corner of his prison of broken glass and vegetables, he sat down and curled into a fetal position. The labor had taken his mind off the fear, and though he felt chilled, it was not long before he fell into a fitful sleep.

Light came again, and with morning, it was time to go to work. There was still no sign of help. No voices, no machinery, no sounds at all, except for his own attempts of freeing himself. Resigned to the situation, Jason began the task of beating the jammed 2 x 6 in earnest. He was still chilled, but he could live with that. His stomach growled for something to fill the space in its convoluted, acid filled confines. That, at least, was easily taken care of with a jar of canned beans, and another of California peaches. The day may not have been filled with the joy of living, but at least he was alive. Clutching the end of his new shelf, he aimed carefully at his antagonist, the wedge. With all of his strength, Jason banged at the wooden lock holding him a prisoner. With each blow, pain streaked through his body with red fury, but he continued throwing his weight into the task at hand . . . ridding himself of the board holding him captive. His efforts were not without success, but for every blow that moved the wedge, five did little but cause pain. Still he worked, breaking two more of his precious shelves. The day's light began to fade once more.

"How many days have I been here?" he wondered, as he swung the board yet again.

With a crash, the 2 x 6 gave way. The steel door moved on its hinges enough for him to look out into a world of chaotic wires, pipes, flooring, ceiling fixtures, and furniture. It was as if his house had folded in upon itself. Something else rolled into his small cell, something that earnestly renewed his panic. An odor, which had been but a whisper before now, engulfed him as the door swung open. The scent of oily smoke, tainted with roasted meat, wafted into his small underground room. This time the shivers running up and down his body were not from the cold. Rather, they were caused by a premonition surrounding the terrible aroma filling his olfactory senses.

Exertion from board battering, coupled with the nausea he was experiencing over the smells emanating from above, made the decision for him. He would spend another night in the safety of his office. Though he had worked like a demon most of the day, he could not eat. His stomach, normally capable of ingesting anything at any time, could not overcome the smells. He curled into a ball and tried to rest. Sleep was a long time coming, but finally fatigue overcame the imaginary pictures flashing before his eyes.

Awakening on his third morning, Jason was starving. He downed two jars of tomatoes and the last can of peaches. The smell, though still apparent, was not as evident as the day before.

"Maybe I'm getting used to it." He grimaced at the thought. On his sleeve, he wiped the last of the syrupy peach juice. He felt dirty with sweat and blood. "My kingdom for a bath," he laughed ruefully at himself. His head was still sore. The leg wound had never been serious; however, under the cut, the tissues were still tender to the touch.

Gazing through the door, the half-light reflecting off what remained of the Collyar's home, he thought, "All in all, I guess I'm pretty lucky to be alive. I guess I can stand a few hurts." Looking back into the cement bomb shelter, he thanked his lucky stars he had been playing Doom. "What, three or four days ago?" he wondered.

He moved forward into the basement, dodging the debris of a dead house piled in disarray. Carefully he slithered around broken timbers, bent pipes, and shattered bricks. Gray light shining through and around the splintered pieces of the once comfortable house began to show a pathway upward. With determination, Jason started his way to the surface. It took him over an hour, but finally his head breached the basement wall, and he looked out on his front yard. It was a scene from hell!

As he pulled himself over the edge, his mind was screaming, "No, this can't be. It just can't!" His neighborhood could not collapse like a toy Christmas scene. All the neighborhood homes were rubble; a mirror image of his own. Trees were down everywhere and the street was nothing but cracked asphalt, rising skyward in places. Fires blazed on the horizon. The most noticeable were to the southwest, where flames, hundreds of feet high, licked the sky. There was little breeze, and what did stir, filled the air with ash, creating a half-light. What little of the sun's rays filtered through the smoke, failed to warm his heart or body. Jason stumbled a few feet and sat heavily on the grass, his mouth gaping open and his body slack. It was as if a giant grabbed him by the collar and was shaking all the life from his body.

"This isn't happening," he kept telling himself. "I'll wake up and it will have been nothing but a nightmare. A dream brought on by the action in Doom. This isn't real. Nothing like this could be real . . . nothing!"

Sometime later, Jason's faculties began a slow shift into first gear. How long he had been sitting, staring into nothingness, his mind a blank, he did not know and he didn't care. Jason staggered to his feet, walked a few steps and relieved himself on the stubble of a small jack pine. The horrid smell, he knew, came from the fires. Everywhere he looked was devastation of monumental magnitude. Houses, smoke whisping from their ruins, filled his view. Looking down his street, he could not see one remaining structure. Few trees stood and no living thing moved. Greasy black smoke boiled from the direction of the Twin Cities, and uncontrolled fires raged in every direction. His lungs filled with the soot of burning flesh and dying trees, of gas pumps and manufacturing plants. As his mind lurched with every new assault, his primal instincts seeped into his conscious mind telling him to survive. Sick to his stomach, but gaining the strength needed to persist, Jason looked up into the overcast heavens.

No one could survive this mess, he thought. Just as quickly, he remembered he had, indeed, made it through whatever wrought this havoc. Maybe others then? Starting down the street, he spotted the ruins of Jennifer's house where Sally had told him she was going to play.

Slowly at first, Jason moved toward the smoldering ruins of what had once been his neighbor's home. Now he was running, dodging a downed maple tree, tripping in its branches, and scraping himself off the ground to run to the edge of the crumpled house. Screaming at the top of his voice for his sister brought no response. Jason stepped closer to the basement's edge and peered into the rubble.

"Oh my God! No, no! This can't be happening," kept storming through his brain like a runaway freight train. He could plainly see Sally's crumpled body lying amidst the destruction. She was skewered, like a raw shish ka bob, on a sewer pipe.

Jason, staggering under the kaleidoscope of sights, began to cry. He cried as he retrieved his sister. He cried as he found a garbage can lid and dug a shallow grave in their back yard, and he cried as he buried her. He cried, not some weak whimper, but tears that rolled from his soul. He wailed great sobs of grief for his family, who he intuitively knew was dead, and for himself for being left alone. Rivers of salty tears rained down his cheeks. He didn't try to stop them. The pain was too massive to try to hide away in some fake macho niche of his mind. He felt the pain of being alive; when he knew he should have been with those he loved. He felt betrayed that they had left him. His heart, if anatomically possible, would have broken, but since the heart kept pumping, Jason cried.

*****

Doctor Benjamin Duke, Margaret, and Gilmore sat on one side of the small conference table in Gilmore's office. Across from them were the newly elected tunnel leaders, each wearing an armband of varying colors. Gilmore introduced the bands as an identification tag; a quick means of knowing in which tunnel the wearer lived.

Several days had passed since the strike, and things below were returning to a semblance of normalcy. There was damage of course, but nothing irreparable. Their main concern was the nuclear reactor. Built under strict specifications to withstand the strongest and most violent of earthquakes, the reactor had survived. However, the Operations Room, at the wheel's Hub, did receive minor damage, mainly to delicate computer components. The outer rim of the wheel sustained several cave-ins as well. Though the fallen rock alone did not cause a threat to those living within the confines of the wheel, the broken and dying plants they crushed, and the fact the entire rim's lighting system was out, did. The seven people sitting at Gilmore's conference table were there to discuss what was to be done.

Doctor Duke opened, "Okay, we're not in immediate danger. We have more than enough oxygen to last us several months, even with the current foliage loss. However we've got to get the lighting fixed, and very soon. Without proper lighting throughout the rim, we're going to rapidly start losing more and more of our vegetation. We've got to clear the rim and fix the lighting as soon as we possibly can."

To Gilmore's surprise, the man who had helped him settle the turmoil in Charlie tunnel during the quake turned out to be that shaft's chosen leader. He was now glaring at their overlord. Jack, wearing the blue band of Charlie tunnel, did not care for Gilmore one bit. It was evident in his body language, as well as the intensity which blazed in his eyes. His demeanor was as cold as the rock that outlined the walls of Gilmore's office.

"Well, what do you want us to do about it?" Jack Mossmen asked mordantly.

Noting the tone and inflection in Jack's voice, Gilmore turned to face him directly, eyes glaring. "Fix it, of course." His voice was chiseled from iron.

"It's going to be difficult to move the heaviest of the boulders," Doctor Duke stated flatly. "We'll have to break the larger rocks by hand before we can move them. Once we have the passages clear of debris, then we can set the electricians to work repairing the lighting problem."

"Who's going to do the rock breaking?" Jack asked.

"We'll divide into sections, pie like," responded Gilmore. "Each tunnel will be responsible for the outer ring clockwise. In other words, Alpha will clear to the start of Bravo, Bravo to Charlie and so on. We'll equally divide the necessary shovels and picks between each working party. Broken rock will be transported to a point midway between Charlie and Delta, since that is where the worst of the cave-in's occurred."

"Now wait a damn minute," interrupted Jack. "What is that going to do to the oxygen levels in our tunnels? Are you thinking Charlie and Bravo are expendable?"

"Of course not." It was Doctor Duke who answered. "The entire rim is what supports our oxygen levels, not any one part."

Margaret, who had been quietly listening to the tone of conversation, looked at each member sitting before her. Trouble is brewing and it is going to start with Charlie tunnel, she thought. Wrinkling her brow, she ran her small fingers through rich, brown hair. I wish I'd died with those above. At least then it would have been over quickly, but now it's going to be slow plodding to my grave. Much too morbid thoughts for a good psychologist, she thought. Looking around the room, she wondered at the rock walls of Gilmore's office, filled with diagrams of the huge wheel in which they all now lived. One wall, however, was blank except for what appeared to be a door. Strange, she thought. I wonder where it leads?

"I don't like it, not one bit, that you want to close down part of our rim," Jack was saying. He looked to the woman, wearing Delta's green. "What do you think? Your tunnel is going to be affected as much as Charlie's."

`The young woman glanced first at Jack and then at Gilmore. "Let's wait and see what happens."

"Thank you for your confidence," Gilmore said, nodding to the woman from Delta. "Okay, let's get with it." Turning to Doctor Duke, "You're in charge of arranging the work parties and setting them up on the job. Report their progress this evening."

"Sure! When's evening?" the doctor retorted. His remark softened the atmosphere somewhat, but there was little doubt Jack was not happy with the entire situation.

The group slid their stainless steel chairs from the table and stood, glancing at each other as they filed from the small room. There was tension among the members, but each realized the rim must be cleared if any were to survive.

By late afternoon, work had been in progress for several hours. Many of the larger boulders had already been broken into smaller stones, and transported to the ever-increasing pile of rock between Charlie and Delta tunnels.

Jack, a tall, lanky man of twenty-eight, worked like a man possessed. It appeared he was everywhere at once, his slightly balding forehead shining under the lights. Just watching him, with his insatiable energy, drew comments of approval. Jack radiated his capability to steer those around him to their highest potential. Had he been in the Marine Corps, he would have been a commander's dream as a Sergeant's Major. He bantered, joked, and joshed his way from task to task, taking time to encourage each man and woman as he passed. It was hard, backbreaking labor, accomplished by flashlight and work stand lights. He made sure he spent more time with Delta's crew, getting to know them as well as his own squad. Throughout the day, he laughingly took verbal jabs at Gilmore's authority. Those who heard his quips laughed and went about their work. Jack was gaining popularity and he knew it. He was not only aware of what he was doing; he was carefully cultivating each rim worker's support. Jack wanted as many as possible of the fifteen hundred he lived with under the great Rocky Mountains to know him personally.

Doctor Duke meandered through the huge outer part of his home; the rim. He did not know the majority of his fellow dwellers who were working and sweating to clear the rim of rock and stone. He was not a people person, never had been, and never would be. His world had been confined to small offices, classrooms, and, of course, his heavenly stars. He was extremely uncomfortable in the leadership role he had been forced to assume, but he was doing the best he knew how. The problem facing him, as he walked the rim, was convincing those who broke stone not to damage living plants in the process. In the course of clearing the heavy, fallen boulders some of their precious herbage was being damaged or destroyed. His solemn face drew nods of acceptance, from the workers, but little else as he explained about saving the plants. By the time he returned to his cubicle, Doctor Duke was tired, very tired.

Hugging Margaret closely, Ben felt the glow of love surge through his very soul. "I'm way over my head with this Chief of Staff thing," he whispered in his wife's ear.

"I know, I know," Margaret whispered back. "But, my love, you are doing a fine job, and there are a lot of folks who realize how important your knowledge is to the survival of us all. Don't let this get you down, and most especially, don't let Gilmore wear on your nerves."

"He can be so damnably unreasonable at times. He makes decisions without consulting any of us. That upsets people. People like Jack Mossmen, from Charlie tunnel."

"Yes, I've noticed Jack's resentment, but his is more intense than most. Do you have any idea why?"

The couple moved to their small couch, the only place to sit comfortably in their living quarters. There was little to brighten the single room. The only mementos on display were two unassuming pictures . . . one of Margaret's parents, and a single snap shot of Doc Ellis.

Glancing toward the frames, Doctor Duke said, "I miss the old man. If only he could be here with us, I think we would have a far better chance of enduring the transitional months. I know you can feel the tension, and I know I do, but I have no idea how to cope with its effects."

"The man to watch is Mossmen," Margaret stated with emphasis. "He is an organizer, and it's obvious he has the confidence of his tunnel. That could be a good thing, but if he chooses to use his popularity to gain a power base, we might have a problem."

"What are you saying?"

"Only the obvious. Observing Gilmore and Jack this morning, I could sense more than just mistrust on Jack's part, but I can't put my finger on it. It worries me though."

"Okay, enough of this, what have you been doing this fine tunnel day?" her husband asked, wishing to change the subject.

"I've been counseling quite a few of our fellow moles on the virtues of being alive under tons of mountain rock. Frankly, that period during the strike has caused a mass paranoia about living under ground. Many of our companions are in need of help psychologically, just as we predicted would be the case."

Benjamin looked at the small woman sitting by his side. You could not call her pretty, certainly not cute, but to him she was the most beautiful woman God ever put on earth. "You, my lovely wife, are too fantastic for words." With those words, he leaned over and kissed her warmly. She returned his kiss with equal tenderness.

*****

Sitting next to the freshly torn earth of his sister's shallow grave, Jason cried himself out. There were no more tears, but sadness settled upon his heart like a stone, a hurt that could never be totally wiped away. It was late in the afternoon when he looked down at his sister's small grave . . . a grave he had dug in hurried desperation. "Goodbye my little Sally," he whispered softly, "I hope you knew how much I loved you."

Gathering himself from the ground, Jason looked around his neighborhood once again. This time, it was with determination, the type born from the need to overcome all odds and endure. Though he could see there was little chance of many living through whatever ripped his world apart he realized, with more certainty, others must be alive. Pondering where people might gather under these circumstances, he concluded it would be in a building that might possibly withstand such a monumental disaster.

"Something downtown," he thought. "Maybe the courthouse, a school, a church, any large cement structure."

With renewed strength, Jason started through the labyrinth which, until a few days ago, had been his home street. He wove around and over trees, cars, parts of houses, and even whole or torn bodies of neighbors and friends. It was just over two miles to the center of Anoka, and as he turned south on 7th Avenue, he became numb to the sights around him. There was too much death, too much destruction for any one individual to comprehend or understand in a lifetime, much less in the short period that had elapsed since his escape from his basement. As he approached Main Street, the sound of lawn mower engines began to hum in the fast-closing evening light.

"No. Not lawn mowers, they're portable generators," he realized. "If there are generators, then there are people!"

Jason stepped his pace up to a half trot. He would have moved faster, but the debris was too concentrated. He passed the TCF Bank on his right. Glancing at the ruined structure, he actually smiled at the sight of money lying in piles amongst the ruins of the building. The safe, an integral part of the building's construction, was broken open to the world. Jason did not care, and neither had anyone else. What good would money be in the ruined world that surrounded him? No, the generators' reverberations were far more important.

The courthouse, a substantial public building, had not totally survived the havoc, but it withstood the ravages enough to provide shelter. It was here Jason heard voices as he mounted the steps. Entering the hall, he was met with the drawn, ash white faces of two dozen or so men, women, and children. In their eyes, he saw the reflection of his own trauma. No one seemed to notice his entrance. They all huddled over a radio, while several generators hummed in the background.

"...East Coast has reported. From the disaster descriptions, which stations in Tennessee and Kentucky have given us, we fear there isn't much left of the coastal states from Maine to Florida. We know most of the Gulf States were swept by two or three mammoth tidal waves. If they were the residual effect of some great waves that hit the East Coast, nothing would be left. From the West Coast, we get the same . . . nothing. We know there were at least five major earthquakes reported to have shaken hell out of Colorado, Wyoming, and Idaho. The general consensus is that the St. Andrea fault finally gave way. Unfortunately, we have had no communication with anyone in California, Oregon, or Washington. We know a quake traveled up the Mississippi River basin. Indications are that the river simply does not exist any longer. Towns and cities along the entire river's length disappeared, or are in such devastation that for all intents and purposes, they are gone. Little is known what has happened to Europe, or any other country, for that matter. What few reports the HAM network has been able to glean tell of much the same sort of mass destruction worldwide.

> *To repeat, we know an enormous asteroid hit the earth three days ago. Where exactly this massive space invader hit we do not know, but its effects have been felt worldwide. If you are listening to this broadcast, do not, I repeat, do not expect help or aid of any sort. The entire United States has been devastated. You are on your own.*
>
> *This is KRCP radio, broadcasting from Del Rio, Texas, with 100,000 watts of pure power. We'll be back on the air one-hour from now to bring you up to date on any new information. This is Rick Owen, out."*

Except for the drone of the generators, the hall was deathly quiet. Each face stared into another with the blankness of incomprehension. Jason stepped forward, his rubber-soled shoes sounding like a tree falling in a quiet wood. "I'm Jason Collyar," he announced to no one in particular. "Is that true what he said on the radio?" Is the whole country like here? That's pretty hard to believe, don't you think?"

Dirty faces turned to stare at Jason, each with less expression than the one next to it. A big man of around sixty, his arm wrapped over the shoulder of a withered, sharp-nosed woman, looked sternly at Jason. "Son, believe it. Our world has come to an end and God will be sailing in on the clouds."

The man's words were like blows from a heavyweight boxer. Jason suddenly felt very tired. He was bone weary tired. It was the exhausted weariness that saps the very will from muscles and nerves. Moving slowly to a corner near the others, Jason, his back against the wall, slid into a fleshy heap on the floor. Sleep came instantly, a dreamless sleep. A slumber that attempts to heal the heart and soul.

CHAPTER 6

Decisions

Jason woke with a start, his mind fully alert.

"Sweet Jesus, son! We thought you had up and died on us. I'm real glad to see you ain't dead."

Jason was looking into the smoky blue eyes of the skinniest man he had ever seen. The man's face was lit from ear to ear with a stained tooth smile, and the joy in his voice was obviously genuine. "Nope, I guess I'm not dead yet, and frankly, I don't intend to be."

"Damn straight! I'm Jake, and from your entrance two days ago, I guess you'd be called Jason. Well, Master Jason, I'm right proud to make your acquaintance."

Smiling up at the man called Jake, Jason said, "I'm hungry."

"Ain't we all? Come on, son, get yourself up and we'll head to the supermarket for some vittles."

Struggling to get his feet under him, Jason stood. Every part of his body hurt. The cuts on his leg and head were healing for the most part, but the physical exertion he'd placed upon himself since being trapped in the bomb shelter was finally catching up with him. "I can't remember ever being so stiff, not even after football practice."

"Heck, boy, you've been a lyin' on that there hard floor for two days, what'cha expect?"

"It's hard for me to believe I slept for two whole days, but I was sure tired. Has there been any more news about the rest of the country?"

"Not much to fill you in on, lad. That there Rick feller just keeps a yammerin' about how the country sort of disappeared. Don't ya fret about it none now. Ain't nothin' ya can do about it no how, so let's go get somepin' in your belly."

Man and boy moved through the entrance of the Anoka Courthouse. Remnants of clothing, bedding, and other personal articles were strewn in various places, the belongings of other inhabitants of this strange home for the dispossessed. The only people Jason saw was a woman with two small children cowering in a corner. He nodded to her, but received no response.

"She's been like that since she arrived." Jake motioned to the woman's position with a toss of his head. "Reckon she might be ailin' from the trauma or such. The kids be okay most of the time, but I get tired of their yammerin' and cryin'. Her Hubby must be out gatherin' the daily grub for them. Fact is, that's where most everyone is, gatherin' food and scroungin' for gas for the generators. The town's a shambles, but there's still gear around we can use to make life a tad more comfortable till we figure what to do permanent like."

"Jake, what happened, do you know? I mean, what happened here in Anoka and the Twin Cities?"

"Don't reckon I know much more about that than you do, but from the talk I've heard, we've been struck by one helluva earthquake. Couple of the folks have been down to the river, but it's plumb gone. I ain't seen it, ya understand, but them that has says ain't nothin' but river banks with no water."

"No way! How can a river just disappear?"

"Got me! God didn't ask me for no advice, and I sure as heck ain't got none no way."

The two were slowly making their way west on Main Street, dodging cars, downed streetlights, piles of broken glass, and the dead. "What are we going to do about all these dead people lying around?" Jason asked. He was surprised at how he had adjusted to the hundreds of bodies scattered everywhere. "The stench is going to become overwhelming soon. As a matter of fact, it's getting pretty darn ripe right now."

"Ain't much we can do, boy. Thing is, the sun ain't as bright or hot as it should be this time of year, but them carcasses are going to drive us out of here soon. I figure to get in the country somewheres. A place where there ain't a house for a mile or two. Course, the problem is getting supplies hauled."

"My God, I can't believe it," Jason exclaimed in utter disbelief. They were standing in front of the Rum River Bridge, "You mean the Mississippi looks like this?" he questioned, pointing to the bare trickle of water flowing south under the twisted remains of the two-lane bridge.

"Yep, that's what I've been told. Peers the earth done just swallered her up, don't it? After we get some food in your belly, why don't we go have a look at the mighty 'Sip' for ourselves?"

"Yeah, I'd like that," Jason nodded his head.

They backtracked to Second Avenue, where they turned northward. Jason could see the downed sign of a Country Market about a half a block away. The sign appeared to be suspended in midair, cocked sideways with no base. As they walked closer, he could see that it had fallen across a heavy cable of a stoplight that had somehow withstood the tremors. He could also hear voices, the chatting of men and women at work gathering their provisions for the day.

The parking lot of the large supermarket was a mess of tangled cars, shopping carts, downed light poles, and the ever-present dead. As they walked closer to the doors, Jason could see bodies stacked in a pile outside the entrance.

"Guess shopping with the dead wouldn't be much fun," Jason said quietly to Jake.

Though the very idea of so many deaths sickened him, the vast number of corpses he had seen since escaping from under his house somewhat numbed him to the revolting sights.

In the store, Jason went to work finding something to feed the emptiness in his gut. He realized only packaged or canned goods were safe to eat. The smell of spoiling meats and vegetables, mixed with the decay of the dead outside, did not enhance his appetite. Still, nature overcomes such obstacles. It was an odd feeling, moving almost silently through a store that would normally be humming with activity. What had once been a thriving supermarket now was a shambles of spilled food, downed shelves, and spoiling vegetable matter. He encountered a few of his fellow "shoppers," smiled and said "good morning," but received little response in return. Passing what had once been a large cereal section, he grabbed a box of Cap'n Crunch that had survived the quake. Continuing down the aisles, he stuffed handfuls of his favorite cereal into his mouth and searched for canned meats, potato chips, sodas, and sweets.

Jake watched in amazement as the boy chose his breakfast of junk food.

"Boy, you ought to get some real food in ya. That stuff ain't gonna stick to your ribs for long, ya hear?"

Jason nodded absent-mindedly. Now sitting on the floor in the middle of the canned meat's aisle, after finding a can opener in the housewares section, he was busily stuffing Sour Cream and Onion chips in his mouth while opening a can of corned beef. He could not remember ever being so hungry. But then, he realized, he had not taken any nourishment for two days, and only canned peaches and tomatoes in the last week.

"Slow down, son," Jake said flatly. "You gonna make yourself sick."

Jason looked into Jake's pale blue eyes, and recognized the old man was right. He took a deep breath and forced himself to bite, chew, and swallow at a more relaxed pace. "Thanks, Jake! And thanks for helping me out."

Jake smiled down on his companion, thinking this young man might have the potential for helping others. There was going to be a lot of help needed, if making a life from the destruction that surrounded them was going to be possible. He liked Jason, and hoped the two would find some way of staying together for a while. "When you're done stuffing your face, we'll wander about and see if we can figure our next step, okay?"

"Sounds good to me." Jason smiled up at the man through a mouthful of corned beef.

*****

Sitting in Charlie Common Area Two, one of the four common areas each of the main living tunnels possessed, Jack Mossmen was discussing recent events with several of his fellow spoke dwellers. It had taken three entire twenty-four-hour days to break and move the rock in the rim. Jack spent as much time as he possibly could during each shift, ostensibly to help with the work, but Jack had other reasons as well. He wanted to get to know as many of the wheel's inhabitants as he could, but more importantly, he wanted them to know him. At the very least, he wanted his name to become commonplace throughout New Land.

"I don't know," a diminutive woman of twenty-eight was saying, "He has been making a good deal of right decisions. Besides, who of us could possibly see what was going to happen once we got down here?"

"Sure, he's made good decisions. I won't debate that. But he does all the decision-making without consulting any of us, not even the elected tunnel heads. That's what concerns me," Jack answered. "I just feel we should have an elected leader, not some self-styled ex-general who was set up as a dictator over us all. We wouldn't let that happen above ground. Why down here?"

"Because that was the way it was explained to us before we accepted life under the mountain instead of possible death above. I signed that paper, and so did you," the woman retorted. "Why do you want to upset the apple cart now?"

"I don't want to upset the apple cart. I just want us to have more say in what goes on down here. At least think about what I'm saying, okay?"

As Jack's conversation progressed, Doctor Duke was inspecting the electrical work in progress. The rock removal had gone well, but rewiring the massive greenhouse, which was the rim, was slowing to a snail's pace. The tons of rock which had broken under the stress of multiple quakes, ripped miles of wire feeding electricity to the hundreds of lights which shone on the rim's vegetation. Finding the breaks was hard enough, but splicing and securing them was a prolonged procedure. Already, plants were beginning to droop from lack of sufficient light. Doctor Duke was worried as he toured the work in progress. He knew each of the workers realized how important it was to get the lights back on, but he still encouraged them to hurry as best they could.

Striding around the outer circle of their home, Doctor Duke turned into Charlie tunnel, heading toward the Hub and Gilmore. Each living tunnel was much like another. The doors of housing cubicles faced each other, opening into a small room with little but a chair and beds. Each room accommodated two men or women, who, until one or the other found a mate, would live together with little or no privacy.

Dispersed every twenty doors, a common area was located for convenience, gathering and entertainment. As the tunnel approached the Hub's outer corridor, access to administrative, medical, and all other offices necessary to conduct business could be found. Dining facilities, two per tunnel, were centrally located on either side of the tunnel. The two dining rooms had their own kitchens, cooks, and waiters. Waiting tables worked on a revolving work schedule, and included all inhabitants, each serving a month slaving in the galley. Already, that edict from Gilmore was causing problems. Those individuals holding positions of authority thought they should be exempt from the menial task of serving others food. Gilmore stood firm on his decision, but it was well known that each tunnel was doing much as they well pleased when it came to their individual eating areas.

Doctor Duke was musing on the problems and layout of each tunnel as he moved down Charlie. As he passed Common Area Two, he glanced in to see Jack and the others talking. Jack looked up, smiled, and went back to his conversation.

Seems every time I see Mr. Mossmen he's in some deep discussion with five or six others. I wonder what he's up to, the Doctor thought to himself. Margaret may be right about him. Still, I don't want to jump to any conclusions.

Arriving at the Hub's outer passageway, all thoughts of Jack Mossmen left his mind as he saw Gilmore hurrying toward his office. "General Gilmore," he beckoned.

Gilmore turned; his eyes ablaze. The red flight suit-styled tunic he had chosen to wear as a sign of his leadership was crisp and military sharp. "Doctor, what's up? Whatever it is, I hope it's good news. I could use a little agreeable information this morning."

Catching up with the big man, Doctor Duke asked, "Why, what's the problem?"

As they turned into the Hub's master control room, Gilmore made a quick scan of the control panels and technicians at work. Clustered together were men and women, dressed in white tunics signifying a Hub worker. Gilmore hurried to the group with strides only a man of his stature could make without appearing to run. "What's it doing now?" Gilmore asked.

A stocky man, without a hair on his head, looked up into the eyes of his boss. Neither of the men's eyes wavered from the other. With equally strong personalities, each was secure in his position of responsibility.

"It has stabilized for now, but we still don't have any idea what made the temperature rise," the bald-headed man answered Gilmore.

"How high has it gotten? Is the complex in any danger?" Gilmore queried.

Doctor Duke now realized they were gathered around one of the control panels that regulated the reactor. Apparently, the nuclear reactor, that crucial force which made possible their life below the mountain, was acting up.

"It is only about a hundred degrees above normal, but it's the 'why' that has us all concerned. We have a crew down with the hot box now, but so far nothing!"

"But we checked everything out after the strike and found nothing wrong. Do you think it has something to do with the quakes we experienced during the strike?" Gilmore pressed.

The bald-head lowered in thought, as the man stroked his chin gently with his right hand, pulling an imaginary beard. "Yes, I would think that something has been shaken up inside the reactor itself. Possibly part of the cooling system, but we know it's leaking neither coolant nor radiation. For that matter, we can't find anything openly wrong, but there are two possibilities. One, the temperature sensing equipment is wrong, or two, something is restricting the coolant liquids from circulating properly." He stopped talking just long enough to stare directly into Gilmore's eyes. "Don't ask me to tell you which or what until we've," his hands motioned toward the eight or nine co-workers around him, "have had ample opportunity to check everything out down to the last nut and bolt!"

"Right! Please inform me the minute you have something concrete, and for God's sake, keep this information within the confines of this room. Understood?" Gilmore drew himself up to his full six feet four inches glaring at each man and woman in the room in turn. They certainly got the message.

Gilmore spun on his heel, bumping into his companion. "Okay, Doctor, let's go to my office and we'll talk."

They walked in silence, each man busy with his own thoughts. As they climbed the stairs to Gilmore's office, Duke looked back. The white coated, young scientists were already returning to work. They were trying to find the problem that could destroy New Land should it go untended. He shook his head. Could life above be any worse than this, he wondered?

"Okay, what's your problem?" Gilmore asked, with a bit of sarcasm. "Something serious, I suspect."

Shaking the negative thoughts from his head, Doctor Duke stared at the ex-general. "Well, it isn't as critical as what's going on in the Hub, but it could be a problem if we don't get it solved soon. The electricians working in the rim are having a slow go of it. There was a great deal more damage done to the wiring than we first expected, which is making it difficult to get any power to the lights. Without the lights, plants will begin to die, without the plants we're going to have to start making oxygen from water, a process I would rather not contemplate at this time."

"What's their prognosis? How long will it be before we can restore at least partial power to the system?"

"I can't give you a hard time, but it will be several days yet. Plus, we have plants wilting already."

"Would more help speed repairs?" asked Gilmore.

"Possibly, but I doubt it. We have our best electricians in there now, and they understand the criticality of the problem. About the only thing additional people could do is locate breaks, but we'd still need the technicians to repair them."

"I see. Any other pleasant bulletins for me this morning?" Gilmore asked.

"Nothing quite as dramatic as nuclear power plants overheating or dying plants. However, there is one other thing I would like to discuss with you."

"What's that?"

Looking across Gilmore's shoulder at the door behind his leader's desk, he considered how to answer Gilmore's question, and wondered what contents might be held wherever the door led. Shaking the thought from his head he answered, "It involves Jack Mossmen of Charlie tunnel. He's been a very busy individual, talking to everyone and anyone who will listen. He made it a point to work like a horse clearing the rim, and in the process, made a lot of friends. General, he doesn't care much for you, and I believe he would be more than willing to undermine your decisions at any opportunity."

"So! Just what are you trying to say, that he is a subversive?"

"No. At least not yet, though Margaret agrees that the man is trouble, and she isn't normally wrong about such matters. I just feel he is worth keeping an eye on. We have enough to deal with right now. We certainly don't need for him to usurp your decisions."

"I understand," Gilmore replied. His black skin shone with irritation as he said, "You know I will not tolerate insurrection in the rank and file, and believe me, I have the means of solving such problems." He gestured toward the door behind him. "Please, Doctor, keep an eye on him and an ear to the ground."

*****

Jason, sitting on the steps of the courthouse, was watching the sunset. It was not much of a sunset. The haze of dust which blanketed and dulled the colors was also responsible for the cooler than normal June temperatures. The young man shivered, thinking he had better go "shopping" for warmer and cleaner clothes. He hadn't washed his hands in days, much less taken a bath.

"I must stink like a skunk," he thought to himself. "Tomorrow I'll walk to Crooked Lake and take a bath, put on some new clothes, and look around for some transportation. An ATV is what I need, something that will go just about everywhere."

His mind pondered the events of the day. After breakfast, such as it was, he and Jake wandered toward the Mississippi. Both of them wanted to see for themselves if the mighty river had indeed gone dry. Though beginning to adjust to the devastation, which surrounded him everywhere he went, he still could not quite assimilate it all. They slowly strolled the six blocks south from Main Street, down 5th Avenue to River Lane. Indeed, the river was gone! Wet mud, old tires, and dying vegetation were all that was evident of the once flowing river. Stepping to the river's edge, Jason threw a large rock at the muddy bottom. Like a magician making a rabbit disappear, the stone vanished instantly.

" Geez! What happened?" He looked to Jake.

"Don't know son, but ya sure as heaven ain't gonna cross that mess of mud."

The pair turned north along the bank, hoping to find the East River Parkway Bridge intact, but there was not so much as a piling left of the original four-lane structure.

"We're pretty near cut off from the cities," Jake observed.

"Yeah, I know," Jason, said sadly. He really wanted to cross to the cities and have a look at what had happened there.

From the river they headed back through downtown Anoka, noting most of the supplies they would need to leave and start a life in the country would be free for the taking. Goods were not the problem . . . fuel was. Without electricity, gas pumps did not work, but they could siphon from the hundreds of cars and trucks scattered everywhere one looked. Yes, they decided, it would be far better to get out of any metropolitan area. Even a small town was going to be a living nightmare, caused by the decay and rot of hundreds of corpses that were, as the Bible put it, returning to dust.

As the afternoon turned to evening, they backtracked to the Country Market for their evening repast. Others had gathered in the supermarket as well. Jason met many of them this trip. Most, like him, were trying to understand what had happened to their lives. With the exception of the family with two kids, all had lost a husband, a wife, a child, or all three. Despair, sadness, and the feeling of utter hopelessness permeated their attitudes. They ate because their bodies told them to, not because they wanted to live. Surprising even himself, Jason discovered he was glad to be alive, no matter how the others might feel. No doubt Jake's presence helped bolster those feelings. The man's upbeat perspective of their situation was rubbing off on his own countenance.

"Hey there, Jason. Good old Rick boy is 'bout to speak his nightly say so." Jake was calling for his new friend.

"I'll be right in," Jason yelled back.

With one last look at the dying sun, Jason mounted the cement steps into the anteroom room of his town's courthouse. "Tomorrow, I'll get a bath," he said aloud to no one in particular.

The scene upon Jason's entrance was much as it was the night of his arrival. All but a few of the courthouse's inhabitants were huddled around the radio. With the generators droning in the background, KRCP's Rick was rattling off as much new information as he had available.

> " *. . . a new report from South America. Apparently, they have had things as bad or worse than the U.S. The only voice communication I have received is from a Ham operator located somewhere in the rain forest of Brazil. He was with an oil expedition when the strike occurred. He says*

that everyone is dead or dying, whole rivers disappeared, mountains tumbled, and cities were swallowed entirely into the bowels of the earth.

Information from the Mediterranean area suggests Africa is gone, presumably the continent the asteroid hit. It is the same in southern Europe . . . cities gone, hundreds of thousands dead or dying, and no one to give aid. We are on our own, folks. What you got is what you got, so use it well, and start thinking about your next step.

The news from what is now the new southeastern U.S. isn't good. Apparently, the mountains of the East Coast now represent the coastal beaches of our nation. Georgia, Alabama, Kentucky, and Tennessee are reporting cases of a sickness that seems to have appeared since the strike. The few doctors available haven't a clue as to what is causing it, but hundreds are dying. Reports indicate that it starts much like the flu, but appears to quickly infect the internal organs. The resulting internal bleeding cannot be stopped. So, it appears our trials are not over yet. I can't tell you how this new virus, or whatever it might be, is transmitted, but it is deadly.

This is Rick, transmitting from KRCP's 100,000-watt tower of power, Del Rio, Texas. Out!"

Blank eyes continued to stare at the radio, as if to will its speaker to spout more words, rather than the hissing static, which it now produced. Their attention on the small black box was shattered by three rapid blasts from a shotgun. A woman screamed and fainted. As the small crowd turned, they witnessed a tragic, yet predictable, scene before them. A small, brown-haired lady lay slumped with her two children, each with their heads blown apart by the explosive power of a 12-gauge shell. The man standing before them was fighting to reload the weapon.

Jake sprang forward like a young deer, trying to reach the man before he could chamber another round. He almost made the forty feet, but not quite. The man, a wicked, hysterical smile on his face, placed the barrel in his own mouth and pulled the trigger. Blood, bone, and oozing gray matter plastered the ceiling. Jake sagged to his knees, and hung his head.

"Oh Lord, it's done started," Jake cried. "I figured we'd have folks killin' themselves, but to do your whole family?" He turned on his knees, looking up at the others slowly gathering around him. "We're alive, ya hear? Alive! We can make it, but we've got to work together. It ain't over till it's over."

Jason moved swiftly to his friend's side, gathering him by the shoulders and helped him to his feet. He had been surprised at the speed with which older man moved, but in his arms, he could feel the strong, sinewy muscles that covered the frame of Jake's thin body. "It'll be okay, Jake. No one else is going to kill themselves tonight," he whispered into Jake's ear, as he noticed tears trickling through the time-etched lines of his face.

"Yeah, okay! I'm okay now," Jake said. He looked directly into the eyes of each of those around him. "We'll make it, but we gotta have a plan!"

Jason echoed the statement, "A plan, and soon. The dead are going to drive us out of Anoka." He was standing by Jake, speaking with authority and strength springing from inside him somewhere. " Jake says we should plan to move into the country, somewhere away from any town, but that means supplies. Lots of supplies! Everything . . . food, clothes, fuel, and gear. I think we should all try to find ATV's tomorrow, something to haul ourselves and our things onto a farm, any big farm."

"But what about this new disease the radio talked about?" a fat, dour woman in a dirty tent of a dress asked.

"We'll worry about that when the time comes. For now we have to think of what to do about tomorrow, not next week or next month," Jason retorted.

I knew the boy was a leader, Jake was thinking to himself. These folks are gonna be damn glad to have this young buck around.

The room was settling down as a man asked, "What are we going to do about them?" pointing to the corner.

"They are no more and no less victims of this whole rotten, doom's day tragedy. I suggest we put them outside with the rest of the dead. We can't begin to bury or even show too much concern for all those that have died. We have to worry about those of us that are alive," Jason replied. "I know that sounds harsh, but we are living in a harsh world right now, and that's the way we have got to look at it . . . care for us, the living, not those that have passed on." Jason's words were not that of a teenager, rather a clear thinking man. Where he had gotten his inspiration, he could not fathom.

"The boy's right," Jake said. "Look at us, and this here mess we've been a livin' in. Shoot, we've made this room no better than some animal's den. Listen to the boy."

As if infused with a new lease on life, there was movement within the group. Two men moved to the bloody corner of the anteroom and started dragging the small dead bodies toward the door. Moments later, other men in the group moved to help. They were gentle with the dead, but quickly removed them from view of the others.

Eyes which were dulled with pessimism took on a shine of possible hope. They had been zombies. Now there was a spark, a glimmer of life. The room seemed to grow. The light from oil lanterns and weak electric bulbs appeared to brighten the room. Hope, like laughter, was infectious, and the people living in Anoka's courthouse were encouraged by Jason's words. Perhaps life could be forged from havoc, if they all pulled together and worked at it.

CHAPTER 7

More Decisions

Jason was walking back to town. He had gotten up early, long before any of the others. Not even disturbing Jake as he had gathered his clothes together and headed for the courthouse door. The prior evening's experience had been a drain on all of them, but at least they were now willing to help each other get ready for a major step toward survival. After the bloody shooting, and his spouting off their need to hang together, the older men and women seemed to be looking to Jason for advice. The fact that he was but fifteen years old did not seem to create doubts in their minds regarding his knowledge of what should be done. Jake, too, was the focus of those seeking advice. Between their combined efforts, well into the wee hours of the night, they had calmed the fears of many, and given hope to all.

Leaving the downtown section of Anoka, Jason headed for Crooked Lake, but then decided that Charlotte Lake was closer. Though it was just around the corner from his home, he remembered his own words of the previous evening, "Let the dead go, worry about the living." He raided a small department store en route down Main Street, appropriating new pants, shirt, underwear, socks, boots, and a warm sweater. The sweater was becoming increasingly a necessity, as the days were not warming above sixty-five degrees, and the nights were twenty degrees cooler.

It did not take him long to make the trip to the lake. On the way he detoured around a small pack of dogs, which were devouring the remains of a man and woman who'd died when a falling tree smashed through their windshield. The dogs did not look like they wanted to be interrupted during their feasting, and that was just fine with Jason.

As he walked to the lake, he thought it funny how the destruction around him was already beginning to take on a tired aura . . . like it had been there forever. In just a week's time vegetation was creeping around broken foundations and downed trees. Dust, something all too prevalent in the air, was settling on vehicles and broken buildings alike.

The world was cloaking herself in a gray mantel of death, and the rotten smell permeating the air reinforced the mood that the scene produced.

Arriving at the lake's edge, he found the placid blue waters soothing, even with the carnage that lay scattered on its shores and beaches. The lake represented something familiar from his past. A place he'd ice-skated, searched for treasure and crawdads, and even kissed his first girl, though he'd only been eight at the time. Now trees lay broken and twisted in the shallow waters of Charlotte Lake. There were even several bodies visible along the shore. Carnage or no, familiar or no, Jason decided he needed a bath. The cool water of the lake felt heavenly when he dived beneath its surface.

He spent over an hour frolicking in the water, finally using the bar of soap he had pocketed at the department store. He scrubbed his skin with such ferocity, that it shone pink from the tortured cleaning. It felt good to be clean. On the bank, he donned his new clothes, laced up the boots and looked southerly at what should have been the Twin Cities' skyline. The fires, at least visibly, were now out, but a huge cloud of thick, oily smoke hung over the area, giving it a mystical aspect straight from the pages of a Grimms Brother's fairy tale.

Now he was on his way back to the courthouse and breakfast with Jake at the Country Market. *I feel good for the first time in days,* he thought to himself. *I think maybe, just maybe, I'll live through this mess.*

He walked west on Grant Street, a different route than he had come. Jason was hoping to find an ATV in someone's yard or garage. *Good luck on finding a garage intact,* he thought, as he glanced at buildings caving in upon themselves.

The scream was not loud, but it was frantic in its need. Jason cocked his head to the left. The scream appeared to be coming from in front of him. He sprang into a run, new boots crunching broken shards of glass that littered streets and yards. He tried to imagine what could be the cause of such a plea for help. Turning left on 4th Avenue, Jason headed directly back into the heart of Anoka, dodging debris as he ran. He continued to hear the call for help, now mixed with an angry man's voice.

The dusty, red sun shone on what was left of an ancient brick building, which had been the Baldwin Chiropractic Center and Ye Olde

Milk Factory. Jason slid to a stop, catching his breath as he surveyed the setting. In front of the structure, its roof sagging under broken timbers, a large man stood amongst the rubble of brick and board holding a boy by the throat. The teenager was swinging completely off the ground, helpless as the man held him in a near death grip. He was kicking wildly at his antagonist and mouthing pleas for help, which were now but a whimper compared to his earlier screams.

The big man yelled into the young black face before him, "Why are you alive, you lousy little bastard? Why are you alive when all my boys are dead? All four of them! Why are you alive you lousy, no count little bastard?"

Jason moved within twenty-five feet of the two and yelled, "Hey, mister! Let the kid go." He wasn't sure just what he could do in this situation. The man looked huge, at least six feet or more, with the build of a TV wrestler. "Mister, let the boy go!" Jason repeated, with more authority than he felt.

The assailant stopped shaking the boy long enough to swing a cruel blow to his solar plexus. The impact of the large fist would have doubled the youth in half, had not the vicious giant been holding him by the shirt collar. "What makes you special?" the man raved.

There was no doubt in Jason's mind that the big man intended to kill the boy. Already blood covered most of the boy's face, seeping from wounds inflicted by pounding fists. He moved closer to the two, cuffing the man on his shoulder, "Mister, for God's sake, stop it," he pleaded.

The dirty, blood smeared man turned slightly to his left. He let go of the black boy's collar with one hand, and in a sweeping motion swung sidearm, hitting Jason squarely on the jaw. "Shut up, you little prick. You'll be next."

Jason did not see the blow coming, and was unprepared. Staggering under the weight of the impact, he fell to his knees in surprise. He shook his head to clear the fireworks that were exploding behind his eyes. Moments passed before he realized that the man had forgotten all about his presence, and was once again busily slamming the boy against the broken brick wall . . . still mouthing his obscenities.

Jason hurriedly cast about for a weapon, something to down the madman before he killed the black boy. Not more than a few yards to his right lay what appeared to be a large stick. His hand reached for it, wrapping around the smooth wood of the shop's mahogany flagstaff. The pole, now a weapon, was five feet, two inches long, with a brass ball attached to its end. The ball glittered golden, even in the weak sunlight, as Jason lifted his stave into the air. In one smooth motion, Jason swung the staff behind him as he rose from his kneeling position. With both hands grasping the end of the pole, he whipped it over his head with all the strength he could muster. The brass ball sunk into the man's skull, making a smushing sound like a watermelon hitting the ground at a 4th of July picnic.

The brute stood upright for several seconds, tittering on his heels. Then, with little drama, he merely crumpled to the ground, dropping his intended victim like a sack of potatoes.

Clutching his weapon, Jason moved to the boy's side. "Can you hear me?" Jason yelled, as he gently rolled the boy over. The youth's face was covered with blood, his eyes were clouded, and he was as limp as a spoonful of Jell-O. "Can you hear me?" he repeated.

"Yeah, I guess so," came a weak reply. "Am I dead now?"

"No, I don't think so," Jason smiled down, "but you're beat up pretty badly. Can you sit up?"

"I'll try, but I hurt everywhere."

"I can imagine. What was the guy beating you up for anyway?"

"Dammed if I know. He just came out of nowhere and started yelling at me about being alive and his kids all dead. Then before I knew it, he had me by the throat and started pounding the hell out me."

Jason was wiping blood off the young man's face with his new shirttail. He helped him into a sitting position, leaning the teenage black boy against the ruins of the shop's wall. "What's your name?"

"Billy. Billy Ball. I live up on Enchanted Drive, north of here. What's yours?"

"I'm Jason. Jason Collyar. What are you doing here in Anoka? Enchanted Drive is closer to Oak Grove than Anoka, isn't it?"

"Yeah, but I couldn't find anybody alive up that way, so this morning I headed for Anoka, hoping to find something besides dead bodies down here."

"Well, you've come to the right place. There's about thirty of us set up in the courthouse. Do you think you can walk?"

"If I have to, I suppose I can. Jesus, that guy really tried to kill me. Do you have any more crazies down this way? If so, I think I'll take my chances further north."

"I can't promise that we don't have any more nuts in Anoka, but at least we've got good folks too. We did have some guy kill his whole family and himself last night, but I don't think we will see much of that anymore. What do you think? Want to come meet the rest? They'll be collecting food at the Country Market by now, and it isn't too far away."

"Sure. Give me a hand up."

Jason reached under the smaller boy's arms and helped him to his feet. Then, without giving it a thought, retrieved the staff. Hefting the strong pole in his right hand, he planted its end on the ground, held it away from his body at a forty-five degree angle, spread his feet apart, and held his head high. He felt strong, stronger than ever in his life . . . with the staff in his hand. "Let's get going," he said quietly to Billy.

With little or no thought to the dead man, his brain oozing dark red blood into the dirt, the two boys moved south down 4th Avenue, heading for the Country Market and something to fill their stomachs. It was not that Jason didn't care about what he had done. He fully realized that he had just killed someone he did not even know. However, he had already rationalized his actions as something the times demanded. Jason walked with the staff in his right hand, using it as a walking stick. It clicked rhythmically on the pavement.

*****

Gilmore slumped in his office chair; feet draped on the edge of his stainless-steel desk. He was deep in thought, most of which involved the unpleasantness of being in charge of the fifteen hundred souls living in New Land. Though the planners and architects of the caverns had given thought to practically everything The Few would require, it could never become a real home for sun-loving humans.

"Hell, I've spent days underground in Korea," he spoke aloud to himself.

When Gilmore was a Lt. Colonel, he had been stationed in Seoul. He was a small part of the Army's contingency to protect South Korea against an invasion from the north. He had served three years with the Koreans, and it had been one of the best tours during his long career.

Those years were filled with beautiful Korean women, long strolls through the wondrous city of Seoul, and enjoying the countryside and people who made it their home. He learned and understood the hatred the Koreans had for the Japanese. The Koreans had loved their trees, even before the Japs had come in the '30s and cut every living twig to the ground.

He laughed to himself as he remembered the saying the Yanks had about Korean law. "Better to get caught killing someone than to be arrested for pissing on a tree." There was a lot of truth in those words.

Now, sitting in his underground office, he reminisced about CP Papa. CP Papa was a gargantuan command post cut into the side of a mountain, south of Seoul. The drive up the mountain followed a winding road of beauty seldom seen anywhere in the world. CP Papa, with its living quarters for over a thousand solders, men and women, had office spaces not unlike where he now sat. CP Papa was much like New Land, but with one large difference. There you could leave the confines of the caves when and if you wished. New Land, though similar in capabilities and design, was to be home for the rest of his life. He would never again tread greenery, nor enjoy the warmth of the sun. It was downright depressing when he gave thought to the situation.

"If I'm prone to these kinds of thoughts, it's no wonder there's rumbling in the tunnels. I've got to decide how to get their minds off our immediate plight and onto something else," the big man said to the stone walls.

Since the reactor started its cyclic overheating, the situation in New Land was not uplifting for its inhabitants. The problem with the nuclear hot box persisted, though technical experts worked on the dilemma twenty-four hours a day. The consensus was that a portion of the miles of cooling conduit had been pinched during the quake. Unfortunately, an inspection of the myriad of coils did not show a collapse. Nonetheless, this did not rule out the possibility of inner wall compression, as the tubing was composed of three separate layers. The question remained . . . if the cooling system was being restricted due to failure of an inner wall, why could it not be found from an exterior examination?

Another theory, one not accepted by many, but which had to be considered, was that something was shattered internally. If this were the case, say a pump component, then they could expect problems of a more serious nature to develop. Regardless of the cause, the overheating of the reactor occurred on a regular basis . . . about every six hours. Since the temperature regulation of New Land was dependent on the reactor's cooling system, the overall temperature of the tunnels was increasing. Because the elevated warmth felt good to most of The Few, there was little concern . . . that is, until the cave walls started sweating.

The engineers who designed the climate control for New Land had ascertained the exact temperature the core of the mountain retained. Then they had calculated, within a few degrees, how much warmth could be added before condensation would begin to develop. With those figures in hand they had then designed the reactor's heat exchanger to provide New Land a constant climatic temperature of sixty-five degrees Fahrenheit. It was a bit on the cool side, but had kept the tunnels dry. But now . . .?

A knock on his door brought Gilmore sharply out of his daydreaming. "Come!"

The Doctors Duke stepped into their boss' office. "Good morning, General," Margaret said.

"Good morning to you." Gilmore swiveled in his chair as he spoke, feet hitting the deck with a thud, and eyes flaring.

"To what do I owe this unexpected pleasure? It is not often that the two of you visit me at the same time."

Doctor Benjamin Duke coughed the cough of a beginning cold. "It's the dampness, sir. The humidity may be doing wonders for the surviving plants in the rim, but it isn't doing the people in the tunnels any good. It appears we didn't leave the flu or cold viruses topsides when we moved into the mountain."

"Yes, I've noticed a lot of our population coughing and hacking their way through the tunnels. This must be caused by the increased dampness?"

"Undoubtedly so," answered Margaret. "I have been in conference with the medical staff most of the morning. The general opinion is that we have nothing serious to worry about. However, with the increase in unhealthy individuals, there is always the possibility that we could lose a great deal of our work force."

"I recognize the problem, Doctor, but I see little we can do about it, unless you and the rest of 'medical' can formulate a cure for the common cold. We will muddle through I am sure. Now I have a question for you. How is the overall mental attitude of The Few from your perspective?"

Margaret sat down across from Gilmore, her husband taking up a position behind her. She wrinkled her brow in concentration, and absently whisked a hand over her brown hair. "Well, I would say, the adjustment to living underground has been pretty much as I expected. Though the screening process was detailed in personality traits, thoughts toward religion, sex, national unity, and a myriad of other potential intricacies, no psychologist could predict what life would be for us after the strike. Studies done on astronauts spending long periods in the isolation of a space vehicle provided solid information about our present situation. However, there was one difference. A difference, which could not be factored as part of our intended life style. That is, the astronauts knew they would be returning to the real world. We don't have that luxury."

"I know! As a matter of fact, I was just thinking the exact same thing right before you two arrived," Gilmore mused. "But what can be done about it? Nothing! We are stuck here for the duration."

"The consensus is that we try to reinstate as many normalcy's to our life as possible. For example, entertainment such as movies, holidays, picnics, and the like."

Gilmore's eyes drilled holes into Margaret. "Where are we going to hold picnics, in the control room? Just how do you and the other experts think we can implement such treats?"

"It not unsolvable," Doctor Duke answered. "For instance, the portion of the rim that was used for storage of the debris after the strike could be dedicated to a picnic or outing area. With work, proper lighting, and the careful arrangement of rock and plant, the area could become a peaceful rest zone. In fact, we could even arrange to have a small pool or brook."

"Are you serious?" Gilmore looked and sounded astonished.

"Absolutely," Doctor Duke said flatly. "Of course, the area would not be large, nor could it accommodate more than thirty to forty people at one time, but it would be a very special spot, one that could be built voluntarily."

Gilmore shook his head in disbelief. "If you think this will help, then see to it. What else have you to report?" he asked, glancing again toward Margaret.

"The good news about our wards is that there is nothing wrong with their sex lives. We have seen a rapid increase in couples 'coupling,' so to speak. This is a healthy sign that adjustment to the New Land is, in fact, taking place. Each of the four administrative sections has reported a dramatic rise in request for movement from one cubicle to another."

"Wasn't that something we expected?" Gilmore asked.

"Yes, it was. However, it does raise the issue of marriage and monogamy. I understand this was not to be a consideration. It was thought we should work out any necessary form of social structure deemed appropriate as we learned to live in New Land. However, as a psychologist, I have genuine concerns. The society we left above was based in large part on the Christian ethic of monogamy. I'm not sure we should allow that ethic to break down."

"And why not?" Gilmore asked. Having been a bachelor all of his life, enjoying the fruits of as many ladies as he could, the thought of being able to move from one bed to another without moral judgment seemed a proposition to be viewed with anticipation, not fear.

Margaret glared intently at her boss. She knew he had never married and that he had been known for his womanizing, though he'd always acted with discretion. "Because, whether we want to believe it or not, we are creatures of habit. Humans have always needed a moral base from which a societal structure could be built. The Few have been infused with the Christian ethic from the day they were born. Though they may try to overcome that ethic, guilt will appear. When that happens, we could see recalcitrant behavior develop."

"Can't we let dead dogs lie regarding this issue? Why not see what happens before I institute rules and regulations concerning the personal sex lives of New Landers. As you've said, humans tend to figure this sort of thing out."

"As you wish, but I suggest you keep a very close watch on the situation. If it explodes, we could have major social upheaval," Margaret firmly stated.

As the conversation among the three major figures of New Land continued, Jack Mossmen was moving. Humming to himself, he paid little attention to the water dripping down the walls lining the passageway of Charlie Tunnel. He had been to see Gilmore about the condensation forming everywhere. He'd asked the "boss" what he intended to do about the situation, but now, moving toward the rim of his tunnel with what few possessions he owned, he didn't much care one way or the other. Most of the contents of the bundle in his arms were clothes. Passing common area number two, he glanced in to nod good mornings to the dozen or so men and women talking within. One of the men winked at him knowingly as he continued down the tunnel to his new cubicle, and Heather.

He had met Heather only a few days before, but they had found themselves extremely compatible. She was beautiful, with auburn hair that hung to her shoulders, eyes so blue that they truly were turquoise pools of reflective water, and her body was straight from the pages of Playboy. Jack, not a very handsome man, thought he'd died and gone to heaven, for she had invited him to move into her cubicle a short two days after they'd met, and now he was on his way. He had forgotten his battle with Gilmore altogether, at least for the time being. He was in love, or at the very least, heavy lust!

Heather lounged on her small bed. She was deep in thought, her exquisite eyes closed to the harsh glare of the overhead light. "Jack's a good catch," she mused. "He's a mover and shaker . . . a man able to provide me with extra niceties. He might even be able to get me out of working in the damned kitchen."

The door swung open and Jack stepped inside. "Good morning," he said, as he stepped into the room. "How are you this fine day?"

"Now that you are here with me, I'm fine," she smiled, as she got up to close the door behind Jack. "Put those things down and give me a hug."

Jack did as he was told. She moved into his arms, and tilted her head to meet his lips. The kiss lingered long enough for Jack to steer her to the bed, where he began unzipping her smock.

****

Jason spied Jake leaning against the broken door frame of the Country Market. "When did you start smoking?" he asked, as he helped Billy move around the tangled mess of the store's parking lot.

"Well, ya know, I stopped about three years ago, but don't figure it'll hurt none to start again, seein' as how it don't seem to make much of a difference no how. What's that you got with you?"

Billy was leaning heavily on Jason's shoulder. Though none of the inflicted wounds were serious enough to cause permanent damage, he did not feel very good at the moment. "Jake, I'd like you to meet Billy Ball from Oak Grove."

"Right pleased to meet ya, boy," Jake smiled.

Billy's reaction was immediate. His dark brown eyes blazed to life, and he shook off Jason's shoulder, standing erect and defiant. "I am not your boy," he quietly said, with unmistakable menace.

Jason recoiled in surprise. "Wait a minute, Billy. Jake calls me boy, too. Don't get all up tight about it."

Billy looked at Jason and relaxed slightly. "Oh. Sorry. Guess I overreacted!"

"Not to worry none, son, I reckon just 'cause the world's gone to hell in a hand basket don't change the way people think none," Jake said as he reached out to clasp the hand of the teenager. "I'd say you don't look none too good, all banged up and such. Where'd ya find him?" he asked, turning to Jason.

"About two blocks up that way," Jason answered, pointing north on 4th Avenue. "He was getting the proverbial crap beat out of him by some crazy son of a bitch."

"What happened to the other guy?" Jake removed a handkerchief from his coat pocket and was gently wiping blood away from Billy's right eye.

"He' dead!"

Jake rolled back on his heels, a look of utter disbelief screwed tightly on his deeply wrinkled face. "You kilt him?"

Jason lowered his head, the impact of his deed hammered home as he told Jake the story. As he finished, he looked into Jake's eyes for forgiveness, like a son to his father.

Jake stood silent for a moment, looking from one boy to the other. "Reckon ya did what needed doin'," he said quietly. "That the weapon ya holdin' there so important like?" He nodded at the staff in Jason's right hand.

Jason looked at the wiry old man, and then at his staff. "Yes! I think I'll keep it with me for a while. It might come in handy."

"I reckon it might at that," was all Jake said, as he looked hard into Jason's eyes. "Let's get you boys some chow, and then we've got work to do." Looking at the ebony skinned boy of thirteen; he saw the strength of survival radiating from his eyes. He'd had plenty of contact with blacks over his years, and this lad, with his kinky, short-cropped hair like a Brillo pad, radiated the same leadership qualities that Jason emanated. "I'm gonna like these lads," he thought to himself.

Billy ate like a horse. Hurt or not, he was hungry. Jason recalled the first time Jake had brought him to this same store, just a few days past. "How long ago was that?" he asked himself. "Three, four, eight days ago?" He could not remember. Time seemed to have little meaning. Survival was paramount!

"Jake, we've got to start getting the necessary equipment together for our move. Have you talked to the rest?" Jason asked, waving his hand around the grocery store.

"Yep. I done talked to them this mornin', though we all wondered where you wandered off to. You're right. Today's the day we gonna make our commitment. Soon's ya finished tryin' to eat every darn thing on this aisle, we'll get down to business."

Country Market was alive this morning, not like the other times Jason and Jake had sought sustenance in the food filled aisles. The courthouse people felt a purpose in their lives once more. Infused with hope, provided a plan of action, and ready to leave the destruction and rotting flesh smell of Anoka, they collected their morning meal in haste. Each knew there was work to be done and supplies to be accumulated before they could be on the move.

Jake made it clear to each of them the necessity of filling their clothing bag with strong work clothes, warm sweaters, coats, hefty boots, and top of the line work gloves. Clothing, tools, and equipment of all sorts were to be brought back to the courthouse, separated into categories, and inventoried. Transportation,of any sort was still of prime importance. ATV's seemed to be the best alternative, but where to find some forty odd all terrain vehicles presented, what seemed, an overwhelming obstacle.

"Ya said you were a lookin' for an ATV when ya run across Billy?" Jake asked Jason, as they were leaving the Country Market.

Jason shifted his staff to his right hand and gave a quick glance at Billy to make sure he was moving all right, "Yes! I came down Grant Street, but there was no sign of anything we could use there. Besides, garages and storage buildings were mostly trashed, like everything else."

Billy, his head hurting and muscles aching, said, "You looking for four wheelers?"

"You bet! We need a bunch of them to move us into the countryside." It was Jason who responded.

"I know where we can find what we need. There is a Honda snowmobile and ATV outlet in Oak Grove. I can't remember the name of the place, but it is supposed to be one of the largest distributors in Minnesota. If you want, we can head up there this afternoon."

Jake stopped dead in his tracks, "Boy, ya be a lifesaver. Jason, you and Billy boy head that way right now. We can get the two of ya outfitted with other stuff later. Right now, this here crowd needs transportation more than anything else. If ya find what we'll be needin', hurry on back and let me know. Ya hear?"

"Billy, are you feeling up to a hike? It's at least four miles to Oak Grove, and the going isn't easy." Jason faced his friend.

"Probably do me good. Walking off some of these hurts, I mean. Sure, I'm ready."

The three separated. Jake headed for downtown Anoka where others were gathering to make their first assault on department, sporting good, and hardware stores. The boys headed north on 4th Avenue on their way to Oak Grove.

*****

After the Dukes left his office, Gilmore sat thinking about their discussion, and the need to bring a semblance of normalcy to tunnel life. They were right, of course, but how and what could be the first steps in that direction?

"A party." The idea hit him from the blue. "A *We Survived Party!* ' " Grabbing his Tunnel Communications beeper box, he punched the call button for each of his tunnel heads, then sat back and waited for them to respond. He smiled to himself; "I could use a party as well. I wonder if we could get one of our engineers to construct a still? Have a little bubbly for the inhabitants of our underground home?"

Thirty minutes later his office was filled with staff and tunnel leaders. He explained the idea to them like an excited teenager looking forward to his first big date. The idea was received with enthusiasm from the entire group. Heads bobbed in affirmation from the moment he began explaining his idea, and it was, indeed, the first directive he'd issued and received with unanimous approval. Even the ever-spiteful Jack Mossmen appeared to be impressed with the thought of some rabble rousing.

"How soon do you want the party to kick off?" asked a cHubby engineer, with a nervous tick over his left eye.

"As soon as possible," responded Gilmore to the leader of Alpha tunnel, noting the man's smock was a wrinkled mess. I have to quit wanting everyone to look military, he thought.

"Well, if you want us to build a still and produce some form of alcoholic beverage, you'll have to wait at least a week. Even then the spirits won't be of an aged quality, believe me."

"I know, I know," Gilmore nodded. "Just do the best you can. I don't want cases of booze, just enough for each person who would like a taste or have a sip to tickle his throat."

" I understand," the engineer agreed. "Still, it is a tall order, but we'll give it a try."

"Good, good," Gilmore smiled. "Now, I'm open to any ideas that will help make this a memorable event." He looked around the small room for responses.

CHAPTER 8

To Your Health

Jason was sitting next to his sister's grave. Billy, never too far from his friend's side, had moved off down the street out of respect for Jason's need to be alone. Each boy wore a dust mask over his mouth and nose. The masks were impregnated two or three times a day with perfume, as the stench of decaying bodies were too much for the senses to handle.

"Sally, I'll be leaving soon," Jason said aloud through his mask. "We've almost got everything we need to head for the country, though it seems every time we get enough supplies for our group, more people straggle into Anoka. We have over a hundred men, women, and kids living in the courthouse now. Who would have believed it? Anyway, Jake says we've got to hit the road, regardless of more folks arriving every day. We're going to leave messages for any new arrivals, and trail signs for them to follow. Oh, Sally, I wish you were going too."

A slight breeze stirred the leaves on the few remaining maples lining his street. Jason sat quietly for a moment, glancing around at what used to be his home. "I don't know where Mom and Dad are," he again spoke aloud. "I guess they got caught in the cities. Mom's note said she was going to visit Dad when she finished shopping, and that was on University Avenue, right next to the Mississippi. Did I tell you that the Mississippi is gone? Well, it is. Can you believe it?"

A dog barked and Jason looked up startled and cautious. Dogs had become a problem in the last week. Jake said they were reverting to their pack instinct and that made them dangerous, and not to just the dead, but to the living as well. A couple of days ago, one of their numbers had been killed by a pack of wild dogs. A woman named Clare, Jason remembered silently.

The sound of the dog's barking was moving away from Norwood Street, causing Jason to relax back into his one-sided conversation. "Sally, I just came to say goodbye. So much has happened since the quake that I can't begin to tell you all of it, but I do miss you." A tear was dribbling down his cheek, and he brushed it away unthinkingly. "I had to kill a man, something I would have never thought me capable of in a million years, and I've made new friends. It's really strange, this new life without you and Mom and Dad. God, but I miss you so!"

Jason shifted his mask to better cover his nose, and lay back on the grass, which was once his lawn. Closing his eyes, his thoughts drifted over the events which had occurred since he and Billy had left for Oak Grove. Billy, though badly beat-up, had led them north off 4th and on to 7th Avenue. They'd then hiked up Round Lake Road for what seemed miles, and finally turned east into the town. It had taken them a while to search out the Honda dealership, because Billy was not sure exactly where it was located. In the end, they had stumbled across the store by accident. Clone's ATV and Snowmobile was every thing Billy said it would be. There was a veritable wealth of ATVs, plus all the accessories to go with them. ATVs of all sizes, makes and models lined the showroom and a fenced area behind the store itself. Though the building had been severely damaged during the quake, it fared better than most, and the inventory was primarily intact. They had excitedly roamed the store, picking the biggest, most powerful four-wheelers they could find for themselves.

"Have you ever ridden one of these things?" Billy had asked.

Jason's answer had been no, but that had not deterred them from climbing aboard the machines and firing them up for a quick ride around the block. Back at the outlet, they had gone to work in earnest, sorting through the accessories for anything that might prove useful. In the end, they had elected to hook trailers to the rear of each of their machines, filling them with spare tires, tools, and a couple of winches. They checked the oil, siphoned gas from a car, and began the trip back to Anoka.

Though fun, riding the four-wheelers proved more difficult than they had expected. They had to detour constantly. Where they had been able to walk with little restriction, other than inconvenience, riding required them to deviate extensively from a straight-line route. Still, the ATV's crawled over obstacles such as light poles, roofs, and other debris with ease. They had not considered the possibility of a flat tire until after they'd left Oak Grove. Neither knew how to change the big, knobby wheels that plowed their way over the destruction they were driving through. They'd been fortunate in they had not met any problems on their way home. When they finally arrived back at the courthouse, it was well after dark. Jake met them on the steps, his smile beaming around a clenched cigarette.

"Well, bless my soul," Jake had exclaimed. "Ya done found us some honest to no kiddin' transportation."

It always surprised Jason how Jake's voice boomed from such a skinny chest, but his outburst had drawn the attention of those inside, and they'd filed out to admire the new ATVs.

A new wave of hope spread throughout the group gathered on the steps. Here before them was a fast, efficient means of getting out of town. Jason and Billy explained in detail what they'd found, and where it was located. Jake decided they should leave at first light with two men loaded in each trailer, and one riding double with Billy and Jason. That way they could have six more ATVs by mid-morning, and most of the machines parked in front of the courthouse by the end of the day. On each trip they would bring back as many spare parts, tires, front-end blades, tools, and whatever else they could find to be sorted and stacked as part of their traveling equipment.

The next day had gone as scheduled, with no mishaps or major delays. Before the first group left in the morning, Jason jury-rigged a makeshift scabbard to the side of his machine. Throughout the multiple trips made to Oak Grove, he could be spotted by the golden glint of the brass ball swinging to the motions of his four-wheeler.

The next two days went well. Groups were assigned by Jake and Jason to gather the remaining needed staples. Finding enough clothes for their growing community was not a problem. The Sport Shack down the street from the Courthouse provided enough clothing, boots, and foul weather gear to last them for a long time. Finding sufficient unspoiled food was another problem altogether. The Country Market, used now for several weeks, was beginning to have empty shelves. Jake didn't seem to be too concerned about this dilemma. He figured the group could raid other markets as they traveled. However, hardware such as gas cans, hammers, nails, and a thousand other bits and pieces necessary to build or repair a future home had been difficult to find. Downtown Anoka had no real hardware store, but in the end visiting gas stations, car repair shops, and sorting through what was left of Anoka's homes located enough equipment. The small community was working as a team, all of them anxious to leave. By midweek, the smell had become overwhelming from the rotting, bloated bodies littering the town. That was when they had started wearing masks saturated with perfume. The perfume helped, but could not totally hide the stench. The night Jake announced they would leave in four days was also the night they received their last broadcast from KRCP.

The moment the broadcast started, they had all realized something was wrong. Rick sounded like death warmed over, and that, as it turned out, was almost the case. Rick had, for several days, been warning of the sickness spreading throughout the mid-west. Now, he explained, it had arrived in south Texas. Rick was dying; this would be his last broadcast. Before he signed off, Rick told of the disease sweeping rapidly across the U.S., and how he would be in contact one day with a small community struggling to survive, only to receive static the next. Before he left the air, Rick flatly stated he felt it was the end of everything. Life on earth was done, at least for mankind.

That night, deep in depression, Anoka's survivors huddled together. A new fear had come into their lives; as if what had already transpired was not enough. The next day saw a flurry of activity from every individual. Final arrangements for the transport of generators and other large pieces of equipment were made. Trailers were designated to carry specific supplies, such as medical, fuel, clothing, or food. Now it was late in the day after Rick's announcement, and Jason had grabbed his staff, mounted his ATV, and driven toward his home with Billy motoring beside.

"Jason?"

The sound of his name being called brought Jason suddenly back to reality. "Over here, Billy," he called.

He gathered his staff close, as he moved into a kneeling position over Sally's shallow grave. "Rest in peace, little sister." Jason patted the ground where his sister rested.

"Are you okay?" Billy asked, as he walked over to his friend.

"Yes . . . No, Damn it, I'm not. I just don't understand why this all happened. I don't understand why my sister is dead, or why my Mom and Dad are dead, or why God killed or destroyed everything worthwhile in this world." Jason was near rage, his voice crying out to the heavens where he knelt. Pushing himself up with the staff, he yelled, "Dammit, why?"

Billy moved closer, stepping gently, and placed his arm around Jason's slumping shoulders. "I don't have an answer to that. Nobody does. I guess its best not to think too much about it, cause if you do, you'll go fruitier than a fruitcake."

Jason seemed to deflate like a punctured inner tube. Then, drawing a deep breath, he turned to Billy. "You're right! Thanks. We'd better get back, Jake will be wondering where we've run off to." Looking down one final time, his blue eyes shining with tears, he spoke softly, "So long, little one."

The two moved to their waiting ATV's and swiftly drove down the street, heading for the courthouse.

*****

Every tunnel was reverberating with the sound of revelry. The *We Survived Party* was in full swing, and if the level of laughter and chatter could make a judgment, then it was an overwhelming success. Gilmore's idea had been well received at its announcement by all fifteen hundred New Landers. The Chief of Engineering succeeded beyond his wildest expectations in producing a rather fine grade of whiskey. Though it had aged but a couple of days, no one seemed to care. Besides, it was being mixed with all manner of fruit drink concoctions. Each tunnel decorated their party areas in themes. Delta's green tried, with some success, to have a springtime appearance, while Bravo's gray was attempting a Halloween theme. The decorating had been fun, and provided a welcome diversion from the day's routine.

The party idea had given Gilmore and his staff time to work on the reactor problem without constant complaints. In the past week, hundreds of man-hours were spent searching for the coolant problem . . . without success. The morning of the party found Gilmore in conference with his nuclear experts. They had told him there was nothing more they could do without shutting down the reactor, a solution not to anyone's liking. Without the reactor on line, all services to New Land would be effectively rendered inoperative. There would be no electricity. Without electricity, there would be no lights, plumbing, or water. Without the reactor on line, there would be no heat for the caves, making living conditions a nightmare. Still, if they were to fix the problem, the reactor had to be shut down. Gilmore queried his experts on the length of time the repairs might take, but he could not be given a definitive answer. The dilemma, in this instance, was that no one knew for sure what the difficulty entailed. The only thing certain to the men and women sitting around Gilmore's office was it would take longer to repair than the inhabitants of New Land wished to endure.

The most persuasive argument against shutting down the reactor had come from Doctor Duke. He had explained, in detail, the possible loss of plant life without electricity to power the lights throughout the rim. He had illustrated how they had lost around twenty-five per cent of their flora during the strike, and to lose more so soon could put the entire community in jeopardy. His reasoning had been the ultimate case upon which to base the group decision . . . leave things as they were, at least for the time being.

Now it was evening, though in reality, there was no real morning or evening, just a variation shown by a clock. It made no difference to the festive mood, which radiated throughout New Land.

Gilmore, dressed in an immaculate red tunic, moved easily through the Halloween mood of Bravo tunnel's common area. He was in his glory, as he nodded and smiled at the faces that swept past his six four frame. He knew very few of those who stopped to greet him, though he occasionally ran into a familiar face, but he was making every possible attempt to be accepted. Regardless, though he honestly was trying to be just one of the 'guys', his military, crisp look, and his role as the ruler of New Land, held him aloof.

An entourage of yellow tunics followed Gilmore as he moved about the common area. Yellow had been chosen as the color for his major staff members. He had asked them to join him as a group to visit each of the parties, and now they, too, were enjoying the food and drink offered them by the tenants of Bravo tunnel.

Gilmore turned, speaking over his shoulder, "What do you think? Time to leave here for Charlie?" He was speaking to Doctor Duke and Margaret.

"Yes, it probably is. We've been here for over an hour. Great party though, don't you think?"

"You've got that right," Gilmore answered. He began moving slowly toward the headman. "George, this has been a great time. Thank you for having us." He waved a hand indicating his staff members. "The gray of Bravo can be justifiably proud of their Halloween decor. Thanks again."

George Blaksen, elected head of Bravo, made a mock bow and grinned broadly into Gilmore's eyes. "We thank you for honoring us with your visit. It has been a pleasure having you, and if you get tired of the other tunnels' events, please feel free to return for another drink."

"Why, thank you, George. We just might do that. But for now, I'll bid you goodnight."

Shaking hands with several men and women as he made for the exit, Gilmore thought he liked George, and that he might want to give the man more responsibility.

Walking around the Hub's outer tunnel, Gilmore felt better than he had since his arrival in the caverns of New Land. *I might be able to bring this whole plan off after all,* he thought to himself. *Lord knows, if anyone can, I can.*

Walking rapidly to pace the bigger man's stride, Doctor Duke said, "I think people are really having a good time. This was a fine idea you had."

Margaret voiced an affirmation of her husband's comment. "You made some allies this evening. This party has made you into more of a real person to many, and that's advantageous to us all, particularly with the reactor problem we're having."

Turning to look Margaret in the eye, Gilmore said, "Why thank you, Margaret. I'm pleased I have finally done something right in your eyes."

"General, I have never been your adversary. I'm just trying to keep you advised about my appraisals of the overall social attitude."

"Margaret, I have never doubted that, or you," Gilmore answered, in a serious manner. Stopping to face her for a moment, he stated, "I trust the opinions of you and your husband more than anyone else down here. No, please believe I've never had any uncertainty whatsoever about the two of you."

Margaret nodded her acceptance of the compliment.

"Now, enough of this serious talk. Let's get on over to Charlie's party." Gilmore was already on the move. "I must admit, I am thoroughly enjoying myself tonight."

The group reached Charlie tunnel, where '50s music, along with laughter and happy chatter, echoed from the damp walls. They turned into the first common area, which was decorated to resemble a high school gym. Jack Mossmen was standing by the door, his thinning hair combed flat against his head. Seeing Gilmore and his staff approaching, he moved to intercept.

"Why, General, what a pleasure to see you this evening," he smiled with tight lined lips, barely showing a hint of teeth. "Let me escort you to the bar."

"Thank you, Jack, it would be a pleasure," Gilmore smiled politely.

The two men moved slowly through the crowd; an imposing black man to whom Jack's lanky six foot two inches looked small by comparison. Reaching the makeshift bar, Gilmore ordered the house special . . . homemade whiskey and orange drink. He realized, as he sipped, that he was beginning to feel tipsy. It was a pleasant feeling, particularly after the intense strain he had been under for the past couple of weeks.

"Jack, your people seem to be content this evening. Have you had any complaints I might be able to help with?"

"No, I can handle most of our own problems without bothering you," Jack replied strongly.

"Yes, of course you can, Jack." Gilmore gazed at the other man with a thoughtful look. Indeed, he thought, "here is a man of whom I must be careful; just as Margaret warned.

In another part of the party room, Ben and Margaret were in a deep conversation with a small group of men and women.

A plain and oddly pretty woman of twenty-five asked, "Doctor Duke, living under the mountain is driving us all somewhat nuts, much more so than any of us ever dreamed. Are you absolutely positive we can't open the big door to the outside?"

With a resigned sigh, Ben started his well-rehearsed spiel once more. It seemed he had spoken the words a thousand times, and yet nobody in New Land wanted to believe what he said. "The big rock hit in the central part of Africa. The understanding of all of the scientists involved in solving what to do about this catastrophic event agreed on one point . . . the collision of The Devil's Face and Earth would bring about another ice age. The resulting dust and debris thrown into Earth's atmosphere would totally block the sun for fifty years or more. No animal life could or would be able to withstand the climatic change. Thus, we have New Land. These tunnels are to be our home."

"But why don't we send someone out?" the woman pressed.

"I suppose we could, but the chance of contaminating our community with an agent, virus, or bacteria which could infect either us or our plant life is too great. We just can't risk breaking the rather sterile environment which we have made for ourselves."

"Yes, I suppose you're right," the woman said sadly. "Still, I wish you and the rest of General Gilmore's staff would give it some consideration. Frankly, " she turned her head and nodded toward Mossmen, "Jack thinks we should give it a try."

"Well, I don't think it would be a good idea at all, and I would fight such a recommendation to the fullest. But Jack is certainly welcome to his opinions." With his final remark, Doctor Duke sidestepped the woman, and moved in the direction of the bar. Margaret caught her husband's arm, and the two left the group to mutter among themselves.

"I don't like those kind of thoughts mousing their way around New Land," Margaret whispered.

"Nor I," Ben answered. "I particularly don't like Jack Mossmen pushing for that sort of major change to the overall plan we established, and which he was fully aware of prior to joining us."

They reached the bar and ordered. As they picked up their glasses, Gilmore and Jack elbowed their way back through the crowd for another drink.

"Having a good time, Doctor?" Gilmore asked Ben.

"Yes, I think I am." As Doctor Duke answered the General, the most astonishing woman walked into their midst, taking Jack by the arm.

With a smile that could have launched a ship, Heather asked, "Well, Jack, aren't you going to introduce me?" She was looking squarely at Gilmore, who stood agape.

With a hard tone, one that unmistakably conveyed his not wanting to introduce Heather to anyone, much less to those before him, Jack said, "Of course. Heather, this is General Gilmore, our esteemed leader, and his Chief of Staff, Doctor Duke. The lady is Margaret, Doctor Duke's wife."

Gilmore reached out to shake Heather's hand. "I am very pleased to meet you, Heather. I don't believe I have seen you before, but the pleasure is certainly mine now."

"Why, thank you," Heather sighed, her voice sounded like a clean spring morning.

Jack tensed, his body noticeably taking on the appearance of a fighter ready to attack. "Heather and I are living together," he stated flatly, looking at Gilmore.

There was a long second of silence, and then Jack turned to face his lady. "Heather, we haven't danced yet tonight." With those words, Jack took Heather by the arm and began to lead her to the small dance floor. She went without question, but she glanced briefly over her shoulder, giving Gilmore a "come hither" look of encouragement.

"God Almighty, that is one helluva beautiful woman," Gilmore said to no one in particular.

The party continued around them.

*****

Jason and Billy turned left onto 7th Avenue, their most direct route back to the courthouse. Rounding the corner and accelerating south it became apparent, as they passed Johnson Street, that 7th was no longer accessible to travel by ATV. The Highway 10 four-lane overpass and the railroad bridge had finally succumbed to the damage received during the quake. The road was piled with rubble composed of cement and reinforcing steel bars. They would have to detour around the mess.

"I'm sure glad we weren't under there when those bridges came tumbling down," Billy yelled over the noise of their engines.

"That's for sure," Jason screamed back. "Let's turn down Grant and take 4th into town."

As the two pulled up in front of the courthouse, several men were gathering on the steps. There were worried looks and hushed conversations being exchanged within the group.

"What's up?" Jason asked lightly, as he shut down his machine, grabbed his staff, and made his way toward the men.

The assembly grew silent. A man stepped forward with a serious look on his cHubby face. "Jake wants to talk to you two. He's down by the Rum River Bridge. You'd better talk to him."

The tone in the man's voice said things were far from right, and if Jake wanted to talk to him away from the others, somethin was really wrong. Jason, with Billy at his side, hurried off in the direction of the bridge.

"Over here, boys." Jake's voice was no more than a whisper.

Jason looked around, finding Jake in the fading light by the faint glow of his cigarette. "Jake, what's going on? Those guys at the courthouse looked like they'd lost their last friend."

"That ain't far from wrong," Jake answered.

Billy and Jason were now standing in front of the older man and could see the deep lines of concern engraved on his skinny face. "Jeez, what's wrong?" Jason asked in alarm.

"Sit ya down and we'll talk."

The boys settled themselves on the ground, close to Jake's feet. Viewed from outside, one might have thought of a teacher lecturing his students. They looked up into Jake's eyes questionably.

"We've got real problems, lads. Ya know 'bout that sickness Rick's been yammerin' about? Well, seems as if it may be here with us. We done had 'bout fifteen folks git what appears to be the flu this afternoon. Them's that got it are as sick as I've ever seen. I mean, they're sick, sick."

Jason's face went ash white. Oh, my God, no. Not this, he thought silently. "What are we going to do?" he said aloud.

"Ain't no longer a question of what we gonna do, boy," Jake said quietly. "If this here disease is as bad as old Rick says, then it don't matter much one way or tuther. But if you, me, or Billy boy here survives this mess, it will be a miracle. Fact is, lad, I ain't feelin' none too perky myself. That's why I wanted to talk to you without all the others around."

"What are you driving at, Jake?" Billy asked.

Jake sat in silence for several moments. He looked into the faces of each of the young men before him. I've done gone and got soft hearted 'bout these two, he thought to himself, as he snubbed out his cigarette, only to light another. "Jason, you and me been honest with each other from the very first time I done kicked ya awake. Well, I ain't about to beat around the bush with ya now. If I croak and you two don't, ya gotta have a new plan."

Jake held his hand up in a stopping motion as Jason started to say something.

"Hold up there lad, don't be interruptin' me. This is hard enough for me as it is. I just . . ." Jake suddenly doubled over in a coughing fit, his cigarette spewing from his mouth. He continued to cough for several minutes, unable to stop long enough to catch a decent breath. Spittle ran from the corners of his mouth, as Jason rushed to his friend's aid.

Pounding on Jake's back, Jason kept repeating in an urgent voice, "It's okay, Jake, it's okay. Come on now, relax."

Jake, his coughing spent, collapsed into Jason's arms. Jason hugged him tightly, feeling the older man's bones poking through his skin. Rocking back and forth slowly, Jason was thinking how much he had come to love this skinny old man, with his funny way of talking and wise counsel.

Sucking in a long, deep breath, Jake shrugged out of Jason's grasp. "I'll be all right now, boy. Thanks."

Reluctantly, Jason released his arms from around the shoulders of his comrade. "Are you sure? That was quite a coughing spell you had there."

"Yeah, I'm okay," Jake answered, as he lit yet another Marlboro. "Ya know I wouldn't lead you wrong, least ways, not on purpose, don't ya?" he asked, looking back and forth between Jason and Billy.

"Of course I do," Jason answered, taken aback.

Billy was nodding an affirmative with wonder and fear in his dark eyes.

"All them plans about moving to the country and settin' up a new life, well forget it," Jake said flatly, pausing to let his words sink in. He could read the utter astonishment on the two faces before him. "If this sickness comes to us, like Rick said, then we all might be dead in the next few days, and it don't make a tinker's hoot no how. But if you should live through it, ya gotta make new plans. Think about it, boy. Ya notice the days ain't been warmin' up none. I reckon it must be nigh on to July or such by now, and it still ain't been above sixty-five or seventy degrees. The sun just ain't able to poke its way through this here haze and dust. I figure it's gonna be the same all dang summer, and if that be the case, winter gonna be so cold, nothin' gonna live through it. Don't matter where you're holed up in Minnesota. Ya gotta get yourself south, down in my country."

"But what about all our planning and all the gear we've collected?" asked Jason in disbelief.

"Never mind about that stuff now. It ain't important. If you make it through the next few days and I don't is what counts. Now listen up good like, here's what I want ya to do. First, get yourself over to the armory." Jake stopped to take a breath, and again held his hand up to stop an interruption. "I know what you're thinking, lads, but we've gotta look at things realistic like. I know I've said over and over, 'No guns.' But things done taken on a different complexion in the last few hours. The dogs are gettin' more bothersome everyday, and it's gonna git worse before it gits better. As long as we remained in a big group, we probably wouldn't have no real trouble from them, but if it gits down to just a couple of folks left, a good shotgun's gonna come in real handy. Believe me!"

Jason nodded his head slowly. "But, Jake, you're talking like you won't be around, and I don't like you thinking like that."

"Don't make no difference what you like or don't," Jake spoke sternly. "You gotta accept facts, boy. You get yourself a shotgun. Cut down the barrel, cause it ain't for hunting, it's for killing up close like. Ya understand me?"

"Yes, sir," Jason answered solemnly. "But, Jake, I just couldn't make it without you. We've lost everyone else in our lives," he motioned to Billy as he spoke, "and the thought of you not being around would be just too much."

"I 'preciate the way you feel, boy, but facts is facts, and the fact is I may not be around much longer." He began coughing again, but it didn't last as long this time. He continued to explain what he wanted his young companions to accomplish in the next few hours. "Once you have weapons and ammunition, hitch up a trailer to your four-wheelers and load them with food, clothes and tools. Don't worry none about such things as nails and the like, just things necessary to fix your ATV's. After you're done with the loadin', hide 'em. Don't let none know where you stashed 'em, cause I have a feelin' things is gonna get rough around abouts here in the next couple of days. Ya understand what I'm tellin' ya?"

"Yes, sir, but why hide the ATV's?" asked Jason.

"Cause, I reckon there's gonna be those that's gonna want to hightail it out of here if we do git the sickness. I don't want them takin' your transportation."

"But," Billy interrupted, "if what Rick said on the radio is true, we'll be dead along with everyone else."

"But what if you ain't?" Jake coughed. "Besides, if anybody's gonna live through this thing, its gonna be some young whippersnappers like you. I just want ya to be ready. If I make it, then I'll be goin' with ya, but seein' as how I feel like leftover rotten eggs right now, I'm not thinkin' that'll be the case."

"Jake, please don't talk that way," Jason moaned. "You'll be with us, you'll see."

"I do love your attitude, Jason boy, but we'll just have ta wait and find out. Now off with ya while ya still have a little light. Make for the armory and do as I told ya." Jake's thin body convulsed into another coughing fit.

"Not without you, Jake, and that's final," Jason said sternly. We'll help you back to the courthouse, then we'll get busy."

Jake looked into the blue eyes of the boy talking so much like a man and said, " Okay, lad, but let's not make no habit of this sort of thing, ya hear."

Billy and Jason gathered their friend up by his shoulders, each to a side, and began walking the short block back to the courthouse. Arriving a few minutes later, they found more men and women gathered on the front steps and surrounding sidewalk. The group was waiting their return in silence. Now they wanted to know what to do about their latest impasse. They all seemed to ask questions at once.

Jake shrugged off the helping hands, stood tall, and took command of the situation immediately. "Whoa there. What's all the yammerin' about? Yeah, I know we got some sick folks in there," he pointed to the courthouse door, "but that don't mean we've got the sickness that's been killin' everybody. Heck, might be we gotta cold bug come down from Canada. So stop y'alls bellyachin' and let's help those that need it." He began walking through the crowd and into the courthouse with his questioners in tow.

Jason held Billy's arm, as the group disappeared inside. "Let's do what Jake said."

With those words he spun on his heel and moved off rapidly across the street.

The National Guard Armory had not been a large structure before the quake. Now it appeared even smaller. The roof had caved in, as well as the back wall. They entered with caution, hoping the rest of the building would not crash down on their heads. By poking around in the rubble of bricks, glass, desks, typewriters, and blackboards they eventually found what they were looking for . . . a weapon storage area. Just as Jake had indicated, there was a multitude of shotguns and rifles scattered about, with ammunition aplenty. Jason hefted an M12 shotgun to his shoulder with knowing grace, assuming a field-shooting stance.

"Have you shot one of these things before?" Billy asked.

"Sure! Well, not one as heavy or quite like this, but I've shot a 12-gauge before."

"That's great, cause I haven't ever even held a gun before, much less fired one," Billy said with doubt.

"No sweat. I'll teach you. Now, let's find a hacksaw."

"I know where there are about a dozen of them. I helped inventory them a couple of days ago. Be right back." With those words, Billy dashed out of the building.

Jason continued to look around, picking up a pistol and deciding it might come in handy as well, if he could find bullets. His eye caught several scabbards stacked in a corner. "With some slight modifications, I can rig these to mount on the four- wheelers," he thought. Hanging on a wall over the scabbards was a large rifle, with the biggest scope he had ever seen.

"What's this?" he said aloud, just as Billy returned.

"That's a sniper scope and gun," Billy said, catching his breath. He had run to the cache area behind the courthouse and back. "I saw one just like it," he said, pointing to the weapon in Jason's hands, "in a movie. Pretty cool, huh?"

"Yeah, but I don't think we'll mess with it. Let's get these barrels sawed off."

The two friends worked together for the better part of an hour; until they were satisfied they had what they needed in the way of firepower. They loaded their guns and ammo into trailers, and carefully smuggled them into a safe hiding place near the TCF Bank. Then they began collecting the other items, per Jake's instructions. It was late when they entered the courthouse, thinking they would have a thousand questions put to them about their activities in the past couple of hours, but that was not the case.

The refugees of Anoka were all sitting in their own selected areas, looking like surgical rag dolls in their perfumed masks. Little was being said, and what was could hardly be heard. The sick, now dozens of them, were being attended by others. Snyder's Drugstore, just across the street from the courthouse, had been raided of every cold and flu remedy on its shelves, and though the medications helped relieve the symptoms for a while, not one individual was showing any sign of recovery. Fear, deep-rooted fear, shone in the eyes of everyone in the room.

CHAPTER 9

On the Move

Two generators hummed in the background, providing electricity to the dimly lit anteroom of the courthouse. People lying or sitting around the room and halls of Anoka's house of law could be heard snoring softly or moaning in pain. It was a chamber of resignation and hopelessness. No sound of laughter, no chatter of children at play, not even the sound of crying over the loss of a loved one could be heard. Only the cold drone of generators, and men and women shifting for comfort. It was the final house of the dead. The room was not even filled with sorrow, for sorrow meant caring, and these individuals no longer cared about anything, including their lives. It was over. No more hope. No more dreams of a new start in the country. No more of anything except the resignation that death stalked close by.

Two days had passed since Jason and Billy had taken Jake's advice and hooked trailers to their four-wheelers, filled them with supplies, and then hidden it their survival gear in the hodgepodge of rubble behind the TCF Bank. It had been two nightmare days of watching new friends and companions sicken with a disease that ate at the internal organs like the maggots infesting the bloated bodies littering the streets and buildings of the world. The quake had been over almost as fast as it had begun, leaving few alive, but in the weeks that had passed, they had at least started to adjust to the horror. But this? Watching others sicken, unable to help in any reasonable manner, and in the end seeing them die an excruciating death in pain so fierce, screams of agony could not even be voiced; it was a form of purgatory. Only their faces manifested the magnitude of the suffering caused by their organs destroying themselves. Already, over forty of their number had died and been carried outside to join the other cadavers from past weeks. All but two were sick now.

Billy was squatting in the middle of Main Street. He was absent-absentmindedly staring into a small fire, which was weakly heating water to a rolling boil in a blackened pot. The fire had mesmerized him into a semi-hypnotic state. His mind meandered into a cocoon of darkness where there were warm wonderful things of indescribable nature soothing his over stimulated senses. It felt good to drift within the void, The sizzling of water bubbling into the fire brought Billy rudely back into awareness of the real world . . . a gray, dusty world filled with the smell of putrefied flesh. Shifting his mask quickly from his face, he emptied on the pavement what little contents his stomach held. Bile stuck in his throat like the acid it was, to cause a burning pain. His vomit was not the type he had seen the last couple of days. That heaved from the dying was filled with black blood. No, Billy's disgorge was the result of the disgust and horror he had been forced to watch. Billy was sick of death.

Wiping his lips free of ropy liquid on his jacket sleeve, he lifted the heavy pot with a gloved hand. Slowly he began walking back into the repulsive room of death, which had filled his world for the past two days.

Jake had wanted a cup of coffee, and Billy had warmed the water to please the old man. There was no more cooking inside, not with the cries of anguish and the slippery floors covered with blood and puke. He moved slowly, careful not to disturb those lying in pain. Jason and Jake were in a corner, a candle flickering over them casting an ethereal glow about the two.

Jason, sitting with his back against the wall, held Jake's skinny body in his lap. Tears rained down the boy's face in rivers. He had removed his mask, oblivious to the smells and sounds around him. He hugged the old man tightly, his chin resting against the sunken cheeks of his friend.

"Jake, please don't die. Please, please don't die," Jason murmured. "You just can't die. It's not fair. Oh, God, it's just not fair."

"Hush now, boy," Jake said in a waning, yet surprisingly strong voice. "It'll be over soon, but we done did our best. Didn't we now?"

Sniffing a tear, Jason cuddled the dying man tighter still. "But what am I going to do without you? There isn't anyone else."

"Ya got Billy, and there will be more, yer just gonna have to find 'em." Jake's voice broke and wheezed as he spoke. "Jason, lad, ya listen to me good now, ya hear? Don't ya be hangin' around this place frettin' over me. Ya git on that machine of yours and head south. Promise me, lad, you'll head south."

"But where? I've never been south of Wisconsin. I don't have any idea where to go."

"Now, listen here," Jake spoke with forced strength. "I know you can do it, Jason. Ya gotta do it. It don't make no never mind where ya been, just follow your instincts. I got faith in ya, boy. You just up and move down the road. Let it carry ya where it will. Just move south out of what's gonna be a cold winter. Promise me, boy."

"I promise! I'll try. Dammit, Jake, just don't die."

" 'fraid I don't have much say so in the matter," Jake said, as a thin trickle of blood ran from the corner of his mouth. "Jason, lad, I hurt so bad. My guts is tearing 'emselves plumb apart."

"Hold on, Jake," Jason whispered. "Billy's coming with the water. We'll make that cup of coffee for you."

"Think, lad, it's done too late. Promise me, Jason, head south. Live a good life, and fight the good fight. I got faith in ya, boy, and damned if I don't love ya some at that."

Jason struggled to pull Jake closer, to protect him from the inevitable. "I love you too, Jake." With those words, Jake's skinny, disease-ridden body went limp in his arms. "No, Jake. Please, no!"

This time, there was no answer. Jake was dead.

Billy was standing above the two; his eyes wet with tears, shoulders slumped in defeat. "What are we going to do now, Jason? What are we going to do now?"

Long moments passed before Jason turned an inconsolable face up to his friend. He ran his fingers through the thin, tear-dampened hair of the man he had cared for most in the world since his family's passing, and murmured in reverent voice, "We're going to bury Jake, and then we're going to head south, just like I promised."

"Bury Jake?"

"Yes! Billy, I can't treat Jake like the others, he is . . . was special. Will you help me?"

"Of course I will. Jake was special to me too, you know," Billy said with a trace of irritation.

"I'm sorry. I'm just so sick of the dying and death, and it just wasn't fair to lose Jake."

The two scrutinized each other, blue and brown eyes steeped in emotional sorrow for Jake and themselves.

Finally, Jason gently rolled Jake from his lap, laying him carefully on the hard courthouse floor. He moved to his knees, and leaned over, gently kissing his friend on the forehead. "I'll do as you say, Jake. I only wish you were going with us, to lead and guide." With those words he stood and stepped over to face Billy. With emotion, which came from the root of his soul, he placed a hand on either shoulder of his black comrade and said, "Billy, it's you and me now. There's nothing left we can do here. We could wait till everybody is dead." He waved a hand about the room, replacing it on Billy's shoulder. "But for what purpose? None! We're a team. For some reason we've been spared from the sickness, so let's do as Jake made me promise . . . head south right after we bury him."

"I'm with you, Jason. I always will be," Billy answered in a serious, ardent voice.

The two clasped each other tightly. Their bonds were sealed, their paths locked as they clutched . . . two teenage boys, rapidly becoming men, were now brothers preparing to take on what was left of their world.

"Let's do it," Jason exclaimed, as he released his grip on Billy and reached down for his mask.

Gently they hoisted Jake into their arms and left the courthouse, which had been their home. They walked down to the trickle of what was left of the Rum River. There, near the bridge where Jake had gone to think and smoke his Malboros, the boys dug a shallow grave and laid their mentor to rest. They did not say words over his grave, but rather stood silently over their handiwork, each wrapped in a blanket of his own thoughts. Each said goodbye in his own way. Together, as one, they raised their heads, nodded to one another, and quickly stepped off for the TCF Bank and their four-wheelers.

*****

Jack was sweating from the exertion of his lovemaking. Still holding Heather in his arms, as she breathed slowly in sleep, he looked upon her with loving eyes. She is so beautiful, he thought, so very beautiful. I could lay in her arms forever and never tire of looking at her.

Carefully, so as not to wake her, Jack untangled himself from Heather and the bed. It was morning. He had wakened earlier and gently roused his woman into making love. Though she had been sluggish, he had enjoyed the feeling of her sleepiness while ravishing her body. She had fallen back to sleep immediately afterward, but he had not minded. She would be there for him to love when he returned to their cube later that night.

He was quiet as he brushed his teeth, shaved, and performed his toilet. Slipping on his blue tunic, he thought, "blue tunics," what next? He fought the latest edict from Gilmore's office, but lost that battle as he had all the others. Now each tunnel had been directed to wear a colored tunic, replacing the armbands. Not only did he have to suffer the indignities of a colored tunic, but also there were three rings on his left sleeve signifying his being a headman. Jack fumed, "Is it apparent just to me that he is organizing us into a poor version of an army hierarchy?"

The fury in Jack's thoughts followed him as he made his way to the Hub, where a meeting of the tunnel heads had been called the night before. Bursting through the door, he stopped short to take a few deep breaths and calm his churning emotions. Looking about the large operations room always humbled him into a respectful mood. The displays, control panels, rows of blinking LEDs, and computers crunching numbers were an awesome sight to everyone who entered the control center of their world. The view would have stirred anyone examining its wonders, but to think their very lives depended on this room and those who pushed its buttons made its marvels all the more vivid.

Jack paused long enough to take account of those present. Each of the tunnels was represented by their headman or woman dressed in gray, green, or brown. Then there were the Hub engineers and scientists garbed in white, with diamond shaped patches sewn on their left sleeves indicating their relative rank. Six or seven yellow tunics mingled with the rest, three rings on each sleeve making them on an equal par with his headman stature. Standing above them all, one red tunic, five broad rings adorning his left arm, stood Gilmore.

"Jesus, it looks like a bloody rainbow in here," Jack muttered to himself, as he moved into the group.

"Ah, I see we are finally all here," Gilmore voiced loudly to catch the crowd's attention. His eyes glared into Jack's, conveying the message, 'don't be late for my meetings again' "I've asked you here to discuss the reactor problem. As you are aware, our power plant, the very heart of our underground home, is not functioning as it should. Though the situation has not gotten any worse, it is still a nagging quandary in that we do not know what is causing the overheating, and therefore have no idea if it will reach emergency status in the future."

"I thought you had already decided not to repair it," Jack interrupted.

"Yes, that is correct." Again, Gilmore frowned. "Yet, I feel the ultimate decision should be considered by all of my staff and commanders . . . leaders. Each of you was provided a printout of our predicament yesterday. I hope you have taken the time to review those papers and can now present me with your thoughts."

"Sir." It was Bravo tunnel's Blaksen speaking. "The tunnel heads conferred yesterday evening, and in this case, we believe your decision was appropriate in every respect. We feel, unanimously, that we should live with the conditions now present rather than shutting down the reactor. If the cooling problem becomes worse, then we feel shutting down may be the only reasonable thing to do, but not until then."

"Thank you, George. I appreciate your candor. Are there any here who do not feel as the headmen?"

The Hub remained silent, except for the shuffling of feet. "Good, then it is settled. However, there is one more thing. I have, on anticipating your decision in this matter, directed engineering to begin cutting small trenches along each tunnel wall. This should drain the condensation away from the living and works paces and into the rim. The rise in humidity within the rim, Doctor Duke assures me, will do the plant life nothing but good, and of course that will help keep the dampness level down in the tunnels."

There was a general nodding of approval from the multicolored assembly.

"Is there anything else?" Gilmore asked. "Okay then, back to your duties." Gilmore spun on his heel and strode for the stairs to his office.

*****

Later that morning, Margaret sat behind her desk in her small office. Settled across from her was a tall, very handsome man of twenty-nine. His brown eyes glistened with tears as he spoke quietly to his doctor.

"I'm sorry, Doctor Duke, I don't normally cry like this."

"Don't worry about it, that's why you are here. We can get through this fear, if only you'll talk to me about Phil."

Taking a deep breath and wiping his eyes, he began, "I don't know when it started, but it was shortly after the party. As a matter of fact, I woke the next morning feeling like the walls were closing in on me. My chest tightened as though steel bands were being twisted about me, and my heart began to pound at a thousand miles an hour. I just lay in bed wanting to scream, but too embarrassed to utter a sound. Finally, after several minutes, I got control of myself and got up."

"Has anything like this happened to you before, say as a child?" Margaret interrupted.

"No, never. I've had nightmares before, but nothing like this."

"Have you ever had any problem with claustrophobia?"

"None that I can recall, but if that's what this is, I don't like it. You see, since the first time that morning, it's happened over and over. I don't know, maybe six or seven times a day, and each time it gets worse. My roommate saw me have an attack last night. She's the one who suggested I come talk to you."

"How are you adjusting to tunnel life, Phil? I mean, are you staying busy?"

"I'm doing as well as the others, I guess. I'm an electrician and have been working in the rim for several weeks now. You know, fixing the wiring and lights. I met Abby shortly after we came below. She's really a super gal, and there are a lot of men looking to gain her attention. Plus, I have been with several other of the women in our tunnel." He gathered a fold in his blue tunic to indicate he was living in Charlie. "Actually, I've been rather enjoying myself since the strike. Not to be hedonistic, but it is rather nice having several women to each man. You know what I mean?"

" I believe so." Margaret wrinkled her forehead, raising her eyebrows, thinking of Phil's last remarks. Just as quickly, her mind shifted to the medical problem before her and she said, "What I think we have here is a very bad case of claustrophobia. The whole thing is new to you, so you are reacting to its effects with more anxiety than would normally be the case for someone who had been experiencing such assaults all their life. I'm going to prescribe a mild tranquilizer, nothing that will knock you out, just relax you when you have an episode." Margaret was hunched over her desk scribbling on a small piece of paper.

"Will it go away, do you think?" Phil asked with a plea of hope in his voice. "This thing is driving me nuts; besides, I don't want to be worrying Abby. We think she might be pregnant."

"Honestly, I don't know, but your records," she pointed to a brown manila file folder on the corner of her desk, "would indicate it should go away, that is. You're in excellent physical condition, and since you have never had this sort of problem before, I would think it is just a temporary thing. If this doesn't help, come see me again." She handed him her prescribed medication.

"Thank you, Doctor," Phil said, as he reached for the script, and started to get up from his chair.

"Just a minute, Phil. Did you say your roommate may be pregnant?"

"Yes. She's missed her period, and is experiencing a mild case of morning sickness every few days."

"Has she been to Med yet?"

"No. Not yet. We didn't think it was necessary for a few more weeks. You understand, we would like to be sure before we bother the doc."

"Ridiculous," Margaret exclaimed. "You see that she makes an appointment today. This could well be the first child of New Land. Do you understand me?"

Phil, taken aback by the strength in Margaret's voice said, "Yes Ma'am!"

"I'm sorry, Phil, it is just we want to make sure this baby, if Abby is pregnant, has every possible care we can provide. You will see that she gets to a doctor today or tomorrow, won't you?"

"Yes, I'll take care of it. Will there be anything else?"

"Yes. Please make an appointment to see me in a couple of days. Let's hope the anxiolytic will help. If you have a serious attack, call on me day or night."

"Thank you doctor," Phil said as he scraped his chair back to stand. "I really hope this thing won't last long and I'll be able to get on with my life. I hate thinking about being a problem to anyone."

"Don't worry about anything like that. You're not being a problem." Margaret smiled up into the dark, handsome face of her patient. "Now, get out of here and have Abby make an appointment."

After Phil had closed the plastic door to her office, Margaret sat in quiet reflection. "A baby in New Land, and so soon," she thought. "I wonder why this Abby didn't want medical assurance immediately? Strange!"

Getting up from her desk, she crossed the small, rock-hewn room to the door. She paused, deep in concentration, "Why?" she said aloud. It bothered her that an intelligent woman would wait for conformation and medical assistance. Something isn't right here, she thought. And why would a healthy, strapping man like Phil suddenly start feeling the effects of claustrophobia? Lord knows we performed enough psychological testing to weed out anyone with a tendency in that direction. But here he is, an anomaly to my analysis. I wonder, are there more?

She was moving rapidly down the hall. She wanted to speak with the head of New Land's medical team. Deeply absorbed in her own thoughts, she burst into Newton Blazedale's office without knocking. "Oh, excuse me!" she said, with utter shock.

Doctor Blazedale, his pants down to his knees was not executing a normal physical examination on the raven-haired lady bent over his desk. Margaret backed quickly from the room, shutting the door quietly behind her. She leaned up against the tunnel's cold, damp wall catching her breath. Standing there but a moment or two, suddenly she began to chuckle, then to laugh. Unpredictably she began to see the humor in the situation. "No locks on doors, few men, many women. This type of thing is going to happen on a regular basis in New Land," she thought aloud between breaths and laughter. "I might as well get used to it, and so will everyone else."

The door opened and Doctor Blazedale, having completely regained his composure said, "I'll see you later this evening, Gloria."

The oval eyes smiled up at the doctor. "Of course." She turned to Margaret; "You're the shrink, right?"

Margaret's eyes lit up with irony and laughter, "The shrink? Well, yes. I guess I am at that," she nodded, thinking of what she had interrupted.

Gloria smiled back, rocked forward on her toes to kiss Doctor Blazedale on the cheek, and then walked off without another word.

"Come in, Margaret," Blazedale said, holding the door for her. "I would ask that you knock next time. Might be less embarrassing for all concerned."

Suppressing a laugh, Margaret said, "I wasn't embarrassed. In fact, I thought it was downright funny. More importantly, I think we'd better get used to this sort of thing. It's bound to happen on a regular basis. Our community is so lopsided with women, every man is going to have to host a number of women, and there isn't much privacy. Loving, the way we were accustomed to above our present home, will become something of the past. In fact, I have concerns about how we, as a society, are going to handle this issue. Handle it emotionally and psychologically," she said in a serious tone. "But that's another subject altogether, and not the reason I came to visit you."

Doctor Blazedale moved to his small couch, settled himself down into its folds and crossed his legs. " Just why did you burst into my office?"

Still standing, Margaret looked down on the Chief of Medical Service. "I wanted to know if you have any reports of pregnancy."

"Pregnancy? No, none that I have heard. Why do you ask?"

"Because I just left a patient who claims his roommate is in a family way. This may be our first child in New Land."

Blazedale stood excitedly. "Really? Who? Why haven't I heard about it? Has she been to see a doctor?"

"That's my point. She hasn't seen a doctor. She wanted to be sure first. I've directed Phil, Phil Fagan, to see she receives an exam today or tomorrow. The real question is why she didn't immediately go herself. Still, this could be an exciting event for all of us."

"You bet it is. I'll personally see her, along with the obstetrician, of course."

"That would be good, and please let me know what you think her mental attitude might be, as well as her physical well-being."

"I'll do that. This is big news for all of us, isn't it?"

"I hope so," Margaret said. "I hope so!" She grinned at the man before her, laughing inwardly to herself; "I'll see you later today? Should you hear anything that is, and I am truly sorry I broke in on your morning's activities the way I did," she giggled girlishly.

"Don't worry about it," he grinned.

Margaret returned to her office still wondering why Abby had not gone to Medical as soon as she had an inclination she might be pregnant.

*****

Jason braked his four-wheeler, stopping alongside the road. He turned the key off and stared off into the distance. Billy parked beside him, shutting down his own machine.

"What's wrong?" Billy asked.

They had been on the road most of the day, and the pale sun was beginning to dive for the western horizon. Traveling was arduously slow, although both boys knew how to get to 694, the beltway around the Twin Cities. Quake damage to roads and highways was extensive, but that had not been the real problem. The closer they had journeyed to the cities, the more over and underpasses they had to traverse. Piles of broken cement blocked their route. Detouring was never easy, even on the four-wheelers. Add car wrecks, as well as semi-trucks jackknifed on and off the road and traveling became a nightmare.

"It is going to be dark soon. We've got to find some shelter," Jason stated.

"There was a gas station and a MacDonalds about half a mile back," Billy ventured.

"Yeah, I saw it. It's probably better to go back to something we know is there than to drive on. Billy, is the smell worse here, or am I just imagining things?"

Billy slid his mask down and took a shallow breath. "Holy Mother, are you right about that! It must be the Twin Cities."

Both boys eyed the gray smoke still drifting with the breeze above what had once been St. Paul and Minneapolis.

"It must have been worse for them," Jason said absently, with little emotion. "Let's get going."

"Hold up a minute." Billy was covering his mask with perfume. "Let me get this thing back on."

The two started their engines and began the trek back to a Union 76 station they had passed earlier, arriving just as the sun began to dip below the horizon. The station was a shambles, as was the Golden Arch next door.

"Boy, could I go for a real 'Big Mac'," Billy mused. "With tons of special sauce and a sesame seed bun."

"Dream on," Jason replied, as he scooped two cans of tuna from his trailer. "Somehow, I don't think we'll be eating Big Mac's ever again. Help me with these cans, will you?"

"Yeah, sure. What do you say we get a fire going?"

"Sounds good to me. I'll round up some wood."

The two set about preparing their evening meal. Little was said. Both boys had retreated into their own worlds. The sun slipped behind a line of clouds, and then disappeared altogether. Though its light was obscured by particles of dust suspended in the air, the sunset was spectacular. Weak shades of pink and purple crisscrossed the horizon . . . nature's watercolors brightening a sad world.

Taking a bite of tuna and rice, Billy asked, "Where to tomorrow?"

"I don't really know," Jason sighed. "I've only been to La Crosse once, and that was several years ago. We need a map."

"Well, we're probably in the right place for that," Billy replied, as he heaved himself to his feet and set down his bowl. "This gas station must have some maps, don't you think?"

The 76-station looked like a bomb had exploded in its center. Oil cans, tools, chunks of gas pumps and glass covered the area like confetti. The only structure left standing was the lube pit. They'd used the pit to park their four-wheelers and set up a temporary camp, and for the first time they were using their small Coleman cook stove to heat their meal. However, it was the small blaze from the campfire that provided warmth and companionship. The stove, along with sleeping bags, cooking utensils, lantern, knives, axes, and other camping necessities had been taken from Anoka's sporting goods store, or from the piles of gear gathered for their move into the countryside. Between the two trailers, there was enough food to keep them on the road for several days.

"Yeah, here's one," Billy exclaimed. "Looks like it covers Minnesota and Wisconsin."

"That's good for a start. What else can you find?"

"Here, this one is for Illinois and Indiana. What do you think? These ought to get us down the road a piece, and we can always find more if we need them."

Jason took the two maps from Billy, and began to unfold the one marked Minnesota and Wisconsin. "These will do." He spread the map on the ground next to their lantern, leaned forward, and began studying the red and blue lines. His blond hair fell over his eyes and he absently brushed it away. "I've got to get this hair cut. It's getting longer than my sister's," he said to no one but himself. Looking up at Billy, he said, "Look here, if we continue around 694 we'll intercept Interstate 94 heading southeast to Chicago. That's as good a place to start south as any, and we don't have to cross the Mississippi."

"Fine with me," Billy replied lightly. He studied the map intently for a moment and continued, "We still have to cross a river near Hudson though."

"It's the St. Croix River. I've never seen it, but I have read several articles about it in my Dad's fishing magazines. It even has sturgeon over a hundred pounds swimming in it. Still, I figure we'll have a look at the bridge tomorrow and if we can't cross, then we'll think of something else. Is that okay with you?"

"You bet! It feels good to be on the go. You know, like we are doing something. Do you think we'll run into anybody else along the way?"

"I don't know, but it does seem possible. If we lived through the sickness, then I suppose others did too. What I can't figure is why we didn't get sick with the others. Think about it, everybody got sick. The old, the young, everybody but us. Why not?"

"Maybe we're just immune. The important thing is, we *are* alive." Billy poked the fire with a stick, causing it to flare momentarily. "Where do you think we'll end up?"

"I don't know," Jason said, as he leaned back against his four-wheeler. He looked out at the pale stars that struggled to brighten the dark night. "Jake said head south to his country, and I don't even know where he came from. I guess we'll know when we get there, maybe Georgia or Alabama." He rolled his staff onto his lap, and ran his hand down the smooth wooden shaft. "Let's get some sleep. It's going to be another long day tomorrow."

They both got up and walked into the darkness, away from the fire, returning after relieving themselves beside the devastated gas station. Earlier, they had spread their sleeping bags near the fire, and with words of goodnight, the two crawled into the downy softness the bags guaranteed.

It was deep into the night when they bolted upright, unraveling themselves from their bags. The howling was close, much too close.

"Dogs!" Jason whispered. "From the sound, lots of them." He glanced over at Billy.

Billy's eyes shown white in the dim light of the fire's remnants. "How close?"

"Too darn close," Jason said. "Let's get the fire going."

The two hurried to pile sticks back onto the embers glowing before them. The fire sputtered and caught. Flames licked at the darkness as they piled on larger branches. Jason rose from his knees, where he had been blowing into the fire, and reached for his sawed-off shotgun. Billy did the same.

The dogs yowled again . . . a sound that sent shivers up Jason's spine and raised goose bumps on his neck and arms. "They're right outside the fire's light," he mumbled, as he backed up to Billy.

Back-to-back they stood, each facing out. "Don't you think you should have shown me how to use this thing?" Billy said, shaking his weapon. "I'm not going to be much good to you if I can't hit anything."

"Just point in the general direction and pull the trigger. Then pump and do it again."

The first dog leaped into the circle of light on Jason's side. His shotgun roared, sounding like thunder on a quiet afternoon. The dog disappeared, screaming in pain. Billy opened up; firing three shots as fast as he could eject the spent shells. He learned quickly how to get another load into the weapon's chamber. Again, the bravest of the pack tried to close the distance, and again shotgun fire split the darkness. Dogs whined in pain and death. The pack had enough and backed into the darkness away from the torment, which came from getting close to the red glow of firelight.

They stood there, back-to-back, two teenagers, friends, companions. It was deathly quiet. No sound of crickets or frogs, just their own heavy breathing. Jason moved rapidly to his trailer, grabbed more shells and threw Billy a half dozen as well. "I think they're gone for now," he said quietly. "But one of us better keep watch."

Wiping the sweat which suddenly appeared on his face, Billy nodded his head in agreement. "I'll take the first few hours, Bro, I couldn't get back to sleep now if I tried. Geez, that wasn't fun at all. I would have never believed dogs would have gone so crazy so fast."

"They aren't crazy, just turning into what they used to be . . . hunters."

"Well, that might be, but I don't like the idea of us being the hunted. Go on, go back to bed and get some sleep."

"Okay, but are you sure you'll be all right?"

"Yeah, I'm fine," Billy said, as he snuggled down against the big rear wheel of his four-wheeler. "I'll wake you in a couple of hours."

Morning came dully, the sun pushing its way above a dusty eastern landscape. Jason stabbed at the fire and wiped the sleep from his eyes. He had taken the last watch when Billy gently awakened him some hours before. He stretched and set a match to the stove. Its burner burst into blue flame. Pouring water from a five-gallon Jerry jug into a coffeepot, he anticipated how good the strong brew would taste. The thought brought a pang of sadness as he remembered how Jake had introduced him to the wonders of caffeine.

Smelling the coffee perking, Billy's brown eyes opened slowly. "God, I don't want to get up this morning," he grumbled. "Christ, did we do that?" he yelled, sitting upright.

Jason glanced in the direction Billy was pointing. Three dead dogs lay near what was left of the fueling island. The dogs looked like they had been attacked by a chainsaw. "The shotguns did a real job on them, huh?"

"That's putting it mildly," Billy responded. "I think I'll keep this beauty really close." He patted his gun. "It might come in handy again soon."

They had their breakfast, drank their coffee, and packed for the day's ride.
*****

Doctor Blazedale was furious, his face red with frustration and anger. "She doesn't want to have a baby," he said to Margaret. "She thinks bringing a baby into tunnel life isn't fair to the child. Dammit, Doctor, I thought you tested all these women before they were allowed on the final list." His anger flared.

Margaret was sitting behind her desk, updating her patient files, when Doctor Blazedale burst into the room. Her petite face screwed into indignation, her shoulder length hair framing the fury she was feeling inside. "Just what the hell are you implying? What gives you the right to judge me?" Her words shocked her as much as Blazedale, for she rarely, if ever, used profanity of any sort.

Stunned back into reality, the top man in the medical department stepped away from the woman's desk. "I'm sorry," he said, and meant it. "I just can't fathom this woman, Abby. She is beautiful, intelligent, and definably pregnant, but she's acting like she lives in hell, rather than here in New Land."

"She isn't alone," Margaret said. She, too, was regaining her composure. "Many of the men and women I have been treating have suggested much the same feelings. The symptoms are manifested in a variety of forms, but what it all boils down to is they don't like living underground, without the possibility of ever getting out."

"You've got to be kidding. Every single one of these people knew what they were getting into before we passed through the big door topsides. What has changed?"

"Nothing has changed, physically speaking, but during our testing we could not accurately predict what would happen to the mind once we were entombed. There had never been studies done which could provide us with conclusive details regarding living under a mountain for generations. The fact is, they are now realizing the sun will never shine again on their faces. That's the predicament in a nutshell . . . an extreme case of cabin fever."

The young Chief of Medical paced around the small room, finally sitting down on a corner couch. He crossed his legs and threw his head against the backrest. "What can I do to help?" he said, with resignation. "And again, I am sorry for the outburst."

"I really don't know. I have spoken to General Gilmore about the problem. In fact, he admitted he is having many of the same thoughts. My hope is it will be a stage we must pass through. Rather like a rite of passage. As for Abby and her child-to-be, we must ease her mind about the situation. Why don't you ask her to come see me? Perhaps I can abate a portion of her mental anguish."

"Okay, I'll do that."

"By the way, how does the fetus look?" Margaret asked.

"The baby is, of course, just in its second month, but it appears to be growing normally. The important thing now is to get her in the right frame of mind." He stood, rubbing his forehead and temple. "Damn, I've got a headache."

"Perhaps that young lady from your office can help," Margaret grinned mischievously as she spoke.

"Oh Lord," was all Blazedale said, as he took his leave, quietly shutting the door behind him.

Margaret, left alone, tried to think of a solution for Abby and the rest of The Few who were suffering from an underground life. I'd better report to Gilmore on this latest development, she thought.

*****

The six-lane highway had just split. Now there was a large island between the east and west bound lanes. Once they had cleared 694 and headed almost due east on I-94, the road began clearing somewhat. They still had to make detours, but overpasses no longer hampered them. They were about three miles short of the St. Croix when Jason pulled to the side of the road and stopped.

"Billy," he yelled over the noise of his motor, "look at that." He was pointing to what was left of a show yard of sailboats.

"Wow! What a mess. Let's go have a look."

Shutting down their engines, they ambled up the hill to a Hunter 37 lying on its side. The boat looked huge and, in fact, it was. Especially lying on its starboard side. Jason asked, "Have you ever sailed, Billy?"

No. Have you?"

"No, but it is something I have often dreamed about. You know, something to look forward to in the future. I wonder what happened to the ocean and all those boats sailing on it when the asteroid hit?"

"Yeah. It must have been pretty bad for them, but at least it was over quick. Don't you think?"

"I suppose so," Jason answered, as he turned back to the highway. "Guess we'd better get going. Wouldn't it be neat if we could get that," he glanced back over his shoulder at the big cutter sloop, "on the river and just float south?"

"Dream on," Billy laughed.

Cranking the four-wheelers back into life, Jason led off for the St. Croix, dodging a smaller sailboat lying in the road. The sun continued to climb as they slowly traveled down the road, arriving at the two bridges spanning the raging river at mid-afternoon. The St. Croix was a swollen torrent of muddy water and moving debris. Trees banged into the pilings that supported the cement bridge above the boiling cascade of water. Not long ago, this had been a beautiful river separating Minnesota from its neighbor, Wisconsin. If the Mississippi had gone dry, then by the looks of the river flowing before them, the St. Croix had tried in vain to swallow it whole.

"That's one heck of a river," Billy exclaimed in utter awe. They'd pulled up to the foot of the eastbound bridge and were sizing up their next move. "I sure hope we can get across one of these bridges, cause we sure as heck aren't going to float across that." He was pointing at the swirling waters.

"Me too. Why don't we walk this one first before we try taking the four-wheelers across?" Jason was already striding away from his vehicle, the staff tapping the ground in front of him as he walked.

"Good idea," Billy said, joining Jason's side.

The two walked in silence, dodging craters in the bridge's roadbed large enough for a man to fall through. By the time they had gotten halfway across the bridge it was evident they could bring their machines at least to the center span.

"Let's get the 'wheelers," Billy said. "We can ride them this far, and then walk the rest of the bridge. "

"Okay. In fact, I think we ought to ride them as far as we can, at least till we find something which looks like it might give way. So far, the bridge seems to have taken the quake pretty well."

It took them an hour to make it into Wisconsin across the bridge, but it had been done with no mishap. "We did it, our first big hurdle Jason exclaimed happily, "that felt good."

"I know what you mean," Billy answered. "Like we did something important. So, this is Wisconsin. It doesn't look much different from Minnesota," he laughed. "Where to now?"

"Shoot, I don't know. Let's just head on down the road till we find a place to spend the night. It's getting late anyway."

The big diner had been advertised on several billboards, not one of which remained whole. But they'd been able to piece the ad together, and now it was looming on their left, a big gray and white building with a dozen or so semi-trucks scattered in pieces around the parking lot. Twelve blue and orange flags fluttered in the breeze above what was the restaurant side of the two-story structure. They had to cross the meridian separating the four lanes and climb a steep embankment on the other side to reach what was a large Union 76 truck stop. As Jason topped the rise, the hair on the back of his neck stood on end. He could tell something was wrong. He stopped his four-wheeler and climbed up on its seat. Standing on the black vinyl, he scanned the building and the multiple pump islands. He could see the sign attached to the front of the restaurant. It read, "Riverside" carved north-woods style on a large plank of wood, and stained dark mahogany. A large chain saw carved statue caught his eye for a moment. It was of a sea captain standing straight and tall overlooking the parking lot. The captain's dead eyes, recessed deep in the dark face told him nothing. Jason could not identify the cause of his concern.

"What's the matter?" Billy asked, pulling up beside him.

"I don't know, but something isn't right. I can feel it."

The scream pierced the quiet like an arrow, and the sound of dogs in attack could be heard along with the terrified wail.

"It came from behind the diner," Jason yelled, as he drew his shotgun from its scabbard with his left hand, filling his right with the staff. "Come on, let's go."

Billy grabbed his gun, and ran after Jason, who was already heading full tilt for the diner. Jason rounded the corner running as fast as his legs could carry him, but pulled up short, skidding into the wall and banging his shoulder. Pain snapped through him like a knife, but the sight before him was worse yet.

Two girls huddled against the wall, one protecting the other. The larger girl, her jacket ripped to the elbow, held a hunk of 2 x 4, which she was swinging with all her might at the attacking dogs. Five of the blood-crazed animals were trying to get past the swinging board to her throat and the screeching girl behind her. A third person, unrecognizable from Jason's angle of view, was being torn apart by the rest of the pack. He started to raise the shotgun, but knew instinctively he would kill the girls as well as any dogs.

"Jesus Christ," Billy howled in his ear.

Jason hesitated but a moment, then, dropping his gun, he raised the staff over his head and ran shrieking into the melee. The brass ball crowned a dog on its head, splitting it like a melon. Jason did not notice. He was lost in the fight. He would not remember how his staff struck again and again, or the pain of his leg being ripped open by angry fangs. The staff swung out time and again, hitting gray, brown, and white bodies . . . breaking bones, splitting skulls, and causing panic in the pack's ranks. It was over almost before it started. The dogs that could, ran out of sight, tails tucked low between their legs. Jason fell to his knees, exhausted.

The girl dropped her board and turned to console the smaller person behind her. Assured that the huddled figure was going to be all right, she ran to the torn figure lying on the ground near Jason. She turned the broken and torn body over. "NO!" she protested in pain. "David, no. Not you too."

Regaining some of his composure, Jason stood. He moved slowly to stand over the two on the ground. Billy joined him, putting his arm around Jason's shoulders to stop the wobbling of his friend's legs. "Are you okay?" he asked with concern.

"I guess so." Jason reached down to pull the girl away from the bloody rag doll who had once been David. "Come away now. Here, let me help you."

The girl tightened and shrugged the helping hand away. Then she started to cry . . . a soft pitiful cry Jason recognized as if it were his own. "Please, come away now . . . you can't help him anymore."

She leaned back and looked into the eyes of her savior. Tears rolled down her cheeks in a great flood of sorrow, but there was a return of understanding. "You're hurt," she said, flatly.

It was true, Jason realized. He looked down at his right leg, which was now beginning to throb with a passion. "I'll be all right."

"Oh, sure," the girl spoke angrily, "Mr. Macho. Let's move him inside," she said to Billy. "Sarah, Sarah, the dogs are gone now. I need you to get me the first aid kit from the truck."

Jason was leaning heavily on Billy's shoulder. The world swam before his eyes, his Mom, Dad, and Sally revolving in erratic patterns in his mind. Suddenly, his reality turned to darkness, as he slumped to the hard asphalt pavement. Jason passed out cold.

CHAPTER 10

Changes

Margaret sat in an uncomfortable stainless-steel chair in front of Gilmore's desk. She was studying the big man with concerned eyes. Gilmore had been under a great deal of strain for months, even before their final move into the depths of New Land. The pressure was beginning to tell around his dark eyes. His hair was graying even more than his years told, and he was becoming more aloof, if that were possible. He asked her to sit while he finished some paperwork that needed attending, and she had done so quietly.

Looking up from his desk, Gilmore smiled, his perfect teeth shining in the overhead light. "What can I do for you, Margaret?" he asked her softly.

"Thank you for seeing me on such short notice," Margaret smiled back.

"You know my door is always open to you and your husband," the big man stated with sincerity. "Is something wrong?"

"No, not really. I just thought you might want to know that we have New Land's first baby on its way."

"Why, that's wonderful news. When did all this happen?"

"It came to my attention quite accidentally, actually. I was treating a patient for claustrophobia when he casually mentioned that his roommate might be pregnant. She had not seen a doctor yet, so I had him get her to Medical that same afternoon. That was the day before yesterday. Doctor Blazedale confirmed the couple's suspicions."

"That's great. Do you think it would be a good idea to announce the event to the entire community?"

"No, not yet. We do have a bit of a problem."

"Oh God, I might have known. Can't anything go on down here without a major crisis of some sort?" Gilmore slumped back into the recesses of his chair. "What's the trouble? And please don't tell me the baby has two heads or something terrible like that."

"No! No! Nothing quite that serious. Still, there is a problem. It seems the lady in question doesn't want to have her baby in the tunnels. She has flatly stated to Doctor Blazedale that she doesn't think having a child underground would be fair to the infant."

"And why the hell not? She sure as hell knew what she was getting into when she joined the Few." Gilmore asked angrily.

"I'm not entirely sure, but it has to do with the change of attitude in a lot of New Land's inhabitants. You yourself even admitted to a touch of cabin fever not too long ago. Remember?"

"Yes, I recall, but that doesn't mean that I want to give up living or carrying on life's processes."

"That may be the case for most of us, but there are those that are having a harder time adjusting. I think that Abby, that's her name, is one of the latter. That's the bad news. The good news is that I will be seeing her in my office later this afternoon. I hope that I'll have more information about the situation then."

"Good. I'm glad that you have become involved in this affair. By the way, if you know who the father is, could you enlist his help?"

"No real problem there. Phil Fagan is his name. He's an electrician living in Charlie tunnel."

"I should have guessed it. If there is a problem involving people, they seem to always come from Charlie. I'm beginning to think the air is different in that tunnel or something like that. Maybe it is just my imagination, but it seems most of my problems stem from Jack Mossmen's domain."

"Be that as it may," Margaret went on, "Phil, her mate, seems to be a reasonable individual, with enough intelligence and concern for Abby to help me convince her having the baby will be best for her and everyone else. At least I hope I can enlist his aid."

The door burst open, allowing the bright lights of the control room to flood Gilmore's office. A smiling, excited face appeared in the doorway. Benjamin Duke came striding purposefully into the office, drew a chair from under the conference table, and plopped his thin body down.

Gilmore looked at Doctor Duke in utter astonishment. "Well, Doctor, that was quite an entrance. Have you forgotten that knocking is generally considered the appropriate measure before entering my office?"

His tone was agitated, but he was, in fact, more amused than angry. Benjamin Duke, during their association with each other, had never been as spontaneous as this volatile entrance. Just what *is* happening to people down here anyway? He kept that somewhat disturbing thought his own.

"Sorry for the intrusion," Doctor Duke grinned, his mood not dampened, "but I have some news that should put a smile on your face."

"Is that so?" General Gilmore was trying to remain stoic to the effervescence of the man before him, but was having difficulty not warming to the situation. "Just what in the world could brighten your world so much?"

Margaret, too, was shaken by her husband's dramatic entrance. "Ben, you look like the cat that swallowed the canary. What is it that has put such a radiant smile on your face?"

"The recreation area is completed. Not only is the work all done but it's absolutely beautiful. The volunteer workers have truly put their hearts into the effort."

"What are you talking about?" Gilmore looked puzzled as he phrased his question.

The smile fell from Duke's face. He looked like a small boy whose teddy bear was taken from him. "Why, the park area you said we could build in the rim. Don't you remember?"

"Oh yes, now I recall. You mean you actually were able to construct a mini park . . . pools and everything?"

"Yes! Yes!" Inspiration was back in his voice, and he brightened once more. You have got to see it for yourself. It's splendid. The water diverted from the walls to the rim made the final touches extraordinary. There are flowers, trees, and even grass. The reflection pool is about twenty-five feet across, and there is even a small beach with real sand. The sand was made by pulverizing rock." Duke was trying to tell the two listeners everything at once. Words were spilling out of him faster than he could clearly enunciate. "You've got to come see it to believe it."

Margaret got up from her chair and moved to her husband's side. She smiled down at him with love, bent at the waist, and gave him a kiss and a hug. As she held him close, she whispered, "I haven't seen you so excited since old Doc Ellis told you he wanted you as his assistant."

Doctor Duke returned the embrace and smiled back. "I know I seem like a kid in a candy store, but it really is quite grand."

"If you two can stop loving up each other for just a moment, perhaps we could all go have a look at this wonderment of New Land. We, all of us, could use a boost in spirits." Gilmore was already on the move, striding to the door, flinging it open and moving down the steps into the maze of flickering lights of the Hub. "Well, are you coming?"

Leaving the Hub, they accessed the rim by way of Delta tunnel. "The plant life seems to be doing very well," Gilmore stated.

Doctor Duke, almost jogging to keep up with the big man before him said, "Yes. The entire rim has made a spectacular recovery from the damage it received during the strike. I think the increased moisture in the air, caused by the reactor's problems, has been a big help. Certainly, the additional water drained from the walls of the tunnels to the rim has increased growth, as well as providing water for our reflection pool." He was pointing ahead.

Gilmore stopped in mid-stride . . . his mouth agape. "My God, you weren't kidding."

Before them was an oasis constructed under ground. Electricians had provided a stunning array of lighting, which through its effects, turned the entire area into a scene from Eden. The theme centered on the still pool of blue water, which was lit from above and below causing it to shimmer realistically. A small, but well-defined beach of bleached sand edged the pool for more than three-quarters of its circumference, while the rock wall of the rim bound one full side. From this rock, loving hands carefully constructed a parapet of broken stone so uniquely that it appeared to be part of the original cave wall. Flowing from the top of the palisade, a waterfall streamed down, falling into the pool in a million sparking diamonds. Again, the glimmering cascade was highlighted with carefully placed lighting. Beyond the small beach, vegetation of all sorts represented in the rim had been conscientiously transplanted. Where plant life looked haphazard throughout the rim, here it blended with the surroundings, providing a true oasis effect straight out of an MGM film. The final, yet perhaps most stunning impression forced upon the mind, was the awareness that there was a sun overhead. How a sun had been placed in a blue sky, studded with puffy white clouds, Gilmore had no earthly idea.

"My Lord! " He turned to Doctor Duke, who was smiling from ear to ear. "This is a miracle." He stopped, and cocked his head listening. "You even have birds singing."

Margaret was still trying to catch her breath. She stood awed by the vista before her, for it appeared as a panorama and not just a section of the rim it was. "How? How in the world did you accomplish this, and why didn't you tell me?"

Still beaming with joy, Doctor Duke looked from his wife to Gilmore. "Isn't it marvelous? As it started to come together, I just couldn't believe it myself. I tried to keep it a secret from both of you because I wanted to make sure that it was all going to actually be true. We finished it yesterday evening. I ask you, isn't it just too much?"

"You've got that right," Gilmore mumbled, still too overwhelmed to say much else.

The group carefully walked into the small paradise created by those who lived underground; yet, though surrounded by rock, so vividly remembering what it was like to see the sun. Almost reverently, they touched the water, sand, and foliage.

"Is the pool deep enough to swim in?" It was Margaret who asked. "It looks so real, so deep."

"No, I'm afraid not," the smile fell from her husband's lips. "The water is only about twelve inches deep, but it does look real doesn't it?" He smiled again.

Margaret went to his side, "Yes, my love, it looks real. You have done something very special here. The entire population of New Land will thank you."

"Not me. It was just my idea, but it was the talents of some very special people from every tunnel that has made this so fantastic."

"I don't care who, what, or how, I just think this is great, " Gilmore said with enthusiasm, as he strode over to shake the doctor's hand with vigor." You have done it again, Benjamin. Thank you. Thank you from the bottom of my heart. When can we open it to everyone?"

"Any time. It's ready, but we will have to limit the number of people using it at any one time. I suggest that we announce it on the tunnel view vision tonight, and then have each tunnel arrange for scheduling. I'm sure we can work it out. I figure as soon as the newness of it wears off, scheduling will become much easier, but undoubtedly it will be used more than any other facility we have in New Land."

"I don't doubt you on that point," Gilmore replied.

*****

Jason awoke suddenly, every instinct alive and ready to move in an attack. The last thing he remembered was snarling dogs . . . dogs that threatened to reduce him to ground meat if given half a chance. He tried to move, but could not. His arms and legs were restrained by something. Fear gripped him as he began to struggle in earnest.

"Lie still, you bloody oaf, or I'll clobber you."

The voice was soft; the words, though harsh in nature, were spoken with warmth. Jason tilted his head forward enough to see the girl who had been swinging a 2x4 at the pack of dogs. His memory flooded back, and he cringed as he thought of his part in the drama.

"Where am I?" Jason asked.

The girl paused, holding a needle and thread before her. "You're on a table in the restaurant, and I'm just finishing the last stitch on your leg."

"You're sewing my leg?" Jason quizzed with some disbelief. "Do you know how?"

"No, but I'm learning as I go." She smiled down at him reassuringly.

Jason studied the woman child before him. Her hair was like corn silk blowing on a summer day, full and rumpled. Blue, intelligent eyes shone with life from a heart-shaped face. She was tall, perhaps five feet, eight inches, and already her body bloomed with womanhood. He could see her breasts straining the light green sweater she wore against the cool summer days. Jason thought she was the most beautiful girl he had ever seen. Resting his head back down on the hard table he said, "Okay, stitch away. Yeouch! That hurts."

"Don't worry, that's the last one. Why do you think I had your friend here strap you down? I was afraid you would wake while I was in the middle of a stitch and I'd poke the needle somewhere besides the wound."

A smiling black face came into view. "How you feeling, Jason?"

"Not so good, particularly with needles being stuck in me."

"I'm finished. What do you think Billy? Will they hold?" The girl asked seriously.

Billy studied the neat sewing of the six-inch gash that ripped along the inside calf of Jason's right leg. "You did a fine job. I know I couldn't have done what you did." He started untying the bonds that held his friend steady.

Jason sat up and started to swing his legs over the table's edge.

"Oh no you don't." The young blond hurried to intercept him. "You're going to lay right there until I can get a bed made up for you. That gash was deep and we had a devil of a time getting the bleeding to stop. You're not going to ruin my handiwork by trying to roam around."

The expression on her face told Jason she meant every word she said. There would be no denying her on this issue. "Okay," Jason moaned softly, knowing that she was right. "But I sure don't want to stay on this hard table."

"I've got that taken care of," Billy smiled. Though he was not as tall as Jason, nor as full-bodied, he still possessed a great deal of strength. He lifted Jason in his arms, straining under the load, grunting his way to a makeshift bed atop what had once been a buffet serving line. The gleaming chrome lighting fixtures looked down on Jason with no light or warmth, but the mattress felt wonderful under him, and, as Billy elevated his leg on a cushion, he realized how much it hurt, and just how serious the wound might be.

"How bad is it?" Jason asked.

"Bad enough," his doctor offered. "But if you'll stay down for a few days, and if infection doesn't set in, I think you'll be okay." She moved to Jason's side and examined her handiwork. "Yes, I think you'll heal nicely." She turned to leave.

"Wait! I don't even know your name," Jason exclaimed.

The blond hair swept gracefully through the air, as she turned to face Jason once more. "Mary Lynne Rette," she said softly, gazing down into Jason's eyes. "And I want to thank you for what you did. That was a very brave act." She reached out and touched his arm. "My sister, Lorrie, and I will be forever grateful."

"And what about the boy?" Jason already knew, but asked anyway, hoping.

"David is dead," she answered flatly, but a tear welled at the corner of each eye. "Now that you are taken care of, I've got to say good bye to him."

"Wait," Billy spoke up. "I'll help you." He shot a questioning glance at Jason.

"Good idea, Billy. I'll be okay. Go help her."

After the two had left, Jason looked around, adjusting the pillow under his head. He was lying on a narrow serving island, which appeared to be about fifteen feet long. Over the top of his bad leg, he could see a brick wall and what appeared to be the entrance to the kitchen.

"That must be where the smell is coming from," he thought, "probably meat or vegetables which have gone bad."

Looking to his left, he saw a huge clock on the wall. It had stopped, its oversized hands showing ten thirty. The immense clock reminded him of his grandfather's pocket watch or of an old train conductor standing on a platform hollering, "All aboard;" watch in hand. He rested his head back on the pillow, closed his eyes, and drifted into a fitful sleep, dreaming of golden haired, heart-faced girls.

Jason awoke sometime later to the sound of voices. "I'm hungry," he said.

"Well, that's a good sign. I'll get a plate for you." It was Billy who spoke. Sliding out from the booth the three were sitting in, he made his way to the Coleman stove on a table close by. "How does canned vegetable soup sound to you?"

"Fine," Jason said as he sat up, bending at the waist. He did not want to disturb his leg. He glanced over at the two girls still sitting in the maroon, vinyl covered booth.

"Let me have a look at you," Mary Lynne said, as she slid from behind the table.

"It feels better, but it's still throbbing."

"Here, I brought you some Tylenol 3 with codeine. My mother always carried a bottle in our first-aid kit when we traveled. They should help the pain."

She handed the small white tablets to Jason as Billy returned with a bowl of steaming soup and a cup of coffee. Jason dry swallowed the tablets, took spoon in hand, and began ladling hot soup rapidly to his mouth. The last time he had been this hungry was when Jake had taken him in tow to the Country Market his first morning at the courthouse. The four fell silent. Standing next to Jason, Mary Lynne spooned soup from her bowl while watching Jason eat. Billy and Lorrie continued with their own meals at the table.

Jason, his ravenous appetite overcoming the need for speaking, gulped mouthfuls of the hot liquid like it was his last meal. Finishing his last spoonful, he, looked at Mary Lynne and asked, "How did you get here?"

Mary Lynne sat her empty bowl down next to Jason, and absently combed golden hair from over her eyes with her right hand. She gazed off, unseeing, at the far wall. "Lorrie, David, and I were on a trip with our folks. We go every year in the spring. Our grandparents have a cabin on Leech Lake, up in northern Minnesota."

Jason nodded, "Yeah, I know where Leech is We, I mean my folks had a cabin on Ponto Lake, not too far from Leech. Where were you coming from?"

"Bloomington. Bloomington, Illinois. Anyway, we stopped here for breakfast when whatever happened, happened. It was awful . . . trucks turning over, people screaming and dying. Our folks," she stopped and looked down at her patient, "were killed when a semi crushed them between two trailers. When it was over, those of us who were okay huddled together wondering what the hell went wrong."

"Yeah, we know the feeling," Billy said.

"Anyway, we were able to keep things going here for a while. There's a big generator out back, and it came on automatically when the electricity went off. There were about fifteen of us still alive then, and we cleaned up the mess, buried the dead, and tried to get information on what happened. Billy, here, actually filled us in on more facts than we have had until now. Several of our numbers went in search of others, but none ever came back. Then everybody started getting sick, just like what happened to your group. Lorrie, David, and I were the only ones left."

"Where are all the bodies?" Jason queried.

"We buried everyone at first, but as there became fewer of us, we just dragged them back into the fields surrounding this place. There were just too many of them for us to handle." She lowered her eyes and head, as if to ask for understanding.

"You did the right thing. How long have you been here alone?" Jason asked.

"I'm not real sure, a week or two at least. Mr. Dixon, he was sort of our leader, died three or four days before the dogs and you two showed up. God! I don't know what we would have done if you hadn't been here."

"From what little I've seen, you'd have made it okay," Billy declared. "Jason, these two are some kind of courageous ladies."

"Thank you, Billy, but it's my sister that's the brave one, not me." Lorrie spoke for the first time, her voice a crystal whisper in clarity and sincerity. "If it hadn't been for her, I don't know what we'd have done." She held her blue eyes steady on Billy's. "If only David could have . . ."

"David's gone. We can mourn him, but we have to go on." Mary Lynne left Jason's side to gather her sister close. Over her shoulder she asked, "What are we going to do?"

"We'll head south, just like Billy and I planned, and we don't want to waste much time in getting gone," Jason answered immediately and with authority.

"You'll not be going anywhere for a few days. Your leg will split open and then we'd have a real mess on our hands. Still, I agree with you about going south. Do you have any idea where?"

"No, not really, but we'll know when we get there."

The late afternoon's twilight was fading, and with its passing, the room darkened. Billy walked to the cashier's counter, where he had placed the Coleman lantern, and began pumping pressure into the tank. He touched a match to the mantles, which turned orange, and then a dazzling white. Light flooded the room causing broad shadows to dance on the walls. Images of fishnets and float balls were distorted by the lantern's glow throwing peculiar shapes throughout the room. Outside, the wooden captain stood night watch, his eyes forever staring to the southwest.

"Billy, tomorrow will you try and round up another four-wheeler for Mary Lynne and Lorrie? If you can find one, we'll make better time than if we have to double up."

"Sure, I'll have a look. Anything else?"

"Yes," Mary Lynne said emphatically, "I need to find a library."

"A library?" both Jason and Billy questioned at the same time. "Why?"

"I need some first-aid books. I mean some really in-depth books on first aid. That wound of yours," she said, pointing to Jason's leg, "has made it perfectly clear that we are going to have to know how to take care of ourselves medically. If I'm going to have to sew you up every other day, I'd better learn the right way of doing it, don't you think?"

"Yeah, I suppose so," Jason laughed. "However, I hope not to make a habit of this sort of thing."

The small group talked for a while longer, with Lorrie entering more frequently into the conversation as the evening wore on. They unanimously agreed that Jason required a few days' rest, but they needed to be on their way as soon as possible. Their biggest concern, for the time being, was the roaming dog packs. As long as they were inside the 76 Station they were safe, but once outside they were at the mercy of an onslaught. Billy showed the two girls how to operate the pump Model 12's, and how to reload.

"Not that I'm an expert on these things, but I did learn to shoot in a hurry when I had to," was his comment.

As they talked, a full moon rose to bathe the parking lot in weak, dust-filtered light. A dog bayed at the great orb, his tenor howl keying a note of sadness in each of the Riverside's residents.

*****

Charlie's main recreation hall was abuzz with activity. Small groups were gathered at a scattering of tables playing cards, Yahtzee, or similar games. Still others stood visiting, swilling glasses of fruit juice. Laughter and good-natured jibing filled the air. It could have been a social gathering at a local small town community center, and in a way that's just what it was . . . several miles underground.

In a corner, well away from the Hubbub of the main gathering, two men sat close in hushed conversation.

"I don't blame her one bit for not wanting to have her baby down here. Even with the new Oasis to soothe the spirits of most of these sheep," Jack Mossmen gestured to the crowd, "New Land is still a nightmare. What are you going to do?"

"I don't know, and it really isn't my decision to make. It's Abby's. She wants to have an abortion, but no doctor in Med will even consider giving her one, and a self induced abortion is far too dangerous," Phil Fagan stated with emotion.

"Have you thought about trying to get her topsides?"

"Are you kidding? What are you talking about? We would die in a heartbeat."

"How do you know? That's what Gilmore and his flunkies want us to believe, but is it really so? I don't know and neither do you." Jack looked around the brightly lit room. "Look at them, Phil. You would think they've forgotten what it's like upstairs. Well, I haven't, and I don't intend to."

"Even if we wanted to try to get topsides, how would we go about it? The gate is monitored twenty-four hours a day, and rumor has it there are electronic surveillance devices between the tunnels and the great doors."

"Frankly, I don't have any idea, but if I were to find a way, would you be interested in trying?"

"I don't know. I just don't know. I'll talk to Abby about it," Phil said seriously, his handsome face wrinkled in contemplation.

Jack started to say something else but stopped as Heather walked to their table. "Heather, please join us," he said, standing and grabbing a chair from the table behind them. "Phil and I were just talking about the Oasis, and what a wonderful addition it is for all of us," he shot a warning glance in Phil's direction. "You look wonderful, as usual."

Heather did look wonderful. The blue tunic could not hide the richness of her body; in fact, it did more to show her supple curves than hide them. Men's eyes from all over the room had followed her progress across the room.

"And who might you be?" She smiled at Phil.

"This is Phil Fagan, one of Charlie's finest. Phil, this is Heather."

"Nice to meet you, Jack," Phil said. "You, Jack," turning to face the man next to him, "are the envy of every man in New Land. But you must know that already."

Jack laughed. "Thank you for the compliment to the both of us."

While the three talked quietly in Charlie's recreation room, Margaret was preparing her office for a visitor. She had asked Abby to see her this evening, four days since seeing Phil for the first time. Now she was dimming the lights to soften the harshness of the stainless furniture and the lack of a pleasing decor. She wanted Abby to feel at ease with her. She wanted to be able to reassure her that the birth of her child was a happy event to look forward to, not a dreaded condemnation for the child. She had just finishing rearranging the cushions on her small couch when she heard a light knock at the door.

"Come in."

The door opened slowly exposing a young woman of medium height, coal black hair, full lips, and dark eyes. By any standards, Abby was very pretty. The tentative expression on her face clearly suggested she wished to be anywhere rather than at the door to Margaret's office. "Doctor Duke?" She asked quietly.

"Yes, please come in Abby, and please don't call me Doctor, I'm just plain Margaret," she smiled warmly.

"Thank you," Abby answered, as she slowly entered. As she closed the door behind her, she glanced over her shoulder as if looking for a means of escape.

"Abby, please sit down." Margaret intuitively sensed the *fight or flee* mindset the other woman must be feeling. "It was good of you to come and see me, I've been looking forward to meeting you. Phil thinks the sun rises on your head, and I can understand why. You are indeed a lovely woman."

Abby looked around the room, noticing the dimmed lights and subdued atmosphere, shuffled to a straight-backed chair and sat down rigidly. "Doctor, er . . . Margaret, I am not sure why I am here. I don't feel there is a thing wrong with my mind. You are a psychologist, aren't you?"

"Yes, I'm a psychologist, and I don't think there is anything wrong with your mind either. That's not the reason I wanted to talk to you." Margaret purposefully sat on the couch, catty corner to her guest. She did not want to place the desk between her and this woman. "I am, however, very interested in the event which is going to take place in your life, and quite frankly, in the lives of all of us in New Land. I hope you can understand that?"

"Yes, I suppose so." Abby shifted her chair slightly to face Margaret. "But I think you should know that I feel very strongly that *I* have the right to choose whether I should have this child or not. It's not the doctors, General Gilmore's, nor your choice, it's mine." These words were spoken in a raised voice, with determination and frankness.

"I can understand your feelings, but I must admit I don't understand why," Margaret said with concern. "We, you included, had some understanding of what it might be like living in New Land. The very reason there are such an over- abundant number of women was to perpetuate mankind. Granted, life here is not exactly what any one of us totally expected, still we are the survivors, and it is somewhat a duty for all of us, and to humanity, to have children."

"Why?" Abby interrupted. "What have we, buried under so many miles of rock, got to offer future generations? Nothing! That's what. No, I was wrong to accept the offer to be among the Few in the first place. You and the government made it sound like such a heroic thing we were doing, but it wasn't heroic at all. The real heroes died with the strike. I don't want to bring new life into this underground world, period."

Margaret was taken aback by the resolve the young woman was manifesting. The soft light could not hide Abby's ridged resolve etched in her brow.

"I want an abortion," Abby finished.

Margaret studied the woman before her. How do I convince her to have the child, or even to want it? She wondered to herself. Aloud, "Abby, I think I understand your concerns, but you must be aware that no one is going to endorse your wishes, nor provide you with the means. I'm not trying to be hateful, only speaking the truth of the matter."

The dark-haired woman hung her head, "I know. I'm caught in a Catch 22 situation. It's making me crazy. Oops," she brightened, "I didn't really mean crazy."

Margaret laughed softly, "I know. What can I do to help? I mean, if we both realize that abortion is, in fact, out of the question, what can I do to help you feel better about having the child. I won't kid you, the thought of living out generations underground is bothering more people than yourself, but it is my opinion we are going through a transitional period. The full realization of spending our lives here in New Land has had different effects on different individuals, but I see it as growth, not loss of hope. If you could accept that premise, then we might be able to find comfortable ground for you to stand on regarding your child."

Silence filled the small rock hewn room. The two stared at one another . . . each searching for an answer from the other. Margaret could sense the great sadness Abby felt. Abby on the other hand knew that Margaret wished only to be of help.

"I will try," Abby said simply.

Phil had excused himself several moments before, leaving Heather and Jack alone at their corner table. They were talking quietly, while Jack held her hand. He rarely was seen in public without some sort of bodily contact with her. He was a jealous person by nature, and he wished everyone to know that Heather was his. Heather made no attempt to dissuade either Jack's actions, or the reasons for such overt behavior. She had no desire to be pawed by men of lesser stature than her present choice of a bedmate. The room suddenly hushed, causing the two to look up. General Gilmore was walking through the entrance.

Jack got to his feet, almost knocking over the chair in which he was sitting, and strode for the big black man. "General Gilmore, what a surprising pleasure," he pressed with a tight-lipped grin. "What can we do for you?"

General Gilmore, a huge grin spreading across his face, looked down on the smaller man. "Why, thank you, Jack. I was just out walking; trying to get a bit of exercise and thought I might drop by for a fruit juice. Is that all right?"

"Why certainly."

"Slumming, are you General?" Heather interrupted Jack, smiling a beautiful smile that hinted of distant pleasures. She had quickly joined Jack, upon seeing who the cause of the sudden hush was.

"Certainly not. Heather, isn't it?" Gilmore smiled back.

"Yes, it's Heather," she said, taking Gilmore's hand. "Won't you join us?" She turned to Jack, "please get the General a glass of juice." And then, without another word, she led him back to their table.

Jack stood watching the two for a moment, jealousy and hatred blooming in his mind, and then, trying to shake off the mood, moved for the bar. As the glasses were filled, he continued to eye the newcomer and "his" Heather with disdain. He could kill Gilmore right now, he thought.

Upon Jack's return with the juice, the three passed the better part of an hour talking about New Land, the Oasis, and the nuclear reactor.

Heather kept asking questions of the General, acting as if every word he said was the most important thing she had heard in weeks. Jack added little; the conversation was between Gilmore and Heather.

As Gilmore began to say his good-byes, he felt a pressure on his thigh. It was obviously a small foot pressing lightly through his tunic. "Well, it is time, ah . . ." he glanced directly at Heather, who was smiling warmly, "that I should be going. Thank you for the conversation and the hospitality." The foot left his leg with a gentle kick.

"Please come more often, we love seeing you," Heather cooed.

Jack, with iron in his voice said, "Yes, certainly come again."

With a quick look over his big shoulders, Gilmore strode rapidly out of the recreational room. He was smiling broadly, new thoughts banging around in his head.

*****

Billy spent most of the next day looking for an additional ATV, to no avail. The new morning was a sunny one, or at least as sunny as it now got. Jason remained on his makeshift bed atop the buffet-serving island, and Mary Lynne and Lorrie were beginning to gather what few belongings they thought they might want to take with them when they left. It had been a busy day. Now they were gathered for their evening meal. Billy was cooking his specialty; rice and tuna. The girls were unimpressed.

"This is a specialty?" Lorrie asked, with a slight smile upturned on the corner of her lips. "I would hate to see what he figures a just plain old meal might be," this directed to Mary Lynne.

"Oh, it isn't really that bad, particularly if you dump enough ketchup on it," Mary Lynne quipped.

"Come on guys, it isn't that bad," Billy said, looking like a kicked dog.

"Don't worry, Billy, I love it. It is one of my all-time favorites," Jason joined in on the teasing, letting grains of tuna covered rice fall from his mouth as he talked.

"You're gross," Lorrie quipped, and laughed.

It was good for them all to laugh and kid each other. Until now, the situation had been so serious there was little room for emotions that led to laughter. This unexpected light mood dug deep into their souls, lifting many of the burdens each carried.

The four continued their joking throughout the meal. After the dishes were cleaned, and the cooking gear stored, Billy asked, "Jason, have you thought any more about where we go from here?"

"Yes. I think, weather permitting, we should plan to leave here the day after tomorrow. I should be well enough by then to ride. I've been studying the map, and it appears that Madison should be our next stop for a major re-supply, although we might be able to find a library," he glanced at Mary Lynne, "in Eau Claire. I think we should be able to make Madison, certainly, within a week's time. Though it will depend on the road conditions. Does that sound all right to you?"

"Yes, but there is one thing that is concerning me," Mary Lynne intoned.

"What's that?" Jason asked.

Flies," she answered.

Jason looked at her and the other two with disbelief written all over his face. "Flies, what in the world are you talking about?"

"Haven't any of you noticed the increase in flies around here? It isn't so bad inside, but outdoors, there seem to be flies everywhere," Mary Lynne questioned emphatically.

"Come to think about it, there are a lot more flies than I remember, even at the worse time the bodies were decaying," Billy reflected. His hand was stroking his chin where a soft stubble of a beard had recently sprouted.

Jason thought for a minute, "Of course, the maggots."

"Maggots?" It was Mary Lynne's turn to be confused.

"Yes, maggots. All the dead bodies were becoming infested with maggots, and now they are finishing their life cycles as flies. If I'm right, flies are going to become a major problem, especially around urbanized areas."

"I don't relish the thought of battling hordes of flies," Lorrie interjected.

"Nor I," Jason agreed. "But what can we do about it? Let me think."

The four sat studiously for a few moments, each weighing possible solutions. Jason, his mind awhirl, suddenly sat upright, groaning under the pain the movement brought to his leg.

"Mosquito netting, lots of mosquito netting. If we could find netting at a hardware, or even a Army/Navy surplus store we could fashion protection for ourselves."

"Of course," Mary Lynne acknowledged. Better yet, we could possibly find beekeeper hoods. My Aunt Louise used to keep bees, and she had these helmet-like arrangements you could wear over your head to keep the bees out. But where could we find such things?"

"I don't know, but it is a darn good idea," Jason replied. "Shoot, there might be that kind of net in local hardware stores. I'm sure there are plenty of people around here that kept honeybees. Regardless, we sure want to be on the lookout for them."

"This is making me sick," Lorrie said flatly. "You mean, we are going to have to put up with flies, along with everything else?"

CHAPTER 11

Troubles for All

Jason swung his legs over the edge of the stainless-steel buffet island. Pain shot from his calf to his brain like a bullet leaving a 357-magnum pistol, but he kept moving. The island was a good nine inches higher than a normal table and his legs dangled over the edge, causing blood to rush to the healing wound. It throbbed, but the stitches held, as did the mending tissue.

"Damnation, this hurts. Do you suppose someone might give me a hand?"

Billy rushed to his side. "I thought you wanted to do it by yourself," he said, as he gently helped Jason to the floor. " That's what you said."

"I know, but I didn't realize how far it was to the floor," Jason said, through clenched teeth. He put more weight on his right foot, "Geez, what did that dog do to me, anyway?"

"He took a bloody big hunk out of your leg is what," Mary Lynne grinned at him with compassion. "Careful. I don't want you to rip those stitches."

Jason moved slowly, taking a tentative step on his injured leg. He felt every movement like it was knife cutting tendon and bone, but he made himself keep walking forward. After two or three steps, the pain subsided somewhat.

"I guess I'll live," he stated without emotion. "But I'm not sure I want to." He turned to Billy, "I think you're right, one more day won't make much difference. Anyway, I need to stretch my leg before I try to ride. Will that be okay with the rest of you?"

"Of course it will," Mary Lynne answered. "You would just slow us down the way you are now. Besides, it will give Lorrie and me more time to sew the netting Billy found yesterday."

Favoring his aching leg, Jason continued to move about the room, using tables and the tops of booths as support. "Billy, what else did you find at the farmhouse, anything useful?"

"No, but I did find some canned peaches. Lorrie said she liked peaches," he said, smiling at the petite blond.

Lorrie returned his smile, and said, "Thank you, Billy, it was very thoughtful."

Jason groaned, "Is this love in the making?"

Billy blushed, though you could barely tell through his dark skin. Not so with Lorrie, who had turned beet red at Jason's suggestion.

Mary Lynne just smiled, and told Jason to hush as she stepped over to the booth in which she'd been working. She sat down and began cutting a square from a large piece of olive drab netting. "Lorrie, come on over here and help me with this."

The younger girl stepped to her sister's side, as Jason continued to move about the room . . . stretching his sore leg. Billy quietly slunk through the front door, on his way to service the four-wheelers. The restaurant had taken on a homey atmosphere in the last couple of days. The four worked well together, eating and sleeping in the safety of their small domain. Tables and chairs had been arranged for comfort and a living room effect. Billy had moved booths together in a manner so they could be used as beds, divided by the tan partitions that had been used to separate the main dining room from the buffet line.

Jason moved to a chair near the two girls. He sat silently, studying their handiwork. Mary Lynne, he mused, was not only pretty, but a tower of strength as well. Her hair fell around her face and into her eyes, and she brushed it away unconsciously. Though tall, she was well proportioned, and moved with perpetual grace. Lorrie, on the other hand, was small, almost diminutive. Her blond hair, not as long as her sisters, was nonetheless alive in the sunlight that struggled through the windows. Intuitively, Jason knew she did not have the mettle of her sibling; still, there was a quality, an aura about her, which told there was more to her personality than might meet the eye. He felt comfortable around these two young women, and was more than pleased to have both as traveling companions.

"Mary Lynne, how old are you?"

Stopping her needle in mid-stitch, she turned to Jason, smiled and said, "Sixteen. Why do you ask?"

"Oh, no reason. I'm fifteen, and so is Billy. Well, he almost is anyway. Lorrie, how old are you?"

"Fourteen," she responded, puzzled.

"I can't figure it out. In Anoka, everyone died, the young and old alike. Yet, Billy and I didn't even get sick. Now, we find you two, and the same thing happened here. I wonder what is in us that makes us different from the others. Do you think it might have something to do with our ages?"

"Who bloody cares?" Mary Lynne responded. "It was horrible to watch, but I'm just as glad to still be alive, particularly since you two arrived." She looked straight into Jason's eyes with earnest intent. "Really pleased."

Jason was at a loss for words. He just met her gaze and felt his insides turn to mush.

The next day brought a cold rain, which persisted until late morning. Jason took the additional time to stretch his leg, while the others packed and repacked the gear they planned to take with them. Billy drove the ATVs into the remains of a grease pit, and loaded and unloaded the trailers a half dozen times under the stringent supervision of the sisters. Over a week had passed since Jason had waded into the fury of the dogs, and it was time to head south.

"Let's do it," Jason proclaimed. "The rain has stopped, so let's hit the road and see how far we can get today."

Billy drove the wheelers around to the front door, making last minute adjustments to each trailer. Jason limped to the door, looked for the last time at the big conductor's clock on the wall, and turned, searching for anything he had left behind. Leaning heavily on his staff, he made his way to his ATV.

*****

Jack glared at Heather, as they lay on their small bed. They finished their drinks shortly after Gilmore left; now, back in their cube, he was seething. "For God's sake, why do you have to flirt with every man who so much as looks at you? It's like you enjoy upsetting me."

"Don't be ridiculous," Heather said vehemently. "You can't keep me locked away in this hateful hole of a room twenty-four hours a day, and besides, I like men. I always have. If you can't stand me being sociable, then there is the door, mister. Nobody is holding you here." She was mad, and it showed in her voice and her face.

Jack, taken aback by her outburst, shrunk back across their bed. "I'm sorry, honey, it's just I love you so much, it's hard for me to see you around other men. I promise to do better. Honest!"

Heather immediately softened. Getting the apology from Jack was enough to assure her control over the situation. "Go to sleep and forget it, do you understand?"

"Yes," Jack said with contrite acquiescence, and rolled closer to her lovely body. She did not pull away, and he thought that was a good sign. "I'll really try."

Heather smiled to herself, as she rolled her back to the man in her bed. Soon, she thought to herself, I'll have General Gilmore eating out of my hand. I could see the look on his face as he left. He's mine; he just doesn't know it yet.

At the exact moment Gilmore's alarm went off at eight a.m., there was a knock on his private door. "Come in," he yelled, I'll be out in a minute, I haven't gotten dressed yet."

The Doctors' Duke opened the door, and entered General Gilmore's outer chamber. It was nothing more than an anteroom to his quarters. Gilmore's living spaces were spacious by New Land standards. Margaret looked through the arched doorway into the living room. It was as sparsely decorated as the rest of Gilmore's quarters. There were no pictures or knickknacks to brighten the cubical. The room reflected the man . . . no frills, no messing about, rather straight to the point. Wearing a red robe, Gilmore entered the room, his hair rumpled, and his face still heavy with sleep.

"Well? This had better be good."

Margaret grinned, thinking to herself that Gilmore might be human after all. "I just wanted you to know I talked with Abby last night."

"Abby? Abby who?"

"You know, the woman who is going to have a baby."

"Oh, of course. I'm still waking up," Gilmore said, as he wiped sleep from his eyes. "So, anything new there?"

"Not really, but I think I may be able to help her. It will be an arduous task, but we at least established a rapport between us. I'm sorry about waking you."

"That's okay, I should have been up several hours ago. I usually am, but I had a late night. What have you got, Doctor? Anything devastating?"

"Well, Margaret told me she was coming to visit, and I did want to let you in on some of the latest gossip. You know I'm still working on the Oasis. Just the finishing touches, nothing you can really see."

"Yes, go on."

"Well, as I've warned you before, this Jack Mossmen, head of Charlie tunnel, is still in the lime light."

Gilmore sighed. "Always Charlie. What's with him anyway?"

"I'm not sure." Duke moved further into the room, rubbing his chin thoughtfully. "It's just the people I work with seem to think he's trying to figure a way of getting outside."

"Outside what?" Gilmore asked. Then realizing the full extent of the comment, he said, "You've got to be kidding. He isn't that stupid, is he?"

"I don't know. You've had more contact with him than I, but I'm just telling you what rumor control is saying. I don't know if there is any truth to it or not. Still, I wanted you to be aware."

"Thanks to you both for the information. Now, if you don't mind, I'll be getting dressed." With that, Gilmore turned on his bare heel and headed for his bath.

After dismissing the two doctors, Gilmore ran his bath, which was another luxury granted the leader of New Land. No other living space had a bathtub, only small showers. He eased himself down into the hot water. The sudden temperature change burned at his skin, but it felt especially gratifying to the big man this morning.

He'd returned to his spaces, after leaving Jack and Heather, with thoughts rushing through his mind, none of which related to the ruling of New Land. The woman was beautiful, more exquisite than any woman he had ever known. She obviously been flirting with him from the moment he entered the recreation room, and the clincher was the foot on the leg bit. But why, he wondered. She had a tunnel head to bunk with, why him? Of course, the answer was obvious. He would have liked to believe it was just for himself and not his position, but he knew that was not the case.

Gilmore scrubbed his face with vigor and thought, what will I do if she really comes on to me? It could cause even more problems between Jack and I. But, he's a big boy, and why shouldn't I have the pleasure of a woman along with every other stud running wild on the women of New Land? He laughed to himself. How long has it been anyway . . . since I have slept with a woman? Too long, that's for sure.

With great care, Jack Mossmen was winding his way through the only cave leading away from the rim. This tunnel, he knew, led to an elevator room, which in turn could hoist him to the first floor of New Land. He had traveled down that elevator on his arrival. Now he was looking to see if there was a passageway cut through rock where a man could travel on foot. He scouted the area for TV monitors or other devices that might detect his presence, but could not find any obvious contraptions.

Jack had left the warmth of his bed and Heather's body to explore this shaft before the vast majority of New Land's inhabitants were up and about. He wanted to be alone. He was not anxious to answer questions of anyone as to why he might be roaming around the entrance tunnel.

At a monitor located in a corner of the Hub, a technician noticed a flickering light. It was red, and it indicated movement in the tunnel leading to the elevator shaft. Damn, another dust ball or something has set off the intruder alarm, he thought to himself.

The triggering of the motion monitor had not been an unusual occurrence in the past month. The system's sensitivity had been set too high, and the least amount of activity set the warning light blinking.

I've got to have someone repair that darn thing one of these days. But who is going to intrude anyway? What a stupid waste of money and time. He laughed silently, I guess money wasn't a real concern . . . not much need for it now.

*****

The road was clear during most of the afternoon. The two ATVs were making good time, eating up ten to fifteen miles each hour. Jason's leg hurt like a fire was burning inside his skin, but he was not making an issue of it to the others. The countryside had taken on a completely different appearance from what they had become used to in Anoka and even around the diner. The earthquake had not had much, if any, affect on their new surroundings, but something had swept the area. No trees remained; at least none of any size. Buildings were razed, and even where farms stood deep in a valley, it was rare to see a barn, home, or silo that was not damaged.

Though the map Billy carried showed many small, rural towns between Hudson and Eau Clare, most could not be seen from the interstate highway. What few villages they passed were little more than stubbled foundations gathering dust. Surprisingly, there was scant debris. Each wondered aloud during the day's ride as to where all the wreckage might be. When the road passed between a hill or rise, dunes of decaying grass, trees, brick, and board rose in drift like fashion. This, too, was a mystery. As the day wore on, and they drove deeper into the hill country of Wisconsin, more mounds of rotting material and bodies caused them to detour overland. The countryside looked like a dirty pot, scoured clean, yet with streaks of grease still running down its aluminum sides. And like a pot full of greasy stew, left for days in a sink, each dune they passed erupted into a cloud of blackness as flies filled the air. The four travelers were grateful for their head nets, even though beyond these hills of trash, the winged pests were not as prevalent.

Jason pulled alongside Billy moments after detouring around one of the dunes. "Stop for a minute, Billy." Jason was conscious of the gentle, tightening of Mary Lynne's arms around his waist. It was a pleasant sensation; one he had enjoyed the entire day.

"Let's find a place to spend the night," Jason hollered over the engine's dissonance. "My leg is really starting to bother me, and, besides it's getting late."

"You bet," was Billy's cheerful reply. He turned to Lorrie, "Hang on."

Billy led off looking for a place to hole up for the evening. It was another half-hour before he spotted what was left of a gravel driveway leading to a large farmhouse hidden deep between the undulating hills. The house was obviously old, but had been well maintained; though now the paint was peeling from every side but the front, which faced north. A huge barn, looking to be an acre in size, sat behind and to the right of the house. Dozens of outbuildings were scattered further behind the barn, but now only remnants of their presence remained.

Nine silos, each over seventy-five feet high, stood like missiles pointed toward heaven. The paint was gone, exposing the polished metal below, which reflected the weak evening sun in shades of pink.

The two ATVs pulled to a stop in front of the farmhouse. The four looked up in awe at the multi-gabled house. Its upper stories, studded with square outcroppings and framed windows, overlooked a clean landscape. The quiet admiration of the teens was broken by the unmistakable sound of a cow mooing. They all turned to look at each other and then at the barn.

They had not seen any life during their ride from the diner, and the cow was a surprise. Getting off their four-wheelers, they bunched together and start walking slowly for the barn.

"Wait a minute," Billy said, and ran back to his ATV. "I want to get my shotgun." He returned on the run.

Mary Lynne looked at the weapon with disdain. "It's just a cow, for cripe's sake. What are you planning to do, shoot the poor thing?"

"No, but I've learned to expect the unexpected, and I want to be ready for whatever might happen," Billy said, his guard up.

"He's right, Mary Lynne, we can't be too careful," Jason whispered, shifting his weight on the staff. "Come on, let's find out what's ahead."

The four slowly made their way for the barn's huge doors, which they found slightly ajar. Billy reached forward, grabbed the big door to his right, and pulled. The door swung easily and silently on its mammoth hinges, opening enough for Billy to poke his head through the gap. He jumped back in amazement, knocking Jason off balance."

"Who's out there?" someone yelled from inside.

"We've got more people," Billy said.

They swung the door full open, and moved out of the light and into the barn. The two groups viewed each other as if they had just stepped out of the twilight zone. No one said anything for a moment, and then voices all erupted at once.

"Where did you come from? Who are you? Is that your cow? Where are we?" It was like a dam bursting, and everyone wanted to speak his piece at once.

"Hey, one at a time," Jason yelled above the din.

The barn just as suddenly fell silent. Jason stepped forward and said, "I'm Jason," holding out his hand.

A pimply-faced boy of around fifteen stepped away from his companions. He took Jason's hand and said, "I'm Tom, and this is my sister, Carol," pointing to a grime-covered girl of thirteen. Gesturing to the other boy, he said, "Jim is his name. We found him here on the farm. He doesn't talk, at least not to us."

Jason introduced his companions and then pointed to the cow, which was watching the exchange with doleful eyes. "That's the first cow we've seen. In fact, it's the first animal of any kind we've seen, except for the dog packs."

"We were just trying to decide what to do with the cow. Jim has been taking care of it, but we thought we might kill it for the meat."

Jason looked around the great expanse of the barn. It smelled of warmth and sweet hay. He looked into the rafters far overhead. There were a few birds twittering among the lofts, scolding those below. Turning his gaze back to ground level he noticed a wealth of farming equipment . . . tractors, mowers, bailers. He took a minute to view the interior of the barn before framing his answer. "Fresh meat would taste wonderful, but what does Jim want to do? It's his cow, after all."

Jim stepped forward, looked Jason in the eye, and motioned with his hands to the cow's stomach.

"She's pregnant," Mary Lynne exclaimed.

Jim nodded emphatically, smiling at Mary Lynne.

"Well, that answers that question," Jason said. "I won't kill anything that might be bringing new life into this world, but you do what you want."

Jason walked from the barn. The others followed, leaving the cow to her own devices.

Later that evening, their camp set up inside the house, Tom related his and his sister's story. He and Carol lived in the small town of Wilson, about ten miles from the farm. They had not had an earthquake, but a south wind had blown with such strength that the land had been swept clean. They had heard the wind building and, thinking it was a tornado, hidden in the family's root cellar. When the winds died, and they'd left the safety of their underground refuge, they found nothing left of their home or family.

"Everything was gone . . . the house, barn, animals, trees, everything. It was as if a giant had taken an eraser and wiped the land clean," Tom recited in a monotone.

He and his sister made it into town, where others had gathered, those who lived through the gale. Life was hard for the survivors, with little food or water, but they had been able to get a few nearby wells back on line with hand pumps, and local root cellars and basements had provided enough canned goods for the group to eat. No one knew what had happened, but they figured the Red Cross or someone would come to help eventually. No one had come!

Then the sickness had hit, killing everyone with the exception of Tom and his sister.

"Were there any other teenagers in your group?" Jason asked.

Yes, a few. I'm not sure how many though," Tom answered.

"Go on," Jason said. "I'm sorry I interrupted."

Tom continued, telling of their decision to leave Wilson and ending up on this farm the day before Jason arrived. They had found Jim sitting on the front porch staring out into nothingness. It had taken several minutes for them to get the mute to acknowledge their presence, but he had finally come around.

After Tom finished his narrative, he asked Jason for their story, which he then related in detail.

"So that's what happened. A damned asteroid. It must have been a whopper, and you say the sickness was spreading all over the country, killing everybody. Why not us?"

"I have no idea, but it's got to be something to do with our ages. Look around; we're all between thirteen and sixteen. Why us? I sure as heck don't know. I'm even unsure about the age thing, now that you say other teenagers died in your party. Still, I guess we shouldn't worry about it too much."

The others were listening to the conversation as well, soaking up the tale. Billy shook his head, and asked, "Jason, what are we going to do now? We don't have room for three more people on the four-wheelers."

"Tom, we're heading south, as I said. You're welcome to join us,"

Leaning back in a big overstuffed chair, Tom looked to his sister. She nodded an affirmative. "Yeah, I think we would like to go with you."

Jason looked around the boxy living room where they now sat; its pictures of relatives, pets, and family outings gazed down on him from cabinets and shelves. He shifted his sore leg on the ottoman where it rested. "What about you, Jim?"

Jim, looking pale and withdrawn, glanced nervously at Jason. He stood, and began walking around the room, touching lamps, chairs, even pictures hanging on the wall. Finally, he strode purposefully to face Jason. He shook his head vigorously, and opened his arms to the house, then patted the wall.

"I understand," Jason said. "You want to stay at home, but if you do, you might not make it through the winter by yourself."

The boy shrugged with resignation.

"Okay then, we'll head out tomorrow with Tom and Carol in the trailers, but we've got to find other transportation soon."

"There's a big truck and land excavating equipment park about four miles down the road," Tom ventured. "We might be able to get something there."

"That's the best news we've had all day," Billy said.

*****

"What do you think?" Phil asked Abby. "Jack was very serious about it. He thinks I might be able to get topsides."

Abby and Phil were sitting on the small couch that graced the rock wall of their cubicle. Like most of the living quarters in New Land, theirs was sparsely decorated with little more than pictures of parents and friends left behind . . . dead. Abby's skill with needle and thread had done wonders with the bedspread, a multi-colored, patchwork comforter. The colors brightened the entire room.

"It sounds almost too good to be true, is what I think," Abby replied. "Besides, what if we should make it and Gilmore is right? What if the world is freezing over or something even more drastic? You know they would never let us back in. Or would they?"

"Why not? If the place is a mess, we would only confirm what they have been telling us. We certainly wouldn't be any worse off than we are now. Besides, I could go alone first, then come get you if it was okay."

"It certainly sounds like it might work, that is if Jack can find a way out. If he does, I'll give you my decision then. Is that okay with you?"

"Of course. Heck, he might not even find a way up. We'll just wait and see."

Gilmore's day passed without major incident. He believed it was one of the first calm days since The Few moved below. He felt good after his morning bath and a breakfast of toast and coffee. Paperwork was light, and the Hub quiet. As the morning wore on, he felt the need to just wander, perhaps even head for the Oasis. He had not been back since its grand opening a week earlier. It had been an enormous success from the beginning. Again, he thought how lucky he was to have a man like Doctor Duke helping keep New Land on an even keel.

He pushed a tiny button recessed into his desktop.

"Yes sir," a voice echoed through the office.

"I'm going for a walk. If you need me, just beep," he told the duty engineer in charge of the Hub's control room.

"Yes sir. Have a good time. We'll keep things under control here, don't worry."

Gilmore nodded, switched off the computer before him, and stepped lightly from the room. He bounded down the steps and into the outer passageway like a whirlwind. He made a full lap around the Hub's outer tunnel, acknowledging those he passed en route. It took him over forty-five minutes to walk the substantial ring, but the exercise felt great. Approaching the entrance to Charlie tunnel, he made a rapid decision. He turned into Charlie's passageway and strode for the rim, waving hellos to those using the recreational areas.

Heather saw the big man as he made his way by recreation room two. She had been playing cards with two other women and losing. She did not return Gilmore's wave with the others. Rather she toyed with the cards, feigning intense interest in the next play. She allowed a reasonable time to pass before she excused herself from her colleagues, saying she had a headache, and hurried down the tunnel in the direction she'd seen the big man take.

Gilmore walked straight to the edge of the Oasis, again in utter awe at what the workers had accomplished. There were several couples mingling among the trees and others lying on the blanched beach. As they began to feel his presence, there was shuffling as people quietly gathered their belongings and disappeared, most leaving toward Delta tunnel rather than have to pass their leader.

Gilmore sighed, "Damn, leadership is a lonely comrade!"

"I beg your pardon?" Heather cooed softly.

Gilmore started. "You scared the hell out of me," he smiled, as she slipped up from behind. "It is very nice seeing you again so soon."

Heather presented him with a flawless smile, placed a hand on her hip and let the hip swing to one side slightly, "Yes, what a pleasant surprise." She stepped forward, closing the distance to bare minimum, and took both of his big hands in hers. "Care to enjoy the Oasis with me?" she asked.

"That would be wonderful," Gilmore responded, noticing an unwanted response developing under his red tunic. "Have you been here before?"

"Jack brought me for a few minutes the day it opened, but that was the only time, and it wasn't for very long. Jack thinks this project was designed to cause problems for Charlie and Delta tunnels."

"That's ridiculous. That man wears on my nerves sometimes."

"I know what you mean," Heather sighed. "But he's been pretty good to me. Let's walk."

The two strolled hand in hand into the Oasis. The sun was where it would have been topside around eleven o'clock in the morning, creating shadows on the inner wall of the rim. They paused by the pool, each viewing the manmade splendor of the cascading waterfall.

"It's truly beautiful," Heather squeezed Gilmore's hand. "Isn't it?"

"It is every bit of that and more," Gilmore confided. He turned to her, looking down on the lovely upturned face, "Almost as beautiful as you are."

Heather held his gaze, never wavering. Then, closing her aqua eyes, she reached up on tiptoes, her lips awaiting his kiss. It came lightly at first, then with power and strength. Her mouth parted, allowing his tongue to search for hers. She found herself drowning in his massive arms, sinking in a pool far deeper than the one before them. She had never been so deeply and emotionally kissed in her life. Here was a man who could tame her, bring her to her knees with the very strength she admired. She drew in a noiseless breath of yearning as he pulled away from her.

"We can't be doing this," Gilmore said huskily. "You're spoken for, and I have made it a point never to interfere with another man's wife or girlfriend. All it does is cause problems."

"Damn! No one is getting married here, and I can and will be with whomever I please," Heather chastised him. "You want me, don't you?"

"Right now? Yes, more than anything, but I don't want to cause any problems which aren't absolutely necessary."

Heather reached up, grabbing Gilmore behind the head with both hands. His head bent to meet her lips once again, this time with even more urgency than before. Their knees folded, and they slowly fell to the soft sand, holding tightly to one another. They did not make love, rather they kissed, they talked, and they drew from each other what they both lacked.

Jack Mossmen sat in his cubicle drawing a diagram of the area he had explored earlier that morning. His sketching was stiff, but detailed. He had found the spur tunnel, a small opening leading at right angles to the elevator's entrance cave. He had spent over an hour investigating the offshoot, finding it was a series of inclines leading to multiple steps. He'd climbed several of the blocks of steps, and walked the inclines, finally deciding it would be the same all the way to the top. It would take many hours to negotiate the climb, for it was over five miles straight up, and there was no telling how many miles it might be via the back switching steps and inclines. Nonetheless, it could be done by a person with proper motivation. These thoughts, and others, passed through his mind as he continued to sketch.
*****

Morning broke with a dusky sun struggling to provide light and warmth to a battered planet. Jason awoke early, before the sun struggled above the windswept horizon, and positioned himself to view the sunrise. Now he understood what had happened here. There had been no earthquake, but winds with enough strength to blow buildings away must have been just as devastating. Certainly, it explained the dunes of debris caught between the sharp roadbed trenches that had been cut through the hills years previous. Looking to the north, he viewed a barren landscape, devoid of life, but he knew life was there, ready to spring forth once more.

As the sun labored to warm his face, an idea came to him unexpectedly. "Billy, are you up yet?" He banged his staff on the porch floor and yelled again, "Hey Billy, come on, get up."

Billy staggered to the screen door. The screen had left with the wind, but he pushed on what was left of the frame to walk outside. "Geez, I thought something was wrong," he said, seeing Jason sitting peacefully on the porch steps. "What do you want?"

"Billy, if a truck in the park Tom was talking about has something with a plow attached to the front, we might be able to make better time."

"What do you mean?" Billy looked and sounded puzzled.

"Think about it. If we could push the junk creating roadblocks off the highway, we wouldn't need the ATVs. We could use some other vehicle, like a truck or RV. That way we would have our transportation plus a place to stay every night all wrapped up in one. What we could do is send the bladed vehicle out an hour or two before the rest of us left. That way the road would be clear. What do you think?"

"I think it's a great idea, if they have a truck big enough to push the crap off the road. I guess we'll have to wait and see."

"Billy, maybe this place won't have one, but you can bet we'll find one somewhere. After all, the road department would have snowplowing stations along I-94. All we have to do is look for huge piles of sand or what's left of them."

"You're right," Billy exclaimed excitedly. "I saw one of those places yesterday. The wind had blown most of it down to the size of a kid's sandbox, but you could still make it out. I'll keep my eyes open today."

The door slammed shut. "What's the matter?" Mary Lynne asked.

"Nothing. Jason just had another brainstorm is all," Billy smiled.

Mary Lynne moved rapidly to Jason's side, and kneeled. "How's your leg this morning?"

"Better, and it seems to be healing cleanly. I'm going to have one heck of a scar though."

"Not as big as if I hadn't sewn you up," Mary Lynne said as she produced a clean gauze bandage and hiked Jason's jeans over his knee. She rebound the wound, nodding her head with satisfaction. "You're a fast healer, Jason."

Jason smiled at her from his vantage point on the steps. "Mary Lynne, how do you do it? You look as fresh as a daisy, even after you just got up. I guess you know how pretty you are?"

Mary Lynne swept the hair from her face and smiled back at him. "You're a bloody idiot. Now come on, let's get some breakfast."

After eating, they loaded their gear in silence with Jim watching every move intently. The big farmhouse, which had looked so inviting the afternoon before, now had a strangely saddened guise about it.

The ATVs were running, their motors a discordant in the silence. Jason, leaning on his staff, walked to face Jim. The boy had tears rolling down his cheeks.

"Are you sure you don't want to come with us? We'll make room, and don't worry, we'll find more four-wheelers."

The sad looking lad shook his head no, chin hanging low on his chest. "Good luck," he muttered softly.

Jason, surprised by the words, stepped forward and took the smaller boy in his arms. "And to you, my friend."

He released the crying boy, turned, and made for his vehicle. As he climbed aboard, Jason felt Mary Lynne's arms encircle his waist. Shifting to first gear, he spun out of the driveway. He did not look back. He knew Jim would be standing there, his world gone.

"He'll be okay, at least for a while. He just wants to live in a familiar place. Don't blame yourself," Mary Lynne softly said. "You're a very special person, Jason Collyar."

CHAPTER 12

STRUGGLING

Phil had just finished his shift with the electrical engineering department. He enjoyed his work, and was known to be very good at what he did. He was stripping off his blue tunic when there was a light rap at the plastic door.

"Come in."

"I don't want to disturb you, but can I talk to you for a minute or two?" It was Jack Mossmen, and he was carrying a small briefcase.

"Sure. Come on in. What's up?" Phil asked.

Jack stepped beyond the green door, closing it gently behind him. The small room looked much like his own . . . sparse. "I've got something to show you. Are we alone?" he asked, glancing toward the tiny bathroom door.

"Yes. Abby is at work and won't be back for several hours yet. Please . . . sit down."

"Thank you."

Jack sat on the couch and began opening the briefcase. He removed a sheaf of papers, leaned forward, and handed them to Phil. "I want you to have a look at these and tell me what you think."

Phil took the papers, glanced briefly at the top sheet, and whistled quietly through pursed lips. "Are these what I think they are?" he asked, moving slowly to the corner bed. "If they are, then you've been a busy man."

"They are," Jack stated flatly.

Phil spread the papers out on the multi-colored bedspread. He studied them closely for several minutes, tracing his finger along the sketches of the elevator tunnel, and the side spur that led to the surface.

"I didn't go all the way up, of course, but I drew in what I think it might look like. You can see there are a succession of inclines honed from the rock, with each ramp ending at the base of a series of steps. Each bank of steps has approximately thirty footfalls, leading to yet another inclined ramp. I moved up at least six such progressions and have no reason to believe it isn't the same all the way to the surface. What do you think?"

"I suppose you are right, but if you are, then it is one helluva long way to the top."

"Yeah, I realize that. I gauge it to be over five miles of steady climbing, but it most certainly could be done. Done by you."

Phil turned to stare at the man beside him, a thin wiry man with slightly balding, dark hair. It was the eyes that caught and held him mesmerized. They were the eyes of a ferret, shifty and dangerous. Yet here was a way for Abby and him to have their baby outside the damp tunnels of New Land.

Eyeing the papers on his bed, he said, "Yes, I could do it. Let me talk to Abby. Can I keep these to show her?" he asked, waving his hand over the drawings.

"Certainly, but for God's sake, don't let anyone else see them. Make sure they are well hidden whenever you leave here. Do you understand?"

"Absolutely. We'll keep the secret. You can count on it," Phil said, with strength.

"Good. I'll talk to you later, after you've had a chance to discuss it with your lady. This is it, boy! We can do it." With that Jack stood, gave the younger man a stern glare of authority, and left the room.

Abby took off work early, not because she wanted to, rather because she had been asked to visit Doctor Margaret Duke. She was walking around the Hub, having left her office at the entrance to Charlie tunnel. She was an administrative assistant keeping files on the constant shifting of The Few's living arrangements. It was a boring, unrewarding job, but it was what she had signed up for when she'd agreed to live in New Land, something she was now very much regretting. Passing an entrance to the Hub, she stopped and glanced inside. It was a spectacular array of lights and cathode-ray monitors. It never ceased to amaze her, what the engineers and scientists had done to create their home under a mountain. She noticed General Gilmore. He stood out among the many white-cloaked technicians scurrying around the various control panels. Gilmore, tall, black, strong, and decked out in a perfectly fitting, sharply creased red tunic was in conversation with a bright faced, young engineer.

Abby shook her head and thought, "Why me? Why must I have the first child in New Land?"

She continued walking, her steps slow and paced.

Gilmore had seen the woman stop, not knowing who she was. Nor did he care who she might be for he was discussing the reactor problems with his Chief of Engineering.

"Okay, I understand that there has been no change in the overheating problem, but I still don't like having the situation hanging over our heads. It's like a time bomb set to explode and no one has a clue as to what time the clock was set."

"I know what you mean, but I am much less concerned about the problem now than I was. The very fact nothing further has developed since we first experienced the overheating is a good indication we will not have further problems," the smaller man said.

"I suppose you are right, and everyone seems to have adjusted to the new temperature and the additional humidity. Plus, the water runoff has provided us with a beautiful recreational area. Have you seen the Oasis yet?" Gilmore asked.

"I certainly have. It is somewhat of a miracle, don't you think?"

"I do indeed," Gilmore nodded. "By the way, how is the rest of our system holding up? I mean, have you had any problems I haven't been informed of for some reason?"

"No," the Chief Engineer said, shaking his head. "We have had some minor problems with our motion monitoring system. The sensitivity is set too high, but repairing it is of little concern at the moment. We'll fix it when we have the chance."

"Very well," Gilmore replied. "I'll be in my quarters."

With purpose, Gilmore stepped off for his rooms. His pace was hurried, even more so than was normal for him. He knew Heather would be waiting for him when he arrived. They had planned their rendezvous before separating at the Oasis the day before. It had been all he could think about since. Heather's beautiful face burned its way through all other thoughts.

Arriving outside his quarters, he took a deep breath and opened the door. Heather was standing in the living room, her blue tunic around her ankles. Gilmore stood in shock for a moment, then moved rapidly from his door to stand before her. She said nothing, but the look in her eyes was unmistakable. He swept her into his arms, bent his lips to hers, and carried her to his bed.

*****

Little had been said since leaving the farmhouse. Even Billy was not his normally jovial self. They had been traveling for better than three hours, but had not made more than five miles. The added weight in each of the trailers, along with the debris trapped between hills had slowed progress considerably. After pulling onto I-94, and turning east, the terrain had taken on characteristics of a roller coaster, as it undulated over the barren, denuded Dells of Wisconsin. Dust clogged the road, not enough so they could not tell where the roadbed lay, but enough to create clouds of ash behind them.

When they topped a rise, the view in all directions was much the same . . . rolling knolls stretching their crowns as far as the eye could see through the dust-laden air. Where trees once prevailed there was nothing but stumps surrounded by the broken hearts of the proud oak, pine, and maple. From a distance, the once mighty forests appeared like so many scattered boxes of toothpicks, strewn haphazardly over acres of farmland.

Leading the group, Billy rounded a gentle curve in the road and pulled to a sudden stop. He pointed ahead, as Jason's ATV pulled alongside.

"There, that's what we have been looking for," Billy cried over the engine noise.

Before them was an overpass, with its associated exit to a state road. Off to the right of the exit, there was a hundred thousand square feet of truck park. The tremendous winds had blown the mammoth road trailers on their sides and stacked them two and three high. At first glance, Jason had little hope of finding what they might need, but felt closer examination was necessary.

"Okay Billy, let's have a look," Jason yelled. Turning to Mary Lynne he said, "Keep your fingers crossed. It doesn't look too good, but we can hope."

Mary Lynne smiled at him, and gave a thumb's up sign with her right hand. "Hope breathes eternal," she said.

"Yeah, right, " Jason hollered, as he toed first gear and motored off after Billy.

The park was a hodge podge of twisted aluminum and steel. Trailers had been blown from the southern to the northern end of the huge asphalt parking lot. As one trailer stacked against another, they had formed an eighteen-wheeler ridge line. As more and more of the semis slid into the barrier, others toppled or rolled over until the last two rows had a potpourri of tractors and trailers from which to choose a vehicle in running condition.

"What a mess!" Lorrie exclaimed. "Do you think any of them will do us any good?" she asked Billy.

"I don't know. What do you think, Jason?"

"I don't see what we are looking for. You know, a truck with a plow. What good would a semi do us?" Jason was speaking to himself as much as answering Billy's question.

"Jason, over here!" It was Mary Lynne. She had wandered into the maze of broken vehicles with Tom and Carol.

"Is this what you're looking for?" she asked, as her face broke into a wide grin.

As Jason and Billy ran to her, they could immediately see what had captured her attention. Sitting wedged between two trailers, which resembled wads of tinfoil, was a dump truck . . . a dump truck with a massive snow wing attached to its front end.

"Yah-hoo," hooted Billy and Jason together.

"You'd better believe that's what we're looking for," Jason sang out, as he ran to Mary Lynne and wrapped her in his arms. "I could kiss you."

"Then why don't you?" Mary Lynne said softly.

Jason dropped her like a stone. His eyes were full of shock and disbelief. "What?

"Why don't you? Kiss me, that is," Mary Lynne said, smiling gently.

Jason stared at her a moment, then turned and ran off toward the others, leaving Mary Lynne smiling slyly behind him.

It took the rest of the day to release the dump truck from its prison. By using semi- tractors to push or tow as necessary, they were able to disengage the big snowplow. The hardest part had been figuring out how to start, shift, and drive the big tractors. The transmissions on the giant, long haulers had ten forward gears, which they ground like hamburger until they eventually got the hang of shifting. They learned of fifth wheels and driver's seats that shaped into dozens of different angles and contours. By the time their prize was purring smoothly on the tarmac, they were all covered with dirt, grease, dust, and dead tired.

"This dumper is a thing of beauty," Billy said to the group, as he climbed down from the dump truck's cab. "I haven't tried to figure out how the blade works yet, but it can't be all that hard, certainly not like those things," he pointed to the cab of a semi-tractor with Joe Bob still imprinted in bright blue letters on its driver's door.

"Well, you can figure it out after supper, I'm starving," Jason stated. "Let's get some grub on the table."

They were cleaning up the dishes and pots from their canned chicken and rice dinner, when Lorrie asked of Mary Lynne, "You really like him, don't you?"

"Who?" her sister questioned, without looking up from the dish pan she was drying and silently cursing the ever present dust that continued to settle on every thing.

"Jason, of course," Carol teased.

"What gave you two that idea? He's okay, but just another boy as far as I'm concerned."

"Right," Lorrie giggled.

Full dark enveloped the truck park before Jason and Billy, having discovered how to operate the hydraulic snowplow, returned to the camp they'd set up earlier. The black asphalt stole what little light the rising moon tried to produce. In the distance, dogs could be heard howling, chasing their evening meal; more than likely each other. The six teenagers huddled around a small, but bright fire. The red-orange flames provided warmth against the evening's coolness and protection from predator attacks.

"I'll take the first watch," Jason stated. "Then Billy, followed by Tom. Tom, do you know how to use a shotgun?"

"Sure. I hunted with my Dad every year since I was ten."

"Good. When it's your watch, just grab my gun. Okay?"

"You bet."

"Let's hit the rack. It's going to be a long day tomorrow." With those final words, Jason picked up his weapon and staff and moved off to sit braced against the dual rear tires of an eighteen-wheeler. The tiny camp was quiet almost immediately, with only the sounds of heavy breathing emanating from the sleeping forms rolled in sleeping bags.

Jason rubbed his sore leg. The stitches had held well. Mary Lynne has done a fine job of tending to me, he thought to himself. "Did she really want me to kiss her this afternoon? And what did I do but run away like some stupid dork," he said aloud.

"You're not a dork."

Jason almost jumped out of his skin. He had not heard Mary Lynne slide from out of the darkness. "Geez, you scared the crap out of me."

"Sorry, I just couldn't sleep and thought I would join you for a while. Is that all right with you?"

"Sure," Jason said shyly.

"You're not a dork. In fact, I think you're about the most special person I have ever met. You came out of nowhere swinging that staff of yours saving Lorrie's and my life one day, and the next you're hugging a poor, lonely boy goodbye. Jason, you are very special."

"Not really."

"Yes, really! Don't you see? You have become our leader without so much as any real choice being made on our part? You are a natural and I feel we are all going to need your leadership for a long time."

"Why do you say that?" Jason asked. He was puzzled, having never given the subject any thought. He just did what he felt was right.

"Don't you see? Tom and Carol aren't going to be the only ones we're going to find as we move south. It's more bloody likely we'll have a caravan by the time we make a stand, wherever that might be."

"You're serious, aren't you?"

"Very!"

"Well, we'll see. But for now, let's take it a day at a time," Jason declared.

Mary Lynne settled in next to Jason, touching his shoulder with hers. "Yes, one day at a time. That's a good idea, but we'd better think about it anyway. Besides, if it does work out where there are dozens of us, I'll really need a decent first-aid book. Do you think we can detour into Eau Claire when we get there? The town is big enough to have a library."

Jason shifted his position so he could look into Mary Lynne's eyes, "Of course we'll find a library." He paused, started to say something else and stopped. "Er . . . this morning, I mean . . . you know, I mean . . . did you really want me to kiss you?"

Mary Lynne could feel his discomfort. His embarrassment was evident in his voice and on his face. She had known boys before. In fact, she had lost her virginity the year before. Now she was sorry for those previous encounters. She did not quite know why she felt remorseful about her sex life, only that she wanted to be perfect for the man-child before her.

"Yes, I very much meant it, Jason."

Jason sat very rigid, unsure of what he should do. He had survived an earthquake, killed a man, watched people die, buried his own sister, and been half eaten by a dog, but this had him completely confused. He thought Mary Lynne was the most beautiful girl he had ever seen. Her golden hair and full lips danced in his dreams, but never had he ever fantasized she might care for him. He leaned forward slightly, wrapped his arms around her shoulders, and drew her to him. Mary Lynne gave no resistance, but melted into his arms.

They kissed, a tentative kiss initiated by the one who knew little of such intimate matters. When they separated, their eyes met and held for a long moment. Jason would not fathom the mystery for some time, but for now the kiss held a promise of much more in his life.

"Hey, you two, what's up?"

Billy's timing could not have been worse if he had planned it for a year.

"Nothing," Jason said angrily.

"Geez, I'm sorry. You don't have to bite my head off," Billy griped.

"I'm sorry. You just surprised us. Is it your watch already?"

"Yeah. Why don't the two of you get some sleep?"

"That's probably a good idea," Jason said, as he helped Mary Lynne stand. See you in the morning."

*****

The two women sat much as they had on their first encounter, Margaret on the couch and Abby sitting rigid in a chair. Margaret had not tried to soften the room this time, thinking Abby would see through this attempt to put her at ease. She did not want the woman to feel she would try to deceive her in any way.

"How have things been going the last couple of days?" Margaret asked, quietly. "Have you given any thought to our last conversation?"

"What else would I be thinking about? You'd think nothing is as important as this baby is. I'm damned if I do, and damned if I don't."

"That's not true, and you know it," Margaret responded, with more venom in her voice than she intended. "I thought we'd agreed to work on the situation together."

"Sure. That's easy enough for you to say, but it's my body, and I don't have a say in what I want. I still don't believe having the baby is the right thing, at least not down here."

"Okay! I'll accept that as a given, but what if you were living as you used to? What if we'd never moved into New Land, and you were in your own apartment? What if you'd met Phil on a blind date, or something like that, and he fathered your child? What would you do then?"

"That's not a fair question," Abby snapped. "We aren't in those circumstances and we never will be again."

"Again, if?" Margaret pressed.

Abby, her eyes showing her anger and frustration, stood and whirled about the small office. She felt like a caged animal. "I don't know. I just don't know what I would do under those conditions. At least I would have a choice. Here, I have none."

"Have you ever thought of being a mother?" Abby softly questioned.

"No! Have you?" Abby stopped her pacing, pivoting to face her antagonist.

Margaret never flinched, keeping her eyes level with Abby's. "Yes, many times," she almost whispered. "But there has never seemed to be the time because of our careers . . . but yes."

Abby deflated like a balloon, sinking back into her chair.

"What if I were to have this child? Can you give me any assurance of what sort of life it would lead in the wet tunnels of New Land?"

"Of course I can't, but whatever way he or she might grow up it will be quite different from what it might have been before the strike. However, if you stop and think about it, the child will know nothing different. New Land, these caves and tunnels, *will be home.* Not knowing life as we have, will not make any difference to the child whatsoever.

"I guess I hadn't thought of it that way before," Abby said, with a somewhat surprised expression on her face. "Am I being selfish?"

"I can't answer that question for you; it's something you'll have to work out for yourself. Perhaps, more importantly, you must decide if you want to be a mother. If the answer to that question is yes, then all else is secondary. You can raise a child in New Land, or anywhere else for that matter."

"I think I understand. I'll give it thought along those lines. Thank you Doctor, I mean Margaret."

"Fine. What say we grab some lunch? I'm hungry. That is, if you would care to join me?"

Abby studied the woman before her with new interest. "I would enjoy having lunch with you, but let's not talk about babies. Okay?"

"Promise," Margaret said, crossing her heart.

By late afternoon, Gilmore had decided his concerns about seeing another man's girlfriend could go to hell. He wanted Heather, wanted her to be waiting for him every day, just as she'd been that morning. Never, not in his entire life, had he felt such deep, gut-wrenching turmoil over a woman. Heather sparked more than lust, and there was plenty of that to go around for both of them. Their lovemaking had not been frantic, as it might have been with any other first time encounter, rather it had been powerful, strong, and fulfilling. Fulfilling beyond anything he'd ever experienced. Heather infused him with a desire to be with one woman and one woman only. Accepting his needs were one thing, how to handle the situation which might develop with Jack Mossmen, was another.

"What do I really know about Jack?" Gilmore said aloud to his bathroom wall. He lay soaking in the tub, his second scrub in a day. "Other than the fact I have never liked nor trusted the man, I know damned little about him."

Gilmore catalogued what he did know about Mossmen. Their first encounter had been during the strike. The man had been terrified until he had slapped him into action. Then Jack turned up as headman for Charlie, where it seemed ninety percent of New Land's problems arose. Moreover, both Dukes had been warning him about Mossmen practically since the strike was over, and the Dukes were rarely, if ever, wrong. Add to these facts Jack's intense jealousy concerning Heather, and he was a virtual powder keg ready to explode.

Earlier, Heather had told Gilmore of the jealous streak Jack exhibited before she had left his side. "I know he is capable of violence, and I'm afraid our being together might push him over the edge," she had said.

Right now, Gilmore was not very concerned about physical violence. He was never one to be afraid of another man . . . never had been. It was the disruption of Charlie's leadership that most worried him. Would . . . could Mossmen create a riff in New Land's social structure to the extent it might usurp his command? This, he thought, was the critical issue.

As General Gilmore lay in his tub, thinking of ways to avoid having his leadership challenged, Heather was resting on her own bed in Charlie tunnel. She was debating whether to tell Jack about her decision to move in with Gilmore or just pack and leave a note. Of course she could let someone else tell him. She was quite sure they had been seen at the Oasis, and it was just a matter of time before someone told Jack. She was afraid of what the man might do to her, regardless of how he found out. If she just walked, at least then she would be under Gilmore's protective arm, but that might infuriate Jack even more. Ordinarily, none of this would have bothered her. She had set her sights on Gilmore from the moment she'd met him during the *We Made It* party. But then it had been for personal gain. Now she knew she was more concerned for Gilmore than herself, and this was a completely new sensation. She fell asleep, as the ramifications of the situation ran through her mind.

"Who is the best electrician we have for this sort of problem?" the Chief of Engineering asked his younger assistant.

The man, in a white tunic, standing before the large, cluttered desk of the Chief of Engineering thought for a moment and said, "Phil Fagan from Charlie."

"Fine. Get him working on the motion sensor system tomorrow," the Chief said, as he bent to the paperwork before him, dismissing his assistant in the process.

*****

Morning broke with a heavy, dust burdened dew on the ground. As Jason and the others unwrapped themselves from their sleeping bags,

153

Tom was stirring the fire into life and brewing coffee on the Coleman stove.

"Good morning, everyone," Tom said cheerfully. "Did we have a good sleep?"

"Right, sure. It is always so much fun trying to sleep on hard pavement," Carol groaned at her brother.

"We'll all feel better after a breakfast of canned hash and oatmeal," Mary Lynne piped in.

"Oatmeal. Yuck!" Jason wrinkled his nose, and stuck a finger down his throat. "I hate oatmeal. It always reminds me of something I've eaten already, not something *to* eat."

Mary Lynne stuck her tongue out at him, and the rest of the group laughed.

After breakfast, the boys started the dump truck and moved it to an overturned pickup.

"We ought to be able to siphon the gas out of here," Jason said, pointing at the smaller vehicle. How much fuel have we got left in the ATVs?" he asked, turning to face Billy.

"Enough for the morning, but that's about all. We need to find more gas. Too bad the dumper doesn't run on diesel; we sure have plenty of that around," he said, waving his arms indicating the vast numbers of semis.

Jason retrieved the siphon tube from his trailer, and stuck it down the refill spout of the pickup. Then, squeezing the bulb, he started transferring gas from one truck to the other. He was just finishing this task, when he heard the sound of small engines. He cocked his head, listening intently.

"We're going to have visitors," Jason yelled to the others. "Stop and listen."

All ears could now hear the approaching vehicles.

"ATVs," Billy said, pointing to a cloud of dust.

They could see four red machines rapidly approaching from the west on I-94. Billy moved rapidly to his own four-wheeler, grabbed his shotgun, and pumped a round into the chamber.

"Hey, the camp," a young voice screamed from above. "Are we glad we made it in time! We thought you might have left already."

"Hey yourself. Come on down and join us. Take the exit, then the first right turn," Jason yelled back.

Moments later, four red ATVs, one a three-wheeler, were parked beside Jason's and Billy's.

"I see we had the same idea," a tall, freckled-faced, red-haired boy of sixteen said good-naturedly, pointing to the accumulation of ATVs. "We camped on a rise about a mile back, and saw your fire when it got dark. We left early to try and catch up with you."

Jason had retrieved his staff about the time Billy had gone for his shotgun. He now shifted it into his left hand, stepped forward, and offered his right to the tall redhead.

"Welcome."

The newcomers' stories were much the same as their own, with small variations. Now, they were traveling in the hopes of finding others alive. They had not made any plans regarding their future or where to go.

"You're welcome to join us," Jason offered, after explaining his plan to head south.

"That would be great," the tall, redheaded, Bob said. "What's the dump truck for?" The boy pointed to the plow laden truck.

Jason shared his idea of scouting ahead and clearing the road for the ATVs. Then he turned to Billy. "You," nodding to his friend, "had better climb aboard that dump truck of yours and start pushing on down the road if we hope to make miles today."

"On my way, boss," Billy smiled. "Mind if I take Lorrie with me? Tom can drive my 'wheeler.'"

"Fine with me," Jason grinned.

The group broke up, each to tend their particular chores of making ready for the road. Mary Lynne sided up to Jason as he was packing his trailer.

"Told you so," she smiled knowingly.

"Told me what?" Jason questioned.

`'"That there would be others, and here they are. We're getting to be quite a clan." She took his hand in hers, "It's just the beginning, Jason. Just the beginning."

Jason had let an hour pass before he gave the group an okay to mount their ATVs to follow Billy, and since their return to the road, they made better time than he expected. Even with the six ATVs strung out behind him, Jason was pleased with their progress. Importantly, his leg was not bothering him as much as the day before.

By noon, they could see a dust cloud not far ahead. Jason appraised correctly; it was Billy shoving aside debris.

The only morning problem stemmed from the lack of head nets for their new companions. The young drivers were constantly complaining about the flies. Mary Lynne assured them she would rough together headdresses for them when they stopped for lunch.

The group caught up with the dump truck shortly before one o-clock. Billy had swung his rig off an interstate exit, and plowed his way into a RV sales lot thirteen miles west of Eau Claire. The town's name was Elk Mound, but there was little left to the once thriving community. RVs, like the semi's the day before, had ended up stacked against the interstate's man-made overpass. RVs of all sizes and shapes lay sprawled about randomly. There was one that caught everyone's eye immediately. It was as large as a bus, and though the paint had mostly been scoured from its polished aluminum, you could still make out *ARROW VAN LUXURY* etched on its side. It sat slightly tilted against several other RVs, but it looked as if it could be righted.

"This is what we've been needing," Jason yelled in excitement. "She's a beauty. Billy, you never cease to amaze me. How do you find whatever we need at just the right time?"

"Just lucky I guess," Billy grinned ear to ear, pleased with Jason's compliment. "Besides, that's not the only one that looks in good shape. There is another identical one just around that pile of junk," he pointed further down the stack of RVs.

"Okay, this is as far as we go today. We've got lots of work to do to get these things on the road, so let's get cracking," Jason ordered good-naturedly.

The boys began sorting through the wreckage, freeing the two RVs they had chosen to be their living and traveling quarters. The girls were requested,

by Jason to round up as many gas cans as possible, as well as anything in which gas and diesel could be carried. Then they began siphoning what they could from the wrecked and torn vehicles on the lot.

The work went faster than the day before. The snowplow made short order of clearing paths, and the power of the truck pulled the RVs free from the pile. By mid-afternoon, they had their new homes-on-wheels and running. Each vehicle was new with a complete book of instructions stashed in their glove compartments. The boys pored over these pamphlets, learning how to start the gas refrigeration, fill water tanks with water and the sewage system with biodegradable chemicals, and topping off the propane tanks, which they found to be charged already.

Water was more of a problem than the fuel. They had been carrying 10 six-gallon Jerry Jugs of water, which had been filled the last time at Jim's farm. To top off the hundred and fifty gallon tank in each of their new buses would require some thought. Jason figured they could use the propane stoves until their tanks ran dry, after that it would be back to the Colemans, since one-gallon cans of white gas could be found at most any hardware store.

The ATVs were not to be left behind, Jason decided, even if they had to spend more time holed up in the RV lot. He would find trailers on which to load the four wheelers, and then tow them behind the big buses.

By dark, Jason was dead on his feet. His leg was throbbing, but not enough to keep him from supervising and helping prepare the traveling homes for the road. As Billy moved the last of their gear into the bigger bus, Jason limped to the temporary kitchen, and sat at Mary Lynne's improvised table constructed from an inverted car hood stretched between a stack of tires.

"You could have cooked in the bus," Jason said to the girls preparing their evening meal.

"It was just easier to cook outside tonight, at least until you are finished packing and working on the RVs," Mary Lynne said, as she looked up from the frying pan where she was warming canned beans. She studied Jason a moment, noticing the haggard look on his face. "You look like death warmed over," she said, moving to his side. She wrapped an arm around his shoulder, taking note of his torn shirt. "Come on, you bloody fool, sit down and have some supper. And take your shirt off. I'll get you another from the bus."

Jason did what he was told, too tired to disagree. He struggled out of his shirt, slipping on the warm, wool plaid Mary Lynne handed him. "Thanks," he said, without feeling. "I guess I really am worn out."

"Well, it's little bloody wonder. You have been pushing like a madman for days, and you're still recovering from that dog bite." She leaned down to inspect the wound.

Jason jumped and howled when she pulled the taped bandage from his calf. "I wish you'd warn me when you're going to do that," he grimaced.

Mary Lynne gently probed the tissue surrounding the gash. The stitches were starting to rot away, and she could tell they were not really needed now anyway. She noted the ragged edges around the wound were still red, puffy, and tender to the touch, but there was no sign of infection.

"Jason, you've got to stay off this leg and give it a chance to heal," she said with concern. She looked up into his face. His eyes were already closed, and his breathing regular in sleep. Mary Lynne brushed a lock of blond hair from his eyes, leaned down, and tenderly kissed him on the forehead. "My lovely Jason," she whispered.

"Can I help?" Billy asked, as he kneeled down beside the two.

"Yeah. Will you carry him to bed in the bus?"

"Sure." Billy started to gather him into his arms, stopped, and turned to Mary Lynne. "You love him, don't you?"

Mary Lynne returned his glance. "Yes."

"So do I," Billy said. As he spoke, he hefted Jason, struggling under the larger boy's weight and carried him to their bus.

CHAPTER 13

Rats, Flies, and Bullets

Phil Fagan was just starting work on the task he had been assigned earlier that morning. He could not believe his luck, or the coincidence of the whole thing. His supervisor had designated him to repair the motion sensor devices throughout the rim and elevator tunnel. In fact, as he had been told, he'd been specifically requested by the Chief of Engineering . . . a real feather in his cap, he'd been assured. It would be a big job, one that would have him digging around in every nook and cranny of the rim and the entrance to the elevator shaft. If Phil believed in omens, then this was straight out of a book of witchcraft.

He started his work in the rim, slowly tracing wires into the elevator shaft. He did not want to give the impression he was too interested in any one area, and besides he needed to get a broad feel of the system beyond the schematics he had been provided. The idea was to be able to knock the elevator shaft's sensors out without affecting the rest of the system. To do that would require the rerouting of certain wires in a manner that could not be easily detected by another electrician, at least without close scrutiny. It could be done, but it would take time.

There were two possible methods of ensuring he would not be detected moving through the elevator's tunnel. He could remove the motion-sensing units, saying they needed to be adjusted in his lab, or he could rewire the entire system, as necessary, providing himself a cutout switch to be used in the future. In the end, Phil decided to combine the two. He would remove the four sensing units from the elevator shaft, taking them in for repair, though all they actually needed were minor adjustments. As he feigned repair on the small units, he could rewire the system with a cutout switch so it would not alert technicians in the Hub when and if he chose to try leaving the confines of New Land for the uncertainties of the outside.

It would take him several days to accomplish the chore, but that would not raise any suspicions; besides, he had not talked to Abby about his latest visit from Jack Mossmen. Abby was more distant than usual, withdrawing into herself, and because of her distance, he had not brought the subject up. Now, however, he had the means of getting them topside without anyone the wiser. It was time to make their decision one way or the other.

Jack Mossmen sat at a dining table with several other men. They were finishing a breakfast of reconstituted eggs, smoked ham, and grits.

"I detest grits," a good-looking man of twenty-five said distastefully. "I have never understood what southerner's see in them. Heck, you might as well be eating cream of wheat, and I don't like that either."

Jack nodded his head disinterestedly, acknowledging the man's comment. He looked over the crowded dining facility, its long communal tables filled with men and women dressed in the blue tunics of Charlie tunnel, preparing for the day's activities. He was hoping to see Heather and finish his breakfast with her. She had just been getting out of bed when he was ready to leave, having gotten up and finished his toilet an hour before. Something was bothering her as they had gone to bed the night before, and no matter how many times he asked, she would not tell him what it was. He hoped they might be able to discuss the problem over breakfast, but he could not find her in the crowd.

"I'm sorry," Jack turned his attention back to the man who hated grits. "I wasn't paying attention. What were you saying?"

"I was just wondering when you would be moving in with someone else?"

Jack stopped his fork in mid air; eggs mixed with grits fell to the table with a soft splat. "What did you say?" Jack asked, his voice hushed and dangerous.

"I said, are you planning to move in with anyone else?" The speaker was looking down at his plate when Jack asked him to repeat his question and failed to see the surprise mixed with rancor reflected in Jack's eyes.

"Why would I be moving?" Jack asked slowly.

The man glanced up to meet Jack's gaze. The look he received was almost physical with intensity, causing him to drop his fork and sit upright in his chair. "God damn, Jack. I'm sorry. I thought you knew."

"Knew what?"

"Hey, now! I didn't mean anything." He could sense Jack's temper flaring, and that he might be on the verge of physically striking him.

"It's just that Heather was seen with Gilmore in the Oasis, and they weren't just talking."

The last word had not left the man's mouth when Jack's right fist struck him squarely on the jaw. Jack, in one swift movement, stood and swung a roundhouse blow of tremendous power. The man tumbled over backwards in his chair, crashing on the hard rock floor like a hundred-pound sack of flour. He did not move, nor would he for several minutes. His world was wrapped in the darkness of unconsciousness.

The commotion drew the attention of everyone in the dining room. Men and women stood to see what caused such an outbreak. Jack pivoted in place several times, glaring with red flaming eyes, daring anyone to say or do something. No one did. Jack was their headman, their tunnel leader, and either out of fear or respect of his position no one moved.

The room was silent as Jack hurried out of the room, leaving others to clean up the mess of eggs, grits and ham that had been flung from his table when the man toppled. He left behind, also, a room filled with questions . . . questions about what had taken place.

Jack did not care what anyone thought. He was in a rage. His mind seethed with the dark poison of jealousy as he made his way down the long tunnel to his room. Reaching the door, he ripped it open, tearing the top hinge from the plastic. His head tucked low in anger; Jack's bright red face was a noticeable contrast to the blue of his tunic as he stormed into the small enclosure.

Heather was just finishing her shower, rubbing her blond hair vigorously with a thick cotton towel. Droplets of water still clung to her naked body, dripping silently on the yellow bath mat beneath her feet.

"You God damned whore," Jack shrieked. "You miserable little bitch, you're nothing but a tramp."

Heather looked up in astonishment, a towel spun turban fashion over her head. She did not see the blow coming until it caught her full force on the nose. She fell into the bathroom, knocking the back of her head against the sink, and spraining her right arm as she reached to break her fall.

"You no 'count bitch," Jack wailed again, as he leaped atop her, his fist raised to strike.

The blow came hard on her left cheek . . . knuckles cut deep below her eye. Again, her head snapped back, this time against the hard rock wall. Heather felt herself falling into a well of darkness, but could dimly see the two men behind Jack grab him as he was readying to hit her again. They had little room to maneuver in the small doorway, but were able to stop the assault. Like a terrified animal, she wormed her way through the thrashing legs of the three men, escaping into the main room. Though the blows to her head numbed her mind, she knew, instinctively she had to distance herself from Jack. Struggling to her feet, Heather ran through the door and down the tunnel, her naked feet slapping the cold, rock floor.

The two men were able to subdue Jack. After a short struggle, he fell limp on the bathroom floor.

"Jesus, Jack, what in hell is wrong with you?" one of the men asked.

"Nothing. Get out and leave me alone," Jack whined, tears filling his eyes. "Just leave me alone."

The two men backed quietly from the room, both shaking their heads in shock at what they had just seen. As they passed through the door, the larger of the two reached up and wedged the hinge back into place, allowing the door to close fully, though it would fall off as soon as the door was moved again.

Jack lay on the bathroom floor for a long time. He curled into a fetal position, hugging his body with his long arms, and gently rocked back and forth as he cried. Then, almost instantly, the crying stopped, and he stood. Looking into the mirror, which covered the wall over the bathroom sink, Jack splashed cold water in his face. The reddened, fury-ridden eyes scrutinizing him from the polished glass were not Jack's, they were some crazed animal's, something from a Stephen King novel.

"I'll kill them both," he whispered.

Heather ran in terror, blood streaming from her nose, into her mouth, and off her chin. By the time she had reached the Hub's outer ring, she was covered in her own blood. Heather did not scream, she just ran, knocking men and women from her path and leaving them in a state of stupefaction, wondering what in Hell was going on. She slowed to make the turn into the Hub's outer ring, and then slid to a stop, seeing Gilmore through one of the many control room entrances.

The big general saw her at the same time, taking a second for the situation to register in his mind, and sprang to her side. Heather collapsed into his arms, safe at last.

Gilmore hefted Heather across his arms and broke into a trot for the medical department. The white-tuniced technicians in the Hub saw their boss run from the room to the injured woman. As he lifted her into his arms like a bag of marshmallows, the Chief of Engineering ran for his communication panel to inform Medical that Gilmore was on his way.

Medical, in the form of Dr. Blazedale, was waiting for Gilmore as he burst into their office spaces. Heather was unconscious as he laid her gently on an examination table. Blazedale, his eyes shaded by his glasses, turned to Gilmore and said, "General, please wait outside. We'll handle it from here."

Gilmore backed from the room, looking like a small boy who had just lost his favorite puppy. He could not be in charge, not here in the emergency room of Med, and that made him feel less than adequate.

"Blazedale, damn you, let me know how she is as soon as you can. I'll be waiting right here. Do you understand?" Gilmore's voice was the complete juxtaposition of his present countenance. He articulated in clear, cold iron and steel.

"Yes, sir, you'll be the first to know. Now please, General, let us do our work," Blazedale said.

Not more than thirty minutes passed before Doctor Blazedale emerged from the emergency room. "She's going to be fine," he said to a pacing Gilmore. "Her nose will be sore and swollen for several days, and we will want to keep an eye on the bump on her head for a week or so, but she should be fine."

"What bump?" Gilmore stopped his pacing and asked intently.

"Heather has two severe contusions on the back of her head. She told us she hit the sink when she fell."

"How did she fall?" Gilmore quizzed through tight teeth. He was sure what happened, or at least had an idea, and his anger was barely contained.

"I think I'll let her tell you. You can go in and see her now if you wish."

Grabbing the doorknob, Gilmore did not acknowledge the doctor as he stepped into the emergency room. He hated the sterility of hospitals and anything to do with them. He disliked this room even more, with its stainless steel cabinets, bottles of oxygen, operating tools, and Heather lying on the examining table.

"How do you feel?" the big man asked softly, gathering her small hand in his.

"Better, now that you're here," Heather whispered, her nose puffy and red. The nurses had cleaned the blood from her face and body, and covered her with a clean, crisp sheet. "But I have felt better," she whispered, trying a crooked smile, but with one eye swollen shut, and a lip split slightly, it was a poor imitation of pleasure.

"What happened?" Gilmore asked, concern deep in his voice.

As the pale, battered woman told her story, Gilmore closed his eyes, remembering his father beating on the one woman he truly loved . . . his mother. He could almost smell the whiskey and hear the slapping blows the smallish black woman received with each successive impact. His mother would take the beating without so much as a whimper. He hated his father at those times, and now he could plainly picture the man's cruel face towering over his mother. He had solved that problem in his life on his thirteenth birthday when he stood before his father, fists balled, and let him know he would never again strike a woman in their house. Now, it would be Jack's turn to learn the same lesson his father had so many years ago

*****

Jason woke from a dream-filled sleep. He could remember the dreams, which kept him tossing much of the night. His family had been at the cabin on Ponto. He could see his Mother through the screen door, and his Dad smiling in at him, a stringer of bass held high. The lake had been cold, when he and his sister swam close to their unsteady dock. It had been all wrong though, because Mary Lynne had appeared with him in the lake, her supple, girlish curves luring him to deeper waters.

Jason shook the sleep from his eyes, realizing he was in a real bed for the first time in months. "How did I get here?" he wondered aloud.

"Billy carried you in after you fell asleep by the fire," Mary Lynne spoke from the other room of the bus. "How do you feel? Last night you looked like something the cat dragged in."

"I'll tell you after I've woken up some," he replied.

Mary Lynne stepped into the RV's spacious sleeping compartment, brushing a strand of golden hair from her forehead. "You look bloody awful."

Jason sat in the middle of the bed surveying his surroundings. The bedroom took up the rear quarter of the van, its light blue wallpaper bounded by oak veneer cabinets and hanging lockers. Mary Lynne sat down next to him and looked around as well.

"Pretty nice, huh?"

"Better than sleeping in a restaurant booth or on the ground, that's for sure," Jason smiled. "Where did you sleep last night?"

"With you."

Instinctively, Jason pulled the bed covers around his waist, realizing he was naked. "With me, . . . but . . . well, you know, I haven't got any clothes on."

"I know. I undressed you, and tucked you in," Mary Lynne said, a coy look crossing her blue eyes, and her smile grew larger yet. "Then I got undressed and climbed in with you. I wanted to make sure you stayed warm."

"You could have left my clothes on. That would have worked too, you know."

"Not near as much fun though." Mary Lynne laughed with throaty mirth. "Jason," she said as she caught her breath, "you're a prude. Do you know that?"

"You think so, huh?" Jason let the covers slip and grabbed Mary Lynne by the shoulders, pulling her down on the bed next to him. "Try this," he chided, and began tickling her along the ribs.

Mary Lynne, not ticklish as rule, began giggling uncontrollably. "Stop it, please. Jason, stop," she forced through her chortling.

Jason stopped as suddenly as he'd begun and, pinning her shoulders to the bed, bent down to kiss her. It was a warm, tender kiss. She stopped struggling, returning the kiss with as much emotion as Jason was giving her. She wrapped her arms around Jason's broad shoulders and pulled him tight. In her mind, she knew she would never let this man go. He would be hers till death saw fit to separate them forever."

The kiss ended slowly. Jason pulled away, much less shy than at their first encounter. He looked down into her aqua eyes, smiled, and said, "You know I'm falling in love with you, don't you?"

"Yes," she sighed. "And I you."

They kissed once more, not with lust or passion, but lovingly, full of concern and caring. It was Billy who once more interrupted a perfect moment.

"Hey, you two, we've got work to do. Come on, Jason, get dressed. I've got breakfast cooking out here." His dark head disappeared around the doorway.

Mary Lynne shook herself free of Jason's embrace, stood and made for the door. "Get dressed, you bloody oaf. I'll help Billy with the food," she said over her shoulder.

Jason, dressed for the day in his new plaid shirt, joined the group sitting around a makeshift table. "Oh, goody. Hash again. Good thing I like this stuff so much, 'cause it seems to be all you can come up with for breakfast," he said, chiding Billy and Mary Lynne.

"Hey, buster, if you don't like it you can fix your own bloody breakfast." Mary Lynne feigned hurt pride.

The group laughed. It felt good to laugh, easing the sadness and many losses they all struggled to carry in their hearts.

"Billy, I want you, Tom, and Bob to take the dump truck to Eau Claire this morning. Find a couple of good size trailers we can tow behind the RVs. They should be large enough to haul the four-wheelers plus cans of fuel. If you want, load a couple of the wheelers aboard. That way you can scout the town for more mosquito netting, canned goods, and any other supplies we can use."

"Okay," Billy said, between bites of hash. "What are you going to be doing?"

"The rest of us will scout the area for a clear lake. I'm sure there ought to be one somewhere nearby. We might even be able to locate a working well. Regardless, we'll start hauling water back here to fill the tanks on the RVs.

`"Sounds good to me," Billy replied, as he washed his empty plate. "I'll gather my gear and be on my way. You guys ready?" He asked Tom and Bob.

"Lead on, oh mighty scout," Bob answered.

Billy punched him on the arm with good-natured enthusiasm.

"Hey, Billy, while you're in town would you look for a library?" Mary Lynne asked.

"Sure, I'll put it on my ever growing list of things to find." Billy smiled warmly, and then continued walking for his truck.

"May I go with Billy?" Lorrie asked Jason softly.

"Sure, if he has the room."

Lorrie did not hear "if he has the room." She was already running after the retreating figures.

Jason, with Mary Lynne holding tightly to his waist, was threading the ATV east on State Road 29. Leaving the RV lot, they made their way across the overpass and onto the two lane, country road. Thirty minutes later, their hope of finding a small lake or pond nearby was all but dispelled though they did locate a livestock watering pond. The quarter acre reservoir was so polluted by dust it was actually silting into a shallow pool. There was no sign of a farm structure, and so they continued searching.

Clouds of sifting finely powdered earth billowed behind their small vehicle as they persisted in their search, winding around the country's byways. Jason saw it first, and braked to a stop, pointing to their left. Highlighted against a dusty brown sky and standing like a lone sentinel guarding a path to forbidden lands, were the remnants of a once mighty windmill.

"What do you think? Do you suppose it's worth a try?" Jason asked, turning to face Mary Lynne.

"I guess so, but I doubt it will do us much good. Most of the tower is gone, and without the windmill doing the pumping, how will we get the water up?"

"Heck, I don't know. Let's give it a try anyway," Jason said as he released the hand clutch and moved slowly off the road toward the well.

A six-foot length of galvanized pipe dripped water into a long, animal drinking trough. The tank was overflowing, creating a muddy mess for several feet in all directions. Sodden dirt filled the bottom of the tank, but the continual overspill kept the water reasonably clean on the surface.

"Jason, how can water still be coming out of the ground? There isn't anything to pump it with."

"Darned if I know. Maybe they had a small earthquake here, too, and the water is now under some sort of pressure."

"Do you think the water is safe to drink?" Mary Lynne asked.

"Well, we've been drinking the water we gathered at Jim's farm and it came from a well a lot like this one, and besides, it's coming from underground. Yeah, I think it's safe enough. The problem is . . . how do we haul it back to the buses?"

"We don't," Mary Lynne said. "Let's bring the buses here. Then we can siphon the water into the tanks just like we do the gas."

"I guess we could try, but it would be a rough trip across the bypass for the buses, and I sure as heck don't want to lose them now." He paused to think. "Yeah, I think you're right though. Let's give it a try," Jason said, as he took Mary Lynne's hand and started back to their vehicle. "Hey, look at that."

Jason was pointing up into the northern sky. Gliding high above was a bald eagle, its great wings soaring on the air currents. Suddenly, it folded its wings and disappeared behind a hilltop.

"What a wonderful sight, and it means there is more life around than we thought," Jason remarked with some excitement. "What do you think?"

"I'm sure you're bloody well right. If the eagle is able to find food, and if it has survived this long, then there have got to be small critters for it to eat."

"If there are critters, as you put it, for them to eat, then we might be able to find some fresh meat for us as well. Boy, would hamburger, chicken, or pork be wonderful. I think I've forgotten what real meat tastes like."

"Me too," she said, climbing on the back of the ATV.

The trip back did not take as long as the one out, and they arrived to expectant faces. After explaining their situation, Jason climbed into the seat of his bus, and got the engine running. One of the new arrivals, a boy of fifteen with jet-black hair, got behind the wheel of the other.

The drive across I-94's median gave them a couple of heart stopping moments, but they were able to reach the security of the blacktop without incident. The trip to the windmill was a learning experience for the two boys. The converted passenger buses had power to spare, located over their rear, dual wheels, and big rigs took some getting used to driving.

At least, Jason thought, the big RV's sported automatic transmissions, and that made driving them a world easier than the semi-tractors. When they arrived at the windmill site, the group emerged with smiles of accomplishment on their faces.

"Okay, let's get busy," Jason yelled, as he pulled a hose from the belly of his RV. The hose was standard equipment on both vehicles, and by connecting the two together; they were able to easily reach the water tank. Mary Lynne rigged a filter over either end, using a pair of Carol's pantyhose. Jason asked why in the world Carol was carrying pantyhose with her, but only received a stare of "keep your thoughts to yourself." He let it drop like a rock, not wishing to raise any of the young ladies' ire.

The trough held over five hundred gallons of water, and even with the silt present on the bottom of the tank, there was ample clean water to fill the one hundred and seventy-five-gallon tank onboard each bus. It took most of the afternoon to complete the task, as the siphoning was steady, but slow. When both tanks had been filled to the top, the young crowd stripped to their underclothing and leapt in the tank for a good scrub down.

Mary Lynne kept trying to get everyone to skinny dip, but shyness and the fact no one knew anyone very well kept the group from shucking to their birthday suits. It felt wonderful to splash and wash in the big tank. Days of road grime peeled from their bodies in sheets. It was nearing three p.m. before they dragged themselves from the cool water, and began coiling the hoses. It proved to be difficult turning the buses around, and in the end they had to drive another two miles before finding a secondary gravel road on where they could maneuver enough to get the big rigs pointed in the right direction.

The buses, their diesels straining under the difficult meridian crossing, alerted Billy and his crew of Jason's return. Jason pulled in next to the dump truck and exited out the side door with the rest of his passengers. He was anxious to find out how Billy had fared.

Billy stood next to his truck, the mammoth snow wing towering above him. He smiled broadly at the sight of Jason striding across the pavement, puffs of ashy dirt exploding under his shoes.

"Well, how did it go?" Jason called as he advanced.

"You know me. Send this lad on a search and seizure expedition and you get what you asked for," Billy beamed proudly. "Heck, I even brought Mary Lynne half the books in the Eau Claire library."

The two walked around the truck, Billy leading. "Just have a peek at those."

Billy was pointing to the trailers he had brought back. One had been towed behind the truck, and now sat off to the side. Bob was laying a makeshift ramp from the bed of the dumper to the pavement so they could unload the trailer sitting in the truck bed.

"I figured we might as well keep the rain off whatever you want to haul," Billy said, pointing to the fully enclosed trailers. "Well, what do you think?"

"They're great," Jason responded. "Just what we needed. Did you find anything else we can use?"

"You hurt me to the heart," Billy said, clutching his breast with both hands. "Of course I found goodies. Did you think I'd come back empty handed?"

Jason smiled warmly at his friend, "Okay, okay I get your point. Let's see it."

"Hey, you two, how about giving us a hand." It was Bob who yelled at them as they talked between themselves. "We need some help unloading these damn things."

Jason and Billy ran to the aid of the three boys trying to unload the trailer. The 16 x 8 foot, tandem-wheeled towable slipped down the ramp with the four boys easing it along from behind. By the time they finished, all of them were sweating like racehorses.

"I could sure use a shower," Billy said, as he opened the rear doors of the trailer.

"Well, I have a surprise for you. You can take a shower tonight. I've got both buses filled with water . . . enough to take a short wash down."

"That's great. Now come on, I want to show you the goodies I brought home with me. What do you think?"

Jason looked in astonishment at a pile of supplies covering a whole spectrum of needs. There was canned food, filled propane tanks, clothing, additional camping equipment, two Coleman heaters, lanterns, four shotguns, and enough twelve-gauge ammunition to start a war.

"And look at this," Billy said eagerly, as he pulled on Jason's arm. He lifted a corner of a tarp, exposing a pile of bee hood nets. "What do you think of that?"

"Gezz, Billy what did you find? An 'I Need to Survive' store. You've got just about everything we could possibly use in there."

"There's even more in the other trailer. It's probably more than we can haul, but we can sort it out in the morning and pack it under the buses. What do you think?"

Jason shook his head in disbelief. "I think you're a wonderment, Billy. That's what I think."

*****

Phil and Abby sat in their cubicle sipping coffee. It was the end of a long, busy day.

"I don't know, Phil. I've been talking to Margaret Duke, you know, the same doctor you went to for your claustrophobia, and she's really got me thinking,"

"I know, but it's like we are supposed to leave. Jack comes to me with his sketches, and then I get assigned to repair the motion sensor system. It's like someone is telling us something. Besides, we don't have to leave right away. I can rig the system so we could leave anytime we want. Even after the baby is born. Don't you see, we don't have to make a decision right now. We can take our time. If you decide to have the baby, you ought to have medical attention anyway."

"You're right. I can't seem to get anybody's attention about having an abortion anyway. I think I'll have to have the baby whether I want to or not. We could make the final decision after we know if the baby is healthy. Besides, you've been having your own problems. How is your claustrophobia anyway? I'm sorry, I haven't even asked about you, and you were really having some problems."

"I haven't had an attack since the doc gave me those pills. They really seemed to help. I guess she was right, and it was just a temporary thing," Phil answered. "Of course, I have been really worried about you and us, and I think that took my mind off my own problem."

"Not to change the subject, but did you hear what happened this morning?" Abby asked off handedly.

"You mean the thing with Jack and Heather? Who hasn't? I'm surprised Gilmore hasn't taken any action. I would have thought he'd have Jack arrested or something."

"I know what you mean," Abby responded. "He has always struck me as a man of action, but I wouldn't count him out yet. Jack is a shifty sort of guy, and I'm sure Gilmore knows it."

"I knew Jack was more than a little jealous when it came to Heather, but I can't see how he ever thought she would stick with just one man. She is a terrible flirt, and has a body that could stop a freight train."

Abby did a double take on Phil. "And just what have I got?" she asked, pretending to be hurt.

"Abby, you are well aware how I feel about you. I'm probably one of the few men down here who hasn't tried to bed every woman in sight. Certainly I had fun with the ladies before I met you, but since then I feel sort of like a one-woman guy." He smiled a perfect smile.

"Yes, I know, and I'm glad you are the way you are." She moved closer to him, took his rough workman's hand in hers, and kissed it lightly. "If love is possible under all this rock, I suppose I love you, Phil. Whatever we decide about leaving, I know you'll be there with me."

Gilmore stayed with Heather throughout the morning, gently holding her hand as she drifted in and out of sleep. They talked when she was awake, speaking of their childhood, their dreams, and their accomplishments. Heather told how she had grown up in a small midwestern town, attending college at Iowa State, and graduating with a degree in political science. She then moved to Washington, D.C., where she had worked as an attendant to several Democrat senators. Her main job, as she put it, was to stand around offices, parties, and receptions looking beautiful and alluring. She had had little trouble with those duties, and done well for herself.

"I've always been a climber, looking for the easy way to the top. I admit I have used men to accomplish that end," she confessed, smiling weakly. "In fact, you were next on my list to seduce for my own ends."

"I know that. I've known it from the first time I met you. Do you feel the same now?" Gilmore asked seriously.

"What do you think?" Heather answered.

"I would like to believe there is more to our blossoming relationship than that."

Heather squeezed his hand and smiled warmly, "Trust me, there is much more."

Shortly after their conversation, Heather drifted off to sleep once more. Gilmore crept quietly from the room, leaving Heather and the hospital smells behind. He checked with a nurse sitting behind a desk in the reception space of the emergency attending area. Though the examination room looked like any ordinary emergency room with framed and covered walls, the reception room was bare rock. Few areas of New Land had actual finished walls; the medical area was one of those few.

He told the nurse he would be in his office, and she should call him on the tunnel-com if there was any change, and he would return later that afternoon. The nurse, a handsome woman of twenty-seven acknowledged his directions with a nod, and turned back to her paperwork.

Gilmore ignored the questioning glances he received from his staff working in the Hub, and went straight up the stairs to his office. He sat for a long while, his hands folded on the desk before him. He stared at the far wall. The panel of lights indicating the entire layout of New Land glared back at him . . . cold and unrelenting. He debated with himself over his next move. Should he take action against Mossmen? What if he did. What would he do with him? There was nothing resembling a jail. He might order house arrest, but that would mean guards. No, he decided, that would not do.

If he set the precedent of house arrest, particularly concerning an incident in which he was involved, what would the rest of the population think? Neither he nor the many scientists and engineers who designed New Land had figured on a crime problem, and in all fairness, they'd been right. There had been no crime. Yet, here he was having to decide what should be done with a man who had broken a moral statute. Of course, he thought, there was another dilemma. What would Mossmen do?

If Gilmore was to take at face value what his two primary advisors had told him in the past, then he knew there was bound to be more trouble before this incident was tucked safely away. Heather certainly reinforced the fact, Jack was volatile under normal situations, and this was not a typical predicament by any stretch of the imagination. Gilmore knew now, beyond any doubt, the man could be violent. Mossmen had proven his capacity by striking out physically in a very dramatic manner.

There was a knock, followed by the door opening and a balding head poking its way around the plastic panel. "Is there anything I can do for you, General?" the Chief of Engineering asked.

"No thank you, but I appreciate your asking, Gilmore replied. " I'm just sitting here thinking, but I'll let you know if you can help. Thanks again."

"Okay. Just thought I'd ask. Call if you need anything." The shiny head disappeared from view, and the door closed quietly.

Gilmore shifted position in his chair, put his hands behind his head, and leaned back. Perhaps the best thing to do was ignore the whole thing. If Mossmen will let it drop, then we could chalk it up to "just one of those things." It bothered him he was even contemplating letting the bastard off the hook, but he had to think beyond his personal desires. New Land's welfare came first and foremost, and he was personally connected to this problem. But what if Mossmen would not let the incident pass? What if he were to take further retribution against Heather or, perhaps, himself?

He spun in his chair to face the wall behind him. He stared at the door cut into the solid rock, the only steel door in New Land. He reached both hands up to his neck and pulled a small golden chain from under his red tunic. He removed it from around his head and took the medium sized key, which was attached to the chain, in his hand. He turned the key over and over, finally standing and walking slowly to the great steel door. He put the key in the lock and turned. The latch clicked softly, and Gilmore pulled open the door with its U-shaped handle.

He paused, and then walked inside the three hundred square foot room, now dimly lit under blue light. Every inch of wall space and most of the floor were covered with a variety of weapons. Everything from M-16's to grenade and rocket launchers hung, lined in racks, or stored in cartons on the rock floor. Crates of ammunition were stacked near the door, while a gun-cleaning table graced the back wall. It was a small arsenal; one Gilmore had insisted be installed. He was sure no one else in the tunnels knew of this room or its contents, although he had noticed Margaret Duke eyeing it on several occasions.

He walked to the left and opened a small crate. Inside lay fifteen handguns. There were 38's, 45's, and 9mm's to choose from. He picked up a military issue forty-five, yanked back the slide with a knowledgeable hand, and let it slam shut. He chose the forty-five out of his love for the weapon. It was the gun of an officer, or at least had been through most of his career. He was adept in its use and care. He laid the automatic pistol on the cleaning table and unthinkingly broke it down into its main components. After inspecting and cleaning each precisely machined piece, he reassembled the weapon secure in the knowledge it was in good working order. Gilmore tucked the gun in his belt and used a crowbar to pry open the top of another box; this one marked "small caliber ammunition." Once the lid was off, he chose a box of forty-five caliber rounds, opened it, took nine bullets from the box, and loaded his weapon.

Gilmore shut the door to his personal armory and locked it, returning the key and chain to its place around his neck. He unzipped the front of his tunic and stripped the top half from over his shoulders, slipping it to his waist. Gilmore shook his head sadly as he slipped a shoulder holster over his left arm and tightened the Velcro strap across his chest. He slammed the forty-five into the holster and slipped his arms back into the tunic.

"A sad state of affairs," he thought aloud.

*****

Morning brought a flurry of activity around the buses. Jason and Billy supervised the sorting and loading of the haul from Eau Claire the night before. The RV's underbellies were cavernous and could hold a wealth of the gear brought from the city, but they could not hold it all.

Everyone had their own ideas on what should be included as supplies, but in the end, it was left up to Jason to make the final decisions.

Billy explained, over yet another breakfast of hash, that the flies had been horrible in Eau Claire. Clouds of the insects would explode before them everywhere they went. Most of the bodies had decomposed or been eaten by predators, but the flies were still terrible. With these words in mind, Jason noted he needed to issue everyone a bee hood. Billy's additional news was even less welcome.

"We saw hundreds of rats scurrying around the town as well as the flies," Billy explained through a mouthful of corned beef. "I think they've been feeding off the dead, and reproducing at a rate which would put gerbils to shame."

"It makes sense," Jason responded. "They would have survived the winds, hidden away in their holes, and they'll eat anything. Now that they don't have many enemies, they probably are living high on the hog. Do you think they could prove to be a danger to us?" he asked.

"Shoot, I don't know, but there are a lot of 'em. I suppose we ought to keep an eye out for them if we stay near a town," Billy said.

"I hate rats," Lorrie screwed up her face. "They're so dirty and yucky. They scared the heck out of me while we were there, and I sure don't want to go back into that town."

Jason thought about their breakfast conversation during the loading process, and as they finished putting the last bit of gear into the buses, he called everyone together. He spread the road map of Wisconsin out on their makeshift table of plywood and wrecked RVs.

"All along I have thought we would take I-94 into Chicago, but with what Billy told us this morning, it seems to me the best idea is to avoid cities. The interstate bypasses most towns of any size, but if we go to Chicago, we would have to drive through the suburbs, and I don't think that's a good idea. We have to go by Eau Claire, but Billy says I-94 passes well south of the town itself. The next city of any size is Madison, and according to the map, the road passes through the city's outskirts. From there, I think we'll continue on 94 till it intersects I-90, which is what we would have done if we were to go to Chicago, but we'll leave I-90 for I-39 at Beloit and head to Bloomington, Illinois. How does that sound?"

"Do we have to?" Mary Lynne asked, her face crestfallen. "I would rather go anywhere than pass through my hometown."

"I hear you," Jason said. "But according to the map, I-39 passes well to the east of Bloomington itself, and it certainly is the fastest way south."

"Okay, but I wish there was some other bloody way," Mary Lynne answered.

"All right then," Jason said, "it's time for Billy to get the dumper moving. We'll give him an hour to move on ahead of us, and then we'll follow. Billy," Jason turned to face his friend, "you should be able to make good time till you get to Eau Claire, since you have already scraped that section. Do you think an hour will be enough time?"

"Yeah, I think so. I'll push dirt till around four this afternoon and meet you wherever I might be then. I'll take Bob and Lorrie with me, if that's all right?"

"Sure, that's fine," Jason answered, as he picked up his staff, which he had laid on the ground beside the table. "The rest of us will finish hooking up the trailers to the buses. We'll see you this afternoon."

Billy moved off for his truck with Bob and Lorrie in tow. He climbed into the driver's seat and started the big rig. His passengers scrambled aboard and with a wave of their hands the winged dump truck headed out of the parking lot.

Billy was rolling. The dumper was in fourth gear and moving down I-94 at twenty miles per hour, clouds of dust trailing behind off the wing. They had cleared several semis from the road by pushing them with the big blade, making enough room for the buses to pass through when they followed. A tuneless high-pitched whistling came from his pursed lips as he down shifted into third. He was approaching another lump on the road between a steep rise of rock on the passenger's side and a wet meridian on the driver's. He slowed to fifteen miles per hour in anticipation of the thump.

"Hang on, gang, we're going to smash another tree out of the way," Billy warned Lorrie and Bob.

The truck hit a massive rock, its momentum coming to an instant halt, and stalling the engine. Billy gripped the steering wheel with his full strength, but his head snapped forward striking the top of the wheel. Blood covered his face immediately, as he lost consciousness for an instant.

Bob, sitting on the far right, had placed his legs on the dashboard to brace himself for the hit. When it came, his legs took the brunt of the strike. "Holy Mother of God, what did we hit?" he yelled in the confusion.

Lorrie heard the warning from Billy, and tried to support herself by reaching out with her arms against the dash. When the truck banged into the boulder, her arms buckled and she was lifted from the seat with tremendous force and nose-dived into the windscreen. She grunted at the impact and slipped like Jell-O to the floor, her legs twisting around the gearshift lever.

Bob, who had not been hurt, glanced quickly around him, seeing Billy shake his head clear of the fireworks. "You okay, Billy?" he asked.

"Yeah, I guess so," he answered, wiping blood from his eyes. "How about you?"

"I'm fine. Damn, what the hell did you hit?"

"Christ, I don't know, but it sure was hard." He looked over at Bob, seeing for the first time Lorrie's limp body lying like a rag doll between them. "Oh God! Lorrie.

Lorrie did not answer, nor did she move. Billy leaned over and tried to raise her head, but the angle was wrong. He clutched the door handle, pushed his door open, leaped to the ground, and ran around to the opposite side. Bob was already on the ground and the two of them looked in the cab.

"We've got to get her out of there," Billy cried, tearing the bee hood from over his head.

"Easy," Bob said, "we'd better be careful. We don't want to hurt her any more than she already is."

The two worked together, slowly extracting the girl from the vehicle. They laid her down the ground. "What do we do now?" Billy asked, looking worriedly at the odd angle Lorrie's arm seemed to have.

"How should I know?" Bob said, his hands slumping to his side. "I don't know anything about first aid, do you?"

"A little but not much. Let's get her feet up and try to stop the bleeding on top of her head," Billy exclaimed, as he removed his sweater. "Give me your jacket."

Bob stripped off his windbreaker and handed it over. Billy took the two articles of clothing and wrapped them into a ball. Then, lifting

Lorrie's legs, he placed the bundle under her ankles. He ripped his shirt off, the buttons flying in all directions, a few pinging off the side of the truck. He knelt beside the stricken teenager and placed his improvised pad on top of the wound, which was gushing blood into her blond hair.

"Lorrie, you'll be all right, " Billy whispered. " You've got to be okay; do you hear me? I won't have you leaving me, damn it."

Jason left the RV lot an hour after Billy departed. He drove the lead bus, with Mary Lynne sitting next to him in the overstuffed passenger seat. They had been talking about the fact they had no cassette tapes to play, and how they would raid a music store when they came to the next big town. It was enjoyable riding in the luxury of the bus, its engine purring. They were eating up the miles much faster and, in a world more comfortable than on the four-wheelers.

"What's that?" Mary Lynne asked, her voice full of concern. She was pointing to billowing dust not more than a couple of miles ahead.

"It's probably Billy clearing a section of road."

"Shouldn't he be further ahead of us than that?" she asked.

Jason looked at the cloud, and then at Mary Lynne. "You're right. He should be a lot further down the road." He stepped on the gas pedal, increasing their speed to forty miles per hour. He picked a mike from over his head, pushed the side button, and said, "Tom, this is Jason. Do you see the dust cloud ahead?"

The CB had been set on channel nineteen before they left, and Tom reached for his mike. "Hell no. How do you expect me to see a dust cloud down the road? I can barely see you. You're putting up enough muck to hide a 747."

"Okay," Jason replied. "Just stay on my tail. I'm speeding up to forty."

"Roger that, good buddy," Tom laughed.

The RVs slid to a stop behind the dumper fifteen minutes later. Mary Lynne was out the side door before the wheels stopped rolling. They had seen there was a problem as they drove over a rise not more than a quarter mile back. Jason radioed Bob and his crew with the concern he felt.

Mary Lynne knelt beside her sister, examining the gash which ripped across the top of Lorrie's head, and then gently probed her sister's left arm. The arm, Mary Lynne decided, was undoubtedly broken. "You did good, Billy. Get my medical kit from under the sink in our bus."

Billy stood rooted, staring down at the two girls.

"Go, damn it!"

He broke into a run and was back moments later. He handed the kit to Mary Lynne, stepping back to give her room. Jason, Tom, Carol, and the others stood quietly in a circle around the injured Lorrie. They had all seen death and dying and now they thought they were watching it once again.

Lorrie groaned as Mary Lynne administered to the wound, cleaning the dried blood away and exposing a shallow trench of ragged meat and skin. Mary Lynne looked up at Jason.

"Get our bed ready to lay her down, Jason. Billy, you find a tarp, and the rest of you get ready to move her into the bus."

Billy returned with the tarp, laying it on the ground beside the downed girl. "What now?" he asked.

"We'll slide her onto the tarp and then carry her inside," Mary Lynne answered. "Come on, you guys, give us a hand."

After they got Lorrie into the bus and on the bed, Mary Lynne shooed all but Jason outside. She then went to work sewing up the wound, which was not deep or serious in itself, but without care, could develop into something more severe. What she had real concerns about was a concussion. She went to her books and looked up a reference on concussions, seeing there was little that could be done other than bed rest. Then she turned to the section on broken bones. She read for over fifteen minutes before she glanced up from her book.

"Jason, I'm going to need your help. We have got to set the bone in Lorrie's left arm. I don't think it is a serious break, nothing like a compound fracture, but we've got to get the bones aligned regardless."

The two worked together for the next half hour, with Jason doing the pulling required and Mary Lynne ensuring the bone was straightened properly. Finally, they were both satisfied it was back in place. From the medical kit, Mary Lynne produced a gauze bandage impregnated with fast drying plaster. She wrapped her patient's arm carefully, making sure she did not move the bone. The plaster was hard as rock in fifteen minutes.

"Ohh, ahh," Lorrie groaned as she woke into the land of the living. "What happened?"

"Just lay still, little sister. You're going to be all right, but you've got be still. You hear me?"

"Okay, but what happened?"

Mary Lynne explained about the wreck.

"Is Billy all right?" she asked.

"He's fine," Mary Lynne stated.

"I want to see him."

"Okay," her sister relinquished. "Hey, Billy, get in here, Lorrie wants to see you."

Billy came on the run, bursting into the bedroom. "Is she all right?"

"Ask her yourself."

"Oh, Billy, are you okay?" Lorrie asked him as he bent down over the bed.

"I'm fine. Are you all right?"

"I've felt better, but I'll be okay. Mary Lynne says I have a concussion and a broken arm, but they'll heal okay. The problem is I'll have to stay in bed for a few days.

"You scared the shiii, I mean the heck out of me. I'm so sorry, I just didn't think it would be a boulder." He bent down and brushed his lips over her forehead. "You know I would never do anything to hurt you."

She reached up and stroked his cheek lightly, "I know."

Outside, Bob and the others received the news with a sigh of relief. Jason asked if Lorrie could travel, and was told she could, but she would have to stay in bed for a few days.

Jason looked into the dusky sky, glanced at his watch, and said, "Okay, we have daylight left. Let's get the rock cleared and try to push on a few more miles before dark. We've got to keep moving."

CHAPTER 14

Cows and Death

"Geez, Jason, I just can't believe this countryside," Billy said. "What could have done this, anyway?"

"Winds. Winds just like in Wisconsin, but worse." Jason leaned on his staff, gazing at the horizon. "There isn't anything left, is there?"

"It sure doesn't look like it. I'm even having difficulty finding the highway in places. There isn't much blocking it, but at times, the dust is two feet or more. Jason, I'm worried. Do you think we can keep moving?"

"We can't stay here and there isn't anything behind us worth returning to. I wish I knew what month it was. I've lost all track of time."

The two comrades were looking over the plains of central Illinois . . . what was left of the great corn belt. The breadbasket of the world, it had once been called. Now it was nothing but a barren wasteland of blowing dust and ash. Nothing was standing as far as the eye could see . . . not a tree, not a building, nothing. Men, since the first discovery of fertile land in the heart of America, had used every tactic and machine they could devise to strip the land clean of its mighty forest. They had plowed their fields for generations, forever opening more ground to be planted. They had built their pitiful sod huts so the rape of the land could begin, and then erected palatial farm homes on small rises overlooking their handiwork.

When the winds came, after the strike, there was nothing to break the mighty force. Three hundred knots of screaming fury swept the landscape clean. It was as if God decided to house clean the vast plains by grabbing a broom and sweeping everything in His path under a rug.

"Billy, if winds did all this," Jason said, swinging his staff to indicate the expanse before them, "then we need to find somewhere the wind's force would have been broken by some sort of barrier."

"That makes good sense, but where? We don't want to fight the rats and smell of a city, and I don't think a small town would have survived what happened here. At least we haven't seen one that did. Even Bloomington, what we could see of it, was blown away, and that was a pretty good size city."

"Yeah, I know. What we need is a natural barrier, something that could withstand almost anything." Jason leaned on his staff and stared into the distance. "Mountains!"

"What did you say?" Billy asked, not comprehending what Jason meant.

"Mountains, Billy, we have to head for the mountains. Don't you see, the mountains would withstand high winds, even the ones that created this mess? We'll go to the mountains."

"You're right," Billy exclaimed excitedly. "But that would mean we would have to cross the Mississippi, and that might not be possible," his face fell as he spoke.

"No, Billy, we don't have to cross the Mississippi," Jason smiled. We'll head east into the Smokey's. I've read about the mountain folk in the Fox Fire books. I should have thought of it earlier. The Great Smoky Mountains of Tennessee, where moonshine and building log cabins became an art," Jason was speaking quietly, but the excitement in his voice was evident. "Let's get back to the buses. I've got to look at a map."

Mary Lynne was standing in front of the lead bus, which sat behind the parked dumper. "They're coming back," she said loudly. She looked behind her, shaking her head at the knot of fifty teenagers milling around their machines.

Behind the Arrow Luxury Liner, home for Jason, Billy, Lorrie, and her, sat a variety of jeeps, buses, RVs, campers, and ATVs. It had been over two weeks since Lorrie had broken her arm, and the once small group was growing every day. As they moved south through Tomah, Portage, Madison, Janesville, and Beloit clouds of dust would announce the arrival of yet another two or more teenagers looking for others who had survived the devastation. Jason's band provided not only the authority figures they needed but, more importantly, Jason had a plan for the future.

Each day created new challenges for Jason's ingenuity. While two buses and a dump truck had been an easy method of travel, now there was a caravan of vehicles. He sent vanguards out each morning, followed by Billy in the dumper. Roads south were scouted and marked. Danger areas were avoided, so there would not be another incident such as the one that injured Lorrie. The outriders had yet another task; they located food and other necessary supplies to feed, clothe, and maintain the clan's growing numbers. Each small town became a supply depot where no store was safe from the needy raiders. Every evening, stacks of goods were distributed and those not needed immediately were stored in trailers towed behind every vehicle that could mount a trailer hitch. As it turned out, those raids had become doubly important. The group, upon arriving in Illinois, found no towns left to pillage. There were enough supplies for the time being, but for how long . . . that was another question.

The group moved well, considering the maintenance required. If a RV broke down, Jason would detail another running vehicle to stay behind while it was being repaired. That way, should an emergency arise, the distressed group could rejoin the main body. Air filters were becoming an overwhelming problem for everyone. The dust, which was forever on the road and in the air, clogged filters on a regular basis. The further back in the pack a RV was during a day's run, the more likely it would develop engine problems. Lists were made for the scouts, detailing the makes and models of everything that rolled. The situation had, several days before, become so serious that a UPS delivery truck was put into service strictly to carry filters, as well as other gas and diesel motor parts.

Mary Lynne stayed busy tending everything from minor cuts to serious infections. Word of her healing talents spread without help from Jason. Lorrie's rehabilitating arm was enough proof for others to come to her on their own. Each evening, after the fires were lit, meals prepared and eaten, and the watch placed, she would set up shop for as long as it took to tend those who required attention. Many of the younger travelers, those from twelve to thirteen, started calling her Mama Lynne, and indeed her efforts to help keep the clan healthy were not unlike a mother hen hovering over her brood.

As the band grew in size, an attitude change began to unfold. After dinner dishes were washed and stowed, guitars and keyboards found their way to the warmth of the fires. Songs filled the tenebrous night, warding away fears of the next day's turmoil. Laughter, something of which there had been all too little, was now but a joke away. Home was no longer a town or city in Minnesota or Illinois, it was here, where they sat this very minute. Family was not a mom or dad with a sibling vying for their affections, it was the crowd of teenagers who sat around them. Jason's strength as a *man,* his ability to lead without bullying, and his genuine concern for those he influenced solidified a sad rabble of lost children into a group of young adults searching for a new home.

Billy and Jason, Jason's staff tapping lightly on the pavement, walked into the lead bus without a word. Faces turned to look at their neighbors with questioning expressions. A quiet murmur could be heard. "What's going on?" They all wondered.

Jason reappeared in the doorway. He looked at the crowd of expectant faces turned up to him and wondered to himself who had put him in charge. He raised his staff over his head to signal for quiet, waiting for the crowd to settle down. "We're going to turn southeast for Indianapolis," he spoke in a loud, clear voice. "Then head for Tennessee and the Great Smoky Mountains. Billy and I have been studying the maps, and we think we have found the perfect place. It's a town located in the very heart of what used to be Smoky Mountain National Park. It's called Gatlinburg."

"Hey, I know that town," a boy yelled from the crowd. "Gatlinburg is right next to Dollywood."

"I don't know about that," Jason voiced loudly, "but I think it's the best place for us to go. I think, and Billy agrees, we need to get off the flat lands. It's here the wind blew everything away. We need to find an area where there was protection from the wind. Without the wind blowing everything down, we might have a chance at building something new, and the mountains might provide us with that."

There was a moment of silence from the upturned faces, then an outcry of approval.

"We'll spend the night here," Jason went on. "We have to wait for our outriders to return this evening, then we'll have them scout I-74 tomorrow morning. Let's get camp set up."

The clan broke apart into groups with new hope. They now had a name to associate with their destination . . . Gatlinburg.

*****

Jack had not left his room in three days. He sat brooding in a near stupor, neither eating nor sleeping. His beard grew shaggy, covering the face of a broken man. Red, bloodshot eyes gawked from the recesses of blackened sockets, and the odor of coppery blood, both his and Heather's, filled the small cubicle's stale air. His brain boiled with hatred, seething under the pain of desire and jealousy.

His fists clenched and unclenched, fueled with the loathing he felt for himself and General Harold Gilmore. Nothing like this had ever happened to Jack Mossmen. In his own mind, he had always exuded strength and confidence in others. He was a man not to be crossed.

In reality, Jack Mossmen was a conniving, self-important little man with few attributes other than his ability to convince others he was someone of importance. He had fooled Charlie tunnel into believing he was a strong headman by words alone and very little action. Leadership, however, can become the master; a physiological time bomb for someone without real strength of character.

Mossmen hated Gilmore from the day of the strike, when the big black man had humiliated him by having to slap him into action. He vowed at that moment to get even; to bring the big black man down to his level. He tried to undermine Gilmore's leadership, planting a word here and another there to induce New Landers to question edicts presented from the Hub. However, Heather was his crown jewel. Heather, the most beautiful woman in the tunnels, was HIS! The very thought of her being in any man's arms but his own was like a physical blow to the groin. The thought of her being held and kissed by Gilmore created an atomic explosion within his psyche. He would show everyone in the tunnels he was the better of any man, most certainly General Harold Gilmore.

Jack rose from the bed where he was sitting. He stretched, a long-protracted lengthening of his muscles, which had been dormant for so many hours. He glanced about the small room like a caged ferret, his movements jerky and uncoordinated. Mossmen walked into the bathroom and absently urinated, missing the toilet . . . the yellow fluid splashed on the floor behind the porcelain stool. His darting eyes focused on the shower curtain rod, which was nothing more than a steel bar embedded in the rock at either end. The yellow curtain had been ripped away during the fight, and the rod stood bare, but for ten dangling curtain hooks.

Jack grabbed the stainless steel rod and pulled. Lead anchors had been hammered into small holes drilled into the virgin rock. Screws, holding the rod's retaining cup, had been fastened into the anchors. With the force of Jack's pulling, the screws and anchors gave way and the rod broke free in his hand. He gave the rod a flip, causing the curtain hooks to fly throughout the bathroom, landing on the hard floor with metallic pings.

Gilmore awakened early, ate a breakfast of coffee and toast, and went to visit Heather. He smiled at the day nurse as he entered Med, and strode down the hall like he owned the place.

Heather had been transferred to a private room the day before, and though she still looked as if a bulldozer had made a track turn on her face, she felt much better. The room was bright, if not airy, and care had been given to provide the resident with a comforting atmosphere. The pale green wall at the foot of her hospital bed was plastered, a nicety rarely seen in New Land. Soft green provided the visual appearance said to soothe the mind and induce healing. She doubted the veracity of this, but enjoyed the homey atmosphere it provided; something totally different from the stark rock walls of her normal living quarters.

A tunnel viewer, mounted on the wall, ran movies and old syndicated sitcoms twenty-four hours a day, if one cared to watch. There was a personal tunnel-com sitting on the bed stand next to her, along with a pitcher of cool water. The medical staff had seen to her every wish. Still, she wanted out. She wanted to get well in Harold's bed, not cooped up in Med.

"How do you feel this morning?" Gilmore asked, as he walked through the door. Not waiting for an answer, he took her hand in his and leaned over to kiss her tenderly on the lips.

Heather pushed him away saying, "I haven't even had a chance to brush my teeth yet."

Gilmore smiled down on her. "I don't think that makes a bit of difference, do you?"

"No, I suppose not," she sighed, returning his smile. "I'm feeling much better, and frankly, I want to get out of here. I want to lie in your bed, not on this contraption."

"I'll talk to Doctor Blazedale about it. I think I might be able to persuade him to see it your way. We'll see." He dragged a chair from the corner and sat, his brow wrinkling in concentration.

What's wrong?" Heather asked. "You look worried."

"I am a little. Nobody has seen or heard from Jack since the incident. He's holed up in his cubicle and no amount of enticing from friends has coaxed him out. Do you think he might do something stupid?"

"What do you mean stupid? Will he kill himself or something like that?"

"Yes."

"No, he won't kill himself. It's my guess he's brooding. He'll get over it, I think," Heather answered with thoughtfulness and concern. "I'm more worried about what he might do to you. You've got to watch out for him. He can be vicious, as I have learned the hard way."

"I know," Gilmore said quietly, still dwelling over his inner turmoil. "I'll be careful."

The two talked for several minutes more before Gilmore stood and said, "I've got to go, but I'll be back at lunch. Make sure you save me some. This Med food is better than the dining areas. I'll have to find out who their cook is and steal him for my mess," he laughed.

They kissed, a long lingering kiss of expectation and love, and then with a wave, Gilmore stepped from the room. Heather blew him a final kiss as he passed from her view.

Taking his tunnel-com from a tunic pocket, Gilmore began walking toward the Hub. He pushed the code for Margaret Duke's office, hoping she would be at work early. The speaker gave an electronic click and Margaret's voice came on line.

"Good morning, this is Doctor Duke."

"Good morning, Margaret. Gilmore here. I wonder if you could drop by my office this morning. I've got something I would like to talk to you about."

"No problem, General. What time would you like me there?"

"Now, if that's possible."

"I'm on my way."

The small radio went dead in his hands as he entered the Hub, heading for the stairs and his office. He settled behind his chair and began sorting through the morning reports stacked neatly on his desk. A moment later, there was a soft knock on his door.

"Come."

"Good morning again," Margaret said, as she entered and took a seat.

"Thanks for coming. I really want to talk to you about this problem with Mossmen. Charlie is in an uproar, and the son of a bitch won't come out of his room."

Margaret smiled, though with little humor. "I told you he would end up being a problem, didn't I?"

"Yes, but I had no idea it would be this way. Heather and I . . . er, well, it just sort of happened."

"It usually does," Margaret countered. "Regardless, I think Heather . . . you said that was her name?

Gilmore nodded an affirmative.

"I think Heather," Margaret continued, "was a catalyst for the present crisis, but if it hadn't been her, then it would have been something else. The man was looking for any excuse to attack you, although, I did not realize he was as violent as it now appears. I'm sorry I couldn't warn you about that."

"It's not your fault. All my life I have made a concerted effort never to mess with another man's woman, wife, girlfriend, whatever." He shook his head, "I don't know. I just fell head over heels in love with this woman darn near the moment I first laid eyes on her. It's like I'm some damned schoolboy. I know in my entire life no woman has ever had the effect on me she does. Foolishness? Perhaps, but nonetheless it's true."

"Don't be so hard on yourself, General. You're human after all, and love pops up in the strangest places . . . even in New Land."

"Okay, enough about Heather and me. What do you suggest I do to reestablish a semblance of sanity in Charlie tunnel? I've got people who are refusing to work. Some think Mossmen is a madman who should be locked up in a side tunnel, and others think the whole thing is a big joke."

"Do nothing, nothing at all. If you make an issue of this affair, you're going to come out looking like an overwrought lover who wants to get rid of his competition. No, don't do anything. Conduct business as usual, just continue providing us with your good judgment. Charlie will soon see the folly of continuing to make a mountain out of a molehill. Think about it. Most men are sleeping with five or six different women. That's the way it was supposed to be. That's the way we explained it to those who accepted life underground. People realize you haven't tried to bed a woman in New Land until you met Heather. Don't try to make more of this situation than it already is."

Gilmore listened intently to Margaret's comments. He nodded agreement. "That's what I've been thinking as well. I guess I just needed to hear it from you. Thanks for the help."

Jack left his room, yanking the door open . . . the broken hinge giving way once more, this time, causing the door to crumple inside the room. He glanced briefly down Charlie tunnel's long passageway. There were people mingling with each other, walking to breakfast or going to work, all unaware of the potential nightmare standing in their midst with a steel pipe in his hand. He started forward, shoving aside a young woman with enough force to knock her to the floor.

"You damned creep," she yelled after him, not realizing she was cursing Charlie's headman.

Mossmen never heard her, as he moved rapidly toward the Hub. His steps were strong and sure. His pace never wavered, as he strode forward, swinging the steel pipe in an arc by his side. Hearing the shouts of the fallen woman, others turned to see the dirty, bearded face of their leader bearing down on them. They ducked into cubicles and recreation areas as he passed. No one wanted to be intercepted by Mossmen with a weapon in his hand.

Jack reached the outer ring of the Hub, paused momentarily as if in thought, and then, without further hesitation, entered the control room. Duty technicians moved quietly about their tasks, not noticing the interloper as he passed under the archway. Eyes burning crimson with hate, Mossmen started walking for the stairs at the far end of the room.

The Chief Engineer glanced up from his desk, where he was going over the details of the reactor's latest heating cycles. Seeing Mossmen bearing down on him with pipe in hand shook his normal business-like composure.

"Wait a minute, where do you think you're going?" the head engineer questioned, as he stood and moved around his desk.

Jack did not acknowledge the other man's presence. His pace never varied as he continued for the stairs.

Bald head beading in sweat, the Chief Engineer could feel fear channel its way up his spine. Fight or flight adrenaline began coursing through his body as he moved to intercept the demented looking man crossing the Hub. Other technicians stopped what they were doing and turned to see what was going on.

"I said, where do you think you're going?" the chief asked again, this time directly in front of Jack.

Mossmen hitched a step, just enough for his right leg to be planted slightly to the rear. Now in balance, he turned at the waist, gathering the pipe in both hands and swung with all the force he could muster.

The blow caught the Chief of Engineering just below his left ear. Death was almost instantaneous, as the young scientist's eyes bulged in surprise. The powerful impact threw his body against the reactor's control panel. A monitor exploded into flying shards of glass, as the engineer's right shoulder pushed through the front of the screen. The Chief's body fell heavily onto the controls in front of the shattered monitor, his elbow crashing through the delicate electronics. Warning signals began to light up the remaining control boards, and alarms began shrieking.

Gilmore and Margaret heard the second challenge yelled by the Chief of Engineering, the following commotion, and the sound of alarms. Neither had any idea what might be happening as they sprang to their feet. Though a big man, Gilmore could move rapidly and with agility. He pushed away from his desk, stood, and began moving for the door in what appeared to be a single motion.

Jack did not take time to assess the damage he'd done to the head engineer. Even as the man's body flew through the air, Jack plowed toward the staircase. Taking the steps two at a time, Mossmen was half way up when Gilmore's face appeared before him, as the General stepped from his door.

"Arrgghhh!! Jack screamed, as he charged up the remaining steps, pipe held high over his head like an ax.

Gilmore stepped to the side as the pipe arced through the air with an angry hissing sound. The pipe struck the metal hand railing surrounding the small platform. The tremendous force of the sudden contact vibrated through Mossmen's body, delaying his recovery for an instant. That infinitesimal moment of time was all Gilmore needed. He backed to the far side of the platform while unzipping his tunic to the waist. Jack spun to face his nemesis, raising the pipe once more. The forty-five was in Gilmore's hand. The click of the safety sounded like a thunderclap, and the first shot reverberated through the Hub like God's own wrath.

The bullet struck Mossmen in the right shoulder tearing flesh and bone, creating a hole the size of a tomato can. Jack fell backwards into the railing, which held him in a semi-standing position. He looked down at what was left of his right arm, screamed in agony, and tried to spring forward, weapon held in his left hand swinging roundhouse fashion . . . from the floor.

Gilmore fired three more rounds in rapid succession. All three bullets struck Jack in the chest. Gigantic holes opened where organs had once been. The weight of the lead slugs plucked him off the platform like a rag doll, throwing him ten feet over the hand railing. He fell to the rock floor beneath, dead long before he hit the ground. The body twitched once, twice, and a third time, then lay still, blood oozing into a puddle.

*****

Billy's dumper led the caravan of assorted vehicles across Illinois and Indiana using I- 74. The going was relatively easy. Little in the way of obstructions fouled the highway. The vast cornfields of these two states had been planted just weeks before the Devil's Face struck Africa. Though a few brave plants had poked tiny sprouts through the damp soil, there was not enough vegetative material present to be blown from the ground and into piles. ow Billy, along with Lorrie and Tom, sat napping in the cab of his dumper on the outskirts of Indianapolis. Flies hummed around the netting which covered his face. He had long since given up trying to brush the pesky little beasts away. There were just too many of them, particularly near a city the size of the capital of Indiana.

The evening before, Jason had instructed them to push to the northern outskirts of Indianapolis and find a reasonable campsite. The three arrived early in the afternoon at the remains of an interstate rest area. Winds had blown away roofs and picnic tables, yet there was not the total devastation they had become so accustomed to seeing throughout southern Wisconsin and Illinois. Apparently, the force of the gale had not been as strong here as it had further west.

Billy wondered why Jason had not wanted them to push further south, but kept his questions to himself. Jason was more withdrawn as the weeks went by, but Billy knew it had nothing to do with him . . . it was the burden of decision-making which took up so much of his friend's time. He was quite content to follow his directions and provide him with whatever support he might need.

A sharp poke in the ribs brought Billy out of his self-contained thoughts. "Huh? What is it?" he asked.

"Look there," Lorrie said excitedly. She was pointing over the dusty right fender of the dump truck. "Is that what I think it is?"

"If you think it's a herd of cows, then it is." Billy said. "How many do you think there are?"

"Oh, at least twenty or so, but they sure look sickly. You can see the bones popping through their skin from here. Do you think we might be able to get them corralled?" she said, punching Tom on the arm.

"Right," Tom said, wiping the sleep from his eyes. "We'll just leap on our horses and ride off yelling, 'Get along little dogies' and line them up in what's left of the pavilion over there." He was pointing at a large, roofless picnic area.

The scrawny bovines, wandering slowly toward the truck, were destined to become hamburger before The Devil's Face destroyed Indianapolis. The city was formerly home to some of the largest meat slaughtering and packing businesses in the world. When the winds came, these animals were standing in muddy pens, clustered rib cage to rib cage awaiting their turn to move through a chute which would lead to a brain shattering blow. Small earthquakes and high winds destroyed their prison, freeing them to walk what was left of the city. There had been thousands of them then; now this small group of twenty-seven was but one of several small herds roaming the countryside surrounding the city.

"Do you think we might kill one for supper tonight?" Tom asked tentatively. "We haven't had fresh meat in so long I can't remember what it tastes like."

Billy thought for a moment. He was wondering what Jason would do. For sure, he did not know how to butcher a cow, or anything else for that matter. "Tom, I just don't know. Do you know how to butcher a cow?"

"Are you kidding? I've hunted all my life, and butchering one of those puny things couldn't be much different than a deer. We could use the cross beams left on the pavilion to hang the carcass."

"The cows are hungry," Lorrie said. "I think we should find some food for them."

The three got out of the cab and walked in the direction of the moving animals. The small herd stopped to survey the approaching teenagers. Lorrie reached the timid creatures first, reaching out her hand to touch the nearest animal. The cow, either unafraid or too exhausted to run, allowed the hand to stroke its muzzle.

"Oh, Billy, we can't kill them. Look, they're so thin and tired. How could we hurt them? They have been through enough."

"Yeah, I suppose so," Billy answered, reaching out to scratch the cow's flank. "Still, it is meat, and we could use some fresh beef."

While the two approached the cows, Tom dashed back to the truck, retrieving Billy's shotgun. He now stood four or five feet in front of the animal Lorrie and Billy were stroking. "Move aside, you two, we're going to have hamburgers tonight."

Lorrie turned to see the gun in Tom's hand. "No way, Tom. I won't let you." She moved to cover the cow's head with her body.

"Jesus Christ, Lorrie, they're just cows. Now move."

"No, Tom. Let's wait for the rest. Then we'll decide," Billy said, firmly. "Besides, if we do kill a couple, it will be easier to hang them with more of us to work, if that's what you say we have got to do."

Tom lowered the gun. "Okay, but I can't understand you two. It's just a damned old cow, and not much of one at that." He turned and walked back up the rise to the truck.

Lorrie scrutinized her surroundings for the first time since they stopped. She'd become tranquilized by the sameness of the terrain over which they traveled the past few weeks; gentle rolling hills devoid of life, except for an occasional pack of wild dogs on the horizon, or a scurry of rats crossing a water-logged ditch. What she saw now was much the same, though she remembered during the last couple of days there were more buildings left standing. Standing there now, it was her hope to find a farm. On a farm, there might be a silo full of grain.

"Billy, look! There's a farmhouse with a barn." Lorrie was pointing with her healing arm, now out of its sling, to a dirty white frame structure a mile to the east. "Let's get the wheelers and see if there's any corn we could feed the animals."

Billy shook his head. "Lorrie, even if there was something there, how would we haul enough to feed them all?"

"I don't know, but we ought to try. Please!" She gazed into Billy's eyes with her best pleading look, the one that always worked so well. "Please?"

"Okay," was all he said, and began walking to the dump tuck to begin unloading their ATV's

Jason, along with the caravan, pulled alongside the dump truck on the downside of midafternoon. Without direction, they parked their vehicles in a protective ring; something the small tribe of youths had recently began as part of their evening camp down. The new arrivals spotted the cows immediately, causing an immediate debate: should they kill them for fresh meat or not.

Jason, on the other hand, was more concerned about Billy's empty truck and where his friends might have gone with their ATV's. He was relieved to see a dust cloud trailing the four wheelers as they approached from the east.

Billy roared into camp followed by Lorrie and Tom. On the back of their vehicles were fifty-pound sacks of corn, gathered from a partially blown away barn. The farm they visited did not provide much in the way of essentials for the caravan, but there had been corn.

Billy was smiling ear to ear as he shut down his motor. "We've got feed for the cows."

His announcement brought a flurry of questions from the crowd that rapidly formed around them. He explained what had happened and Lorrie's insistence on trying to feed them.

From among the group a voice yelled, "Feed them, hell. Let's kill them and have some meat for supper."

There were murmurs of agreement on the comment.

"No!" It was Jason who spoke firmly. "Lorrie is right. We should feed them, not kill them. We've got plenty of food. Nobody here is going hungry. Look at them." He pointed to the cows trying to dig grass from the dust. "They've been trying to survive just like us. Look at them, damn it! It's been a miserable existence for them."

"So what?" the same voice screamed. "Let's butcher a couple for supper tonight."

"I said NO! There is far too little left living to kill something we don't need. We'll feed them, and if we can find a way, we'll take a few with us to Gatlinburg. Think about it. How many animals have we seen since all this began? Except for an occasional cat, a pack of dogs, or some rats what have we seen? Nothing! That's what. If we are the last humans on earth, we shouldn't kill what is trying to survive with us. No, we won't kill them. Not even one."

"You're crazy if you think I'm going to pass up fresh beef." A path opened, as the leather jacketed, black-haired boy of sixteen strode forward to Jason. His face was covered with adolescent pimples and his brown eyes blazed in defiance. "I'll kill every damned one of them if I want to, and you can't stop me."

Jason glared back at the ruddy face of his adversary. The two boys stood eye to eye, each approaching five-foot, ten inches, their young bodies filled out to near manhood.

Jason shifted his staff to his left hand, the base firmly planted on the ground, "As long as you are with this group, you'll not kill those animals and that's final." He was surprised at himself, for he had never asserted his leadership with such authority. In essence, he was creating a showdown, which was totally out of character for him.

Billy moved to Jason's side, feeling the tension building. It was the first time anyone had challenged Jason's leadership. If there was to be trouble, he would be ready to support his friend. Others too began to shift closer to Jason. He had gathered them together, seen to their needs and given them hope.

"Jason's right," a small girlish voice broke the strained silence. "There's no reason to kill them and every reason to help them."

Heads nodded and voices agreed with the girl. The righteousness of Jason's words were having effect. There were too few living things left on earth to unnecessarily take the life of any creature, large or small.

Lorrie tried to break the uneasiness everyone felt. "Come on, somebody help me with this corn." She walked to her ATV and began struggling with the sack tied on the rear carrying rack.

Several others, boys and girls moved to help her. The confrontation ended as the crowd broke up. Jason nodded to his challenger, "It's over. We don't kill the cows." With that, he turned and walked slowly to his bus, very conscious of multiple eyes boring holes into his back.

The western sky was a vivid pink, mixed with soft purple as the sun began its evening passage below the horizon. A column of smoke far to the west created a cloud, which spread fan-like, high into dusky sky, and it reflected multi-colors that mirrored off billions of dust particles still floating over the world. Jason viewed the sight with emotion, thinking he was lucky to be alive and luckier still to have Mary Lynne beside him as they did their dishes. He reached out and pulled her to him.

"I love you; you know that?"

"Yes, you bloody oaf," she said, giving him a light peck on the lips. "Now, will you dry those dishes so we can go to bed?"

With a wicked glint in his eye, Jason released his love, and turned back to the task at hand. He thought her invitation warranted a very rapid drying of the remaining dishes.

The shot rang out sharp and clear in the fading light. It was a rifle cracking, different from the thunder of a twelve gauge. Heads pivoted and doors opened to see what was happening. Minds formed images of a pack of dogs attacking the camp, and that meant a fight. Jason dropped his dishtowel and ran for the door, yanking it open and dashed out.

Billy was by his side before he could reach the rear of the bus. "What is it?" he asked quietly.

"I don't know," Jason replied, as he scanned the camp. "There!" He pointed to the open field next to their campsite.

Billy looked in the direction Jason was pointing. Standing alone with a rifle at his shoulder was Jason's afternoon adversary, and at his feet, the cow which he and Lorrie had petted.

The entire camp followed Jason, as he ran to the field. The group watched in horror as the rifle swung to point at their leader's mid-section. Apprehension, so thick it could be cut with a knife, filled the cool, night air.

"I killed it, and I'm going to eat it whether you like it or not. There's nothing you can do to stop me."

"Yes, there is," Jason said, almost whispering, his voice like tempered steel. "You will leave this camp now, tonight. You will leave with what you came with, and nothing more. This afternoon we made an important decision about life, and realized we are Earth's Children. You are not welcome with us now or ever again. You *will* leave."

"Who's going to make me? You?"

"No," Jason replied, almost sadly. "Them." His staff made an arc, indicating the thirty or so guns pointed at the killer. "This group made a decision this afternoon. You intentionally violated that decision. You are no longer one of us. You will leave." Jason spoke quietly, but his muscles tensed for action. Suddenly his staff struck out like a cobra, knocking the rifle from the gloved hands of the assassin.

The boy's presence shrunk; all his bravado gone. "You can't make me leave. I don't even have my own ATV. I won't be able to survive alone."

"That's something you should have thought about before you shot the cow against *our* wishes. You are not one of us any longer."

The boy gave a weak attempt to beseech the group for understanding, but received none. His fate was sealed the moment he pulled the trigger. He moved away from the sad looking dead cow before him, and started up the hill toward the camp. The crowd moved slowly behind him. No one spoke as he gathered his belongings and placed them in a backpack. "Can I have my rifle back? At least let me have my weapon."

Jason's eyes held a mixture of sadness and resolve. He did not like what he was doing, but would not back down. "Yes. Take your rifle, then go as you are."

"You're trying to kill me. You know, the dogs will get me."

"So be it," Jason stated flatly. He turned and walked to the blazing campfire not far away. Over his shoulder he said, "I learned something about myself this afternoon." He was speaking to himself, as much as to those gathered around the fire with him. "We are alone on this earth. Yes, there may be others like us, and we may find more as we travel, but we are alone. We have been given another chance. A chance to grow, a chance to give Mother Earth back her dignity, a chance to see all living things are given their right to life as well. I won't say we won't kill, but when we do, it will be for a purpose, and if it is for food, we will thank the animal for dying for our sake. Killing for no reason will never be tolerated again, not if I can stop it. If we are all that's left," he turned to face his peers, who were listening intently, "then we are truly Earth's last children. Let us all try our best to be good to her. She let us live."

The inspiration in Jason's message captured the complete attention of those who surrounded him. His words burned into their brains with the heat of a branding iron.

Jason stepped out of the firelight, walking to face the cow's killer. "I wish you luck, and that's all."

The boy, shoulders slumping under the weight of his knapsack, slowly walked into the night. He did not look back, as the darkness swallowed him.

CHAPTER 15

New Happenings

Word of the tragedy, which had taken place in the Hub, spread rapidly throughout the tunnels. The tranquil mood that had prevailed for many weeks turned to fear and apprehension, as word was passed about the loss of their Chief Engineer and the shooting of Jack Mossmen. Most of the fifteen hundred knew of the altercation, which had taken place in Charlie tunnel the day before. They knew of Heather and of the headman's jealous outrage. The incident had been a topic for gossip, exciting news to arouse everyone's interest. Deaths in their ranks, however, became far more than mere idle talk.

The bodies, not yet removed, were covered with sheets, brought for that purpose by a Hub technician. Gilmore sat behind his desk once more, Margaret on his left side and Doctor Duke on his right. Before him, sitting rigid in the straight-backed chairs surrounding the conference table, sat the remaining heads of their respective tunnels and his primary staff. All wore worried looks on their faces, as they glanced nervously at one another.

"Where did the gun come from, General?" the petite head-woman of Delta asked, breaking the ice-like silence. "We were told there would be no weapons brought into New Land."

"I had them build me a small armory as a prerequisite to my taking command." He pointed to the door behind him. "It is there, and I am the only one who has a key to the door. Considering this morning's events, I feel I was completely justified in having them include an armory."

"Justified my ass. You're a pompous son of a bitch to believe that," spoke Alpha's headman. "If it hadn't been for your screwing *that* woman, none of this would have happened."

Gilmore was out of his chair before the man could finish. Benjamin Duke stood with him, holding the big man back.

"Easy, General, don't do anything rash," he whispered into Gilmore's ear. "Everybody is upset right now. Don't add fuel to the fire."

Gilmore sat back down. "I'll overlook that comment, but I don't want to hear such crap again at this table. I'll remind you it was clearly understood by each of you there were to be more women than men in New Land, and why. I have not done anything that was not expected of all of us. In fact, Heather was, and is, the only woman I've been with since our arrival. My seeing Heather may have triggered what happened this morning, but it would have happened regardless. Jack Mossmen was an unstable individual, one who had no business being part of the Few. The man somehow slipped through the massive testing required for each of us to be sitting here. I hold no one responsible, but I will not tolerate the blame being placed on my shoulders. Is that perfectly clear to everyone?"

Alpha's headman sat down, reprimanded, and in his heart he knew he deserved the words Gilmore had spoken. The table was quiet.

"Okay, we have some serious decisions to make right now. When Jack bashed our Chief Engineer, he fell into the reactor's control console. We have no way of monitoring the reactor's heating problem . . . at least until we can repair the damage. If we can't scrutinize what the reactor is doing on a minute-to-minute basis, we have little control of it. In other words, if the nuclear reactor started heating to critical temperatures, we would have no way of knowing it and what might happen. The reactor could blow before we could shut it down."

"What you're trying to tell us, General, is that we have got to shut the reactor down?"

"Yes, that's my feeling, but I wanted your input before we turn the switch."

"What are the ramifications of such a move?" asked Margaret.

Doctor Duke stood, his small frame imposing beyond its stature. "Of course we've been through this before several months ago, but I will review the facts. If the reactor is shut down for more than twenty-four hours, we can expect the temperature in the tunnels to drop rapidly to around twenty degrees Fahrenheit. We'll easily survive such a temperature drop . . . however, it will be very uncomfortable. The real issue concerning temperature in the tunnels will occur when the reactor is brought back on line. The rise in temperature will cause moisture content in the air, formed by rapid condensation, which will collect on the tunnel walls in quantity. Fortunately, General Gilmore had the water runoff ditches dug some time ago, and those will help."

"It doesn't sound as if we have insurmountable problems," a senior technician broke in.

"No. We can withstand the temperature variations, but remember we'll be without electricity and water as well. We can solve the water dilemma by filling every possible container available to us, but the electricity is another problem all together. I remind you again, electricity is our sole source of light, and though we can live in the dark for an extended period, our plants cannot. Should the vegetation in the Rim start dying, we would rapidly lose the oxygen it produces, and that, ladies and gentlemen, would be a serious problem."

"How long do the engineers believe the reactor will have to be off line?" Alpha's headman asked.

"We're not really sure," Gilmore answered. "It could take as little as a few hours, or as long as several weeks. Since we aren't sure what's causing the problem in the first place, it is difficult, if not impossible, to forecast a time frame."

"I, for one, don't like the idea of shutting down the reactor at all. It seems to me we have been doing just fine, even though we have had some heat variations. Why should we take the risk of losing everything when we might not be able to repair the reactor anyway?" It was the Chief of Supply who questioned the need for a shut down.

"A very good question," Gilmore stated. "I have no real argument for you, except we could lose everything with either decision we make today."

"I'm more concerned about the response of some of our inhabitants," Margaret interceded. "We have a high number of claustrophobia cases where none existed before our arrival. If we black out New Land for an extended period of time, we could see psychological reactions, which might be nearly uncontrollable. I tend to vote for the status quo and not shut down."

Doctor Duke stood and began pacing around the room in thought. "Look," he began. "I know shutting down the reactor is a monumental decision, but I can't agree with Margaret on this issue. Our very existence, absolutely and unequivocally, depends on the reactor. If something should happen, anything at all, that would keep us from repairing the reactor, we will lose everything we came here to accomplish in the first place. I say we must repair the reactor now and then we can forever put it behind us."

His pacing held the complete attention of the small assembly, and his words struck home. There was a general murmur of agreement.

"I'm going to put this question to a vote. I don't want it to be said I alone made the final decision," Gilmore declared. "Is that acceptable to all here?"

There was collective agreement from all present, indicated by head nods and verbal affirmations.

"Okay, all in favor of a reactor shut down, please raise your hand."

All but two hands went into the air. The two dissenters were the head woman from Alpha tunnel and Margaret.

"Let it be noted, we will shut down the reactor," Gilmore said with authority. "It is my wish that we plan the shutdown one day hence. In other words, I want to give each of you the opportunity to talk to your people and explain the situation in full. I will go on tunnel viewer tonight and give the particulars of our decision here, but I'm relying on you to make this crisis palatable. Is that understood?" He paused, ensuring he'd made his point. "Let's get cracking, then."

Phil was nervous from the very moment he had first heard about the shutdown. His claustrophobia had been getting progressively better. In fact, he had not had an attack for over a month, but the thought of living in the dark terrified him. Leaving work this afternoon, he had gone to see Margaret Duke before returning to his cubicle. She, with understanding, had refilled his tranquilizer prescription. Still, the thought of going into perpetual night in just a little over twelve hours was enough to cause him more than a little concern.

"You look like hell," Abby said. "Are you going to be all right?"

"I hope so. I've got to admit, what they're planning to do tomorrow morning isn't something I'm looking forward to with much pleasure."

Abby looked radiant in her third month of pregnancy. Though you could barely see any outward physical signs of a growing embryo, her complexion was even more robust than ever. She felt great, both mentally and physically. Her sessions with Margaret had done wonders for her attitude, and she was actually looking forward to having the child. Now, however, when everything seemed to be going fine, this damned reactor thing was upsetting Phil.

"Honey, it's going to be fine. Just think, if we were able to overcome the baby issue, we ought to be able to handle this. Don't you think? Besides, I'll be right here to help you through any complications you might have."

"Thanks! I know it's stupid, but sometimes it's like I don't have any control. I just can't get used to what is happening to me."

"I know the feeling," Abby laughed, thinking of her baby. She rose from the one chair they had in the corner of their cube, and moved to sit next to Phil on the bed. She reached up with her right hand and smoothed his dark hair off his forehead. "You were here for me when I needed you most, and I'll be here for you."

"I know I've said it a dozen times, darling, but I'm sorry I've caused you so much trouble. I never meant it to be like this," Heather apologized to Gilmore yet again.

"Stop worrying about it, Heather. If it hadn't been now, it would have been later. It wasn't your fault. If anyone must take blame, it's me. I told you that day at the Oasis I didn't mess with another man's woman. So quit blaming yourself." He took her hand across the table, squeezing it lightly. "I'm just glad you're all right. If anything should ever happen to you . . .." His expression softened, and the normal mantle of command disappeared from his features.

The two were having dinner in Gilmore's quarters, the meal served on a red tablecloth spread over a tiny table. Heather had been released from Med earlier that morning, and had arranged for their dinner together. Her face was healing rapidly . . . the swelling nearly dissipated. Gilmore was unable to join her until late in the afternoon. His schedule had been filled with meetings concerning the shutdown due to occur the next morning. It had been a long and exhausting day.

Heather spent her day arranging their quarters into a cozier atmosphere. She added a womanly touch by rearranging what little furniture her man had allowed himself. She was feeling at ease and at home by the time Gilmore finished with his duties.

"What time does it happen?" she asked.

"Oh seven hundred hours. It scares the hell out of me to think we'll be living with flashlights and chemical light sticks for an undetermined period of time, but I guess its got to be done. I just hope everyone stays calm."

"Why shouldn't they?" Heather asked, genuinely confused.

"Margaret thinks we might have problems with a few individuals who have developed claustrophobia. She has honest concerns. If we have a couple go nutso on us, it could be a real problem."

"Why not sedate them now, before the shutdown?" Heather asked.

"Umm, good question. I'll phone Margaret after dinner and see what she thinks about the idea."

Gilmore and Heather finished their meal, the candle Heather had placed on the center of the table burning to a stub. The looks exchanged between them, as they ate, foretold of what would be for dessert. As they moved slowly into the bedroom, leaving dirty plates behind, Gilmore forgot all about speaking to Margaret.

*****

"That was hard, Jason. For you to send the guy off at night, without a weapon, was very hard on you. But, my love, it was absolutely the right thing to do. I'm very proud of you." Mary Lynne gave Jason a bear hug.

"I hope so," Jason said seriously. "I truly hope so."

They, along with Billy and Lorrie, returned to their bus shortly after the confrontation over the cow. Jason had given instructions for the animal to be butchered and the meat divided among those who wanted it. There was a note of sadness throughout the camp after the young man disappeared into the gloom, but it was not so much for him as it was for the cow. Jason's words had struck a chord of humanity. In his short speech, he had brought them together as a family. They felt better about life in general, and what the future might bring. He had called them Earth's Children, keepers of the keys to life, and they believed him. It was the perfect answer to the question they each had asked themselves a hundred times . . . why me, why am I alive?

Twelve-volt lamps gave a warm glow to their rolling home. Through the efforts of Mary Lynne and Lorrie, the once sterile RV was now a home to the four of them. Jason and Mary Lynne claimed the aft bedroom as theirs, while Billy and Lorrie occupied the daybed at night. The arrangement had proved satisfactory to them all.

Jason was just beginning to explain his next step regarding the clan's movements when there was a pounding on the door.

"Mama Lynne, Mama Lynne! Come quick," a high pitched, excited voice screamed.

Billy opened the door. "What's the matter?"

A girl of thirteen, her tangled, dark hair hanging in her face, came into the light. "Jim Anderson cut his hand really bad," the girl breathed heavily, having run from the pavilion to their bus. "It's bleeding all over the place. Please, Mama Lynne, you've got to come."

Mary Lynne was already retrieving her doctoring kit from the closet and moving down the hall to the door. "I'm coming. Where is he?"

"Follow me," the frantic girl said, grabbing Mary Lynne's arm.

The two disappeared into the darkness with Jason yelling after them, "Do you need some help?"

"I'll let you know," Mary Lynne yelled back. "Probably not. See you soon."

Billy and Jason looked at each other in astonishment. "She's become quite the doctor," Billy said. "Is there anything she can't fix?"

"Mary Lynne has always been that way," Lorrie said, as she sidled up to Billy, wrapping her good arm around his waist. "Ever since she was a little girl."

"She isn't a little girl anymore," Jason joined the two. "I don't know what we would do without her. She's been studying her medical books every spare minute, and has learned more about healing than I would have ever expected. In fact, she wants to find a library in Indianapolis to look for books on homeopathic healing. She feels it won't be long before she'll run out of drugstore medications and will have to start relying on herbs and plants."

"Sounds good, but we haven't found many herbs and plants since we left. Just a lot of dust," Billy said.

"I know, and that's what I wanted to talk to you about tonight. Have you noticed damage to towns and farms has not been as extensive as what we saw further north? In fact, I've even seen a few green patches growing on top of hills and knolls."

"You've got better eyes than me," Billy laughed, "but I'll take your word for it."

"Well, it's really Mary Lynne who has been pointing it out to me. She's been scouting for such things. Anyway, I think the closer we get to the mountains the more vegetation we are likely to see. First of all, there will be areas that were protected from the winds, and those same areas probably won't have as much dust gathered on them either. If I'm right, we'll start seeing grass again."

"That would be wonderful," Lorrie piped up, joining the conversation. "I'm getting awfully tired of brown dust."

"Aren't we all?" Jason continued. "What I want you to do," he said, turning to Billy once more, "is to select enough of our scouts for a run for Gatlinburg. The remainder of us will follow you at a slower pace. I want to make sure the Smokeys are the place we want to plant ourselves for the winter. If it's the same in Gatlinburg as it is here, then I think we should head further south."

"I see what you mean," Billy said. "I've noticed it has been cooler during the day than it was. Do you think winter is on its way?"

"I'm not sure, but I'd guess it is late in September, and we don't have much time before the snow flies. I want to be set up with proper shelter and enough supplies to last through what could be a very long cold spell. If you find out Gatlinburg is okay, we can raid Knoxville for everything we need. It's just a day's run from our final destination. What do you think?"

"I think it's a damn good plan," Billy smiled. "I know just the crew I'll take with me. Bob and his bunch can act as scouts ahead of my dumper. It will take me a couple of hours to get it arranged in the morning though."

"No sweat," Jason said. I'll plan to move the main body closer to Indianapolis tomorrow after you leave. We'll set up a camp somewhere on the bypass and send riders into the city to re-supply with what we need. I know Mary Lynne will want to go."

The door opened and Mary Lynne stepped in, followed by the same girl who had banged on the door earlier. "He'll be fine, Jenny. Just let me know if it looks like any infection might set in, okay?"

"Yes," the girl started to leave, then as an afterthought turned to face the group inside. "Thank you, Mama Lynne, you're pretty wonderful. I could never do what you just did. Thanks."

"You're welcome. Now run on home, ya hear?"

"Geez, what did you do?" Jason asked.

"Nothing really. I just cleaned him up and stitched the cut together."

"How many stitches?"

"Fourteen."

"Fourteen!" Jason exclaimed. "What did he do, cut his hand off?"

"No, you great bloody oaf," Mary Lynne smiled. "But he did have a nasty gash. His knife slipped while he was hacking at that damned cow."

As Mary Lynne spoke, a howl from the depths of hell arose not far from their camp. A pack of dogs had scented the freshly killed animal, its blood coloring the air with tantalizing odors.

"I hope he makes it," Lorrie said flatly, thinking about a lonely figure, knapsack on his back, huddled against the dangers of the night.

*****

New Land, its cold rock walls ceasing their continuous dripping, was heavy with blackness. Eerie shadows danced on cubicle and tunnel walls, as men and women moved slowly through the morning holding chemical light sticks, their greenish-yellow glow contributing even more to the macabre atmosphere. Life in the caves below the Rocky Mountains had all but come to a standstill. It was the second day since the reactor had been taken off line. Forty-eight hours of total, absolute, and complete darkness. New Landers moved as if blind, their eyes held wide searching for the tiniest source of light. Without their hand held Chem-lites, they were encased in darkness . . . black on black.

Phil lay on his bed, a near broken man, sweating profusely. From the moment the electricity winked off line, he had become more and more vegetative and less rational. He hated himself for his lack of resistance to something others seemed to be able to cope with adequately. Fear coursed through him. Even the drugs Margaret had provided did little to help alleviate his difficulty. His mind was being stretched beyond its tolerance. Phil needed an escape.

Abby entered the room, returning from a breakfast of dried fruit and cereal. "Honey, how are you doing?" she asked. "Don't you want something to eat?" She moved to the bed and sat next to him.

"No. I couldn't eat anything right now. God, Abby, this is driving me nuts. I just don't know what I'm going to do."

"We'll get through it together," she consoled, gathering the man in her arms and gently rocking him back and forth.

The bed sighed softly, as the two swayed, and the darkness loomed about them. Abby knew in her heart her man was close to his breaking point, and if he did go over the edge, she wondered what might happen.

"If it gets too bad, you could make it to the outside, couldn't you?"

"Don't think I haven't thought of doing just that. The monitoring system is still down; in addition, I doubt they've kept that particular system on line with only emergency power available to the Hub.

If you decide to go, I will support you in your decision, but I won't be going with you. I've just recently come to terms with myself about having our baby down here, and I don't think I would want to chance what you might find on the surface."

"I understand," Phil stated sadly. "But if I found it was okay up there, then I would come back for you and everyone else."

"I know you would."

Gilmore and Doctor Duke stood pensively at the entrance to the room housing the reactor. Here, surrounded by blackness, was a refuge bathed in light. Emergency generators hummed loudly, reverberating their harsh noise down the surrounding tunnels. Several men and women were engaged in the delicate work of dismantling the reactor's cooling system, while others huddled close, talking quietly.

"I hate to think how much oxygen those generators are using," Doctor Duke spoke to Gilmore. "I know they require the light to work, but every minute those damned things run is one less for us."

"I realize you're concerned, but it appears they are moving right along with their work," Gilmore said. "The foreman of this work crew told me earlier they think it will only be a couple of more days before they will have the problem repaired. It has something to do with the triple walled cooling pipe and a heat exchanger. I'm no expert on this sort of thing, but they sounded encouraging."

"Well, if they can have everything back on line in three or four days, we should be fine. We wouldn't begin feeling the effects of oxygen loss for seven or eight days and the plants won't begin to die by then. At least, I don't think they will."

"Has Margaret said anything to you about how our people are handling the darkness and cold?"

"Yes, we discussed it this morning. She thinks, overall, everyone is doing fine. There are a few, like this Phil Fagan fellow, who are holed up in their cubes and sweating it out, but he's an exception."

"Fagan? The name sounds familiar."

"It should. He's the father of New Land's first child-to-be."

"I remember. I didn't realize he was having a problem, but now that you mention it, I do recall it was through his visit to your wife that we found out about the child."

"That's right."

A woman dressed in smudged overalls, holding a clipboard in her hands, interrupted their conversation. "Excuse me, General, but it looks like we have located the source of the original problem. It was as we had expected. The earthquakes pinched a cooling pipe. The constricted pipe, in turn, caused the heat exchanger's computer controller to compensate for what it interpreted as the reactor's core operating below normal temperature. Thus, the computer's solution was to constrict the flow of coolant to the reactor."

"If you say so," Gilmore said. "I don't have a clue what you're talking about, but I'll take your word for it. More importantly, are we still on schedule as far as the repairs go?"

"Oh, yes. In fact, we might be able to speed things up. The main problem is repairing the multi-walled piping. Once that's accomplished it won't take long to be fully operational."

"That's the best news I've heard in weeks," Gilmore smiled.

By afternoon, Phil was not only sweating, though his cubicle was an uncomfortable thirty-five degrees, he was crying as well. Abby had left a few minutes earlier to talk to Margaret. She hoped to persuade the doctor to give her something to knock Phil out completely. His condition had continued to deteriorate throughout the day, causing her to become more anguished over his situation with each passing hour.

"I'm leaving," Phil said aloud, the dark empty room echoing his voice.

With the decision made, Phil felt better, his mind switching channels from fear to resolve. He gathered his issued Chem-lites and two flashlights, throwing them in the pillowcase that he ripped from his damp pillow. He struggled into a warm jacket, fashioned a sweatband from a hand towel, and strode for the door.

Within fifteen minutes, he was passing through Charlie's dining area, grabbing dried fruit, water, and two loaves of bread from the galley. The food found its way into the sack with the lights.

Leaving the kitchen, he made for the rim, using a flashlight to find his way. At the rim, he made a right turn and began struggling through the vegetation in the dark, slashing out at branches and leaves that hindered his progress. Reaching the Oasis, he barely noticed its existence, as the sandy beach crunched under his feet.

Phil's mind was far from the enjoyments the Oasis had brought to so many in the past weeks. His destination, his very sanity, lay ahead. The shaft leading to the elevator was his goal, and upon reaching its confines, he felt safe for the first time since the electricity had been shut down. Phil started up the first set of stairs, which in his mind led to freedom and away from the demon eating his guts from the inside out. Forty-five minutes had passed since he had left his room.

*****

Billy handpicked his scouts from what he knew of their individual capabilities, as well as the vehicles they drove. They would take one RV, a Chevy van camper, and the dumper to haul supplies and provide shelter. Other than that, they took only three and four wheelers, transportation they could use to make detours and side trips while exploring the land ahead.

"Good luck," Jason said, shaking Billy's hand. "I'm counting on you."

"I know. Don't worry, I'll find us the right place. Never you fear," Billy smiled good-naturedly. "Have I ever let you down, Bro?"

"Never, and that's the truth," Jason gave his friend a hug. "Now don't forget, I'll expect a rider the day after tomorrow. You should be in Knoxville by then. I really want to know in what shape we can expect to find the city when we arrive. If Gatlinburg is okay, we'll want to strip Knoxville of everything we can carry."

"Keep your chin up, Jason. It's going to all work out. You'll see!" Billy replied over his shoulder, as he made for his truck.

Within minutes, the small band disappeared over the horizon, trailing a cloud of dust and exhaust. Jason, Mary Lynne, and most of the camp watched them leave, each with expectation welling in their hearts. They were on their last leg to a new home.

Not long after Billy and his crew departed, Jason started the caravan moving for the bypass circling Indianapolis. The small herd of cows, which had remained overnight, now lowed softly, as if to say goodbye to their protectors. The bovines were not the only eyes watching the dust rise from the departure. A lone figure stood a mile behind, cursing each and every member of Jason's party.

"Someday I'll find you again, Jason, and when I do, you're a dead man," screamed the angry teenager, his upraised fist a silhouette against the horizon. "You can count on it, you son of a bitch." He gave one final look to the south, adjusted the shoulder straps to his backpack, and moved across a windswept, dust-covered cornfield.

It was high noon, when Jason signaled for a stop, using the CB to alert the vehicles behind his bus. RVs pulled along either side and began forming a defensive circle of iron and aluminum. The morning's outriders returned shortly after the caravan's engines were shut down for the day. They reported to Jason that there was a water tower approximately three miles further around the bypass. The tower not only still stood, but also appeared to be full of water.

"I think someone must have shut the master valve off or something," said a jacketed outrider.

Jason tightened his own coat around his neck. The wind was biting cold this day, and it had rained most of the morning, adding to everyone's discomfort. "That's great news. We'll plan to stop long enough tomorrow to fill everyone's tanks. You did a good job; thanks for the information."

The boy smiled, and walked back to his companions, just as Mary Lynne joined Jason. She slipped her hand into his, and they stood quietly for a moment, staring at the northern sky. Clouds were rolling angrily over the entire horizon, their black bases bulging with rain.

"I hope it pours cats and dogs tonight," Mary Lynne observed. "It might knock the dust down and clear the air for a few days."

"More importantly, it might help grass poke above this stuff," Jason replied, kicking at the dust at his feet. "I would feel a whole lot better if we had seen more green show up this summer. I think it's getting into fall and it worries me there hasn't been more recovery around here. I hope Billy will have better news."

"You worry too bloody much. Haven't you noticed that there hasn't been as much dust in the air lately. Things are going to be fine, you'll see. Now, come on, let's get our four wheelers and drive into the city proper. I still want to find some books on herbs and plants with healing qualities."

Indianapolis was much like every city they had visited while traveling south. The majority of downtown had burned uncontrollably, leaving grotesque sculptures of charred wood and brick reaching for the sky. It was obvious; the city had been affected only by wind, not a quake. Tall buildings and skyscrapers were broken like twigs halfway up their steel girded frames, the top hanging limply to the north. Streets were littered with hundreds of skeletal bodies, now decomposed or eaten by tens of thousand of well-fed rats, which scurried everywhere Jason and Mary Lynne wandered. The two walked and rode street after street searching for a library to no avail. Mary Lynne was becoming discouraged and Jason wanted to return to the camp.

"We should start back now," Jason said. "I don't want to get caught in the city and have to find our way back after dark."

"Okay, you're right. Let's check one more block then head back."

Jason looked around nervously, his shotgun slung over his shoulder and the staff upright in its sheath. "One more block and that's all."

Not two minutes later, Mary Lynne gave a hoot of pure joy. "Jason, there's a book store, and from all appearances, it was a huge one. Come on, help me look."

Thirty minutes later, in a torrential downpour, the two were on their wheelers heading rapidly out of the city. Mary Lynne's face was sparkling with pleasure, due entirely to the twelve books tucked safely in her saddlebags. These books would provide her with the knowledge she needed to help the clan long after there were no more drugstores and hospitals to raid. They were worth their weight in gold, and she was protecting them from the rain, as if they were her children.

Soaked to the skin and shivering with cold, the two put the four wheelers back on the trailer behind the bus. Mary Lynne carefully brought the precious books inside, checking each one for dampness. As they dried off and changed clothes, the rain continued to pour like a river waterfall. As night fully covered the land with its blanket of darkness, they ate a light dinner while the remainder of the camp found shelter inside their own vehicles. Little activity could be seen, except for an occasional shadow crossing a dimly lit window . . . the downpour creating small rivulets along the roadside, which, in turn, swept away several months of ash and dust in swirling torrents.

By midnight, the road was awash, the water rising from drainage ditches to swirl around RV tires. Jason awoke fearful for Billy and his scouts, hoping they had sought refuge before the storm hit. As morning approached, the rain began to taper off to a drizzle, then stopped altogether. Shortly after six a.m. the clouds rolled away to the northeast and for the first time since Jason dug his way out from under the ruins of his home in Anoka, the sky was blue.

Jason, Mary Lynne, and the entire clan stood in the puddles that covered the highway and gazed in awe at the rising sun. The group felt as if they had been born again, released from the darkness of the womb to physically *feel* light untainted by dust. Jason held Mary Lynne close, feeling the sun actually warm her body, though it was still early morning. The welcome sunbeams felt tangible, touching their skin with tendrils of heat that pulsated like an electric shock. Teenagers throughout the small camp, hugged each other in an expression of pure joy. Not one could verbally characterize the emotion rushing through them, as blue sky and a gorgeous golden globe looked down on them protectively. Earth, their world, was coming back to life, and they were her children.

CHAPTER 16

Blue Skies

The storm which swept the Midwest plains originated over the southern Pacific Ocean. It hit the western face of the Rocky Mountains, and there it began to release the vast quantities of stored water with which it had engorged itself as it passed over warm waters. Rain fell, clearing dust from the air, cleansing the earth of the ash which had fallen steadily since the strike.

Phil could not hear the rain nor had he seen the sky since May, and right now, what went on above him had little meaning. He struggled up stair and incline, hour after hour, his muscles straining with exertion. He had stopped only to munch on fruit and crackers since his arrival at the elevator shaft. Claustrophobia, like a living creature, continually clawed at his innards, the very feeling fueling his resolve to continue lurching upward through the darkness broken only by his tiny Chem-lite. He had no idea of the time or that he'd been climbing for over forty-eight hours, nor did he know that, in the darkness far below, in the tunnels, searchers prodded every nook and cranny for him. Phil had not the slightest notion it would be less than twenty-four hours when the reactor would be brought back on line and the electricity restored. Phil Fagan had one goal and one alone, to reach the great doors, which represented his escape to the outside.

Breathlessly, Phil climbed yet another incline. When he had first started his sojourn upward, he began counting the number of short stairwells he encountered, but gave up and lost track at one hundred and fifty-seven.

"It doesn't matter anyway how many steps it will take to get to the top," he thought aloud, speaking softly through his clenched teeth. "I will make it, I've got to."

It was midday when Phil took his final step into a large dust covered cavern, which was the entrance to New Land. The huge chamber had been used to store vast amounts of goods prior to being moved to the tunnels far below. He ran to the entrance.

He leaned against the massive doors, a fanatical grin spreading across the width of his hollowed cheeks, feeling the sun, heat-soaked metal against his skin. He had made it; he was at the top. Only the thickness of the door itself separated him from the freedom of open spaces, and open space was something he desperately craved. He began searching the face of the door for a handle, lever, or any device that might open the huge structure.

Nothing marred the smooth surface except for what was obviously the joining ridge between two matching doors. He could not remember how the doors opened. Had they opened inward or to the outside? Flashlight in hand, he began sweeping it over the carved rock walls. He let out a sigh of relief, when, to his left, he saw what appeared to be a control station of some sort. He ran to the panel, touching it lovingly, then, with a sinking heart he remembered the electricity was off here, as well as below.

There's got to be a manual backup system, he thought.

It took him another fifteen minutes to locate the crank. It was recessed into the rock wall on the right-hand side of the door. He unfolded the four-foot handle. Its length seemed excessive, but needed the added extension to provide the leverage necessary to move the massive gateway. Phil began cranking.

The gearing mechanism was such that one person could easily rotate the handle, but it required several complete revolutions to move the doors a fraction of an inch. Phil, at first, thought it was not going to work, for even with all the straining effort he used to crank the handle, the massive steel doors would not move. Finally, he perceived, with a feeling of elation, that the doors were indeed moving, though so slowly it was difficult to detect. Suddenly, a crack of light forced its way through the tiny fracture dividing the doors. Phil's heart jumped into his throat. He began spinning the handle with the determination of a man being chased by a demon. Several minutes passed, with only the sound of gears grinding and Phil's heart pounding in his chest.

The opening allowed a rush of sweet, rain freshened air into the cavern. Phil took a long deep breath, filling his lungs to the bursting point. Letting the air from his ballooned lungs out slowly, he savored its taste as if it were a steak freshly cooked on a grill. All thoughts of fear, claustrophobia, and life in New Land vanished as if they had never been. He could see a blue sky, appearing like magic, as he cranked even harder, and then the opening was just large enough. He canted his body sideways and squeezed through. The sudden bright sunlight blurred his vision, but he gawked in wonder at the sights filling his view.

A well-used gravel road wove sinuously toward the eastern horizon. Thousands of trees lay dead, cluttering the slopes where once a great forest of hundred-year-old spruces had bordered the road, its canopy covering the surrounding mountainside. Nature had, however, left much of her greenery intact. There were trees still standing, having survived the tremendous quake the Devil's Face had wrought. The ground, though mostly barren, did have patches of green where hardy grasses attempted a comeback. The Earth was livable. It was not freezing, as Doctor Duke had so ominously predicted; though, it was cool . . . jacket cold. Phil began to dance about, first on one foot, then the other. His joy was overpowering. Ecstasy filled his entire being. It bubbled. It sang. The happiness was a living entity coursing through him.

As the minutes passed, Phil began to glide back down to a level plain of existence. He sat, his back against the opened doors, and ate the remaining fruit from inside his pillowcase. Then gathering his few belongings, he set off down the winding road to explore his wonderful New World.

The great doors stood open, air rushing like a tide into the tunnel beyond. Sweet mountain air raced down the steps that Phil had so recently climbed, carrying on its shoulders the euphoria of expectation and life.

Far below, New Land was spending yet another day engulfed in total darkness. However, the news was being passed by word of mouth that they would soon be able to resume their normal lives. The electricity would be back on tomorrow. There was a feeling of general relief, knowing the reactor would soon be meeting their needs once more.

Abby sat with Margaret in the small psychologist's office. Both women wore concerned expressions, though for far different reasons. Abby knew where Phil was headed, though, she had refused to tell anyone until now. Margaret pressed her for information, and she had finally relented to the pressure. She apologized several times for staying silent and having caused so many people the trouble of searching for her lover, but she quietly hoped he'd made it to the top.

"How long ago did he leave?" Margaret asked sternly.

"I think he left while I visited you for more medication. That was two days ago."

"You know I have to inform General Gilmore and others, don't you?"

"Yes. I am sorry, but I just couldn't tell you then. He was so upset, so out of it. I sincerely thought he would give it a try and come back. Do you think he could have made it all the way?"

"I don't know, but thanks for finally telling me the truth. Now, if you'll excuse me, I've got to let others know. If for no other reason than to stop the search for him."

Margaret was upset, no, downright mad about this latest development. The thought of someone trying to get outside without permission, endangering the entire population of New Land, infuriated her. She walked with a determined pace, head down, mumbling to herself. She was on her way to the Hub, having sent a messenger to find her husband, and another to warn Gilmore she was on her way with disturbing news. It had taken her twenty minutes to assure Abby that Phil would not be harmed or chastised when he returned. Margaret would see to this as his doctor, but she was still steaming about the entire situation.

Benjamin was already seated when Margaret burst through Gilmore's office door. There were several Chem-lites lying or hanging in strategic places, which illuminated the room sufficiently to see both the worried faces before her.

"Your messenger sounded as if the world had come to a sudden end," Gilmore said with no hint of humor.

"In a way it has," a slightly breathless Margaret answered, taking a seat next to her husband. "You're not going to like what I have to tell you, and," she turned to Benjamin, "darling, you're going to like it even less."

Doctor Duke's face was grim, the furrows on his forehead etching deeper at his wife's words. He knew if she was this concerned, something terrible had happened.

"Phil Fagan won't be found in New Land. He's made a run for the surface."

"You've got to be kidding, Margaret. There isn't any way he could do that. The only way up is the elevator, and it won't run without electricity," Gilmore exploded, sitting forward in his chair.

"Not so," Doctor Duke said flatly. "Remember the stairs."

"My God, you're right. You honestly think he would try climbing to the top?" Gilmore looked astounded.

"That's exactly what he is doing. In fact, he has been thinking about it for weeks. It seems our very own Jack Mossmen isn't completely dead yet. Jack was the one who gave him the idea in the first place. He even did the initial exploring of the entrance shaft to the elevator. Jack was the one who told Phil about the steps." Margaret stopped to catch her breath.

The three sat in silence for several moments, locked in their own thoughts.

"We have to assume the worst case . . . that he'll make it to the top and find the hand crank," Gilmore said at last. "If he is able to open the doors, what then?"

"I don't know. I just don't know," Doctor Duke mumbled softly. "We can pray he'll close them again once he establishes it isn't livable outside. My only hope is he'll close them before he freezes to death. If the sun is completely obscured, as we think it must be, then it's going to be damned cold up there."

"Okay, here is what we'll do. Tomorrow the reactor will be up and running. Once we have the electrical load on line, I'll send a detachment up the elevator to check on the doors and Fagan. I don't see there's much else we can do at this time."

"I agree," Margaret responded. "I blame myself for this, at least to some degree. I should have seen it coming."

"No one else is blaming you, and for God's sake, don't go blaming yourself," Gilmore said, closing the meeting.

*****

Jason's caravan of RVs filled the parking lot of an interstate rest area, south of Scottsburg, Indiana, and not far to the north of Louisville. It was mid-afternoon on a beautiful clear day . . . the third since the rain. The group did not move the day after the deluge simply because the roads were flooded beyond what Jason considered prudent for safe travel. No one complained about the delay; it was too wonderful just being able to soak up rays from the sun. Shorts, along with an occasional bathing suit were appropriated from department stores in Indianapolis. Young people, who had matured way beyond their chronological age, now reverted to being teenagers and crazy. It was absurd, for instance, for a group of girls to lie on the rooftop of a bus to sunbathe, when the temperature still hovered in the high fifties. But it made little difference . . . the sun was out and they were wearing summer clothing for the first time since the strike.

The next two days were spent on the road, but they were not able to make many miles southward. Drainage ditches, still filled to capacity, and areas of low lands kept the road dangerously wet. The group moved slowly, stopping frequently to send scouts ahead to determine road conditions. Though they were not putting many miles behind them, Jason was not overly upset. He did not want to rush headlong toward Knoxville, at least, not until he heard from Billy. As they moved around Indianapolis, utilizing bypass 465 and headed south on I-65, Billy's efforts were evident. Semis and cars had been systematically pushed off the road, as had other less weighty obstructions.

Though the sun lifted the spirits of everyone, it was the patches of green that captured Jason's heart and thoughts. The further south they traveled, the more indications of renewed plant life appeared along their route. If renewed greenery was not exciting enough, there were further manifestations of animal life as well. The caravan had passed a small herd of horses, if one could consider three a herd, the day before. The sad animals, their ribs protruding through skin like knobby branches of coral, had been scuffing the damp soil in search of grass. The horses had survived, along with a few cows and pigs, which had been spotted this very morning. These few creatures had endured the winds, quakes, and devastation induced by the Devil's Face and continued to endure; despite the dogs, lack of forage, and swarms of insects. Nature was persevering through it all, and Jason saw his group as a cog in this spinning wheel of continued existence.

By late afternoon, Jason sat with Mary Lynne at a picnic table, his eyes searching to the south. The two were quiet, not wishing to intrude upon the thoughts of the other, but they touched . . . that was communication enough.

Jason stood and cocked his head. "Do you hear something?"

"Yes! It sounds like an ATV heading this way."

"I hope so. I've been worried about Billy and the rest of his group. I thought we'd have heard something from him no later than yesterday," Jason said.

"Me too, but it sounds like we'll get our wish now," Mary Lynne smiled, pointing at a streak of yellow heading their way.

The four-wheeler slowed as it entered the turn off to the rest area, and then stopped at the southernmost RV. There was a brief exchange of words between the driver of the ATV and a person not in Jason's sight. In a moment the engine revved on the four-wheeler, gears meshed, and it came roaring their way, stopping in front of them.

"I've got a note for you from Billy," the driver said, digging in his jacket pocket. "We were east of Knoxville yesterday when I left and everything was okay. Did it rain as hard here as it did for us?"

Jason smiled at the question. "If it came down in buckets on you, then it did. We've been looking for you. Thanks." He took the folded sheets of paper from the boy.

"Is my sister, Lorrie, all right?" Mary Lynne asked.

"She's fine. In fact, she made Billy take her cast off. He said he hoped it would be okay with Mama Lynne."

Mary Lynne smiled, "Yeah, I suppose it is . . . thanks."

Jason unfolded the note and began reading.

Jason,

We were making good time until the rain hit. What a mess after that! Had to lay up a day just to let the flooding go down. I've sent scouts south of Knoxville, but haven't heard from them yet. Knoxville looks like the best city we have seen so far. I think you were right - the mountains blocked a lot of the wind, but there were still a bunch of trees to move, and of course, a billion cars and trucks.

As I write this, I'm camped at the intersection of I-40 and State 66. We have just begun to hit the real mountains and we may have problems we hadn't thought about . . . landslides. Or should I say, rock-slides. There has been a major rock-slide practically every place that the highway was cut into the side of a mountain. Plus, there are hundreds of trees down everywhere. That's the bad news. The good news is there are trees, though they are sure ragged looking. We can see the tops of several mountains from our camp, and they appear to be wiped clean of anything green, but down the slopes and in the valleys, there are real honest to goodness trees. However, because we have so many trees down, we need more help here. Please send chain saws and men, as many as you can spare.

Bob took two of the guys down State 66 and they just now returned. Seems we can't make it to Gatlinburg that way, at least not without chopping our way through rock and wood. So, tomorrow I'll try 321 and 32 (check your map). They are small roads, but appear to wind up the mountains.

Cross your fingers and keep your chin up, brother. It looks as if we are almost home. I'll send another runner back tomorrow evening and let you know what we find.

Billy

"Well, don't keep me in the dark you bloody oaf, what does he say?" Mary Lynne asked excitedly.

Jason gave her the note to read. To the messenger he said, "I'll have to ask you to start back tomorrow morning. I'm sorry, but you'll have five or six more riders with you and a couple of trailers full of equipment Billy asked for. Will that be okay with you?"

"Sure! I was expecting I would have to lead the work crew back. I'll get some grub and a good night's sleep and be off before the sun rises."

"Thanks, I appreciate it. Do you have anyone in mind, as far as who might return with you?"

The young rider laughed, "Yeah, and Billy gave me a list as well. I think he's picked every guy over six feet with muscles to match Schwarzenegger. He wants brawn, not brains for this project. At least that's what he told me."

Jason and Mary Lynne both began to laugh. "That sounds just like Billy," Jason said when he caught his breath. "Okay, pick who you need, but let me know who you plan to take. I plan to raid Knoxville in a couple of days so I need to keep workers here as well."

"You got it," the boy said, as he wheeled the ATV around and motored off.

"What do you think?" Jason asked of Mary Lynne.

"Sounds pretty good to me. Billy seems to be in his usual high spirits."

"God, I hope he can find us a place. It's getting on toward winter and we've got to find a spot to settle."

"I know, but bloody well worrying about it isn't going to change things. Besides, I've got faith in you." Mary Lynne moved to Jason's side and hugged him close, letting her lips brush lightly across his.

Night had fallen over the camp an hour earlier, its blanket of blackness covering the land. Mary Lynne stood before the Arrow's propane stove, warming a can of vegetable soup. Jason sat at the dining table behind the overstuffed driver's seat, bent over a Kentucky/Tennessee road map. He pinpointed Billy's location, and found he was only twenty or so miles from Gatlinburg.

"We're almost home," Jason exclaimed, rising from his chair and moving toward Mary Lynne. His form cast a shadow on the far wall, created by the overhead lamp. He had taken a single step in her direction when the zing of a high-powered rifle slug whizzed behind his head, missing him by inches. The loud, cracking report of the rifle followed instantaneously.

Jason dove at Mary Lynne, knocking her from her feet and onto the hard kitchen floor. Jason landed on top of her, breaking the weight of his fall with extended arms. Two shots followed in rapid succession, each punching holes through either side of the RV. Then silence.

The two lay there for several minutes, each second stretching into an hour. Then Jason rolled off Mary Lynne, crawling to the door. He carefully reached up for the doorknob and twisted it slowly. The door swung open and the self-retracting step thudded into the down position. Jason pulled Mary Lynne across the floor and out of the bus. Once clear of the interior, with its suddenly dangerous illumination, the two crawled behind the dual rear wheel of the big vehicle.

"I'll always be with you, Jason. Never forget that I'm out here somewhere, watching," a disembodied voice yelled from the depths of blackness, followed by a single rifle shot into the air.

It was suddenly still, as if a telephone line had been cut during the middle of a conversation. Minutes passed before doors opened to other RVs.

"It's him," Mary Lynne whispered. "The son-of-a-bitch you told to leave. I recognize his voice."

"Me too," Jason answered. "I guess I have a real enemy. One who isn't going to give up lightly."

"What are we going to do?"

"Nothing. I'm not going to let him dominate our lives. He'll either accept the way things are or we'll eventually find him and take the necessary steps."

"Are you okay?" It was Tom. He had crawled over to their hiding place, and was now lying flat on the ground beside them.

"Yeah, we're okay. Was anyone hurt?" Jason asked.

"No, I don't think so, but it sure scared the crap out of a lot of people."

"Good! I mean, good no one was injured. I think he's gone now, but pass the word we'll be leaving bright and early in the morning. No sense in hanging around until he thinks it's clever to try again." Jason stood, reaching down to help Mary Lynne to her feet.

A thirteen-year-old girl came running out of the night. "Mama Lynne, Mama Lynne, are you okay?"

"I'm fine, Susan, just fine."

"Thank God. I don't know what we would do without you."

"I'm okay. Don't you worry. Get on back home now."

It was over as rapidly as it had started . . . the night folded in around them. Jason, Mary Lynne, and the others returned to their RVs, turning the lights out as they entered. The long night passed without another shot or sound from the woods, but the warning that had been screamed from the darkness haunted many a dream.

*****

Gilmore rolled away from Heather's naked body. They had cuddled like young kittens all night long, each seeking warmth and love from the other. He hated to leave their bed. His need, desire, and want for the woman lying before him was insatiable, and the love he felt was as deep as the tunnels in which they lived. He kissed her gently on the cheek, careful not to waken her. Heather's face was healing to its original beauty, the milky white skin glowing softly under the pale Chem-lite.

Twenty minutes later he entered the Hub

"What's the status?" he snapped, as he passed into the battery-powered light of the control room. "Are we on schedule?"

Several men dressed in their white tunics turned to look at the big man entering their domain. A young technician stepped forward.

"Yes sir, right on schedule. The reactor is coming on line and going through the start-up tests even as we speak. If all goes well, and we believe there are no reasons for it not to, we'll have electricity before breakfast is over."

Gilmore smiled, his first real smile in several days. "That's great, the best news I could possibly have this morning. Send a runner to Doctor Duke's quarters and have him report to me as soon as possible."

"Yes, sir. I'll see to it," the young man said, turning back to his array of lights and monitors for one last check.

Gilmore took a quick look around the control room, and then moved to the stairs leading to his office. Fifteen minutes went by before there was a knock at the door.

"Come!"

"Good morning," Doctor Duke said, as he closed the door behind him.

"The electricity should be back on line soon," Gilmore said, with a pleased look.

"Yes. So I was told earlier. That's good news for all of us. What did you want to see me about?"

"Will you lead the party to the top? I trust you to close the doors and give us a fair assessment of what it looks like outside."

"I anticipated your wanting me to go," Duke smiled. "See." He held up his right leg to show off his boots. "I thought I might wear these rather than the sneakers we have all been roaming around in these past months."

Gilmore returned the smile. "I wish I could go with you, but I have about a million things to take care of here when the power comes back on line."

"Don't worry, I'll take care of it. I just hope we can find Fagan. Of course, he may have never made it to the top. That's one heck of a climb for anyone, much less someone who is having an attack of claustrophobia."

"Well, we'll worry about that when the time comes. I'd hate to have to order anyone to search the stairs to find his body, but . . ." he paused. "Damn it, Mossmen is still causing me more trouble than any ten others. I sure wish the asteroid had hit him square on his brain-housing group when it struck. It would have done us all a great service."

Doctor Duke laughed in spite of himself. "Everything's going to be just fine. Stop fretting and get on with your work. I'll get three other men together from Charlie and start as soon as the power is stabilized."

"Okay. Be sure to check with the head tech in the control room before you leave."

"Right. See you later." Doctor Duke spun on his heel and headed out the door. He felt better than he had in weeks. He'd hadn't had an important task to oversee since the first few days they'd arrived in New Land, and the thought of going topside fascinated him. *I guess I should be thanking Mossmen and Fagan for giving me something to do,* he thought to himself, as he walked out of the Hub and headed for Charlie tunnel.

The elevator hummed smoothly, as the car moved rapidly to the surface. The four men riding upward said nothing as they examined the door before them. Each was wrapped in thoughts of the last five months without the sun. The car suddenly came to a jolting stop, bounced twice on its five-inch around cables, and was motionless. Relays slammed home deep in the computerized lifting motor and the doors slid apart silently. Doctor Duke stepped from the protection of the car to confront the gaping, man size crack in the center of the massive doors.

"My God," Benjamin Duke whistled between pursed lips. "The sky is blue, and there is warmth on the breeze coming through the doors." His voice, barely heard by the others, was filled with awe. "I don't believe it. I just don't believe it."

The men stood shoulder to shoulder, their eyes adjusting to the bright light streaming in from the fissure. Benjamin was the first to move through the doors and into the sunshine. The others followed one by one to contemplate the mountain road, blue sky, downed trees, and green patches. Doctor Benjamin Duke began to cry, the tears running silently down his cheeks.

"I would never have believed it possible," he said, filling his lungs to capacity with the welcome sweetness of earth's natural air. "Look," he pointed to a stand of firs, "there are even trees left and grass. I can't believe it's real."

"It's real all right," one of the men said, and began running down the hillside.

The men forgot what they had been sent to do for the next several minutes, as they bound about the mountainside like young bucks in rut. Everything appeared new, wonderful, and exciting. Every rock, every blade of grass, every standing tree was a gift from God to be enjoyed by them alone. For moments, the men felt they had been granted life everlasting in the Garden of Eden. It was Benjamin who found the footprints leading down the road.

"Phil! Phil Fagan! Can you hear me?" Duke yelled as loud as he could.

There was no answer. Doctor Duke gathered the three men about him and gave each a direction to search. "We'll return here in exactly one hour, so plan your search accordingly. If we don't find him by then, we'll close the doors and report what we have seen to Gilmore. Is that clearly understood?"

The others nodded and moved off. There was a spring in their step and lightness in their calls for their lost companion, who they didn't much care if they found or not. They were outside, in the fresh air and the world was clearly livable. The men knew without asking that they, along with all the inhabitants of New Land, would soon be back on the surface. They could once again live under the eye of the sun.

Doctor Duke knocked on the door of Gilmore's quarters. He knew the General and Margaret would be anxiously waiting for his report, and he had called ahead to arrange the meeting in the General's rooms. He entered without pausing for the occupants to respond and strode into the room like he owned the entire domain of New Land.

"It's livable," Doctor Duke stated firmly, but with a smile spreading across his thin cheeks. "It not only is livable, but there are grasses and trees still living. We even saw deer sign; at least that is what one of the searchers said it was. Personally, I wouldn't know a snail trail from a cow print, but he said it was a deer. I can't believe it. The world is alive and still beautiful, though a bit on the haggard side."

It was a long speech for Benjamin, and he paused to catch his breath. "It won't be five minutes until the whole of New Land gets the word. There was absolutely no way I could swear those men to secrecy, and besides, it's wonderful news."

The small group gaped at him from their seats around the glass dining table in the center of Gilmore's quarters, jaws hanging slack in complete shock. Heather was the first to break free of the spell Doctor Duke cast upon them. She pulled on Gilmore's arm, swung her face to his, eyes wide with excitement.

"Does this mean we can leave? I mean, can we live on top again?" Heather asked excitedly.

"I don't see why not, but we don't want to jump to the surface just yet. We'll have to do some research first, but yes, I think we will be leaving the tunnels soon," Doctor Duke responded, not waiting for Gilmore.

The big general sat quietly for a moment, gathering his thoughts. "I don't understand. You and the rest of your colleagues told us of an ice age. This sounds too good to be true. Have you an explanation?"

All eyes turned to look squarely at Benjamin. "No, I don't. I would have never in my wildest dreams considered this a possibility, but there it is nonetheless. I repeat, I'll have to conduct some testing, but I think it is likely the strike was not as severe as we thought it might be. It is very possible there are hundreds of thousands still alive throughout the world. It's going to be up to us to find them."

"When should we start?" Margaret asked, breaking from a semi-trance. "Is it reasonable to assume we will be topside in less than a month?"

"Hold on," Gilmore interrupted. "We can't just up and move out of New Land. It will take a great deal of planning to make the physical move back to the top. I'll arrange a coordinating committee tomorrow morning. In the meantime, Doctor, you get your research team together and start conducting whatever tests you think are necessary. You'll have at your disposal whatever and whomever you need. Understood?"

Duke nodded.

"Margaret, I would think you're going to have your hands full as well," Gilmore continued.

"No, I doubt that. In fact, I imagine my work will come to a grinding, screeching halt as the news spreads, but I'll certainly keep myself available."

Gilmore dipped his head in understanding and went on. "I'll go on tunnel viewer tonight, along with you, Doctor Duke, to explain in full what has taken place. We'll have enough wild rumors as it is, and we might as well tell them the truth up front."

"I most certainly agree," Margaret said. "In fact, be very sure to explain that we won't be jumping to the surface in the next few days and why. If you don't, we'll have a lot more 'Fagan's' on our hands."

"Understood," Gilmore acknowledged." We certainly don't need that kind of trouble right now."

The conversation continued for another hour, with Gilmore alerting the tunnel vision studio he would be going on the network that evening. There was a universal feeling of hope and wonder around the glass table in Gilmore's quarters.

*****

Jason pulled his bus off the main road and onto the dirt, stopping two miles short of Knoxville, Tennessee.

Brushing a lock of blond hair from his eyes, he picked up the CB mike and broadcast to the caravan behind his intentions of spending the night outside the city. His reasoning was good. A poignant aroma blew with the southerly breeze, and it was even more repugnant after having traveled through the fresh smelling hills of eastern Kentucky. Though the "Blue Grass State" had little grass at all, much less blue grass, the recent rain had swept the air clean.

Jason debussed along with Mary Lynne and went in search of Tom. Tom had been a staunch friend and companion since their first encounter at the farmhouse. "The farm was so very long ago," Jason said aloud to Mary Lynne. "We've come a long way, haven't we?"

"Yes, we have love, and you may be the leader of this rabble, but you're still a great bloody oaf to me," she laughed and poked him in his ribs.

Tom's RV was still running three vehicles behind their lead. The bus idled as its driver went through his routine shutdown procedure. The big diesel fell silent as the two walked into Tom's field of view in front of the windscreen.

"Hey, Tom. I need some help from you," Jason yelled.

"Sure, what's up," Tom answered through the open side window.

"I would appreciate it if you would arrange for a couple extra guards for the night. I don't want another episode like we had yesterday."

"Right. How many do you want beyond the four we normally post?"

"I think three or four more ought to cover it, don't you?"

"Yeah, I guess. Do you think that SOB will return so soon? I mean, we know about him following us now," Tom sounded concerned.

"I really don't know and don't care. Let's just not take any chances. Hopefully we'll never see him again."

Their conversation was interrupted by the whine of a four-wheeler screaming into the camp from the south. The rider, a young man of fourteen, his hair tied in a pony tail flying in the wind along with the leather fringe on his jacket, reminded Jason of movies he'd seen about the Pony Express.

"Yo, Jason," The rider yelled over the noise of his twin cylinder ATV, "Billy sent me."

"I would have never guessed," Jason smiled, walking to the rider's side. "What have you got for me?"

The boy delivered a thick envelope into Jason's waiting hand. "Geez, what did he send, a book?" Jason turned to Mary Lynne; his eyes full of questions.

"I don't have any idea. So, open the bloody thing already."

The two walked back to their bus and sat down at the table opposite each other. Jason tore open the sealed envelope and dumped the contents out. There was a hand written note, obviously in Billy's scrawl, and a brochure. Printed at the top of the multicolored brochure was the name "Holly Ridge Condominiums." Jason looked up at Mary Lynne, his eyes questioning.

She shook her head. "I don't have a clue. Why don't you read the note?"

Jason unfolded the letter and began reading aloud:

Jason,

> *Forget Gatlinburg. The town is an absolute mess. In fact, Gatlinburg has a larger concentration of bodies than anywhere else we've been. The town is small; maybe a mile and a half from city limit to city limit. It must have been a tourist trap or something because there isn't much in the way of stores that sold anything but dumb, stupid, ridiculous trinkets and T-shirts. The streets are choked with skeletons, and the flies, rats, and other critters are as thick as fleas on a junkyard dog. It's awful!*

> *That's the bad news. It just ain't do-able, Bro. The good news . . . we don't have to go to Gatlinburg. In fact, the mountains are just what we hoped for. Ever since we left I-40, and started south on 321 we knew we'd found what you had in mind. In fact, it's even better. The pamphlet I've put with this letter is what we want. It's a huge condo right off 321, on the right. The main building is down in kind of a valley, has plenty of living space with the things we need, like fireplaces and wood stoves, and can handle our whole group, plus a lot more. It's home, Bro, a real home.*

> *My crew will start cleaning up around here tomorrow. We should have it in pretty good shape by the time you arrive. Sam will lead you in when you're ready. See you in a couple of days. Jason, you just aren't going to believe this place.*

> *Billy*

"It sounds wonderful," Mary Lynne sighed. "Jason, you were right, we've found a place of our own."

Jason hung his head in relief. "Mary Lynne, I'm so grateful for everything. We're going to make it, aren't we?"

"Have you ever had any doubts?"

"Yes, hundreds. But now, I think we are going to actually make it through the winter, and many winters to come. How many of us are there now? I know we picked up another group leaving Indianapolis."

Mary Lynne smiled warmly, her heart soaring to her Jason. "We have one hundred and ten survivors following your lead, love, and more coming. That's counting the ones with Billy, and we don't know if he has gathered more around him since he left. You have kept them alive and given them hope every single day, and now you're going to give them a home. I'm very proud of you, Jason."

"No more so than I am of you. Honey, without your doctoring skills, half this crew would be sick or dying." He paused to look long and deep into the misty blue eyes of this woman. "Do you have any idea how much I love you?"

"No more than I love you," Mary Lynne sighed very softly, and took his hand in hers. "Besides, who else would I let father my child?" Her eyes danced with mischief.

Jason stared blankly for a moment. "A baby? You're going to have a baby?"

"Yeah, something like that." She squeezed his hand. "What did you expect? We haven't exactly spent all our nights sleeping." She pointed to the rear of the bus and smiled warmly. "I wanted to have your son, and now I will."

Jason moved off his chair and into her arms. "God or some Great Spirit has blessed me with so much since I met you."

He kissed her with the passion fired by the emotion he felt inside, wrapping his arms around her with the controlled strength only a man could show a woman he deeply loves. If they had not exchanged souls until this moment, then, like the searing flames of a roaring forest fire, their two spirits became one, fusing, bonding, and forging themselves into a substance stronger than a diamond rolling down an ancient stream bed. They were at that moment, and forever more, one.

CHAPTER 17

Ends and Beginnings

The elation, which followed General Gilmore's announcement of the conditions found by Doctor Duke and his search team, was paramount to what VJ-day must have been to those living during the end of World War II. Parties sprang like spring weeds, growing rapidly into full bloom. New Land, its myriads of tunnels and caves hewn from virgin rock, came alive with laughter, song, and bright lights. The revelry lasted throughout the night and into the short hours of morning. The inhabitants, who had lived six months of their lives like a family of well-fed moles, could envision themselves back in God's own sunlight once more.

Duke and a party of fifteen left the depths of New Land for the surface the following morning. The team carried a variety of weather sensing, soil sampling, and biological testing equipment. They did not expect to find anything unusual, but the tests were to be done before beginning a massive movement up from the relative safety of the tunnels. The day went well, with an area of over several square miles being evaluated. In late afternoon, all the Doctor's sub teams returned, and each report made it perfectly clear life could and was being sustained.

All indications were, though winter was fast approaching, life was regenerating. The teams wore heavy jackets to protect them from the frostiness of the mountain air, but their hearts were warmed by their individual findings.

"That's enough for today, let's get everyone inside and on the elevator," Benjamin directed the biologist sitting at a worktable set up earlier. "Tomorrow we'll pick up where we left off."

The pretty young woman nodded an affirmative, and walked off to call her remaining teams in from their work. She returned to Doctor Duke's side.

"It's beautiful, isn't it? Who would have thought we could be living on this planet after the strike? It just doesn't seem possible."

"I know what you mean," Benjamin said. His voice was soft with wonder and admiration for the powers of Mother Nature. "The old gal might be looking a bit on the ragged side, but it's a wonder anything is left at all. Sometimes it's great to be alive, isn't it?"

The woman smiled. "Yes, it is, but it's sad to think of the millions who must have died. I wonder, do you suppose that there are people still living? Do you think there might be survivors trying to make it day to day now?"

"From what we have seen here . . . yes. Undoubtedly there are those who might have lived through the quakes and winds, and I guess we are going to be lucky enough to find out," he smiled.

It was their third consecutive day on the surface, and the weather was holding. The sky remained blue and the sun tried to warm the foot of the mountain where they continued testing. Doctor Benjamin Duke sat silently in a straight backed, folding camp chair, eyes to the east. He felt terrible. His head was splitting; feeling as though some idiotic lumberjack was hacking at his brain with a double bit ax. Adding to the misery, his lower intestines felt like someone was ripping at them with a handful of razor blades.

As Benjamin watched the horizon, other members of his team were slowly returning to the great doors leading to the elevator shaft. They, too, were feeling as if sharp-toothed rats were gnawing at their guts.

Roused from his painful dreamland, Doctor Duke realized most of his party was passing him by. He struggled to his feet, pains shooting through his abdomen.

"Is everyone feeling as rotten as I do?" he asked the group at large.

There were several head nods, as blood shot eyes sought for relief from the pain, which seemed to double as each minute crept by. Without another word, the entire team walked in silence to the elevator, staggered aboard, and someone pressed the down button. By the time the doors opened at the bottom, a man and a woman lay in a heap, clutching their stomachs and coughing up frothy, dark blood. Duke radioed ahead for medical help, only to be told Med was filled to capacity already, but they would send those who could be spared to help them.

Benjamin struggled through the rim's vegetation under his own power. Every step was like walking barefoot on a bed of hot coals. Pain shot through his body at regular intervals, racking the nerves with anguish. He continued to the Hub, placing one foot in front of the other with sheer force of will. As he rounded an entrance door, he was astounded to see the room empty except for the ever-present flashing of tiny lights and the scores of monitors spewing numbers and graphs, the meaning of which he had never known.

As he made his way across the Hub to the stairs leading to Gilmore's office, he heard a loud thud. Something had fallen to the floor above him. He tried to hasten his pace, but could not manage the strength required.

Finally, after what seemed an eternity, Benjamin opened the door to Gilmore's office and stepped through its plastic archway. Dante's Inferno played in slow motion before him, as his eyes swept the room in confusion, fear, and disbelief. Behind his desk, Gilmore sat on the floor like a stone statue. Heather lay in the big man's arms, her once vivacious body deformed into a twisted gnome. Heather was dead; there was no doubt about that fact. Her chin and shoulders were covered in blood, and the expression, frozen on her face, was one of horror and suffering. Gilmore held her body tight to his own, as he coughed his own life's blood onto her corn silk hair.

Benjamin reeled from the sight of the two, but collapsed when he saw Margaret lying like a discarded doll at the foot of the conference table. She was doubled into the fetal position, her eyes staring blankly at its stainless steel leg, which she had spattered with blood during her final coughing spell. Margaret, the woman he loved more than anything in the world, was as dead as Heather.

Benjamin fell to his knees beside his wife and gathered her weakly in his arms. "Oh Margaret, what's happened?" he asked, childlike. He began sobbing uncontrollably, and then coughed blood.

"It's a virus," Gilmore said weakly, red drooling down the corner of his mouth. "Medical has no idea what it is, but it came from above. Mossmen has won after all. That God damned son of a bitch set us up for annihilation."

The big man doubled over in pain and began hacking again. "I'll put an end to this here and now."

He slowly moved his hand off Heather's shoulder and onto a switch he had rigged earlier in the day, as it became painfully obvious the virus would destroy New Land. From the switch, a wire stretched down to the door leading into Gilmore's personal arsenal. The thin wire passed under the door and up the side of a large box. The box's side had but one word stenciled: "EXPLOSIVES."

"What are you going to do?" Benjamin asked.

"I'm going to blow us to kingdom come and back again. We failed. All the technology in the world at our fingertips, and we failed. It's over," Gilmore cried and pushed the button.

The blast ripped through New Land like an atomic bomb. Rock split and crumbled as tunnels began to cave and fall in huge piles of granite. The reactor, designed never to thermally explode was wired to the same explosive devices used in Gilmore's office. It ignited into a wall of flame and radiation. The mountain collapsed upon itself. The government's great hope for mankind died with its disappearance.

New Land, an attempt by man to overcome the odds of nature, had been defeated. A microscopic bug had killed the hopes and dreams of all those who lived within its walls and the government who had placed them in their underground home. A virus which man designed and built himself, born from his continued desire to kill other humans, brought ruin to it all. Nature won Her battle against technology in the only way She could . . . KILL *THE KILLER!*

*****

The two days since Jason discovered he would soon to be a father had been spent stripping Knoxville of everything that might be useful through the long winter months. Every person who could drive confiscated a truck or van. Canned foods, medical supplies, hardware, clothing, bedding, fuel of all sorts, and hundreds of other items were scrounged and stored. The caravan stretched for two miles, as it began its last leg to Holly Ridge, five miles west of Gatlinburg, Tennessee.

They left Knoxville early in the morning. Teenagers, molded too early into adults, sat behind the steering wheels of the latest model vehicles. There would be no more cars, no more noxious gases filling the atmosphere with tons of pollutants for there were no more factories to stamp the metal, or engineers to design the four wheeled planet eaters. These were teenagers who had lived through the hell the Devil's Face had brought upon their lives. They were nothing more than kids, this optimistic clan under the leadership of Jason Collyar, who was but a boy from Anoka, Minnesota. Now that boy saw his best friend, a young black man with an ever-present smile on his face, and an idea in his heart, standing in the middle of a country road at the foot of the Great Smoky Mountains.

Jason radioed for the caravan to stop and hold its position. Setting the parking brake, he stepped from his big RV bus with Mary Lynne by his side. They walked to Billy, as Lorrie came forward to join him.

"It's about time you got here," Billy grinned. "I thought you would arrive yesterday."

Jason shook his friend's hand, and then dropped it to hug Billy to his chest. "God, I'm glad to see you."

"The feelings are mutual, Bro. Now get your buns in gear. I've got something to show you."

As they started to walk up a small rise, the clan gathered silently behind them. The four friends walked quietly to the top of the hill.

Jason sucked in his breath as he looked across a small valley. Sitting on the right-hand side of the road stood a beautiful wooden structure designed to resemble a series of log cabins with adjoining roof lines. In front of Holly Ridge Condominiums, a pond sparkled in the sunlight, lily pads valiantly trying to grow in one corner. An uncultivated field stretched to the south, abruptly butting up to the base of a sheer rock cliff. On top of the cliff stood the remains of several cabins. These remnants of the past had not been able to withstand the winds and now lay in rubble among green patches of grass and newly born shrubs. Hardwood, mixed with evergreens, had been battered and broken but represented life.

Jason moved slowly away from the group, his staff clicking softly on the asphalt pavement as he walked down to Holly Ridge. The young leader's clan stood without speaking on top of the hill. Instinctively, each individual knew this was an important moment. It was if some Great Spirit had hushed the mountains, silenced the birds, and stopped the howling of a distant dog pack.

Jason walked to a place centered between the condominium and its pond. He raised his arms to the sky, the staff he had carried since that fateful day in Anoka held to the heavens in his right hand. His head turned to the setting sun, his eyes reflecting its light as a gust of wind momentarily blew his blond hair in a stream behind him like wheat bending before a squall.

"I claim this spot for the Earth's Children. Let no man try to take it away from us. Let nothing destroy it for us. We are Earth's Children, and this is ours." He slammed the staff into the ground before him. It stood upright, its brass sphere sparkling brilliantly in the rays of the setting sun. *The Children of the Earth had a new home.*